Penguin Crime Fiction
The Fourth Simenon Omnibus

*Editor: Julian Symons*

Georges Simenon wa[...]
At sixteen he began [...]
*de Liège*. He has published over 100 [...]
name, sixty-seven of which belong to the Inspector
Maigret series, and his work has been published in
thirty-two languages. He has had a great influence upon
French cinema, and more than forty of his novels have
been filmed.

Simenon's novels are largely psychological. He describes
hidden fears, tensions and alliances beneath the surface
of life's ordinary routine which suddenly explode into
violence and crime. André Gide wrote to him: 'You are
living on a false reputation – just like Baudelaire or
Chopin. But nothing is more difficult than making the
public go back on a too hasty first impression. You are
still the slave of your first successes and the reader's
idleness would like to put a stop to your triumphs
there . . . You are much more important than is commonly
supposed', and François Mauriac wrote, 'I am afraid
I may not have the courage to descend right to the depths
of this nightmare which Simenon describes with such
unendurable art.'

Simenon has travelled a great deal and once lived on a
cutter, making long journeys of exploration round the
coasts of Northern Europe. He is married and has four
children, and lives near Lausanne in Switzerland. He
enjoys riding, fishing and golf.

Georges Simenon

# The Fourth
# Simenon Omnibus

Penguin Books

Penguin Books Ltd, Harmondsworth, Middlesex, England
Penguin Books Australia Ltd, Ringwood, Victoria, Australia
Penguin Books (N.Z.) Ltd, 182–190 Wairau Road,
Auckland 10, New Zealand

*Le Petit saint* first published 1965
Copyright © Georges Simenon, 1965
Translation published by Hamish Hamilton 1966
Translation copyright © Georges Simenon, 1965

*Maigret et le corps sans tête* first published 1955
Copyright © Georges Simenon, 1955
Translation published by Hamish Hamilton 1967
Translation copyright © Hamish Hamilton Ltd, 1967

*L'Homme au petit chien* first published 1964
Copyright © Georges Simenon, 1964
Translation published by Hamish Hamilton 1965
Translation copyright © Hamish Hamilton Ltd, 1965
Published in Penguin Books 1971
Reprinted 1975

Made and printed in Great Britain by
Cox & Wyman Ltd, London, Reading and Fakenham
Set in Intertype Times

# Contents

# The Little Saint

Translated from the French by
Bernard Frechtman

Part One

The Little Boy in the Rue Mouffetard

# Chapter One

He was between four and five when the world came to life around him, when he grew aware of a real scene involving human beings and was able to distinguish them from each other, to locate them in space, in a particular setting. Later on, he could not tell whether it had been in summer or winter, though he already had a sense of the seasons. Probably in autumn, for the curtainless window was dimmed by a slight blur, and the yellowish gaslight that came from the lamp-post outside, which was the only light in the room, seemed humid.

Had he been sleeping? His body was warm beneath the blanket. He had not been abruptly awakened by any particular sound, he had merely heard behind the curtain, which was only an old sheet that hung from a rod, a familiar panting broken by moans, and from time to time the creaking of the bedspring. It was his mother who slept in that bed, almost always with some-one. On his side of the hanging sheet were Vladimir, then Alice, then the twins, then he himself, each on his straw mattress, and, against the wall, the baby on her iron folding-cot.

Vladimir was a big boy, at least eleven and a half, if not more. Alice must have been nine, and the red-haired twins, who had freckles under their eyes, about seven.

The mattresses lay side by side on the floor and smelled of mildewed hay. The room was filled with other odours which were those of their home, of their universe, and there were also the odours of the whole house and, when the window was open, those from outside.

He had opened his eyes, not out of curiosity, but because he was awake. He had recognized the gleam of the gaslight on the ceiling and through the cloth partition. He had listened vaguely to the panting, then had gradually made out the figure of

Vladimir, in a shirt, kneeling on his mattress and peeping through a hole in the sheet.

Louis was neither surprised nor curious. It was all familiar to him, as if he had often been through the scene without realizing it. But it was the first time that the images and sounds had ever merged into a significant whole.

'Alice!' whispered Vladimir, turning to his sister.

'What?'

'Are you asleep?'

'Almost.'

'Look . . .'

She too was in a shirt. None of them wore night clothes, and they slept in shirts.

'What?'

Vladimir motioned to her to come to his mattress, and she in turn got on her knees and looked.

The twins were breathing evenly and did not stir. Emilie, the six-month-old baby on the cot that had been used by all of them, each in turn, did not yet matter.

Again he heard the muted though distinct voice of Vladimir, who ordered:

'Do it to me.'

'Will you do it to me afterwards?'

Vladimir had lain down with his shirt pulled up above his belly.

'Be careful with your teeth.'

Louis was so unmoved, so uninterested, that he dozed off. When he opened his eyes again, Vladimir and Alice seemed to be sleeping. The twins were still breathing evenly, but the paraffin lamp was lit in the kitchen, the door of which was open. A smell of coffee, spiked with brandy, floated in. Two persons were talking in the kitchen in low voices.

Wasn't it like that in every home, in every house, in every family?

His grandmother had once remarked:

'Louis hardly ever talks. He must be a little backward.'

He did not remember who had answered:

'All the same, maybe he thinks about things. It's children like that who are often the most observant.'

He had paid no attention because he did not know what it meant, but for some reason or other the words had stuck in his mind. There were others too, and particularly images, for even if he really was dull-witted he had not lived till the age of four without seeing what was around him.

But it was rather as if he had wanted to limit the world to as narrow a space as possible.

'If he were allowed to do as he liked, that child would never go out of the house.'

Had he actually heard that comment or had it been repeated to him later? It's not easy to distinguish between what really happened at a particular time and what you were told later on.

He was sure that the hole in the hanging sheet and the business of Vladimir and his sister were a part of real life, despite the vague glimmer from outside. He had seen his brother and sister do the same thing at a later time, in broad daylight, without bothering about him.

There had been a father in the home, a man named Heurteau, Lambert Heurteau, whom he had never known, except for the lone photograph tacked on the wall of the room. He was oddly dressed and was standing next to the children's mother, who was wearing a white dress and a veil.

Lambert Heurteau was not the father of all of them. How old was Louis when he discovered that in most families the children all had the same father? Not in theirs. And not in others in the Rue Mouffetard, where they lived.

His mother's name was Gabrielle Heurteau. Her maiden name was Cuchas. As for the eldest, his real name was Joseph Heurteau, but Louis did not realize until much later, when he went to school, why he was called Vladimir.

Alice's name was also Heurteau.

'It's hard to know who she resembles. In any case, all you have to do is look at the eyes and that sharp nose of hers to tell that she'll go far.'

'Unless she runs a push-cart in the street like her mother and grandmother.'

The twins were Heurteau's too.

'They're the only ones he couldn't disown!'

Why hadn't Louis known the man in the photo and why was he himself called Cuchas? No one seemed to wonder about it, and for years he didn't either. Later, when he knew, he felt completely indifferent.

What mattered most, at first, was the two rooms in which they lived, more exactly the bedroom and the kitchen. During the day, the sheet which hung from copper curtain-rings was pulled back, revealing, on the left side of the window, a very high walnut bed, its two mattresses, its coverlet and the huge quilt.

The image was vague, but Louis would have sworn that he had seen his mother in that bed surrounded by other women, that she had screamed a lot while they kept him in the kitchen and that later they showed him an ugly baby and informed him that he had a new little sister.

His grandmother was present too. He saw her as a very fat old woman whom everyone called Ernestine.

Had he too been born in the walnut bed, and had he sucked his mother's breasts as he had seen Emilie do? Nobody called her Emilie. It was a long time before he knew her name. They simply said 'the little one', the way they said 'the twins'.

'You twins, let the little one alone! Go out and play.'

Much later, and only when he had become an adult, was Louis to remember other images that had not registered consciously and which, perhaps because they had to do with his daily life, had not struck him at the time.

The walls of the room had formerly been papered, but all that remained was patches on which there were still pictures of persons dressed as in the time of the kings. On one of the patches, near the door, was a young woman with very wide skirts who was on a swing. The rest of the wall was dirty, yellowish plaster on which were initials that had been carved with a knife and pictures representing genital organs which someone had tried to rub out. Who had drawn them? Who had tried to efface them?

Not his mother, in all likelihood. When the weather was warm, it didn't bother her in the least to walk around naked in the room and even in the kitchen. When she had not yet put up her big red bun, her hair hung down to her waist, and the bush

14

at the bottom of her slightly plump belly was very fine and fluffy, of the same light shade as Alice's hair.

She was cheerful and often sang while doing the housework, when she had time to do it.

The straw mattresses were covered with a thick, rough brown cloth, except Vladimir's which was bluish. The only sheets were on the wooden bed and the enamelled cot.

'Alice! Go and warm your sister's bottle.'

'Why is it always me?'

Who had given *him* the bottle?

The twins were only three years older than he, and he was four and a half years younger than Alice. Was Vladimir eight when Louis was born?

These questions did not yet occur to him, except a few, the simplest ones, which did not disturb him, because everything seemed natural. Later, much later, he was to wonder how such and such a thing had happened when he was a child in the Rue Mouffetard, but it was out of idle curiosity, a kind of amusement.

It was in 1897 or 1898 that he had observed what his sister was doing so docilely to Vladimir, though it did not interest him enough to prevent him from going back to sleep. It did not surprise him that his mother wore a high corset which left marks on her fine skin, soft skin, or to see some men wearing caps in the street, others bowlers, and others silk top hats. He had heard it said that the family was poor, but wasn't everyone in the building poor and almost everyone in the street, except the shopkeepers, such as his Uncle Hector who ran a butcher's shop at the corner of the Rue du Pot-de-Fer?

'If he hadn't been a fast talker and a good-looking boy, he wouldn't have got around the Lenain girl. Besides, the family let him have her only because she limped. All the Lenains have something wrong with them. The grandfather ended up in an asylum, and as for Azaïs's brother, God knows what he died of. It wouldn't surprise me to learn that Hector, even though he is my brother, had a hand in it . . .'

She laughed. His mother laughed as often as she sang. When she was in bed with a man she began by sighing and moaning, but it always ended with a burst of laughter.

She got up very early in the morning, at times, in summer, at three o'clock. She would wash her face in the kitchen, where there was a copper tap. In winter, she lit the fire before leaving. Louis would sometimes hear her. At other times, when he woke up he would see that she was no longer there.

He knew that she went to Les Halles, the central market, with her push-cart, which she had hired from a certain Mathias who had a yard full of them in the Rue Censier, to stock up with fruit and vegetables. At six o'clock she was on the pavement, facing the shoe shop, while his grandmother installed herself about a hundred yards lower down the street, near the Church of Saint Médard.

At the age of four or five, he was unaware of all that, or rather it was part of a world which was not his, which was only remotely connected with his daily reality.

For example, the stove was, for a long time, more important than his mother and was the focal point of his existence. He did not yet know how it was lighted, or by whom. All he remembered was that his mother, who would be out of breath from climbing the stairs, would cross the room with a bucket of coal whose weight tilted her to the right.

There was no door between the kitchen and the corridor. You had to go through the room. Louis did not mind the fact that their home had only one exit. It was reassuring, because he felt safely shut in, just as he was safe in the blanket at night when he wrapped it around his body.

The stove, which was next to the sink, filled a good part of the kitchen.

'We're lucky to have water on our landing. There aren't many people in this street, even those who are lots richer than us, who have water in their rooms. If only we had gas too . . .'

He knew what gas was, for in the evening he saw its pale illumination in the shops across the street and in certain houses. It was even installed in the yard of the building, or rather in the carpenter's shop.

From his mattress Louis could hear sulphur matches being struck. He liked the smell of them. Then, almost always, his mother would sigh and mutter words that he could not make out, and the smell of sulphur would be followed by that of paraffin,

16

which drowned it, and the new smell in turn was drowned by that of kindling wood and coal. He could have got up to take a look. He did later, around the age of six or seven. Until then, he preferred the mystery of the fire as it appeared to him from his bed, and since it was celebrated very early in the morning, almost always when it was still dark, he would fall asleep again before the end, before the jet of steam spurted from the kettle and the drops that fell one by one into the coffee-pot changed the smell of the room once again.

He was told later when they had tried to put him into a nursery school when he was two years old, that he had not cried but had struggled, and that when his mother had left he had escaped by the window. As he still did not know his house from the outside, he had wandered about among the push-carts and a policeman had finally gone up to him.

'What are you looking for, little boy?'

'I'm looking for Mama.'

'Where is your mama?'

'I don't know.'

'Have you lost her?'

'Yes.'

'What's your name?'

'I don't know.'

'You don't know your name? Don't you know where you live?'

'No.'

He was wearing a little smock, the kind worn at the time by boys his age, and his hair came down almost to his shoulders.

'You're not a girl by any chance, are you?'

'No. That's my sister.'

He had only one, for Emilie had not been born yet.

'What does your father do?'

'I don't have one. I want to go home.'

The policeman, it seems, had taken him from shop to shop.

'Do you know this boy?'

The shopkeepers examined him more or less closely and shook their heads.

'Do you live in the neighbourhood at least?'

'I don't know.'

17

Finally, he had caught sight of his mother behind the pile of vegetables in her push-cart. Or rather, as the story was told to him, his mother had caught sight of him walking hand in hand with the policeman.

'What are you doing here, Louis?'

'I don't know.'

'How'd you manage to get out of school?'

'I don't want to go to school any more.'

'Germaine, would you mind my cart for a moment?'

She had taken him back to the house where the twins were sitting on the kitchen floor playing with blocks. These were not memories of his own. He was unable to remember so far back.

'Even when you were six, they had a devil of a time keeping you in school. You refused to learn . . .'

Perhaps it was not so much that he refused to learn as that he refused to be taken away from the universe which he considered his own and in which he felt safe.

He liked the room that was divided in half by the sheet which hung from a rod, he liked the smell of the mattresses lined up side by side, the portrait of his mother in a white veil and of a man with a blond moustache, the patches of wallpaper, particularly the one with the girl on a swing. He liked, above all, the warmth that the stove gave off in waves, in blasts, the way it roared at times, the glowing ashes that suddenly collapsed into the drawer at the bottom.

'Your son doesn't talk much!'

What would he have said?

\*

He must often have tried later, at different ages, to reconstitute the successive stages of that birth of the world around him. Not because he attached any importance to the matter. It was only a game, though a secret voluptuous game.

He never quite managed to link them up. Images were missing, particularly pictures of himself, for the only photograph he knew was the wedding photo of his mother and Lambert Heurteau that was on the wall. The latter had one hand on his wife's shoulder, and the other, which was gloved and holding the other glove, rested on a pedestal table that fascinated Louis for a long time, until the day he ventured beyond the neighbourhood and discovered an identical table in the shop of a second-hand dealer.

Why did it seem to him, when he contemplated the ill-lit face and pale blond, drooping moustache of that man he had never seen, that he was dead?

'But he's not, idiot. If he were, Mama would be a widow and we'd be orphans.'

'Me too?'

'Not you, since he's not your father.'

'Why?'

'Because he went away long before you were born.'

'Why?'

Perhaps because he had been fed up. Or because their mother had been.

That conversation took place several years later, when he was about eight or nine and dared ask Vladimir questions. Vladimir continued to despise him, but now took the trouble to answer him condescendingly.

'Did they fight?'

'When he drank, or when Mama drank. Haven't you ever heard Mama fight with the others?'

'Did he beat her?'

'Sometimes. Mama was stronger than he and he always ended by getting the worst of it.'

'How do you know?'

'Because I used to look through the hole, and I listened when they drank in the kitchen.'

Vladimir had adopted a defiant attitude. He out-stared everybody and never gave in. He was the only dark-haired member of the family and was taller and more nervous than the others. His long eyelashes fluttered about his dark pupils.

'I don't give a damn . . . He's not my father. Mama was pregnant before she knew him. My real father was a Russian and I heard someone say he was an anarchist.'

'What did he do?'

'He prepared bombs and set them off.'

Before that, Louis must have discovered one of the two

monuments of their flat, the sink and tap, which were almost as important as the stove. On Sunday mornings their mother, who did not work that day, put water to heat in a huge laundry tub.

She had to ask Monsieur Kob, their neighbour, to help her set the tub of almost boiling water on the reddish tiles in the kitchen. Monsieur Kob did not have to be asked twice, for Gabrielle had nothing on under her dressing gown and generously displayed her breasts when she bent.

At that hour, on Sundays, he smelled of cosmetics and wore a gauze appliance to set his black moustache.

Alice, because she was a girl and was less dirty, got into the tub first. She was soaped from head to foot, with her hair hanging in wet locks on her cheeks and hunched shoulders.

Then it was Vladimir's turn. He insisted on washing himself without anyone's help.

'Don't forget to wash your ears.'

'I'll wash whatever I like.'

Then came the twins. At times it was one and at times the other who was first. In the street and at school they were called the redheads, and other children were afraid of them because they were always looking for a fight. At home, on the other hand, they seemed indifferent, as if they did not feel they were members of the family. They had violet-blue eyes and very pale skin, and almost every winter they caught flu together.

'Your turn, Louis.'

The water was already blue and slimy with soap. It did not disgust Louis to be fifth. He was never disgusted. Not by the smells either. Was anyone in the house or even in the street disgusted by smells?

There were no lavatories on the landing. And neither the arch nor the yard nor the stairway was lit up, so that the most important object in the room was a heavy white crockery chamber pot. Everyone used it, the mother first, and also the men who came to see her, who sometimes lived with them for a month, sometimes for a few days, sometimes only for a night.

'Hell! The damned chamber pot is full again!'

This one was a coachman who brought back two bottles of red wine in the pockets of his box-coat every evening. Gabrielle

**and** he did not go to bed immediately. They would sit in the kitchen, which was lit by the paraffin lamp, and, with their elbows on the table, would talk in low voices as they drank their wine. When the mother started laughing, it meant that before long they would be going to bed.

She would lower the wick, which went out a minute or two later, and the room would be lit only by the street lamp opposite the window. Since they lived on the first floor and the Rue Mouffetard was not a wide street, it was rather light in the room. The man, in his shirt-tails and long underwear, would lift up the pot that the children had filled.

'Hell! This God-damned chamber pot . . .'

He would open the window and empty it on the pavement while Gabrielle howled with laughter. She herself poured it into the kitchen sink and then let the water run. The coachman had been with them for almost a month. One Sunday he piled them into his hackney and took them to the Bois de Boulogne. Emilie, who must have been a year old, sat on her mother's knee. Vladimir was perched on the high seat and before long was using the whip.

For years, it was their longest trip. Actually, they never took another one together.

Of course, Gabrielle left for Les Halles very early with her mother and other street-sellers, each pushing her cart. But when the local market began, at the kerb, she spent the rest of the day about a hundred yards from the house.

When Emilie was very little, Alice looked after her, and it was also she who filled the stove and stirred the fire. From time to time, their mother would ask a neighbour to mind her push-cart for a few minutes.

'Here! Put this meat to cook with onions and a dash of vinegar.'

The meat did not come from the shop of her brother, 'Hector the millionaire,' as she called him.

'Ever since that lousy pimp married his cripple and became a boss, he's forgotten that his family ever existed.'

At heart, she did not hold it against him. She was rather proud of him. Isn't that the way things always happen in families, and wouldn't she have done the same in his place?

She had another brother, Jean, who was a bit feeble-minded, a lamp-lighter who went by in the evening with a long pole at the end of which shone a small flame for lighting the gas lamps and who went by again early in the morning to put them out.

'A loafer's job. And yet he was the only one of us who went to school till he was fifteen.'

All of this had registered in bits and pieces. Louis never seemed to be listening. What he heard was always mingled with the hubbub of the street, especially in summer when the two windows were open, the one in the kitchen and the one in the room.

'That one's not interested in anything.'

Perhaps it was true. Nevertheless, certain phrases, certain intonations were filed away in his memory without his bothering to put them in order, to link them up, to try to understand.

'And yet he looks intelligent . . .'

Because of his smile, most probably. A gentle smile, without irony, without meanness, without aggressiveness, a smile that someone once compared to that of Saint Médard, whose church stood at the bottom of the street.

He was happy, he watched, he went from one discovery to another, but, unlike Vladimir, he made no effort to understand. He was content with contemplating a fly on the plaster wall or drops of water rolling down the window-pane.

Certain drops, for example, which were bigger and muddier, caught up with the others by taking a short cut instead of zig-zagging. At times, this went on for hours, against the background of the huge red boot with a gilt tuft that was the signboard of the shoe shop on the other side of the street.

The shopkeeper was Monsieur Stieb, and his name, which Louis was unable to read until much later, was elegantly written out in cursive style on the two windows that framed the narrow door. Louis could see people enter, especially women with one or more children, and it was fascinating to watch them gesticulate without hearing their words. Monsieur Stieb had a square beard and wore a detachable wing collar, a flowing purple necktie, and a frock-coat.

He invited the mothers and children to be seated, got down on his knees to remove the youngsters' shoes, and then began to play a game with boxes, which he went to take from the shelves and from which, with the gestures of a conjurer, he removed shoes of all shapes.

The mother, who held a shopping basket on her lap, would shake her head: no.

'Wait! Wait! I've got just the thing. How do you like these?'

'No . . . No . . .'

No patent leather. No kidskin. Good solid thick-soled shoes, preferably with hobnails!

At the left, in the semi-darkness, thin, severe-looking Madame Stieb would look on with an air of indifference. She was ugly. The redheads called her a sick hag.

She was buried a year or two later. Everyone in the Rue Mouffetard, including the street-sellers, went to the funeral. The shutters remained drawn for three days. When Monsieur Stieb reopened them, there was a saleswoman in the shop.

The shutters were fascinating too. Those of the shoe shop were lowered with a crank that fitted into a small hole in the shop front, and in summer another crank lowered a red-and-yellow-striped awning, the edge of which stopped just above the heads of the passers-by, so that the tall ones or those who wore a top hat had to stoop. Another awning, a solid grey one, obliged them to do the same in front of the tripe shop.

The shopkeepers did not all shut up shop at the same time, and the grocer, whose shop was long and narrow, having only one shop window, was the last to put up two wooden panels which he wedged with an iron bar and then locked before doing the same with the door, so that he had to leave by way of the blind alley.

Louis spent hours at the window, as he did in the yard watching the carpenter in his glass-fronted workshop. Monsieur Floquet was a tall thin man who stopped sawing or planing from time to time to roll a cigarette.

He was probably not rich enough to employ an apprentice, and when he needed someone to lend a hand in order to hold two pieces of wood together, he would call his neat and tidy wife, who emerged from the kitchen in a starched apron.

When, in spring or summer, part of the glass front was open, a pleasant smell of glue and fresh wood emanated from the shop, though it was spoiled a little by that of the building's only lavatory, whose door, on which someone had sawed out a heart, was ajar day and night, revealing on the ground a dirty crockery slab with two places for the feet and a hole in the middle.

Beyond the yard opened still another world, for the building was very large. Though all the tenants were more or less poor, those whose windows overlooked the street were the privileged ones. Among them were even people like Monsieur Kob, who, when he went out, always wore a bowler, sometimes a top hat, and almost always a frock coat. People said he was a laboratory assistant at the medical school and that it was he who cut up the corpses which were not claimed by relatives.

Nevertheless, even in that part of the house there were more old people than young, widows and widowers, especially widows. Some of them received a little help from their children, some had savings, others were on outdoor relief, and at least three of the tenants on the upper floors could no longer manage to go down the stairs.

A kind of tunnel led to the second yard, where the rubbish-bins were lined up. At night, cats and, so it was said, rats too would knock down the not properly placed lids. A stairway, whose bottom steps were of stone, though the rest were wooden, led out to the right. The iron banister was supported by bars that were too far apart, and several children had been hurt. One of them had fallen down two or three flights and had died.

Not everyone spoke French. There were a little girl and her brother who had almond eyes. A tall, thick-lipped Negro lived with a tiny little woman whose skin was as pale as that of the twins. Louis would sit on a step and watch. He rarely asked questions. When his mother came home alone for a meal, she was too busy with the others, and almost every evening there was a man in the room, sometimes a stranger, most often someone who stayed rather long and did not mind playing with the children, as the coachman had done.

Vladimir was the only one who could have cleared up certain points, but he looked at his brother so haughtily and with such contempt that Louis preferred not to ask him anything.

Yet Louis could have denounced him. Vladimir had got into the habit of bringing home in the evening things that did not belong to him, sweets and chocolate which he munched in bed before going to sleep, coins that he hid in his mattress, a penknife that shone as if it were made of silver, and even a lady's watch that he would sometimes put to his ear before going to sleep.

One day Alice discovered the watch, and when Vladimir got home she dangled it in front of his nose at the end of its chain.

'Where'd you get this, Vladimir?'

'Let me have it.'

'Only if you get another one for me.'

'I'm ordering you to let me have it.'

'And I'm warning you that if you don't give it to me, I'll tell Mama. And I'll also tell her that you look through the hole and make me do what she does.'

'She doesn't care. Let me have the watch.'

'I won't.'

'I promise you I'll give you another one.'

'When you do, I'll give this one back to you. Is it gold?'

'It's plated.'

'Is it fake?'

'It's not fake, it's plated. It's almost as good as gold. Listen Alice . . .'

'I won't.'

Vladimir then turned his rage on Louis.

'What are you doing here?'

'Nothing.'

'Were you listening?'

'I heard.'

Vladimir went to get the penknife, which he opened with a meaning gesture.

'If ever you make the mistake of talking about it to Mama or anyone else, I'll puncture you. You know what that means?'

'I do.'

'Come here.'

'No.'

'You'd better.'

Vladimir stepped forward, grabbed Louis's wrist, pulled up

his sleeve, and, with a quick stab, dug the point of the blade into his skin.

'Does it hurt?'

'It does.'

'Well, if I really stab you, it'll hurt even more, and they may have to take you to the hospital. Do you remember the man they found on the pavement last month with a knife in his belly?'

The people who got up early had seen him from their windows, for he had lain in the street more than an hour with-out help.

'All right! So keep your mouth shut. Understand?'

'I understand.'

And Louis walked away from his brother with a smile.

## Chapter Two

Was his memory playing tricks, was it an optical illusion? He had the impression, later, that his childhood had been a suc-cession of periods of discovery, of intense activity, and of periods of somnolence of which he had no recollection, except of a kind of general tonality, sometimes a greyness, sometimes a sort of luminous fog.

The same went for his contacts with people. Some of them seemed, for a time, to have disappeared from his life, though he had continued to see them every day, whereas others, for no apparent reason, entered the foreground, and in such minute detail that they seemed ridiculous.

Such was the case of Monsieur Stieb, whose gestures and facial expressions were so deeply engraved in his mind that he remembered when the shoe-seller had clipped his beard and when he had changed the style of his detachable collars.

Thus, from his first-floor window he followed, without trying to understand, goings-on which for him had no importance but which must have had an enormous amount for Monsieur Stieb. The new saleswoman was dark-haired, full-breasted, and broad-hipped, and she had a well-rounded behind. She dressed strictly in black, as if she too were in mourning. Was she a widow, or a member of the family, Madame Stieb's younger sister?

In the beginning, she served the customers and knelt in front of their stockinged feet, juggled cardboard boxes, climbed up the ladder that slid along the shelves.

Formerly, when there was no one to wait on, Monsieur Stieb would stand at the door of the shop and make pleasant remarks to the women who stopped in front of the shop windows.

But now, as soon as he had a free moment he would disappear with his saleswoman into the back of the shop until, a few weeks later, he started waiting on the customers as he had done before, while the buxom young woman sat in front of the cash register.

Louis did not remember the marriage, which must have taken place during one of his periods of apathy. Nor did he ever know whether Vladimir stole another watch for his sister. At the age of about five, there was a void of several months of which almost nothing remained, except an impression of sun and heat, of the smell of fish and other food that rose up from the street.

Vladimir, who was thirteen, would return from school with a school bag that he tossed into a corner, near Emilie's cot, but Louis never saw him open a textbook or notebook, nor heard him talk about his class or teacher or schoolmates, whereas the twins sometimes sat face to face at the kitchen table doing their homework and learning their lessons.

They were all different. Except for the fact that they lived under the same roof, usually ate together, slept on mattresses that lay side by side, and washed in the same water on Sunday, there were few contacts among them.

Vladimir had black hair, which was thick but fine, with a lock that fell over one eye.

The twins, who were more square-faced and bonier, had their red hair cropped close.

Alice was blonde and fragile-looking, and her chest was beginning to swell a little around the nipples.

Louis could not see himself. The only mirror hung too high on the wall for him and was used only by their mother when she put up her bun.

Louis was short, he knew it, shorter than the other boys his age, and his hair was even finer than his sister's.

As for Emilie, she was beginning to walk in a kind of pen that was set up for her during the day with the mattresses.

Why was Vladimir more present to his eyes than the twins, of whose doings over a long period he had no recollection at a later time?

That summer his mother cut his hair, and he was surprised to see her wrap one of the curly locks in a piece of tissue paper. But though he remembered the lock and the tissue paper, he had no memory of the operation itself and could not tell on what chair or where in the flat he had sat.

He was discovering the Rue Mouffetard, where he was beginning to walk around by himself, with his hands in his pockets. As he saw it, the street was divided into two distinct parts.

To the right of his house, on the way to the Place de la Contrescarpe, the shops were not so closely huddled together. There were fewer dark alleys between the houses and few push-carts along the kerb. It was a foreign world.

In the other direction, towards Saint Médard's, the street became denser, more swarming with people, full of noises and smells, of the cries of pedlars, of piles of food, and of refuse in the gutter.

He often went to see his mother, whose green push-cart he recognized from a distance. On sunny days, it was covered with a piece of canvas that was held up by two sticks and bits of cord.

'Take a look at my lovely peaches, Madame. . . . Don't be afraid. . . . There's none like them in the whole market . . .'

The stock changed every day: peaches, plums, lettuce, string beans.

'Monsieur, try my William pears. . . . Come! Don't be shy. . . . Your wife won't scold you . . .'

A slate was stuck at the top of the pyramid, and between the shafts of the cart was a small board that supported the scales and the metal container.

His mother hardly had time to talk to him. The members of the family never talked much.

'Is Alice with your little sister?'

He wondered whether Alice had ever been to school. His mother would give him a piece of fruit, in other seasons a stalk of tart rhubarb, a few thick-shelled, fuzzy beans, and sometimes a sou. He would walk down the street, jostled by the crowd, stopping at the fish market to look at the heaps of mussels and shrimps and green-eyed fish.

At times he would have to step over a man, unshaven and in rags, who lay sleeping across the pavement beside a pool of vomit.

He never went beyond the church, which was his frontier, and he took no interest in the carriages and omnibuses that rolled by with a clopping of horses' hoofs.

His only expedition beyond the neighbourhood, when the family had piled into the coachman's hackney, already seemed unreal to him. He had seen the Seine flowing, churches, huge buildings, wide streets with silent houses where there were no pedestrians, avenues, and carriages drawn by two and even four horses in which young women, dressed in white, toyed with their parasols. He had caught sight of horsemen in shiny boots, officers with gold epaulettes.

No doubt it was all very beautiful. His mother went into raptures.

'Her whole dress is real lace and she's wearing enough jewels to buy half the Rue Mouffetard . . .'

He was unimpressed. For him, it was outside reality, and he had finally dozed off.

The Dorés, opposite the window, were more real and for a time played an important role in his life. They lived on the first floor, above Monsieur Stieb's shop, but their flat was not like his. It contained at least four rooms, maybe five or six, for Louis could only catch a glimpse when the door happened to be open.

The floors were so brightly waxed that the sun played on them as on a pane of glass, and in certain places they were covered with multicoloured rugs in which dark red predominated.

Madame Doré and her husband were old. They were at least fifty. In summer, their three windows stayed open all day, and a young housemaid in a white apron and white cap would beat the rugs and carpets over the pavement.

Did other residents of the street have a maid? Madame Doré wore a corset which was so stiff that it made her look like a statue. Her tight bun, which was still black, had streaks of grey. She was never seen in house clothes. Her dresses, with wide leg-of-mutton sleeves, were of colours hard to describe, violet, for example with mauve glints, or oak-leaf brown or even lavender-blue.

The two front rooms were the dining-room and living-room, and when Madame Doré sat down to breakfast she was already fully rigged up, without a hair sticking out, wearing a white or black tucker that made her keep her head straight and hold up her chin.

Lots of little dishes and utensils with which Louis was unfamiliar lay on the white tablecloth, and almost every day Madame Doré shook a little bell to call in the maid and tell her to put such and such an object in its right place.

Monsier Doré was fat, had broad side-whiskers, and wore, at home, a snuff-coloured jacket with frogs and braiding.

They almost never seemed to talk. He would read his newspaper in a velvet armchair. His complexion was florid, and after every meal his wife would take a decanter from the sideboard and serve him a little glass from which he drank while smoking a cigar.

They were the landlords of Louis's house and also of the house in which they themselves lived, to say nothing, so people said, of four or five buildings on the street. In summer, when Monsieur Doré left the house he wore a pearl-grey frock coat and was very careful not to soil his patent-leather shoes by walking in the rubbish. He invariably carried an ivory-headed cane, and his eyes were always sad.

It was the Dorés who, in the past, had run the hardware shop a little farther down the street which had been established by Grandfather Doré, who had started as a blacksmith.

For Louis, the Dorés were linked up with his illness and that of his brothers and sisters. By cross-checking, he later established the fact that he was about five and a half at the time. It was after a hot summer, most of which he spent in the street.

After that, there had been a series of storms, one of which was more violent than the others and had transformed the sloping street into a torrent, and as the sewers had overflowed, the street had reeked with a foul stench for several days. Workmen and firemen had even come to dig a trench in order to repair the damage.

When the storms were over, the rain had persisted and got colder every day. He did not know whether it had been in October or November. In any case, they had started lighting the fire in the kitchen stove and the window-panes were covered with steam. He had made drawings on them with his fingers.

One night, Louis, had a stomach ache and went to the chamber pot twice. In the morning, he felt very warm and his eyes itched.

He had not spoken of it to anyone, because it was not unpleasant. He had even gone out for a moment in the morning and had seen Monsieur Doré, who was wearing an overcoat and carrying a rolled umbrella instead of his cane.

'Aren't you eating?'

'I'm not hungry.'

'Have you been on the pot yet this morning?'

'Once.'

'Was it liquid?'

'I don't know. No. Not too liquid . . .'

'If it continues I'll ask the chemist for a remedy.'

No doctor, as far as he knew, had ever set foot in their flat. He knew the one who treated almost the whole neighbourhood, for he had often seen him go by with his medical bag. The doctor was a round-shouldered man with a white goatee who was always dressed in black and dragged along as if he were dropping with fatigue.

The mother went, instead, to the chemist, who would ask her a few questions and sell her a syrup or a powder to be diluted in water or whitish pills that melted on the tongue when you couldn't swallow them and which then left a bitter taste.

'Louis, are you ill?'

Alice was minding the little girl. She never complained about all the things she was asked to do. Nor did she ever play. She wasn't sad, but the expression on her face wasn't the same as that of other little girls.

'No. I only had a bellyache.'

'You're all red.'

He could feel that his skin was getting hotter and hotter, and he went to the window to cool his forehead against the pane. He felt hot and cold. It was both pleasant and unpleasant. He would have liked to lie down, but he didn't dare to, for if he were really ill he would be taken to the hospital. Though no one in the family had ever yet been there, he did occasionally hear it mentioned:

'You know the fishwoman's little boy is in the hospital.'

'What's the matter with him?'

'They don't know. It seems to be something in the head.'

From time to time, an ambulance would stop at the kerb. Men in white would enter a house carrying a stretcher and come out with someone on it, usually an old man or old woman. He had once seen a woman struggling to free herself and screaming:

'I don't want to go there . . . I won't. . . . Help! . . . Don't let them take me . . . Maria! . . . Hortense! . . . Help! . . . If I go, I'll never get out and I'd rather die at home . . .'

Louis had witnessed the scene without turning a hair. The only person who had commented on the incident was a little old woman.

'I understand her, poor thing. No doubt they take better care of you there, but I feel the same, I'd rather die in my own bed too . . .'

Louis did not want to go and die in the hospital and he said nothing that evening, though he had the impression a number of times that the walls were spinning around him. He had nightmares. He felt that he was huge, that he was getting huger and huger, as if he were being blown up, until he filled the room, and he floated.

He did not know how he had floated, but he had lost contact with the floor and was begging them to hold on to him, to help him get down.

When he woke up, his blanket was damp. He felt drained.

His mother had left for the market long before. It was broad daylight and no doubt she was already at her place beside the kerb with her push-cart. Alice, who was sitting on the mattress of one of the redheads with her chin in her hand, was looking at him in a way she had never done before.

'Am I red?' he asked anxiously.

'No. On the contrary. You're all white.'

She seemed sunk in thought and kept staring at him.

'Are you hungry?'

'No.'

'Would you like a bowl of coffee and milk?'

He didn't know. He didn't feel like having or doing anything. Or rather he would have liked to go back to sleep, for his eyelids were heavy and swollen, and he felt bone-weary.

'Do you want it or not?'

He nodded. He heard her moving about in the kitchen, while Emilie crawled on the floor, pushing a tin can. Alice came back with the bowl, helped him sit up, and, when he protested, said to him gravely:

'You've got to do as I say. I'm your nurse. If you don't obey me, you'll die.'

His throat was tight. He tried to drink, but before he had drunk half the bowl he squirted the liquid.

'You can see that you're very ill. If they took you to the hospital, they'd probably open your belly, the way they did to a little girl I know. They took out a lot of pus and then they sewed her up again. She showed me the scar. It's as long as that. It seems they've got a room there full of coffins for those who die . . .'

She suddenly seemed much older than he, and he did not doubt the truthfulness of what she was saying. She spoke with the detachment of someone who knows but can't do anything about it.

'I'm not ill.'

'You are! You're very ill.'

'It's not true.'

'It is. I'll take care of you.'

'What are you going to do to me?'

He already saw her opening his belly with a kitchen knife or a pair of scissors.

'I'll ask the chemist for some medicine.'

'You won't say anything to Mama?'

'Where'll I get the money?'

'There's probably some in Vladimir's mattress.'

'Do you like Vladimir?'

'I do.'

He liked everyone, even the twins, who never paid any attention to him except to make fun of him. They claimed he was too short, that he wouldn't grow up, that when he was old he'd be a tiny little man, maybe a dwarf, like those who lived in the Rue du Pot-de-Fer.

'I don't like him.'

She added, while removing, without surprise, coins and unexpected objects from her brother's mattress:

'He's cruel. Sometimes, instead of sucking me, he bites my pisser ...'

He did not see her leave, did not remember what happened afterwards. When he opened his eyes again, his mother was in the kitchen. There was no man with her. The paraffin lamp was lit.

He felt he had a damp, warm dressing around his chest and stomach, and he had difficulty breathing, probably because the dressing was too tight. In spite of himself, he started groaning, and his mother knelt beside him while the others continued to sleep.

'Does it hurt?'

'No.'

He tried to push aside the dressing.

'I'm choking.'

'Don't touch it. It's good for you.'

She had put her cool hand on his forehead.

'You're already less warm. You're going to drink a little broth I've prepared for you.'

He wasn't hungry, only thirsty, thirsty for very cold water, but he was forced to drink the broth with a spoon. He was so tired that all he could think of was going back to sleep, but he had strength enough to ask:

'Why is everything wet?'

'Because you did it twice in your sheets and I had to wash your mattress.'

It lasted two days. He learned this only afterwards. His grandmother spent one of them in the house, and she too made him drink broth with a spoon. As soon as he opened his eyes, he made sure that he was in their room, still fearing they might have sent him to the hospital. He also made sure that the old doctor wasn't there. Once, he caught sight of Vladimir looking at him, somewhat the way Alice had done, as if he were expecting to see him die and were curious to know what would happen.

'Does it hurt?'

'No.'

'Are you cold?'

'I'm hot.'

'But yesterday you were shivering and your teeth were chattering.'

'Did the doctor come?'

'What for? Would you like a chocolate?'

'No.'

He added:

'Thanks.'

For it was the first time that Vladimir had ever offered him one of the sweets that he swiped from stands and of which he always kept a supply. He was filled with tenderness for Vladimir, for Alice, for the twins, for little Emilie whom he neither saw nor heard, as her cot had been transferred to the kitchen.

The others, the big ones, were strong enough to defend themselves against contagion. At one age or another they had all had the same thing, fever, stomach ache, diarrhoea.

'Thanks,' he repeated more gravely.

He would have liked his mother to be there too, and his grandmother, he would have liked them all to be around him, for it seemed to him that they formed a unit, that they were different from other people, that they alone, all together, had the power of defending one of their members.

He felt very small. The redheads were right. If he lived, if they helped him live, he would remain the smallest in the family.

He was only a child and he was almost frightened at the thought of being a grown-up some day. His mother would be old, as old as his grandmother. Perhaps she would even be dead.

As soon as Vladimir grew up, he would go away and they would never see him again. Then the twins would go away. Why did he think they would marry the same woman?

He himself could marry Alice, so that she would always stay with him. He was afraid of being left alone. If they left him alone, he would die.

People were talking in the kitchen as if he couldn't hear. There were the voices of his mother and of a neighbour, an old woman who lived in the next house. She was a cleaning woman and smelled bad.

'All that's necessary is to moisten his dressing, as warm as possible, every two hours, by diluting a soup-spoon of dry mustard and a handful of bran in a little water.'

Then his mother spoke:

'I've got to go back to work. What with the rain, I've hardly made anything all week. If something happens, Madame Gibelin, let me know right away.'

'You can rely on me, Madame Heurteau. Work is work, and I can understand you, I who've worked every day of my life.'

... If something happens.... If something happens.... If something happens ...

Maybe he was dying, since he no longer felt anything.

He never knew how long his illness had lasted, nor exactly what it had been, for it merged, not only in his own memory, but in that of his brother and sister, with the illness of the others. One day, Olivier, one of the twins, returned from school in the afternoon and complained of a headache. A little later he began vomiting. Gabrielle came home. She made him drink a cup of herb tea, which he threw up, and despite his pleading she wound a damp dressing around his torso.

It was midwinter, since, the next morning – Louis was sure of it – he was kneeling on a chair watching the snow fall, and on the other side of the street Madame Doré, whom he saw indistinctly in the light and shade, was pensively contemplating the same spectacle.

It was an extraordinary period, for while Louis was getting better and regaining his strength, Vladimir announced, with an evil look at his brother:

'That does it, you've passed it on to me too . . .'

Because the children were ill, Gabrielle overheated the flat, and the chamber pot was emptied into the lavatory in the yard ten times a day. Gabrielle was obliged to work, for, as she said, only rich people can buy bread on credit.

Madame Gibelin came for only two or three hours a day and spent most of her time looking after Emilie. Guy, the second redhead, joined his brother on the row of mattresses.

Louis could remember his mother leaving her push-cart for a moment, rushing up the stairs, feeling the children's foreheads, preparing a compress or distributing spoonfuls of a sticky syrup, and then going out again with her knitted woollen shawl tightly drawn over her chest.

'Louis, come and get me if anyone needs me.'

For he was now the healthiest of the lot. His hair, which was finer than ever, was more curly. He spent most of his time looking out of the window or watching the gleaming ashes drop into the drawer of the stove.

Alice was less ill than the others. She too shivered with fever, and at night she uttered moans, at times actual cries, and seemed to be trying to push someone away.

Little Emilie crawled about on all fours from one room to the other, playing with anything, sucking whatever she could lay her hands on. No one realized that she had fallen sick too. She did not look ill and did not complain. She was put to bed, as every evening, in her cot, and as she did not wake up in the morning, Gabrielle leaned over her and then realized she was dead.

Madame Gibelin, who arrived a little later, went to buy a bottle of cognac in the grocery shop three houses away to buck their mother up, and she herself drank quite a glassful.

'You have to notify the district office. They'll send the doctor.'

Louis did not cry and was not really sad. His main feeling was one of surprise.

It was he who had started the series, and it was the youngest of the children who died of the sickness.

The comings and goings that followed disturbed his tranquillity, and he was annoyed with the people who came in, looked at the little girl's white face, uttered laments, gave advice, related personal memories, and asked whether there would be a funeral service in the church.

The old doctor came too, for the first time, with his medical bag. What struck him most was the hanging sheet that isolated the wooden bed.

He sounded the chests of Alice and the twins, without knowing that Vladimir was hidden in the kitchen closet. He asked questions with an air of resignation, like a man who had seen and heard everything. How had it begun? ... With Louis? ... 'Is that Louis? ... Stick out your tongue, my boy.... Don't be afraid.... So you were the one who was sick.... Did you have a stomach ache? ... Did you have to move your bowels often? ... What did you give him, Madame? ... Did you put damp compresses on his chest? ... Good.... Didn't he have headaches? ... Did he recognize you? ... Who had it next? ... Your tongue.... Can you swallow easily? ... Did you have a stomach ache too? ... And then your brother? ... Obviously.... Obviously.... These children ought to have been isolated the very first day.... I'm not blaming you.... In any case, there's no room in the hospital and they wouldn't have been able to admit them.... And you, little girl, do you feel better? ... I bet you began by taking care of your brothers ...'

He looked about for a table, something on which to write, and it was in the kitchen that he wrote out the death certificate and then, as a measure of precaution, a prescription.

'Isn't it you who sell vegetables on a push-cart a little way down the street? I've seen you before. You work in the neighbourhood, don't you? I think my wife often buys from you ...'

When the body was put into the coffin, the children, whether ill or not, were locked up in the kitchen. Louis expected that there would be hammer strokes and was disappointed at hearing only the conversation between the carpenter and his assistant.

It wasn't the carpenter downstairs, but another one, a more important one, who made coffins only.

Had Emilie spent that night with them? He did not remember, just as he had no recollection of other things that were more important than those that had stuck in his memory. In any case, the funeral took place on a windy, freezing morning. The neighbours, who were waiting in the street, held their hats in their hands, and the women's skirts stuck to their legs on one side and waved like flags on the other.

Vladimir was well enough to go out, for he disappeared a little later and did not come back until it was dark. Gabrielle returned home slightly drunk, accompanied by her mother, who tried to force her to go to bed with a hot-water bottle.

'I'm so afraid you may have caught cold at the cemetery . . .'

'No, Mama, it's not on a day like today that I'm going to coddle myself.'

Madame Gibelin had prepared a stew, and everyone ate heartily, even the twins, who were still running a temperature.

'The thing that consoles me is that she didn't suffer, and maybe it's better for her that she was spared this bitch of a life.'

'Gabrielle!'

The grandmother was reprimanding her daughter, who, in order to pull herself together, was helping herself liberally to red wine.

'You're right, Mama. Why worry? Such is life, eh?'

It was not until much later that Louis learned these details, at second hand, from Vladimir, and perhaps Alice had not been wrong in claiming that Vladimir was cruel. One day, she too was to confide in Louis.

'You can't imagine what he forced me to do.'

'I saw it.'

'You mean when he looked through the hole and made me imitate Mama?'

'That's right,' he admitted, blushing.

'That's not all. It annoyed him not to be able to do it like the

39

men, you understand? So he hid a big carrot under his mattress and stuck it into me. I couldn't even scream because of Mama and the fellow who was with her. I don't know how many times I bled and I had a burning pain for several days.'

It would have been necessary to collate all the testimony. That was done, more or less, over the years, in bits and pieces, but Louis would merely listen half-heartedly, as if the truth about the others did not interest him.

He had not taken sides at that age either, when he was about six. His mother, who had once arrived unexpectedly during a fight between Vladimir and the redheads, had asked him:

'Louis, who started it?'

And he had answered quietly:

'I don't know, Mama. I wasn't looking.'

He looked at lots of people and things, but not those in which he was expected to be interested. That same winter, he entered elementary school, after the term had begun.

His first day in the classroom, which was a turning point in his life, ought to have left an impression. He had not the slightest memory of it, though he very clearly recalled trying on blue-checked pinafores at Lenain's, the clothing shop near which his mother set up her push-cart.

He remembered particularly the smell of the materials, the stiffness of the starched pinafore, and, a quarter of an hour later, the sight of Monsieur Stieb, at close range, trying to fit him with high laced shoes.

'They wear them out so fast, Monsieur Stieb! You'd swear they do it on purpose.'

At that moment, he himself had wondered:

'Are Monsieur Stieb and the lady smiling behind the cash register going to get married?'

They did get married, in the spring, discreetly, without a white gown and veil, and the shutters remained close for the three days of their honeymoon.

On the long grey wall was printed: POST NO BILLS. Then there was a building of the same grey, two floors of classrooms, a short flight of worn steps in front of the building, a green door. The pupils did not enter by that door but by a small one in the wall of the yard. In the middle, the ground had been hardened by trampling. A band of paving stones two or three yards wide ran around the yard, and on one side was a covered playground for rainy days.

His classroom was on the ground floor. From his seat in the first row he could see the dark trunks of four chestnut trees. He had been placed in front because he was the smallest in the class.

'Are you sure you're six years old?'

'Yes, sir.'

That wasn't the first day, but the second or third. On the first day he must have taken a seat anywhere, on an available bench. On the walls were a number of maps, though he did not know of what countries, for he had not yet learned to read, but he could contemplate the patches of different colours which were separated by sinuous lines, light blue, yellow, green, and particularly the purplish pink of the biggest patch.

There was a jumble of exciting lines on his desk too, the veins of the wood which stood out in spite of the black paint, and, in addition, the mysterious patterns that pupils had carved with pen-knives over the years.

'What are you looking at, Cuchas?'

'Nothing, sir.'

Whenever the teacher called him by name, some pupil would burst out laughing, as if it were extraordinary or comical.

'What was I saying?'

'I don't know, sir.'

For he had been taught to say 'sir' whenever the teacher addressed him. That was not hard for him, since he was naturally polite and deferential.

'Weren't you listening?'

'No, sir.'

'Why are you in school?'

'In order to learn.'

'What have I put on the blackboard?'

'Strokes, sir.'

'I want you to make the same strokes on your slate. Be sure that they're the same distance from each other.'

He got down to work. He did not rebel, like Vladimir, and

did not, like the twins, loathe school, where they were unable to let off steam except during break. The girls were on the other side of the buildings and had a smaller yard, without trees, for their recreation periods.

The big boys came running out at about ten o'clock and before seeing them he heard the clatter of their hobnailed shoes on the stairs. The twins had already thrown a red rubber ball which the others tried to get from them, and they defended themselves energetically, throwing it back and forth over the others' heads and elbowing and sometimes kicking those who were about to get hold of it.

Vladimir was one of the biggest and walked around the yard with a friend whom Louis knew by sight because he was the son of shopkeepers in the street.

He did not know their name. People said 'at the Spaniards''. They had no shop window. Their shop was a kind of broad corridor, both sides of which were filled with displays of food, some of which Louis would often go to contemplate with even more admiration than envy.

For example, rough, hairy coconuts with a reddish tuft in the form of a goatee. Pomegranates, one of which was cut in two so that the customers could admire the colour of the delicate flesh surrounding the seeds.

He had never eaten coconuts or pomegranates or those tangerines which were preciously wrapped in silver paper.

The oranges were enveloped in crinkled tissue paper, and exotic-looking salamis, flat hams, and dates with plaited stems hung from the ceiling.

It all must have been good, tasty, different from what he ate at home, those little fish that were soaking in a tart sauce, those shrimp salads, those anchovies laid out in such neat circles in casks, the different kinds of nuts, the bottles surrounded with straw, the tin cans of all colours . . .

He was amazed to discover that his Vladimir was a friend of the Spaniards' son, of a boy who lived in the midst of so many good things and who no doubt ate them.

He too was dark-haired and had heavy eyebrows, and his lips were as red as those of a woman with make-up. The two boys kept apart from the turmoil of the others and seemed to be exchanging secrets. Louis could tell from the Spaniard's attitude that he admired and respected Vladimir.

'What are you thinking about, Cuchas?'

'I was looking at my brother, sir.'

'At home you'll have all the leisure you need to look at him. Here you're supposed to work.'

The young boys had break after the older ones. When he in turn was in the yard, he had no desire to play with his classmates or make their acquaintance. The boy who shared his desk, who was also short, barely taller than he, and had a big red pimple on his forehead, went up to him.

'Why do they call you Cuchas?'

'Because it's my name.'

'A name from what country?'

'I don't know.'

'Don't you know what country your father's from?'

'I haven't got one.'

'You haven't got a father?'

'No.'

'Is he dead?'

'I don't know.'

'Doesn't your mother know either?'

The question seemed to him so foolish that he shrugged. He had promised himself to go and look at the dark trunk of one of the trees which had a bump, like a big wart, and to run his hand over it. There were complicated patterns on the bark, like maps, but they were deeply carved and one could stick one's finger into them.

'Where do you live?'

'Rue Mouffetard.'

'What does your mother do?'

'She sells vegetables.'

'Does she have a shop?'

'No. From a push-cart.'

'Is your family poor?'

'I don't know.'

It was true. He had never wondered whether they were poor. Actually, everyone in the building was poor. Even Monsieur Kob, who dissected corpses and wore celluloid collars.

'Those people have to spend their money on clothes,' their mother would say, 'and I'm sure they don't eat as well as we do. Some of them try to act like ladies and gentlemen and then, after bargaining for a quarter of an hour, ask me if I haven't any leftovers.'

'My father works in a bank.'

This did not impress Louis, who did not know what a bank was.

'My mother doesn't work and we have a cleaning woman every Saturday. My two sisters go to a parish school. Are you so short because you don't eat enough?'

'I've always been the shortest.'

'Why?'

'I don't know.'

He never asked himself the question.

After all, if he was always so calm and had a serene smile, perhaps it was because he did not ask himself questions.

'Too bad, because if a big fellow hit you, you wouldn't be able to defend yourself.'

It was already time for the pupils to line up in front of the classroom, take their seats, and make pot-hooks.


## Chapter Three

The teacher was a rather heavy-set, flabby, shapeless, colourless man named Monsieur Charles. That was his family name. He was twenty-eight years old and unmarried. For reasons of economy he boarded with a widow in the Rue Lhomond who mended his shirts and other clothes, which were never new. He had a child's mouth and almost no nose, and one could feel that he suffered from not being good-looking or able to aspire to a minimum of elegance.

From the very beginning, mysterious relations were established between him and Louis, as invisible, on the surface, as an electric current. It was a matter of neither sympathy nor antipathy. Perhaps, on the part of the teacher, whose only vanity, a rather naïve one, was to wear fancy waistcoats under his ill-fitting, threadbare black jacket, it was mainly a matter of curiosity.

He taught two classes in the same room, the walls of which were pale green, and while the little ones were still making pot-hooks on their slates, the second group studied the multiplication table and the history of the Gauls.

Louis applied himself, but without eagerness or enthusiasm. He did correctly what he was told to do and when his neighbour, the son of the bank clerk, left in the middle of the term to enter a private school, the teacher said to him:

'Cuchas, from now on I'd like you to attend to the stove.'

The pupils all burst out laughing. Had the teacher done it on purpose? The stove, a big black cylinder six feet high, the pipe of which went through the ceiling, looked even more monumental when little Louis went to open its firebox and refill it.

Yet those were the best moments of the day. The school was not sparing of coal, as they were at home. Nor did it use little balls of greyish charcoal, but good shiny anthracite that burned with a clear bright flame. It was so beautiful, so fascinating, that Louis hesitated each time to close the cast-iron door.

In the yard, he did not play. He didn't feel like it. He stayed in a corner watching, or digging up pebbles encrusted in the hard ground. The others would jostle him on purpose as they ran by. He sometimes fell his full length, and he would pick himself up without protesting, with neither ill-humour nor rancour, but with a vague smile on his lips, a kind of inner light in his blue eyes.

The two years in Monsieur Charles's class went by so quickly that he was unable to tell later when he had begun to read and write.

For him, it was the trees and the yard that marked the flow of time. The trunks became less black, seemed less rough; then tight buds appeared at the ends of the branches. The sparrows chirped more often, and soon other unfamiliar birds appeared.

'What are you doing, Cuchas?'

The children had got into the habit of pronouncing his name with a stress that made it comical.

'I'm looking.'

45

'May I ask what you're looking at with such attention?'

'The cloud.'

A light pink and white cloud that remained suspended in the pale blue sky, right above one of the chestnut trees.

'I suppose it's interesting.'

'It is, sir.'

The pupils burst out laughing. It had become a game in which Monsieur Charles participated by his unexpected questions, which he asked in a deliberately gentle, insidious voice.

'What is your slate used for?'

'For writing, sir.'

The incident of the marbles took place later, when the buds, after swelling, began to burst with the sprouting of the young leaves. Everyone had begun to play marbles during break, and Louis had some in his pocket which he fingered but, most of the time, dared not take out.

Most of them were fine-veined agates. Others had multi-coloured spirals inside the glass. He had not bought them. Vladimir, who now affected a protective air with him, had said one day, when he was feeling generous:

'You can take my marbles if you like. At my age, we no longer play kids' games.'

Sometimes, however, Louis would take his marbles from his pocket in a corner of the yard and make them shine in the sun.

'Where did you buy them?'

He was being questioned by one of the big boys, a fellow named Randal, who regarded himself as the leader of the main group.

'I didn't buy them.'

'You swiped them?'

Louis could feel that Randal was going to become menacing.

'I didn't. My big brother gave them to me.'

'Well, you're going to give me the yellow one and the blue one.'

'I won't.'

'You're going to give me the yellow one and the blue one.'

'I won't.'

They were surrounded by four or five boys in Randal's gang.

'Did you hear what I said?'

'Yes, I did.'

'You know what's going to happen?'

'No.'

The big boy, who was a head taller than Louis, winked at his friends and then dashed at him. With an instinctive movement of defence, Louis, who was squeezing the marbles, thrust his fist into his trouser pocket, and Randal twisted his arm to make him pull out his hand.

'And now?'

'No.'

They had rolled on the ground among the spectators' legs.

Randal punched and pulled and pushed. There was a ripping sound. The trousers, though they were of thick corduroy, had torn.

'You still refuse?'

'I do. They belong to me.'

'They don't. You stole them.'

One of the corners of Louis's lips was bleeding. Long black legs approached.

'What's going on here? Are you fighting?'

Randal sprang to his feet.

'No, sir. It's him.'

'You mean that Cuchas attacked you?'

Louis stood up too and, running his hand over his lips, drew it away spotted with blood.

'Why were the two of you fighting?'

'We weren't fighting. He stole two of my marbles, a yellow one and a blue one, and won't give them back to me.'

Monsieur Charles studied the faces around him. The spectators said nothing. One or two of them, however, friends of Randal, nodded their heads affirmatively.

'Is it true, Cuchas?'

Then Louis, instead of answering, took his hand out of his pocket, opened his fist, chose the two marbles that Randal had been hankering for, and handed them to his opponent. Randal was dumbfounded. He hesitated to take them. Was Monsieur Charles being taken in?

'Well, Randal, don't you want them any more?'

'I do, sir.'

'You see, there was no need to tear your classmate's trousers and scratch his face.'

'I apologize, sir.'

But everyone could see that Cuchas was smiling, with a smile that was barely perceptible, like the reflection of an inner joy.

'Don't let it happen again. If I catch anyone fighting, he'll stay in for two hours.'

From that day on, the evolution took place more rapidly, though it was barely visible, both among the students and in Louis's innermost heart.

Anyone could kick him as he went by without his hitting back or complaining to the teacher. When, on rare occasions, he brought a roll with a chocolate filling to eat during break, all one had to do was demand it in a certain way and he would give it.

After school, almost all the others would leave in small groups, while he would walk off alone, with his school bag on his back, to the corner of the Rue Mouffetard, looking at the house fronts, the sun or rain on the roofs, anything at all.

His smile was perhaps not a true smile but the reflection of a quiet and almost continuous satisfaction that could have been taken for placidness. Vladimir was not the only one who was irritated by this placidness. Smaller boys than Randal would attack Louis for the pleasure of feeling stronger than someone else.

'I bet if I slapped you, you wouldn't dare hit me back.'

What could he have answered? He took the blow, didn't cry, and even disdained to put his hand to his cheek.

'You don't happen to have a screw loose, do you? Maybe you're a little batty, eh?'

'It's not only that he's batty. Don't you realize he takes himself for a little saint? I bet he goes to mass every Sunday. Maybe he's a choirboy.'

He had never been to mass. Their mother never spoke to them about God except to exclaim, when a misfortune occurred:

'What have I done to that damned God?'

She had nevertheless married Heurteau in church, and there had been prayers of intercession for the dead before Emilie's body was taken to the cemetery.

Nor did he attend the course in religion which a priest came to give once a week after school.

'No!' she had yelled when he had brought home from school the note asking parents whether or not they wished their child to receive religious education. 'So he can talk to you about sin and make you start thinking I'm a bad woman! Religion's for the rich.'

The little saint. The expression had been tossed off during a recreation period and was to stick to him all his life.

'Come here, little saint.... You wouldn't happen to have a top in your pocket?'

For marble time was followed by top time. The chestnut trees were in bloom. They became fuller, with dark holes in their leaves. Monsieur Charles always observed Louis with amazement, and at the end of the school year Louis was surprised to learn that he was at the head of his class.

He did not have the impression of having studied. He was embarrassed by the mocking or envious way his classmates looked at him.

On his way home, as he threaded his way through the crowd in the Rue Mouffetard, the voice of a boy who was running and whom he did not have time to recognize cried out to him:

'Go away, little saint!'

He was not a saint. If he did not swipe things, like Vladimir, it was not out of honesty but because he felt no desire to, or perhaps lacked courage. Too many people might start chasing him, people who ran faster and were stronger than he. He would be taken to the police station, then to prison.

For a time, he was afraid that Vladimir would be locked up. It was after the holidays and during the winter, which was so cold that his mother and the other street-sellers were obliged to light a charcoal burner near their push-carts and keep warming their fingers which stuck out of their mittens.

One morning, when they were all in the kitchen sitting around the table, which was covered with oilcloth, someone knocked at the door. That was a bad sign, for the postman never went up to their flat and nobody came to see them.

'Go and open the door, Vladimir.'

He had to go through the room, since the kitchen did not open on the corridor. Vladimir's mouth was full. They heard him turn the knob.

'Does Madame Heurteau live here?'

The odd thing was that Vladimir, who was usually free with his tongue, did not say a word, and when he appeared in the doorway his face was livid with fear, his features were drawn, he had a shifty expression. Behind him they could see the uniform of a policeman with a weather-beaten face.

'Is your name Heurteau?'

He laboriously drew a piece of paper from his pocket. His hands were stiff with cold.

'Gabrielle Françoise Joséphine Heurteau, maiden name Cuchas . . .'

She was upset too, but not frightened, as Vladimir was.

'If you're from the neighbourhood, you must be new, because I've never seen you. The other policemen can tell you that my licence is in order, that I've never tampered with my weights or my scale, and that it's not like me to cause a disturbance in public.'

Whereupon she grabbed her bowl of coffee and began to drink.

'When did you last see your husband?'

She did not pretend to be dumbfounded. She really was dumbfounded by that sudden mention of her former husband.

'Lambert?'

He looked at his paper again.

'Lambert Xavier Marie Heurteau, born at Saint-Josephère, Nièvre, on . . .'

What struck Louis most was that one of the given names of the twins' father was Marie.

'Wait, let me work it out. Louis's nearly eight. Eight or seven?'

She counted on her fingers.

'He'll be eight next September. The twins are ten. Lambert

up and left one day between the two deliveries, ten or eleven months before Louis was born, so that I even wondered for a moment whether he wasn't his. How about a cup of coffee to warm you up?'

That permitted her to stand up, go to the cupboard for a bowl, and take the coffee-pot from the stove.

'Have a seat.'

There were only enough chairs for the members of the family, but Vladimir remained standing, distrustfully.

'You can see it was ages ago. Two lumps of sugar? Milk? To get back to Lambert, what's it all about?'

'Haven't you ever seen him again?'

'Never. Disappeared. Went off without leaving a trace, except debts in the bars which I had to pay. That seems to be the law.'

'He hasn't written to you?'

'In the first place, he wouldn't have been able to write. He could hardly sign his name.'

'It says here that he was a tile-setter by trade.'

'When he felt like working. I'd say that he was a loafer by trade. He'd hardly be on a job a week and right away he'd injure his hand or foot or get bronchitis – when he didn't argue with the foreman. Bear in mind, I don't hold it against him. He had a weak chest and he used to spit blood. Once a month he went for a check-up to the Cochin Hospital where they made them line up in the yard in the middle of winter. They told him he had to build himself up, that the climate was bad for him, that it would be better if he lived near Nice. Can you see us at Nice? So he didn't believe them. The first thing he'd do when he left the hospital was to go to a bar. When he came back, he was blind drunk and couldn't take his trousers off.'

'Did you argue?'

'Just look at me. Do I look like a woman who argues with people? Ask anyone in the whole street if Gabrielle ever argued in her life! Even with the grumpiest customers, I tell them what I think of them with a smile. He beat me occasionally, but I didn't defend myself, because it didn't hurt.'

'I have orders to take you with me.'

'To the police station?'

'To the mortuary. Some of the down-and-outs in the Place

Maubert have identified him but, since according to the record you're still his wife, you've got to come and identify him officially.'

'Lambert's dead?'

She did not speak in a tragic voice. She was barely astonished, without any sadness.

'Did they finally put him in a hospital? I'm idiotic! If he died in a hospital, you wouldn't be taking me to the mortuary, would you? Well, well! Children, who'd have expected such news when I lit the fire this morning? . . .'

The twins continued indifferently to eat their thick slices of bread and butter which they dipped into coffee and milk. It was about a father they had hardly known. Perhaps Alice remembered his face, his moustache which used to smell of wine or brandy.

Had he ever bounced them up and down on his knees or held their hands and taken them for a walk in the empty streets on Sunday? Did Heurteau even have a Sunday suit?

Alice was particularly interested in the young policeman's ruddy face, and Louis was fascinated by the silver buttons of his tunic, which he was seeing at such close range for the first time and which he would have liked to touch.

'As a matter of fact, how did he die?'

'He threw himself into the Seine from the Pont Marie at about eleven at night. Some tramps who had made a fire under the bridge and who knew him went to inform the river police, but it wasn't till two hours later that they fished out the body more than half a mile downstream. The only thing they found in his pockets was an old dirty military-service certificate.'

'Since we've got to go, let's get going.'

She was looking for her shawl and mittens. Alice asked, in the hollow voice she had got into the habit of assuming whenever she knew in advance that the answer would be no:

'Can I go with you?'

She was quite unmoved. Her face merely looked longer, her features sharper, and her nostrils more pinched. Her mother gave her a look that Louis had rarely seen in her eyes.

'Are you depraved or something? So you feel like taking a look at a corpse?'

He did not attend the funeral. He did not even know whether there was an actual funeral, a ceremony in church, a procession, a coffin that was lowered into the grave with ropes, in a cemetery.

He had once followed a hearse, out of curiosity, to know what it was like. He admired hearses, especially those of second-class funerals, with tassels and silver fringes, with horses attired in a kind of cloak.

He was also impressed by the women who were hardly recognizable behind their crepe veils and who held a handkerchief in their hand. The cemetery was beautiful. It was pleasant to walk in the lanes covered with dead leaves that made an odd sound beneath the soles of his shoes.

In any case, if they had been Catholics he would have liked to be the choirboy in a white surplice who walked in front of everybody and held a long black pole surmounted with a crucifix.

Heurteau was a pauper, a word Louis had often heard but the meaning of which he had only recently learned. Somewhere in the fabulous neighbourhood through which the coachman had driven them one Sunday lived the rich people who, for him, belonged to another species and whom one was not likely to meet in the Rue Mouffetard. Then came the bourgeois, about whom his mother sometimes spoke and who were located, in his mind, in wide, quiet streets and in avenues, such as the Avenue des Gobelins or the Boulevard du Port-Royal where they lived in grey stone houses.

There were also the landlords, for example those opposite, above Monsieur Stieb's shop, who did nothing but collect rent and evict tenants who didn't pay.

The shopkeepers, both the important ones and the less important, lived apart. Last came the mass of the poor, the majority of the people who lived in the street and in the neighbourhood.

The paupers did not have enough to eat every day. When they were ill, they were visited by persons from Public Assistance who gave them bread tickets so that they would not actually die, and some of them, when they were drunk, slept on the pavement with old newspapers under their coats instead of blankets.

Heurteau was a pauper, like the tenants at the back of the yard, like the one whom people had seen from their windows with a knife in his belly.

'What do they do with paupers when they die?'

'They're buried in the paupers' grave. Or else, if nobody claims them, Monsieur Kob attends to them.'

Had his mother claimed Heurteau? He wasn't sure. He dared not ask her. He preferred to imagine Monsieur Kob cutting him up on a big table and carefully laying out the pieces, as on the butcher's counter.

\*

Gabrielle was receiving male visitors again. In fact, there were always such visitors, except during the weeks following Emilie's death. Their absence had been their mother's way of being in mourning.

She also spent a few nights alone after the death of her husband, about whom there had never been much talk in the family but who thereafter was never mentioned again. Nevertheless, the wedding photo in its black and gold frame remained in its place on the wall of the room.

Louis was beginning to be aware of his physical appearance. There was a mirror in the shop window that was full of hats with flowers on them, and he would sometimes look at himself in it. He was really short, much shorter than boys of his age, but his features were very fine. They were not the features of a baby or a little boy but already those of a man, and his bright eyes sparkled. His lips were more curved than those of his brothers and even of his sister. He blushed easily, especially when a passer-by, male or female, caught sight of him observing himself in the mirror. And yet he was not vain. Perhaps, had he been able to transform himself, he would have preferred to be a big, rough, jeering fellow like Vladimir. The day he received his school report, he had merely put it on the kitchen table, without saying anything, and forty-eight hours went by before his mother happened to open it and learn that he was at the head of his class.

'So,' she exclaimed in amazement, 'you're the most intelligent of the lot! It's the first time anyone in the family got first prize.'

Whereupon Vladimir had snapped bitterly and mockingly:

'He's the little saint!'

'What do you mean?'

'That's what his classmates call him. Because he lets himself get knocked around without defending himself. All he does is put up his arms to protect himself, and then he refuses to tell the teacher who hit him.'

'Is that true, Louis?'

'I'm the smallest '

He was lying, and the proof was that his cheeks turned pink. Even if he had been built like the twins, he probably would not have hit back. The blows didn't hurt much. After a few seconds, he didn't feel anything and there was no point getting involved in a fight. Some day they would tire of always picking on the same one and would let him daydream in his corner.

He didn't like people to bother about him, didn't like to be asked questions, to be torn from his thoughts of the moment. He had always been interested in the stove, the stairway, the yard, the carpenter's shop, the stalls in the street, but he was now becoming interested in people too, in his mother, in his brothers, in the faces he saw in the street. However, even with regard to his family he felt untouched, he remained apart, without suffering or rejoicing at anything whatever.

'Monsieur Pliska, a friend of mine.'

Their mother sometimes introduced those of her lovers who spent several nights or several weeks with them. They occasionally played with the children.

Monsieur Pliska, whom she called Stefan, lasted at least two months, which included the period of the Christmas holidays. He was a big fellow of not more than twenty-five, with a powerful build. When he stood in the kitchen, the room seemed too small for him, and the chairs creaked under his weight.

They did not know what he did for a living. When Gabrielle got up to go to Les Halles, he would stretch out on the bed and sleep late, until nine or ten o'clock. The noise did not waken him.

He was very fair, in fact his hair was almost white, and he had orange-coloured skin that was pitted in spots with smallpox marks. He spoke only a few words of French but tried to understand what was said. Without taking an interest in Vladimir or the twins, he had immediately singled out Louis, though he often paid compliments to Alice, whom he pretended to treat as a young lady. He even kissed her hand at times, though there was no telling whether he was being playful or serious.

'Pretty!' He would go into raptures. 'Much pretty!'

Nothing could prevent him from going down to the yard bare-chested, wearing only underpants and an overcoat thrown over his shoulders, and washing himself thoroughly at the tap. When he came up again, he glowed with satisfaction and would hum a Czech song, prepare his shaving brush and sharpen his razor, for he wore neither beard nor moustache.

'It's what?' he asked Louis, pointing to the only mirror in the flat.

'A mirror.'

'Mir-ro-ar . . .' he repeated painstakingly.

'Or a glass.'

'Glass? Why glass? Me drink from glass . . .'

Although he did not mind the cold, he nonetheless appreciated the pleasant warmth of the stove, near which he would sit with a pocket chess set on his knees.

'How you say . . . ?'

Those were his favourite words: How you say?

He outlined a crown on his head with his finger. 'Queen, yes? . . . Queen will take castle . . .'

It was so entrancing, thanks to his mimicry, that within two weeks Louis knew the chessmen, how they functioned, and a few of the standard moves.

'You play? Me give you queen and castles . . .'

It was the only Christmas that the family really celebrated. Other years, they contented themselves with eating forcemeat sausage. On the evening of December 24th, Monsieur Pliska returned with a three-foot Christmas tree which he set up in the middle of the table, and then placed packages on it; a jellied chicken, meat pie, ham, and a bottle of sparkling wine.

For Gabrielle he had bought an enamelled brooch in the

shape of a rose, for Vladimir a whistle that resembled a police whistle, for Alice a thimble which was so light that a needle would probably go through it. It was the intention that counted. The twins each received a top and Louis a box of coloured pencils.

Everyone could have some of the wine, and when he saw the bottle was almost empty he rushed out in his shirt sleeves and came back a minute later with a second bottle and a bag of biscuits.

Then he sang, and after that he insisted that Gabrielle sing too.

'She's woman of my life!' he cried in a burst of enthusiasm, turning to the children after she had sung a ballad of which she remembered only the first stanza and the end of the last.

The street was bright and noisy. The shops were all open, and all the windows were lit up. It was like a canal of light, and Louis went to the window several times to look out, for he was no longer hungry for the biscuits, and the sparkling wine had made him feel a little sick.

Monsieur Pliska's ideas always occurred to him abruptly. Suddenly he would stand up and dash to the corridor as if seized with an urgent need. This time he stayed out longer, so long that when he returned, triumphantly, the children were undressed. He brandished in triumph, while repeating a Czech word, a square bottle covered with unreadable signs and containing a yellowish liquor.

'For Christmas! ... Only Christmas! ... Health, woman my life ... My life always ...'

Gabrielle sipped it warily and remarked that it was strong, but she must have got used to it, for she remained in the kitchen part of the night drinking it. The children, who were overexcited, slept badly. At times they were awakened by Monsieur Pliska's singing, at times by his sobs, and finally by the clang of the bedsprings on which he and Gabrielle collapsed.

He usually disappeared in the afternoon and was away for part of the evening too.

'Me work.... Much work ...'

He would point to his head in order to explain that it was with his brain that he worked. He would also sulk at times, would not say a word for two days, except to explain to Louis, who was definitely his favourite:

'Mother cruel. . . . All women cruel. . . . Men very unhappy. . . . Pliska unhappy . . .'

He had brought an odd-shaped case, with railway labels pasted on it, which remained for a long time in the corner of the room where Emilie's cot had been and in which he carefully arranged his clothes and other personal effects.

What, indeed, had become of the cot? It had disappeared almost at the same time as the little girl. No doubt it had ended up in a second-hand store.

Pliska in turn disappeared, as did his case. Gabrielle did not explain why. She never explained. Perhaps she did not try to explain the whys and wherefores of things even to herself.

For Louis, it was the winter of discoveries. The first of these hardly surprised him. One night when he had awakened with a start from a bad dream and the moon had kept him from falling asleep again, he had gone to the window and leaned against it quietly with his elbows. The big moon lit up the landscape more brightly than the lamp-post and made it look unreal. Four dust-bins, so full that the lids did not close, were lined up on the pavement just in front of the alley.

He had often seen rag-pickers poking about in dust-bins with their spiked sticks and thrusting whatever was still usable into the bag they carried on their back or into a pram.

That night, two people were rummaging in the dustbins opposite, a man and a woman, but they were not rag-pickers, and what they were looking for was crusts of bread, anything edible, which they immediately stuffed into their mouths.

They were not old. They were not wearing rags, like the tramps in the Place Maubert. They were younger than the children's mother, a bit older than Monsieur Pliska. So there existed a category below the paupers who received bread tickets or help from Public Assistance or who could get a bowl of soup at the Salvation Army. When they had finished going through the four bins, they started walking down the street. Without a word, without looking at each other.

The second discovery was more important. To begin with, he knew that Vladimir's friend, the Spaniard's son, was called

Ramon, for when he passed the shop one day he heard the boy's mother call him by name before yelling to him something that Louis did not understand.

Two or three times, while walking in the street after four o'clock, when the lights went on, he had noticed his brother and Ramon strolling along with a self-assumed air of animals on the alert. Not only was Vladimir the taller and more resolute of the two, but Louis could feel that he was the leader and that his companion was his slave.

It must have been a Saturday night, for there were more people than usual in the narrow street which was narrowed even more by the stands that overflowed the shops and by the carts of the street-sellers.

Louis had just spoken to his mother. He was on his way home when he saw Vladimir and Ramon standing on the kerb. They were talking in a low voice, with an expression of self-importance. Vladimir really looked like a leader, and even from a distance Louis could tell that he was giving an order.

Ramon, who was wearing a blue frieze overcoat with gilt buttons, was hesitating and making objections, and finally Vladimir simply shoved him off the pavement by poking him in the side with his knee.

Once again, in the middle of the street, Ramon turned around imploringly but encountered only the hard look on his friend's face. In front of him was a butcher's shop that specialized in poultry and game. A wild boar, which was partly cut up, was hanging from a hook near a garland of wild ducks and other birds that were unfamiliar to Louis, who had never seen them alive or eaten them.

On a stall lay plucked chickens that were marked with a label and, to the left of the door, unskinned wild rabbits.

Two women were waiting their turn. An old gentleman in a bowler hat was being shown some birds at which he kept sniffing.

Ramon waited for the moment when no one was looking in his direction, grabbed a rabbit, slipped it under his coat and started walking very fast while Vladimir, on the other pavement ambled up the street.

Louis followed them with his eyes. They got together in the

dimly lit Rue de l'Arbalète, where Ramon handed his friend the rabbit as if performing an act of homage or offering his tribute of loyalty.

Vladimir took it by the ears, swung it around two or three times and tossed it into the first alley they came to.

Louis then remembered the watch, sweets, and miscellaneous objects that his brother used to hide in his mattress. Did he still collect them? Louis had never since been curious enough to find out. He didn't care. The important thing was that Vladimir had been able to make Ramon steal. Was it actually the Spaniard who had swiped the watch? Probably not. He seemed to be a novice. He had implored Vladimir and had crossed the street reluctantly.

A rabbit that was good to eat was now lying in an alley where rats would soon be squabbling over it.

Louis said nothing about the matter to anyone. He never said anything.

One day he saw a gathering at the head of the street and had no difficulty worming his way up to the front. It was simply a crowd of onlookers surrounding a street-seller, a tall, bony, lantern-jawed fellow with an enormous nose who was contorting his face as if it were made of rubber.

'Now listen closely, ladies and gentlemen, and if the ladies are wise and their husbands have common sense, every family is going to gain a quarter of an hour a day, to say nothing of avoiding three or four fights every week.'

He was not wearing a detachable collar. From a small case, which he barely opened, as if it contained treasures, he took a very high collar with a double lining and, looking as if he were squirming in front of a mirror, attached it with two buttons.

'First and easiest operation, especially if your wife or girl friend lends a hand.'

Another dip into the suitcase, from which this time he withdrew an aggressively purple tie.

'And now for the second morning operation to which elegant men are condemned. Bear in mind that this tie is new and therefore easier to handle than an old one.'

Then followed a comedy which he played with his hands, eyes, neck, mouth, in fact with his whole body, twisting and turning in order to work the tie up between the two flaps of the starched collar.

After which, he gave up in exhaustion, wiped his forehead, and beckoned to a plump, jovial woman in the audience who had a shopping bag under her arm.

'So you, Madame, are willing to be my spouse for a moment. You've nothing to be afraid of. We're in public and I know how to behave. Be so good as to help me get this tie on.'

He had taken her shopping bag and slipped the tie into her pudgy fingers. As she was shorter than he, he leaned forward comically, acting as if he were half strangled each time she raised the flap of the collar.

'And *that*, ladies and gentlemen, is the cause of half – what am I saying? – of three-quarters of family fights, the other quarter being caused by our better half's corset. Unfortunately I don't go in for corsets because police headquarters forbids such demonstrations in public.'

All that remained for him to do was to take from the case a celluloid device to which the tie was attached in the twinkling of an eye. Two or three seconds later, it was set in the collar.

'Ladies and gentlemen, unfortunately not everybody will be able to take advantage of this work of genius which will ensure peace in the family and put valets out of work.'

The case was finally opened. Just as the sale was beginning, one of the spectators nudged his wife with his elbow and, pointing to Louis, who was still up in front, whispered:

'I've never seen such a shrewd look as on that child's face!'

Louis heard him and did not smile. He already knew, in a vague kind of way, that it was not true, that he was not shrewd at all, that he had simply been watching and taking in the spectacle and that every detail of the scene, the man's twisted mouth, the dumpy woman's black polka-dot dress, the wart on her cheek, the expression of the various spectators, was inside him.

He was not laughing at them. He did not think them ridiculous. He had never yet thought anything ridiculous or seen anything not worth watching with interest.

# Chapter Four

Vladimir had stopped going to school. He had not succeeded in getting his diploma. Or rather, no doubt, though he did not bother to explain to anyone – except perhaps to Ramon – he had not wanted to get it, out of protest, out of defiance.

From the very beginning, he had made a point of being at the bottom of the class. He had always been big for his age, and at about fifteen he had suddenly grown almost four inches.

Not only were his clothes tight on him, but he was not used to his height and his movements were awkward. His gait was at times too manly and at times too childish. His face was covered with a dark fuzz that made him look unwashed, and Louis once caught him putting their mother's powder on his face to cover his pimples.

For two or three weeks, he had almost never been seen during the day. He did not wander along the Rue Mouffetard with his Spanish friend, who was now at a *lycée*, where he wore the school uniform. What did Vladimir do with his days? He would come home at night looking, at one and the same time, feverish, arrogant, and depressed.

'When are you going to make up your mind to work?' his mother would ask him.

He would answer like a man who was not obliged to account for what he does:

'You'll see.'

She was definitely worried when she saw him wearing a new suit for which she had not given him money, new shoes, a white shirt, and a wing collar.

'Starting Monday morning, I'll be working for Monsieur Brillanceau as an apprentice.'

'The locksmith on the Rue Tournefort? You want to become a locksmith?'

He had reached his decision alone and had not discussed the matter with anyone, and nobody ever knew by what process or after what experiences he had come to choose the locksmith's trade.

Louis knew the shop, which was not far from his school. It was at the corner of an alley, of which there were many in the neighbourhood, on the side of the street that did not get the sun, and the windows were so dirty, the walls so dark, with hundreds of keys and tools hanging from nails, that a gas lamp burned all day long.

Monsieur Brillanceau had the colour of his trade. He was grey and sad-eyed. A curved pipe, most of the time unlit, was always in his mouth, as if it had been dug into his grisly moustache.

Vladimir started work at seven in the morning. He took with him a canteen of coffee and slices of bread and butter in an old biscuit tin.

Life at home suddenly began to change quickly. Alice was thirteen and, though she was frail, looked older than she was. She had barely passed the examination for her diploma, but refused to continue her studies and stayed at home, where she did the housework and prepared the meals.

'What did you do when you were my age?'

To which Gabrielle replied frankly:

'I'd rather not tell you.'

At times, Alice would replace her mother at the push-cart for an hour. At times too, in the evening, she would disappear for rather a long time, and when she undressed before lying down on the mattress next to his, Louis would get a whiff of an odour foreign to the family, an odour of boy.

She was pale, but pretty enough for people to turn around to look at her as she went by. She was beginning to put on make-up, but ineptly, which gave her a dubious look. With her small pear-shaped breasts and the sparse, blonde down between her thighs, she would strut about nude in front of her brothers, dragging her clothes.

There was a feeling in the air that things were starting to go to pieces. There was no longer the old solidarity in the home, and one night there was a violent scene during which Louis saw his mother in a rage for the first time.

For the past few days she had been coming home with a middle-aged man she called Papa who spent the night with her behind the torn curtain. He was a huge, hairy-chested fellow with impressive hands. He probably worked at Les Halles, for he left with her in the morning, without bothering to wash his face. He had a strong smell and made love very fast, with strong thrusts that shook the floor, after which he crashed down on the bed and sank into sleep.

One night, the fourth or the fifth, Louis was awakened by Gabrielle's shrill voice.

'Let go of her, you son of a bitch!'

It was still dark. The sky was just beginning to turn greyish, vaguely lighting up the room, as did the gaslight from the lamppost. Louis, without moving, half opened his eyes and saw the man's bulk on the bed of his sister, of whom all that was visible was her blonde hair.

'Let her alone, you hear, you pig?'

He kept breathing hard and emitting a kind of laugh. Perhaps Gabrielle and he had been drinking the night before, as she so often did with others.

She tried to pull him off the mattress.

'Get the hell away, you whore!'

Vladimir, who suddenly awoke, punched him on the back of his head with both fists, but the man didn't seem to feel anything. Then Gabrielle, who was in her shirt, ran into the kitchen, came back with the poker and started beating him with it, screaming with all her might:

'You bastard! You pig! You sex maniac!'

He began to groan and got down on all fours with a dazed look, uncovering the body of Alice, who put her hands to her face.

Gabrielle kept hitting him, and blood spurted at the base of his skull, while he staggered painfully to his feet.

The twins, who had not stirred, were surely awake. The scene wavered between the grotesque and the tragic. All the protagonists were in their shirts. For some reason or other, perhaps out of habit, the man had kept his socks on.

He looked like an ox that the killer in the abattoir had failed to knock out with his cleaver. Louis would have sworn, later, that the man's eyes had become red. He stood there with his huge hands open, hesitating to dash at Gabrielle, who was still holding the poker and standing up to him.

'Mama!' screamed one of the twins with terror as the man took a step towards her.

'Don't you worry about me! I'll attend to him!'

The poker rose and came down hard. Luckily it missed his head, grazed his cheek, and landed on his shoulder. There was a sound as of a bone cracking.

'And now, you swine, if you haven't had enough, say so!'

She turned around without hesitating, fearing nothing more from him, picked up the clothes that were piled on the floor, walked to the door and threw them into the corridor.

'Get the hell out of here if you don't want me to finish you off, you dirty rat!'

Then the big shoes were sent flying into the narrow hallway towards which the man she had called papa a few hours earlier was staggering.

Heedless of the neighbours, she slammed the door in his face and when she came back she was still so excited that she knocked over the chamber pot.

Standing in the middle of the room, she yelled at her daughter, who was hiding her face.

'And you, couldn't you scream, you little bitch? Admit you liked it!'

One shitting business, as Gabrielle would say with her fondness for expressive words, brings another. The following day, a letter arrived, something that almost never happened. The principal of the school 'requested Madame Heurteau to be so good as to come to his office regarding an important matter'.

Louis was expecting it. For some weeks he had been seeing the redheads less and less often at break. They left and returned with their school satchels at the usual time, but they did not go to school.

When Gabrielle got home, she was furious, though this time her fury was partly an act.

'You, the two of you, so you imagine I've got it too easy and you've got to complicate my life, is that it? I want to know where you go traipsing most days? You, Guy, answer me.'

He was the more vulnerable of the two, and though they were born the same day he looked younger than his brother.

'I don't know, Mama.'

'You don't know how you spend your time?'

Her hand became menacing and Olivier spoke up.

'We don't like school, Mama. They've got a grudge against us. We're blamed for everything. When someone talks in class, the teacher doesn't try to find out who it was. He says, "Redheads, be quiet!" He doesn't call us by our names, like the other boys. We're "the redheads". And we're always the ones, even when we haven't done anything, who have to stand in the corner. The boys keep away from us and claim we smell of rotten vegetables.'

'Who said that?'

'All of them. They're all against us.'

Because of the vegetables, solidarity was springing up again.

'Didn't you ask them what their mothers do?'

'No, Mama, we didn't.'

That was the twins' shrewd side.

'Some of them are in a dirtier trade than me and I know at least two who earn their living with their behinds. You can tell them that next time. But you've got to go to school, because it seems they've done some investigating, that I'm not a good mother, that I let you fool around and don't look after you. The pompous idiot I went to see who they call the principal threatened to send a report to the police asking that you be sent to an institution.'

'An institution?'

'I think that's the word he used. He meant a reformatory!'

Was there any connection between those events and the habit that Louis began to fall into shortly thereafter of accompanying his mother to Les Halles? He did not ask himself the question. As with many of his ways and acts which were to stand out in his memory, it simply happened one day, without his trying to know why.

One spring morning, very early, before sunrise, while his mother was dressing, he asked her in a humble tone as he lay on his mattress:

'Can I come with you?'

'To Les Halles?'

'That's right. I've felt like doing it for a long time.'

'You need sleep.'

'I won't fall asleep again anyway. Once, Mama! Just once!'

He was not pretending. His intention was to go with his mother just once.

He had already slipped on his trousers and he dressed more quickly than ever. Except in winter, when she lit the fire before leaving, their mother did not drink her coffee at home.

'Are you the one who's going to push the cart?' she joked as they went down the dark stairway where they had to run their hands along the wall so as not to miss a step.

'I'll try.'

It was an exciting experience. In the yard, he already smelled the odour of night, which is not the same as that of day, and he was surprised, as they walked up the street, to see a light. It lit up a narrow, shallow bar in which two dark tables stood near the horseshoe-shaped counter. The bald proprietor was wearing a very white shirt, the sleeves of which were rolled up, and a blue apron.

A woman with a shawl over her shoulders was leaning on the bar with her elbow and dipping her croissant into a cup of coffee and milk. It was a new smell, a new image too, and Louis was happy at the thought that almost everybody was still asleep at that hour.

'Hello, Céline! Ernest, two coffees.'

He placed two glasses, first one and then the other, under the percolator, which let out a jet of steam.

'With milk for the boy?'

'Do you want milk, Louis?'

'A little. Can I have a croissant?'

There was a basketful of them. They had just come out of the oven and were still warm and crisp, and he was allowed to eat four of them, which had never happened in his life.

The owner turned to a shelf and grabbed a bottle at the end of which was a long tin nozzle, and without asking, no doubt following a daily rite, he tossed a dash of liquor into the mother's coffee, which immediately gave off a different smell.

She too was eating croissants. She ordered a second cup, which received another dash.

'You on your way, Gabrielle? Did you sell out yesterday?'

'There was just about enough left to make soup with.'

Everything was different, the sound of footsteps on the pavement, the way the houses looked. Some were four storeys high, two or three with red brick fronts; another, which was painted white, adjoined houses that were only one storey high. An empty hackney went by with the coachman dozing on the seat.

They turned right at the Rue du Pot-de-Fer and entered a yard where they joined other women, among whom was the grandmother. A sleepy little man with a pot belly was in charge. Each of the women picked one of the push-carts lined up against a wall and then went to get her scale and weights in a dark shed.

'Where'd you spend the night, Henriette?'

They yelled to each other, laughed like little girls during break, teased each other, exchanged catty remarks that only they could understand. Some were young and some were old. Most of them were big women with blotchy faces, pudgy fingers, and swollen ankles.

Without waiting, they left the yard and went down the Rue Lhomond. When they passed the Pantheon, the sky was getting lighter, and in the Boulevard Saint-Michel an omnibus drawn by six horses with clopping shoes almost hit the push-cart as it went by.

'You and your hearse!' yelled his mother.

They crossed the Pont Saint-Michel, and Louis, who stayed at the right because Gabrielle wanted him to be nearer the pavement, pushed with all his might. He would have liked to be between the shafts and roll the cart by himself, but he dared not ask his mother to let him.

The Courthouse was dark and empty and only a yellowish-green light shone above the gate of the mortuary.

After the Pont au Change the streets began to get lively. Several omnibuses were waiting to leave. Then, in the Rue des Halles, there were all kinds of noises. He saw carts that were loaded with pyramids of cabbages and carrots, crates full of live chickens and rabbits.

The people there were wide-awake, because activity had started long before, for many of them even before midnight, and beyond the gaslit warehouses, from which issued an unbroken din, a continuous stamping and trampling, yells, calls, oaths, and laughter, stood a little train of trucks behind its engine, which was puffing peacefully.

'Do your feet hurt?'

'No, Mama.'

'Aren't you cold?'

His feet didn't hurt, he wasn't cold, and he was having the greatest adventure of his life. His nostrils quivered without managing to take in all the smells, for they changed every ten yards.

There were vegetables, fruit, poultry, cases of eggs, everywhere, on the pavements, in the gutter, all over the warehouses, and everything was moving, was heaped in one place and then transported to another.

Figures were yelled. People were writing in black pads with violet pencils. Market porters wearing big hats and carrying a side of beef on their shoulder rushed through the streets. Tubs were overflowing with guts. Women sitting on stools were plucking poultry with the rapidity of magicians.

It all looked chaotic, but he would soon learn that, for all the apparent disorder, every waggon, every crate, every cauliflower, every rabbit, every man had a definite place and precise job.

He saw there people of a kind who hung around the Rue Mouffetard, bearded old men in rags, with long hair down to the back of their neck who were carrying crates that were too heavy for them from a waggon to a warehouse while a young man jotted down a check beside their name each time they entered.

The grandmother went by, and Gabrielle yelled out to her:

'It's a good day for red cabbage.'

Why? He realized that she had seen everything, the price marks on piles of merchandise, the vegetables that the other street-sellers of the Rue Mouffetard were already loading on their carts.

'Got to be shrewd in our line of work,' she explained to Louis.

He was grateful to her for saying this, for it was the first time she had ever spoken to him in confidence about her professional life.

'Some women buy anything just because it's cheap.'

She would listen to figures that were quoted as she went by. She stopped, tempted, in front of some crates of potatoes.

'How much?'

Then, without answering, she continued pushing her cart towards a street where the bustle continued, and entered a high-ceilinged shed. On a blackboard, next to the names of foods, were figures written in chalk which a man in a black smock kept changing constantly, the way the teacher did on the dais.

Clerks were working in a glass-enclosed cage. Everything went fast. You have to have your wits about you not to be knocked over by one of the porters, and Louis instinctively held on to an end of his mother's apron.

'Have you got any red cabbage, Samuel?'

'Did you see it on the board?'

'It's not there.'

'Go and ask François. There may be a few crates left.'

She did not change her mind easily, and Louis was pleased to see that everyone knew her and treated her with affectionate familiarity. She got her red cabbage and they started going back, but by other streets in order to avoid those that were too crowded to get through easily.

The sun was up. The windows of the houses were shining. The blues were bluer, the pinks pinker, the reds redder. He began to see cooks and even well-dressed women carrying shopping bags.

They passed three men in evening clothes and top hats coming out of a restaurant in the company of young women covered with frills and furbelows. One of the men who was a little the worse for drink wanted to hire a marketer's horse and waggon at any price in order to drive home.

Louis was pushing with all his might. He felt the resistance of every paving stone. His mother stopped before the Châtelet.

'Wait for me here.'

She entered a wine-shop where she was served a small glass as a matter of course. She tossed down her drink, took a coin from the money-bag under her apron, and threw it on the bar. It was a glorious morning, bursting with life. Everything was alive. Everything was colourful. Everything smelled good and he drank the air rather than breathed it.

'Aren't you tired?'

'Not at all, Mama!'

'What are you going to do till it's time to go to school?'

For at half past six she was already setting up her push-cart in its usual place, opposite the fishmonger's, and she was not the first.

'Don't worry. I'll find something to do.'

His head was spinning, his legs were limp, he was full. He walked slowly up the dark stairway and opened the door of the room, where the twins were still sleeping. His sister was in the kitchen lighting wood for the coffee.

'Has Vladimir left?'

'Five minutes ago. Where have you been?'

'I went with Mama.'

'To Les Halles? She let you? Are you hungry?'

'I ate croissants.'

'Lucky you!'

He was tempted to stretch out on his mattress in order to digest in peace what he had just lived through. His cheeks were flushed, and he knew that if he let himself lie down he would sink into blissful slumber.

He made himself sit by the window and go over his homework. Alice went to wake the twins with little kicks, and they groaned before getting up. They were in their shirts. Their hair was sticking up and their eyes were bleary.

'Hey, little saint, what are you doing?'

'I'm not doing anything.'

They were aggressive as soon as they awoke.

'He went to Les Halles with Mama.'

'What for?'

'Ask him.'

'Just to see,' said Louis casually.

He did not yet know that it would become a routine or that in the classroom he would relish the torpor that kept him suspended between dream and reality.

'Are you dreaming, Cuchas?'

'No, sir.'

'Twelve times twenty-seven?'

'Three hundred and twenty-four.'

A vague smile, which no one understood, would drift over his face.

*

The morning trip to the market behind his mother's push-cart was to play an important role in his memories and his life, but legends grew up around the experience and it became difficult, even for him, to distinguish clearly between truth, exaggeration, and falsehood.

People wrote, for example, that for several years, despite his age and weak constitution, he got up every night at three in the morning, winter and summer alike. But his mother did not always go out at three in the morning. It depended on the season. In the autumn, she would leave the Rue Mouffetard later, for there would have been no point in being at her post with her wares at six o'clock, when there was no one in the street and the lamp-posts were still lit.

There were also mornings when, depending on her companion, she would let herself sleep an extra hour or two.

In any case, Louis himself did not always wake up. It was true that often, as soon as his mother awoke, he did too, that he sometimes was up before her, but at times he would fall asleep again, unless it was a Thursday* or a holiday, or during the holidays.

People also said that the women of Les Halles were so amazed to see a child impose such discipline on himself in order to help his mother that they had nicknamed him the little saint. In what way could he help her, in the beginning, he with his skinny arms? It was for his own sake that he went, in order to renew the wonder of it, to complete his set of exciting images, for example, that of the Seine, which had hardly struck him the first time, of the tugboats that pulled their barges and disappeared for a moment beneath the arch of the bridge, of the

* French children do not go to school on Thursday, but do on Saturday —Translator's note.

horse-drawn canal boats which a carter followed slowly along the towpath. He was constantly discovering images, yellow and green house fronts, signboards, nooks crowded with barrels.

It was not the women of the market but his schoolmates who had nicknamed him the little saint. The term had reached the market by chance. A woman with whom his mother was bargaining over baskets of plums on the pavement had gone into raptures in his presence.

'What a pretty child! He's like a miniature!'

Though he no longer had long hair like a girl, it was still longer than that of most boys and, being very fine, tended to flutter about his face, which thereby seemed all the more delicately designed.

Gabrielle had replied:

'It would be better for him not to be a miniature but a brute like his brothers. The boys in school take advantage of his size and hit him, and since he won't tell who did it they call him the little saint.'

It was also related that he had acquired a passion for chess at the age of six because Monsieur Pliska had sat with him in front of the kitchen stove for a few days and shown him how the pieces moved.

But it was not until a year or two later, when he began to be given spending money for Sunday, that he saved up to buy a cheap pocket chess set, the pieces of which were made not of ivory or wood but cardboard.

When it rained, he would sometimes sit near the window bent over the black and white squares for an hour.

At about that time, the landlord, Monsieur Doré, decided to install gas in the house, and the paraffin lamp, which was no longer needed because of the incandescent gas-mantles that hung not only in the middle of the kitchen but in the middle of the room as well, ended up in a second-hand store, like Emilie's cot.

The mantles, which were delicately suspended from the end of the gas jet, were made of a fragile material and turned to dust as soon as anyone touched them or when they were shaken. They gave rise to a whole series of minor dramas, for on the floor above lived an Italian family from Piedmont with seven or eight children.

The father, a construction worker, wore heavy boots and kept them on when he got home in the evening. He would walk up and down the room, play with the children, and make the ceiling tremble, with the result that the mantles in the room had to be changed twice a week.

'I'm going upstairs to those brutes and tell them a thing or two!'

Gabrielle would go bravely up the stairs, which were now lit by a gas burner with a dancing flame that was at times white and at times yellow. She would knock on the door, and for a quarter of an hour there would be an exchange of insults in French and Italian.

The children would cry, their mother would yelp. Vladimir, if he was at home, would go to the rescue.

Other tenants, disturbed by the noise, would yell at everyone, and once, when Louis had gone upstairs to see what was going on, he discovered through the chink of a door a skeleton-like, glassy-eyed old woman who already belonged to another world and who was telling her beads.

Had it not been for that incident, he would never have known she existed, for she never left her room and it was not until six or seven months later that she was taken away very early one morning, on the sly, in a white pine coffin that resembled the crates in the market.

Vladimir was still working for Monsieur Brillanceau. He wore a cap and a pair of heavy blue overalls. He smoked cigarettes which he rolled and let droop from his lower lip in an affected way.

In the street, he walked with his hands in his pockets, rolling his shoulders with an air of disdain, as if everyone were watching him.

He was losing weight. His face was peaked and the rings under his eyes grew darker and darker. There were evenings when he did not get home until twelve o'clock, and one winter night, which Louis could not place exactly, he did not return until breakfast.

He had a new way of treating the men who spent the night with their mother. He would look them up and down mockingly and aggressively, as if challenging them to pick a fight with him.

One Sunday morning – it was still winter – a tall young man with the head of a musician was drinking his coffee and eating bread and butter with them when Vladimir, who almost always slept late on Sunday, entered the kitchen. His eyes were bleary.

'You're not satisfied with sleeping with my mother, but she has to support you as well.'

He was obviously in a bad temper, ready for anything, ready to bite.

'Keep quiet, Vladimir, and mind your own business. Don't get up, Philippe. Don't mind what he says. He's always like that in the morning and an hour later he forgets all about it.'

The musician nevertheless preferred to leave, and his departure took place amidst an awkward and painful silence. No sooner was the door closed than Vladimir attacked again. Pouring himself a bowl of coffee, he sat down, with his elbows on the table, and snapped at his mother:

'Do you make them pay or don't you?'

'If I made them pay I'd be a whore and your mother's not a whore.'

'Then you're just stupid.'

'I'm a woman, and that's that, and I can't help it if I need a man in my bed. I got married because I thought that was the most practical way. I happened to pick a half-impotent good-for-nothing who spent his time in bars and came home only to vomit.'

'That's no reason.'

'No reason for what?'

'Nothing.'

It was obvious that he had something on his mind, but he checked his anger and chewed away glumly.

'If you're not satisfied with your mother, go and get another one. Aren't you ashamed to talk the way you did in front of your sister?'

He looked at Alice and opened his mouth, but managed to control himself and said nothing. It was only as he left the kitchen that they heard him mutter:

'They're all whores, all of them!'

Twenty years later, Vladimir was to admit to Louis that the

night before that Sunday he had had his first disappointment in love, that he had found his girl, the one with whom he went out and on whom he spent his money, in a corner with a man who was making love to her standing up.

He had pulled away the man's overcoat, which was hiding them, and he had seen. He was determined to fight. The other fellow had run away as fast as his legs could carry him, and suddenly Vladimir, who was chasing him, had stopped hearing his footsteps. The man must have been hiding in the shadow of an alley, of which there were many in the neighbourhood. Perhaps he had rushed into the first house he came to and was sitting on the stairs waiting.

Vladimir had searched for a long time. The girl had gone home.

'I'd have killed him,' he admitted.

He also admitted that for the first time in his life he had cried, he who, as a child, had forbidden himself to shed tears, to let anyone hear him complain.

They got used to the new lighting, which was less intimate than that of the paraffin lamp. Instead of there being a limited circle of light surrounded by a zone of shadow, even the nooks and corners of the two rooms received the same white brightness, which revealed wounds.

They suddenly realized that the walls were dirty, that the mattresses had been patched many times, here and there with cloths of different colours. The ceiling was cracked, and a broad streak of bright white plaster showed where the gas pipe went.

Was it that winter? The following winter? Louis could not remember, not knowing whether he had been in the third or fourth form, for the teacher had changed classes at the same time as the pupils. Louis was always first, though he sat at his desk as dreamily as ever.

He had happened to find, quite by chance, the coloured pencils that the Czech had given him for Christmas and that he used to keep in his school satchel.

The teacher did not resemble the one he had had in the lower forms. He was thin and had a long, curled moustache and long, narrow goatee which he would tug at nervously. He had very beautiful long, white hands with carefully trimmed nails. He probably earned little money, like the other teachers, but nonetheless made an effort to be elegant. Though his tail coat was rather worn, it was well cut and did not come from a ready-made clothes shop. His collars and cuffs were almost always clean and his shoes were of fine leather.

Louis had at first annoyed him with his placidness, with his smile, which the teacher perhaps thought ironic. Then he began to observe him more closely. He would loom up behind Louis when he was writing a composition, would question him point-blank while pretending to look elsewhere.

It was as if Louis were a riddle to him and as if he made it a point of honour to solve that riddle. Perhaps he thought he had found the key to it that morning. It was a market day, and Louis, who was drowsy, was listening to the lesson while drawing one of the pear trees in the yard in black and violet.

He had not noticed that the voice of the teacher, whose name was Huguet, had changed its place, that it no longer came from the dais but from the back of the room. Suddenly a familiar hand seized the unfinished drawing.

The odd thing was that Monsieur Huguet did not say anything to him, did not punish him, but about ten days later, during break, he went over to Louis.

'What are you planning to do when you grow up, Cuchas?'

'I don't know, sir.'

'Isn't there anything that tempts you?'

He searched in his mind, trying hard to be sincere, as he always did.

'No sir,' he finally concluded in disappointment.

'Oh.'

That was all. At about the same time, a week or two later, his mother was summoned again by the principal. The twins had not set foot in school for three consecutive days. There was talk of the police, of the juvenile court.

In the evening, the redheads let the storm break, without flinching. The following noon, they were home for lunch as usual. They did not return in the afternoon. Twice, despite the bad weather, Gabrielle, wrapping her shawl around her, scoured the neighbourhood and questioned the shopkeepers.

The gas in the kitchen burned almost all night long. It was Vladimir who, before leaving for work in the morning, thought of the biscuit-tin. There were six of the tins, with different designs, on a shelf.

The one with a picture of a mill contained the flour, the one with Millet's 'Angelus' the sugar, and so on for the coffee and bags of spices, until the last one in the corner, the one painted all over with pompon roses.

That was the family safe. It contained Gabrielle's marriage licence, the children's birth certificates, a few yellowing papers that were perhaps old letters, the rent receipts, and now the gas receipts too. In short, that was where their mother kept the family treasures, and also a few dozen francs in a man's wallet and small change for purchases in the neighbourhood.

Gabrielle, who had not gone to Les Halles the night before, had already understood.

'Just as I thought. They took the money and left only the bronze coins.'

'Vladimir, what should I do?'

She was addressing him as a man for the first time, was asking him for advice as if he had suddenly become the head of the family.

'They won't get very far. Someone'll spot them and inform the police.'

'Unless they come back themselves, with the money spent. Where could they have slept in such weather? It isn't as if it were summer!'

'They won't come back by themselves.'

'How do you know?'

'I know them better than you. You'll have to report their disappearance to the police.'

'But then they won't give them back to me, especially after what the principal said. They'll be locked up in a reformatory. Vladimir, they're too young!'

Louis was unable to figure out later whether they were eleven or thirteen at the time.

'No hotel will take them without asking them questions. After all, they can't sleep under the bridges.'

She was crying, and Alice began crying too. She was the

closest to the twins in age, since she was only a year and a half older than they. They had played with her more than with the others and spoke freely in her presence, though they were secretive with the others, because she was a girl.

'It's time for me to go to work. Be sure to go to the police station, Mama. Otherwise you're the one who'll have to explain.'

'What do you mean?'

'Nothing. Just go! That's the only way to handle it.'

Vladimir had become a man overnight, and their mother felt it so strongly that she started dressing as soon as he left. She had a Sunday dress which she almost never wore and which lasted her three or four years, a lavender-blue silk gown with a yoke and a high lace collar that made her look like a girl, for her face was fresh, without wrinkles, and she was always ready to laugh.

Instead, she put on her everyday clothes and threw her black shawl around her shoulders.

'Don't forget to leave for school on time, Louis. If the principal asks you any questions, say that you don't know where your brothers are.'

She was still sniffling as she left the room, but her attitude was bolder, and in the street she held her head high as if she were already confronting the inspector. The principal did not send for Louis. Did he even know that young Cuchas and the Heurteau brothers were members of the same family? They were only names among others on his rolls, and he knew only the pupils whom he had to discipline.

It was cold. It was raining. Rubbish was flowing down both sides of the gutter when Louis got home for lunch. Perhaps there was just as much rubbish other days, but on that particular day he noticed it. For him, it was a colourless day, a tasteless day, a day without the usual sounds. He walked in a vacuum, and when he saw his mother and sister sit down at the table in the kitchen, he asked no questions, feeling that they had no good news to report.

'Did anyone say anything to you, Louis?'

'No, Mama.'

'I went to the police station.'

'I know.'

'They're going to try to find them. They were polite. They even offered me a seat. Here's Vladimir! Sit down and start eating.'

'I was telling your brother that they were polite and that the inspector asked me to sit down. He probably has children, because he understood right away and when I suddenly couldn't keep from crying, he came over and patted me on the shoulder.

'They're going to do what they can. It seems they won't find them in Paris. They're used to that kind of thing. Runaways, as they call them, are reported to them every week.

'They asked me if we'd ever lived in the country, if we went there on holiday or if we had relatives there, because that's where children almost always go when they run away from home. Most of them take the train, often a goods train.

'I asked him if they'd be locked up and he said he didn't think so, that I was known in the neighbourhood as an honest tradeswoman who's never violated police regulations.'

'You see!'

'I did the right thing in following your advice. There'll always be the inspector to defend us.'

'Didn't he talk to you about me?'

'Why? Do you know him?'

'Is he a stout man who has a watch chain with charms on it?'

'That's right. You mean you were taken to the police station, and you never told us?'

'I was a child. I was about Louis's age and a cop caught me swiping a handful of sweets from a stand. He picked me up like a rug and took me to the station. The inspector put on a gruff voice. I cried and begged him not to tell you because you had enough troubles without that.'

'Well I'll be damned!'

She was so dumbfounded that she forgot about the twins. It was not until two days later that they were brought back from Rouen, where they had been found huddled behind crates in a goods train. They had thought the train was going to Le Havre, where they were planning to stow away on a boat. They had picked the wrong truck, which had been disconnected at Rouen.

They gave no details about their adventure, spent an afternoon in the police station, and the wallet was put back in its place in the box with the pompon roses. Only two francs were missing.

## Chapter Five

'Listen to me, Guy and Olivier. The rest of you too, because what concerns them concerns all of you.'

Gabrielle was weary. Although events usually left few traces on her and she quickly regained her good humour, the twins' escapade had left its mark on her. She was limp. The children could see, if not how discouraged she felt, at least how tired she was.

'I had another talk with the inspector today. I beg you, Guy, don't look off into space that way as if it didn't concern you. It's a matter of your future, and your brother's too. He's really taken your situation to heart. The school doesn't want to take you back.

'He thinks there's no point in sending you to another one. You'll soon be thirteen and you'll never get your diploma. I haven't got one either, neither has my mother, nor lots of boys who've made good. So, to avoid the reformatory, he advises me to apprentice you. He's found an employer who'll take you, Monsieur Cottin, the printer in the Rue Cardinal-Lemoine.'

That was beyond the Place de la Contrescarpe, Louis's frontier, in a world where he hardly ever ventured.

'I'm warning you that Monsieur is strict, but I've been told he's fair and that he's decent to his workmen. The inspector first thought of separating you. I begged him not to. I assured him you wouldn't be able to bear it. Do you want to become printers?'

They both shrugged.

'I think that's your best bet. Don't you agree, Vladimir?'

'It's certainly better than the reformatory.'

'Well, you start Monday morning. Tomorrow we'll go and buy the clothes you need.'

It seemed to Louis that there was a different atmosphere in the home that evening, a certain constraint, an emotion difficult to define. Was it perhaps the end of a certain kind of existence?

Until then they had lived with each other as in a burrow, sheltered from the outside world, and come what may, their mother was there to protect them. The mattresses, lined up against the wall, formed one big bed, and their mother, though there was usually a man with her, was separated from them only by a sheet that hung from a rod.

There was a beginning and an end, the wooden bed on one side and Emilie's little cot on the other, with the whole brood between the two.

The cot had disappeared at the same time as Emilie. Vladimir had become a man. He appeared at mealtimes only occasionally and led a life of his own about which they knew almost nothing.

Alice, who was fifteen, had already hinted a few times that she was bored being alone in the house for hours on end and that some day she would look for a job. She had become a young lady who went dancing in the evening and brought home foreign odours.

And when the twins started working for Monsieur Cottin, Louis would be the only one who went to school.

Oddly enough, he bore a grudge against the gas. It seemed to him that ever since that hard white light had been installed in the two rooms their life had changed and that part of their intimacy, of the warmth of the burrow, had disappeared. Even the god-stove, on which too much light fell, no longer had its good-natured animal look and one could barely perceive the sparkling of the ashes that fell through the grate from time to time in a fine rain.

Was that the thing that brought him closer to his mother, that impelled him to go to Les Halles with her more often, to spend a few moments near her push-cart when he got out of school? In the years that followed there were bonds between them that had not existed before.

He had become the last of the brood, the last little one. She said so implicitly one day when Vladimir asked why they didn't move to a more comfortable flat where he could have a room. He felt a need to have a room of his own. He did not even have a cupboard but shared the hanging wardrobe with his mother, brothers, and sister.

'What's the point?' Gabrielle had replied. 'You won't be staying with us much longer and you'll be called up for military service in a few years. Alice, I'm sure of it, will marry at the earliest opportunity. The twins are working and don't come home for lunch.'

Louis would often stop in front of the laundry with the pale blue front. Its door was always open, and from it there escaped a special smell, almost as agreeable as that of the bakery. Like most of the shops in the street, this had a narrow front but was very deep, and five or six women worked side by side ironing linen on a long table covered with white thick cotton. Behind them stood a special stove with sloping surfaces on which they heated their irons. Most of them were young, and in summer they probably wore nothing under their white smocks, for he could see their breasts swaying and their hips rolling freely with every movement.

He knew that the name of the woman who ran the laundry was Madame Antoine, that she had started as an apprentice, and that most of the time she stayed in a room at the back where she tagged the linen and made out bills.

The washing was done in the basement, in a cellar crowded with big tanks whose ventilators opened on the yard.

Towards the beginning of autumn, Alice decided to take a job in Madame Antoine's laundry.

From then on, there was no longer a particular time for meals. Had there ever really been one? They all came home at different times. They knew where the bread was. They found cheese, ham, or liver pâté in the larder, which was a crate that Vladimir had covered with wire screening and fixed outside, on the window sill.

On Sundays, Gabrielle continued to prepare a special dish, boiled beef, lamb stew, or more rarely, a chicken that she had managed to get cheap. Yet even on Sunday the whole family seldom ate together, especially if the weather was good.

Vladimir dressed like a man and had bought at the Samaritaine department store a fashionable black-and-white-checked suit with a short jacket which he wore with a stiff collar and a bow tie.

In summer, he sported a broad-brimmed straw hat, which he wore tilted, and for several months he could be seen twirling a cane.

His area of operation had been spreading for some time, and the Rue Mouffetard was now merely a dormitory for him. He would take the train to spend his days off on the banks of the Seine, at Saint-Cloud or Bougival, and spoke of buying a bicycle as soon as he had put enough money aside.

Alice also wore a straw hat, with a much broader brim and adorned with a red ribbon, the ends of which fell down her back.

'Children, where do you expect me to get all that money?'

There had never been so much talk of money before the older children started working. Alice had bought, for the summer, a white dress trimmed with English embroidery, and, as winter approached, she dreamed of a velvet dress that she had seen in the window of the shop run by the Pochon sisters.

On Saturday night, she would go with girl friends to Bullier's, a big dance hall at the far end of the Boulevard Saint-Michel, where she met students. The next day she always had a story to tell. She would be very excited and would mention names that meant nothing to the family: Valérie, Olga, Suzanne Eugène, Roland.

'Roland is the nicest of the lot. He's at the university, where he's studying to be a lawyer, like his father. His father's the one who defended the anarchists who threw a bomb in front of the Royal Tavern.'

There was a great deal of talk about anarchists and bombs, about the underground, a network of tunnels under the streets of Paris where there would be trains that were faster than the omnibuses. Nobody in the family read newspapers. Vladimir would occasionally bring home instalments of a kind of magazine entitled *Nick Carter*, the cover of which showed a square-jawed man threatening someone with his revolver or freeing a girl who was tied to a tree or the foot of a bed.

84

Opposite Saint Médard's was a newspaper kiosk around which other publications hung from clothes-pins, for example *Le Petite Parisien Illustré*, which described, with violently coloured illustrations, the crimes of the week, an old man strangled in the Rue Caulaincourt, the woman poisoner of the Ternes neighbourhood . . .

All this began to exist for Louis on the fringes of his life. Before that time, the world was limited to a closed space which had little by little expanded without his realizing it, somewhat as it had for the twins, who now spent almost all their Sundays on the ramparts.

This reminded him of one of his rare conversations with his mother, for when they went to Les Halles together they spoke very little, despite the fact that the market was a long way off. Louis had never wondered what his mother thought about, though he had noticed that she was not engrossed, as he was, in the spectacle of the street.

She would cross the Seine at the Pont Saint-Michel without being aware of the colour of the light that day or whether there was a current, and she had probably never really looked at the towers of Notre Dame.

She worked. All grown-ups worked, except landlords like Monsieur and Madame Doré or rich people who would go horse-riding, ride in carriages, go to the races in grey top hats, and dine in restaurants with velvet seats and crystal chandeliers.

It was only recently that he had begun to realize this, only since he had started going to the news-stand from time to time to look at the illustrated periodicals.

'What are you thinking about, Louis?'

'Nothing, Mama.'

She pushed the cart along a few more yards of pavement, looking straight ahead with her lovely blue eyes.

'You're an odd little fellow.'

There was an intimacy between them which was composed of a vague tenderness that never manifested itself in words or effusiveness but only in shy, furtive glances or certain intonations.

It was true that he had no recollection of having been cuddled in her arms, the way children were in the books he read.

Perhaps when he was a baby? He retained a vague image of his mother holding Emilie against her bosom, but it was in order to suckle her.

'Are you really thinking about nothing?'

'I don't know.'

'It seems one's always thinking about something, even when a person doesn't realize it. I don't remember who told me that, someone who'd been to school.'

They walked on a little. A red and yellow tram went by them with a clatter. Louis was fascinated by the trams, mainly because of their colours, which enlivened the streets, and also because of the tinkling bells with which they warned pedestrians and the blue sparks they sometimes threw off at the top of their current collectors.

He had recently begun to venture at nightfall as far as the Boulevard Saint-Michel just to watch them go by, for it was nicer in the darkness. All he could see of the people who rode in them was their top hats and heads, as in a Punch and Judy show. They sat silently in a row, side by side, with fixed stares, in the diffuse light of another world, and at every jolt the heads would all bend to the same side before slowly straightening up.

'When your brothers and sister were your age, and even long before, they never stopped asking questions. Don't you ask questions in school either?'

He had to think. The world of school was so far away from that of the market.

'No, Mama.'

'What about your friends?'

'I haven't any friends.'

'Don't you ever play with the other pupils?'

'No.'

'Is it that they don't want to play with you?'

He was embarrassed by her trying, for no apparent reason, to penetrate his secret world. It wasn't a world, but rather a picture book, perhaps a silly one, but he didn't feel like talking about it.

'Don't you like to play?'

'I do play.'

'All by yourself?'

'Sometimes I play chess.'

'That's no game for a young boy.'

'I've played marbles, I've played with my top, I've rolled a hoop.'

Not for very long, but he had played.

'You never laugh. Are you happy, Louis?'

'Very happy, Mama.'

'Wouldn't you rather have been born in another family? Isn't there anything you miss?'

'I've got you.'

She looked at him in amazement, her eyes shining.

'You really love me?'

'I do, Mama.'

If she had not had to push her cart and if they had not already entered the Rue des Halles, where it was impossible to stop in the midst of the traffic, she would probably have kissed him or hugged him to her beautiful bosom. She forced a laugh, a muffled laugh.

'You don't really mean that I'm enough for you?'

'You are, Mama.'

'You're the most charming boy in the world. If only you continue to be happy. If only I could guess what goes on in your mind! With Vladimir, with your sister, even with Guy and Olivier, however tight-lipped they are, I think I can work them out and I'm seldom wrong. But you, you're a mystery. And yet – I oughtn't to say so – you're the one I like best . . .'

She could not prevent herself from adding:

'Although Vladimir . . .'

As if Vladimir, for her, were in a class apart. He was born when she was very young, and she was pregnant with him when she married Heurteau. Vladimir belonged to another race, so much so that though the name on his birth certificate was Joseph, he was always called Vladimir. Was Vladimir the name of his real father? Was he a Russian? Had she loved him? Had he abandoned her?

Questions floated across his mind, as they also did in later years, but he did not really put them to himself. He considered them unimportant and never did anything to find an answer to them.

They had entered Samuel's huge shed, and his mother, who was looking up at the blackboard, seemed ashamed of their unusual conversation.

'What should I get today?'

The blackboard had become familiar to Louis. As soon as they entered the area of the market, his watchful eyes observed the piles of fruit and vegetables, his mind noted the prices written on the labels and those that were yelled out by the fiercely competitive vendors.

'Apples, Mama.'

'Why apples?'

'Because they're red, the kind that children like best. They're not expensive today.'

He did not add that he admired the crimson colour of the pippins, the golden, star-shaped designs that illuminated their skins, their slightly flattened shape.

'How much can I have the apples for, Samuel?'

'How many crates?'

'Enough to make a big pile on the cart. In the Rue Mouffetard, the more there are, the more they attract people. They think you're selling them cheap because you're afraid to have any left over.'

It was true. He had seen his mother waiting for hours trying to sell a few bunches of leeks that were left at the bottom of the push-cart, whereas when it was overflowing with them she didn't know where to turn first.

'If you knock off two sous, I'll take ten crates.'

He felt she wanted to please him and it bothered him all morning in school. At noon, he ran to find out how the apples were selling and was overjoyed to see from a distance that the pyramid had melted. His mother was very vivacious.

'You see, my boy, you've brought me luck. Here! Go and buy yourself a bar of chocolate.'

She gave him a sou, which he dared not refuse, but he was sorry to be rewarded, particularly since he didn't deserve to be, because it wasn't she he had thought of but the apples. He nevertheless bought the chocolate and licked it as he walked up the street. His sister's voice yelled out to him as he passed the laundry.

'Did Mama give you some money? Why?'

'Because I advised her to buy apples and she's sold almost all of them.'

It must have been autumn. The weather was almost as warm as in summer and there were broad rings of sweat under Alice's arms. Only the two of them would be home for lunch. When things were selling well, their mother preferred to get rid of the whole stock before going home and contented herself with a snack, a chunk of bread and a few slices of salami, plus two or three visits to the bar opposite to gulp down a glass of wine.

'Which would you rather have, Louis? Dutch cheese or camembert?'

'Isn't there anything else?'

'There's some currant jam left, but you know Mama doesn't like us to eat it at noon.'

'Then camembert.'

It was a coincidence. It was not a legend that he created later as others were to create legends about his childhood. The chocolate was a point of reference. Louis was not particularly fond of chocolate. It was Vladimir who, when he was Louis's age, had eaten it whenever he could treat himself. When his mother handed Louis the coin, she must have confused him with his brother. When he sat down to eat, he still had the taste of the chocolate in his mouth, so that the camembert seemed less good to him than usual.

His mother had almost indulged in confidences that morning, had displayed more tenderness to him than usual, and he had the impression that she loved him as if he were a warm, soft kitten that was still defenceless.

As they sat and ate face to face, his sister looked sometimes at the window and sometimes at her brother, with a hesitant air.

'Listen, Louis. I think you like me and that I've never done you any harm.'

She was nibbling without appetite and spoke in a forced manner.

'You're a nice boy, you can keep a secret. I've got to tell it to someone and I don't dare say a word to Vladimir or Mama. Vladimir would blow up. And as for Mama . . .'

He waited. He felt embarrassed by the role of confidant, just as he had felt that morning.

'Louis, I think I'm pregnant.'

She was surprised at his being unperturbed, as if there were nothing startling or dramatic about the news.

'Do you hear? Don't you realize what that means?'

'Of course I realize. You're going to have a child.'

'I wonder whether I ought to let it happen. I'm not quite sixteen.'

'Mama wasn't much older when she had Vladimir.'

'It's not the same.'

'Why?'

'I wouldn't even be able to tell who the father is. Sylvie, my girl friend at the laundry, has been pregnant twice. She went both times to see a midwife in the neighbourhood who got rid of it for her. She didn't suffer at all the first time and didn't miss a day's work. But the second time, she was so sick that she had to see a doctor who had to do a curettage. All the same, she advises me to go to the midwife. I'm scared, Louis! What would you do if you were in my boots?'

'Nothing.'

'You'd let it happen?'

'Of course.'

'Even if it meant messing up my life?'

He felt she was annoyed with him for his seeming indifference. What else could he have said to her? Alice would have a child, and that was that.

*

Time passed quickly during that period. He had known long periods, of endless weeks, winters that went on and on though people talked about spring and buds every day. He had known short spells that brought you back to school, which seemed only to have just ended.

This one was a very brief period, and the seasons were so mixed up that later he was unable to determine when things had happened.

He was to remember evenings he had spent waiting for his sister to talk to their mother finally about the child, for ever

90

since she had let him in on the secret he could see that she was getting bigger, that her face was pale, that she had a resigned look.

At the same time he noticed that his mother was receiving fewer and fewer men. Perhaps she even no longer had regular lovers who lounged in bed in the morning, ate with them, and came back in the evening as if they were members of the family.

The twins would come home from work tired, with their finger-nails black and their clothes smelling of lead and printer's ink, and would go to bed early. They went to the shop regularly. Monsieur Cottin would not have tolerated absence. Their attitude nevertheless remained grim and they had a shifty look. They did what they had to do, because there was no getting around it, but they felt like prisoners and some day they would take their revenge.

'Aren't you sleepy, Louis?'

There were only three of them in the kitchen, his mother, his sister, and he. As he did not answer at once, Alice signalled to him and he understood. She was going to talk.

She closed the door behind him. He felt uneasy and did not fall asleep immediately. He expected to hear shouting.

The conversation began in a monotone. There were only some indistinct sounds, and he woke up in the morning without knowing anything of what had followed. He had not heard his mother get up, but she was no longer in bed. His three brothers, who started work at seven o'clock, had left. Alice began at half past six. So he was alone in the house, as often happened when he did not accompany his mother to Les Halles.

There was some coffee left in the flowered coffee-pot beside the fire. He ate quickly so as to have time to run down the street before going to school. He saw Alice ironing with the other girls. She was the third in line, and since he pressed his face against the window she finally caught sight of him. She smiled and nodded in a way that meant it's all right, that is, that the thing had gone off smoothly.

Almost immediately, or so it seemed to him, her pregnancy became obvious and he wondered whether she wasn't exaggerating it deliberately by tightening her dresses at the waist. She walked with her head tilted slightly back, as if to resist the weight of her belly, which nevertheless was still quite small.

'Have you heard the news, Louis?' asked his mother when he went to see her at the push-cart after school.

'I have, Mama.'

'Are you glad you're going to be an uncle?'

'I am, Mama.'

Vladimir, knitting his thick black eyebrows, was the only one who displayed resentment towards his sister.

'You're stupid enough to have done it on purpose! You think you're playing with a doll.'

For Alice had bought wool, knitting needles, and a magazine with coloured illustrations entitled *Layettes* and had begun to knit in the evening, which did not prevent her from going dancing at Bullier's the next Saturday and the following Saturdays.

As for their mother, though she no longer received men, she began to go out at night, on Saturday too, so that Louis stayed home alone that day. She dressed up in a way that, in the past, she had done only on rare occasions. She would take her lavender-blue silk dress out of its cardboard box and iron it, and also her petticoats, and she wore a corset that Louis had to help her lace.

'I'm getting fat,' she remarked. 'If I continue, I'll be enormous. You'd think it was due to my work.'

She had partly unstitched the famous dress in order to let it out, and even then it was tight on her. After powdering her face, putting on make-up, and sprinkling herself with carnation perfume, she would kiss Louis on the forehead.

'Good night, my little man. You're nice, you know! I hope you won't think too badly of me when you're older.'

A few weeks later, Alice had time to explain to him, while knitting slippers that resembled doll's slippers:

'Mama was marvellous. I offered, for her sake and the whole family's, to go to the country and work on a farm or at an inn where they'd have surely taken me on for my board. She could have simply told people that I was tired and she had sent me to live with relatives out of town, or to a nursing-home. I'd have given birth and left the child at a baby farm and no one would have known anything. Mama said no right away, that I had nothing to be ashamed of, that all the shopkeepers in the street, including the most stuck-up, had their first child before they were married or only four or five months later.

'She said to me, "Daughter, look them straight in the face. Carry your egg in front of you like a real female and be sure not to lower your eyes." '

Public works were going on all over Paris and streets were being torn up. Electricity was being installed everywhere. One Saturday evening when his mother had not got dressed up, Louis asked her: 'May I go to the Belle Jardinière department store?'

'It's closed by now.'

'I know, but I'd like to see the arc lamps.'

They talked about the lights in school. They talked about lots of things that he didn't know, about the Eiffel Tower, for example, which he had seen only from a distance, though most of his classmates had been to the top of it.

In summer, many of them took the train to spend their holidays at the home of grandparents or aunts who lived in the country. At least two boys in his class had relatives in Caen and had seen the ocean.

He himself had not been on a tram. He was not bitter about it, was in no hurry to have new experiences, did not try to widen his universe. Perhaps everything outside that limited circle even frightened him. He let the world come to him, little by little, bit by bit.

'Would you like me to go with you?'

'I'd be pleased, but if you've got something to do I know the way.'

Whenever he went to Les Halles, he saw the department stores and, from a distance, the wax dummies frozen in strange postures.

It was an unforgettable evening.

'You want me to dress up?'

He dared not answer either yes or no. She dressed as carefully as she did when she went to meet someone, sprayed herself with the same carnation perfume, dabbed her face with the pink powder, and put on lipstick.

'Don't I look too old?'

'Oh no!' he exclaimed fervently.

She locked the door and put the key under the mat. In the street she suddenly said to him:

'Take my arm, as if you were my sweetheart.'

That had never happened to them. He made himself walk on tiptoe, for he had not grown much. If they had met Vladimir, he would have sniggered, whereas the redheads would have looked away.

'Shall we take the tram to the Châtelet?'

All the lights were dancing in his head. For the first time, he saw people sitting at lighted pavement cafés in the evening. In the tram, he held his breath so as not to lose the tiniest bit of his emotion, and he smiled vaguely at the lady in black who looked funny when the movement of the tram jolted her from side to side. At times she looked as if she were about to doze off and suddenly, just as her head grazed her neighbour's shoulder, she would open her eyes in astonishment.

He saw the famous arc lamps, big globes that shed a bright, bluish light that quivered and crackled. When you stared at one and then closed your eyes, you saw ten, twenty globes in your head and it took a long time for them to go out.

'In the spring, if all goes well, I'll buy you a suit like that one.'

A wax boy with painted hair was wearing a sailor suit with a big white-trimmed collar. He looked as if he were taking a step forward, with his hand out to receive something, and was wearing patent-leather shoes.

'Come. I'll treat you to a drink.'

His mother would occasionally buy him an ice-cream soda in the bars around Les Halles where she would have a glass of wine to buck herself up, but he had never set foot in a real café. There was one opposite the Châtelet with mirrors on the walls and tables with white marble tops. He looked at the crowd anxiously, wondering whether there would be room.

Lots of men stared at his mother as she went by and some of them threw her seductive smiles. She was resplendent. She seemed beautiful to him in the light of the chandeliers that livened her face and made her eyes sparkle and the silk of her dress shine.

'A grenadine syrup for my son and an apricot cordial for me.'

The words were also new to him. He realized that his mother, whom he usually saw pushing her cart, frequented such places. She was completely at ease.

Although she had almost reproached him for not asking questions, he did ask one. There was an object that fascinated him much more than the mirrors and the ceiling on which naked women were painted, much more than the long white and gold bar where the waiters went to pick up the drinks and where a cashier with a cameo on her black dress sat like a queen. The object was a big, bright metal globe at the end of a metal stem.

There was not only one but four of them, in different parts of the vast café.

'Mama, what are those globes for?'

Perhaps he was disappointed by her reply:

'For the dishcloths.'

He got his diploma. Instead of being first, as he had been the other years, he was only third. He had worked neither more nor less than usual. Perhaps he had been more fascinated by the outer world.

His sister, whose belly had grown bigger and whose features had become somewhat puffy, had stopped working on the layette.

'Actually it's cheaper to buy it in a shop.'

The truth was that she had acquired a taste for reading. She had discovered a bookshop in the Boulevard du Port-Royal which had stalls on the pavement, the kind one saw on the quays.

The cheap novels that she read had coloured covers, like the illustrated Sunday papers. They cost sixty-five centimes, and after reading them one could exchange them for others by paying an additional ten centimes. Most of them were dirty, dog-eared, and spotted with grease, but their coarse, yellowish paper had a good smell. She sometimes read as many as three a week, especially towards the end, when she could no longer stand on her feet and iron all day.

Occasionally, when her legs were very tired, she would ask Louis to go and exchange a book for her.

'What kind do you want?'

'You know, a sad one.'

She was not sad herself and was delighted at the idea of having her baby.

'I think Mama's right. If I keep it here, I won't be able to work any more or go out in the evening. I'm too young to live in two rooms with a baby and it's better for both the child and me to send it to a farm. To say nothing of the fact that the open air will be good for it and that I'll go to see it every Sunday.' There were some feverish days. They would buy the newspaper in order to see the classified advertisements and would discuss them in the evening.

'Meaux! It's nice, but it's too far from Paris. Imagine how far I'd have to go just to catch the train.'

They considered Sartrouville, Corbeil, and a village near Etampes, and finally chose a place run by a Madame Campois in Meudon. It was only a few minutes by train from the Montparnasse Station. Vladimir had a regular girl friend and did not go with them. Neither did the twins, who had organized a gang on the ramparts and attacked a rival gang every Sunday.

Their mother had put on her pretty dress. Alice, who was in blue, was wearing a broad straw hat with a ribbon attached under the chin to prevent it from being blown away by the wind. Louis rode in a tram for the second time, went through the gate of the station, and climbed into a third-class carriage filled with soldiers in red trousers.

In Clamart they had difficulty finding the way that Madame Campois had indicated in her letter, or rather in the letter she had asked a neighbour to write for her.

They first went in the wrong direction. The road was covered with a thick layer of dust into which their feet sank. The cornfields were dotted with poppies. The weather was warm. Their skin smelled good. Everything smelled good, the air, the meadows, the barns that they passed, the cows.

They stopped at a farm to ask directions and continued on their way, feeling weak in the knees and overcome by the sun. Finally they saw a man in leather boots and a brown corduroy outfit who was standing at the side of the road and seemed to be waiting.

'Madame Heurteau? Did you have much trouble finding us? It's because we're in an out-of-the-way spot here.'

He pointed down to a house with a pink roof and white-washed walls. The apple trees were laden with fruit. The grass was bright. Two goats came over to look at them before caper-ing off, as if inviting them to play.

'Are they yours?' asked Alice excitedly.

'Yes, they are. We've got a few animals. After all, my wife has to keep busy.'

Chickens were foraging around the white house. There were also ducks and two big ungainly geese, and a few yards from the house was a pond covered with duckweed.

'Rosalie!' called the man.

She emerged from a low room, whitewashed like the rest of the house, and put on her nicest smile. She had a beaming face, enormous breasts, and hips that rolled when she started walk-ing. In the kitchen was a youngster about a year and a half old who was sitting on the floor.

'He's my first. I nursed him at the same time as Doctor Dubois's grandson. My husband's the doctor's coachman. I had so much milk that I could have fed three. Come inside. Sit down and have something.'

The chairs were straw-bottomed. They did not see a stove, but there were ashes in the fireplace where an iron hook was hanging.

'When are you due?' asked Rosalie, looking at Alice's belly like a connoisseur.

'Probably in two weeks.'

'Well, if you ask me, it could happen tonight or tomorrow, or the day after tomorrow at the latest. Don't you think so, Léonard? Come take a look in here.'

Opening a door, she showed them a huge room with windows on both sides, a bed with a white coverlet, and two wicker cradles adorned with tulle flounces that seemed to be waiting. In the opposite corner, next to an enormous wardrobe, was the child's little bed.

'That way, you realize, I can always keep an eye on them. If we agree about terms, you can bring it to me whenever you like, and Doctor Dubois can tell you he'll be taken good care of.'

Léonard allowed Louis to pick apples from one of the trees in the orchard and pulled down a branch so that he could reach it.

'Take a lot of them. As many as you want. There's quite a crop this year. Would you like to see the rabbits?'

There was a hutch full of them and others too in a square of grass surrounded by wire netting where they sat motionless, except for the mechanical movement of their cheeks.

'Would you like to live in the country?'

'I don't know.'

'Do you prefer Paris?'

'I don't know.'

His mother was served a small glass of brandy. Alice dipped a lump of sugar into it. Louis was given a glass of cold water that was drawn from the well in a wooden bucket.

His mother woke him when the train reached the Montparnasse Station. His cheeks were burning and his eyes were feverish. It seemed to him that an important event had just occurred, that the protective cocoon in which he had been enveloped had suddenly cracked, and he felt both heavy-laden and light-hearted.

Part Two

The Little Boy in the
Rue de L'Abbé-de-L'Epée

# Chapter One

Dates hardly mattered in the family. There was no calendar on the wall. They reckoned rather by season, Gabrielle by the fruits and vegetables that succeeded each other on the push-cart, cherries, strawberries, runner beans, and the first peas, peaches which were less expensive in midsummer, apples in the autumn, cabbages and salsify in winter.

The appearance or disappearance of charcoal burners on the pavement was also a sign, as were the days when there was no market because excessive cold, or fog, which remained a subject of conversation for a long time, or ice on the streets or a heavy snow would have made it impossible for the street-sellers to get their loaded carts back from the market and because, in addition, housewives did not go out in such weather.

Gabrielle could not have told the children's dates of birth without consulting the official papers that were yellowing in the biscuit tin, and in order to measure time they would refer to memorable events: the year when the Seine had frozen, the year of Emilie's death, the autumn when gas had been installed, the period in which Vladimir had started working as an apprentice for Monsieur Brillanceau.

Others were added as the children grew up. Some points of reference were common to all of them, others had special meaning for individual members of the family.

In the case of Louis, for example, it was not so much the birth of Alice's child that mattered as his first train trip. The things that constituted his discovery of life, Vladimir looking through the hole in the sheet, then his sister's blonde hair on her naked belly, were more important than Alice's marriage to a boy named Gaston Cottereau who worked in a delicatessen in the Rue de Rennes.

There was also the gap between the little ones and the big

ones and the one between the children and the mother, which had varied several times. For example, Vladimir had been a little one at a time when a certain man was living regularly in the flat, and he must have remembered it, whereas for Louis Vladimir had always been a big boy. He himself remembered only men who came and went, smells, voices, the different footsteps of those who stayed three days and those who stayed a month, of those who ate with them and those he saw only in the evening, so that Pliska, who was only a vague figure in the memory of Vladimir and Alice, remained an important personage for him.

Louis was perhaps the only one, in addition to his mother, for whom little Emilie, of whom they never spoke, had had a real existence, because at that time he spent the whole day at home.

Vladimir and Alice were the eldest. They understood each other and exchanged secrets. Then Vladimir had suddenly become a man whom his mother asked for advice, whereas Alice remained a girl for a while and the difference in age between her and the twins and then between her and Louis mattered less and less.

It wasn't his first day in school that counted but the first time he had been attacked there, when he had refused to give up his marbles. His school record no longer existed, though he could still see the hand of the teacher, whose name he had difficulty in remembering, suddenly coming down over his shoulder and seizing the drawing he had just made of one of the chestnut trees in the yard.

Was it Monsieur Charles? No. Monsieur Charles was the big fellow with the flabby mouth. It was Monsieur Huguet.

The twins' escapade, the first one, the one that had ended in Rouen, had no date, could not be placed. The discovery of Les Halles as he clung to his mother's apron strings was more precise in time and space.

Then there was the conversation with his mother on a bench in a little park where pigeons came begging for bread, which they had not thought of bringing.

Why had they been in a park around the middle of the afternoon? He would have been unable to tell, just as he could not remember the name of the park, which was not far from a hospital.

Yet he had not been a small child at the time. He recalled details of the period when he was six or seven, but certain details of this experience remained hazy.

'You're intelligent, Louis. You learn things easily. You're the only one of us who has a diploma. Tell me frankly, would you like to go on with your studies?'

'I don't think so, Mama.'

'Have you thought of what you want to do later on?'

'Not exactly.'

'What about now? You're less strong than your brothers. I can't see you working in a shop or on a scaffold. If you feel like continuing, don't worry about money. Your brothers are starting to earn wages. I've got good customers and I'm strong on my feet.'

'Thanks, Mama, but I don't feel like it.'

'You can't go on indefinitely following me to the market in the morning and daydreaming the rest of the day.'

'I'd like to work at the market. For Monsieur Samuel.'

'What would you do there?'

'Last year I saw a boy who carried slips of paper from one end of the shed to the other and did errands outside.'

'The Flea!'

'I could do the same thing.'

Monsieur Samuel never wore a jacket or a collar. He was stout and short-legged and his big belly overflowed his trousers, which were held up by pale blue braces. The number of folds of his chin varied, depending on whether he was looking up or down, and a tiny black cap sat perched on the top of his bald pate. With a pencil in his ear, he sat in state in the middle of his shed, the importance of which was not suspected by the people who walked up the Rue Coquillière during the day. To them it was only a porte-cochère.

At night, one noticed the glass vault, as in railway stations, piled-up cases, crates and bags. Three clerks, one of whom was a woman, worked without stop in the glass cage. Push-carts entered, threaded their way through the stock, and came out full, while figures were written on the blackboard.

For years, that warehouse, that little stock exchange for small shopkeepers and street-sellers which was on the margin of the big exchange, the central market of Paris, was going to be Louis's vital element, as water is the element of fish.

He no longer left with his mother between three and six in the morning, depending on the season. He started work at ten in the evening, when men in rags began wandering around looking for a job.

At that hour, the shed was almost empty. There was only the food that had been unsold the day before. Samuel, with his pencil in his ear, would wait for the first waggons, which were drawn by broken-down horses, to come in from the Argenteuil plain or some other rural area.

At first, the shed was lit by gas, but before long Samuel installed arc lamps which were as bright as the ones Louis had seen at the Belle Jardinière.

'No, Victor. I can't pay that price. You know my customers. They're not people that the sky's the limit for, who slip a rebate to the cook or head-waiter.'

He was a lachrymose type and always tried to play on his clients' feelings.

'I feed simple, ordinary people, people who work hard and who don't know that they owe it to Samuel that they've got peaches on the table, just like the bourgeois, instead of having to settle for bruised plums. You fellows from the country imagine there are only rich people in Paris.'

He had several refrains in his repertory which he recited without giving anyone time to interrupt.

'Hello, little one. Come and take a look here.'

For him, Louis was always 'the little one', with no other name.

'This little one, for example! I took him on out of charity, because his mother has God knows how many children and she'll be here tonight with her push-cart along with the others. The grandmother's been pushing hers for thirty years. Little one, go and ask in the office if Vacher phoned up about the leeks.'

It was true that Samuel did not sell to the stores in the smart neighbourhoods but to the vegetable dealers who had only a hole in the wall and a few baskets on the pavement and who stayed open until ten at night.

Louis would come back with a slip of paper. Everything was settled by means of slips that were torn from pads in which a sheet of carbon paper made a copy.

'That's another one who takes me for a philanthropist!'

He would pull his pencil from his ear, cross out a figure, and jot down another.

'Tell them they can take it or leave it!'

Louis would go off again to the paved shed where, when no people were around, his footsteps resounded as in a church. The warehousemen were beginning to receive merchandise. The telephone on the wall, in the glass cage, rang constantly and the clerk would yell into it so as to make himself heard.

'Run over to that robber Chailloux and tell him . . .'

The Rue Rambuteau, the Rue de la Ferronnerie, the Rue Sainte-Opportune, or one of those huge, spectral sheds. He would worm his way with a bill in his hand and find an agent or wholesaler as busy as Samuel.

They would spend two or three hours that way, buying from each other and keeping up to date on the prices, which varied according to what came in, and shortly thereafter the little train from Arpajon would arrive and stop in the street with its goods trucks that smelled of the country.

The shed would fill up with merchandise. They would take on a few down-and-outs to carry loads on their back.

The second year, Louis was already given the job of standing near the main door and checking what came in: so many cases of this, so many crates of that. And, of course, jotting down the names of the producers.

Some of the helpers who were taken on for two or three hours and then went to eat a bag of fried potatoes and a dried sausage at the corner of the Rue Montmartre were young men who had only recently arrived from a cosy house in the provinces and come up against a Paris that was hard and indifferent.

The others, the old ones, whom one saw staggering out of the bars after work, had no more illusions.

Women with big behinds walked back and forth on high

heels, and they would stop under the lighted globe at the door of a hotel.

At a given moment, the tide rose again. The figures that Monsieur Page chalked on the blackboard changed each time that Louis, who went back and forth between him and the glass cage, brought a new slip of paper. No sooner did the merchandise come in than it started going out, not by the cartload but a few cases at a time. He would recognize his mother among the purchasers and would find time to whisper to her as he rushed by:

'Wait a while and take carrots.'

At 8 a.m. the noise and bustle was over, and a man in a blue apron would wash the tiled floor of the shed with a hose.

'See you tonight, little one.'

Louis would go to a bar for a cup of coffee and croissants and would sometimes treat himself to a bag or two of fried potatoes.

When he got home the flat would be empty, and as soon as he undressed he would flop down on his mattress. The other mattresses had disappeared one by one as discreetly as Emilie's cot.

The first to go was that of Vladimir, who had left for Toulon to do his military service and never understood why he had been assigned to the Marines, since he had never seen the ocean except in photographs. He came home several times on leave, and his wide trousers, blue collar, and tufted cap were quite becoming to him.

He had to pass through Paris several times during his training period, but he did not always visit the flat in the Rue Mouffetard.

One spring, around the month of April, two more mattresses disappeared. The twins, who were about fifteen but as big and strong as boys of twenty, ran away from home for good. They left a note on the kitchen table:

'Don't bother informing the police. We won't be back. Goodbye to all of you.'

They had both signed it. There were four spelling mistakes in the note. This time they did not take the money from the tin but only their birth certificates and whatever linen and clothes they had, which did not make up a bundle too heavy for their shoulders.

The room suddenly looked empty. The curtain was no longer in its place. One day when Gabrielle had been in bed with the 'flu, she remarked:

'I wonder why we keep that old sheet. It no longer serves any purpose. Louis, don't you think we ought to take it down?'

It was now he whom she asked for advice. He had taken it down, including, though not without difficulty, the rod, which was too firmly fixed.

'Good God, the room looks so big! I didn't remember it as big as this.'

No doubt she was imagining it as it had been in the days of her marriage with Heurteau, when there was only Vladimir, who slept on the cot.

In the evening, Alice stopped at the threshold, dumbfounded, and likewise exclaimed:

'It's so big!'

No sooner had she lain down than she murmured:

'Look, Mama, would you mind if I slept with you?'

'Aren't you afraid of catching my 'flu?'

'You forget that I had it first.'

The mattress remained unused for a few days, and one morning, when he got home from work, Louis took it and laid it on the dustbins in the yard, when the carpenter had been replaced by another one, for the former had committed suicide. He had been found hanging in the cellar after a two-day search, for he had never used it and, as it was summer, no one had gone down to it to get coal. There was a rumour that he had been neurasthenic. Another resident of the street, Ramon, the Spaniard's son, also disappeared. It was Alice who kept her brother informed of what went on, for he hardly spoke to anyone.

'Did you know he was almost thrown into gaol?'

Louis showed no surprise.

'Such a good-looking, elegant young man, always so well groomed. Well, he belonged to a small gang that snatched handbags from women who were alone. Two others were also arrested, but we don't know their names because it seems they come from good families. Their parents greased someone's palm and the thing's been hushed up. Ramon's been sent to an uncle in Spain, and his parents tell people that he wanted to enter an officers' training school.'

Everything was changing, quickly or gradually, depending on the particular period. Cars, which had been such a rarity that people had gone out of their way to see one, became more numerous than horse-drawn carriages and there were as many taxis in the streets as coaches. People no longer called the underground the Métropolitain, but the Métro, and at times one would see an aeroplane passing in the sky.

One of the women in high-heeled shoes who walked up and down the pavements of Les Halles was younger, smaller, and thinner than the others. She had dark hair and black eyes.

One winter morning, when he had finished working, she had called out to Louis:

'Have you ever tried it, boy?'

He had answered frankly that he hadn't. How had she guessed that he had been wanting to for some time?

'You want me to break you in?'

The expression had shocked him.

'I know how it's done.'

'But you still don't know how nice it is. Come along! I feel like doing it with you. You'll give me whatever you like.'

She had a room on the fourth floor of the hotel whose globe was always lit at night. It was about fifty yards from the shed.

'You're lucky! Since you're the last and I'm going to bed, you'll see me undressed.'

He watched her get ready but kept his clothes on. When she was naked, she lay down on the bed, the coverlet of which was partly protected by oilcloth.

'What are you waiting for? Come here. I'll help you. I bet you're ashamed to show me your tool.'

He shook his head hesitantly. He was keenly disappointed but would have liked not to make her feel bad, not to hurt her. A few moments before, when she was undressing, he had desired her. She had made a mistake in taking all her clothes off, in spreading her legs, in exhibiting a slot invaded by long black hairs.

His mother's was delicate, surrounded by a reddish moss

which stood out elegantly against the whiteness of her belly.

The other slot which he had often seen, and still saw occasionally, his sister's, was barely shaded with blonde down.

'What's happening to you?'

'I don't know.'

'Do I disgust you?'

'No.'

'Well, are you or aren't you?'

He shook his head as he stepped back towards the door and stammered:

'I apologize.'

'That's the limit. I make you a present because you've been eyeing me for months when I pass Samuel's place. And the one time I get undressed – which would give the other girls a laugh – I did it because you're a virgin and I thought it would help you. So the gentleman turns up his nose. Tell me, you undersized little runt, do you think you're . . .'

He didn't hear the rest of it. He tore down the stairs, frightened at the thought that she might run after him just as she was and keep screaming insults at him and that the doors of the other rooms might open one after the other.

When he got to the street, he walked away fast, and it was not until he reached the Châtelet, where he felt safe, that he remembered he had not eaten.

Standing at the bar of a café whose walls were covered with tiles, he dismally dipped his croissant into his coffee and, for the first time in his life, wondered whether he was like anyone else.

Would he have been able to go through with it if she hadn't had such dark hair and a bushy triangle that went up to her navel? She had pretty eyes. She had been nice, at first.

She had called him 'runt'. He had been called that by schoolmates and was used to it. But hadn't she given the expression a special meaning?

Perhaps he ought to have tried it the same day with a blonde or a redhead, to set his mind at ease. He remembered what a woman shopkeeper in their street had once said to his mother when he still wore his hair long:

'Is it a little boy or a little girl?'

It would be a long time before he tried again. He was afraid of discovering that he was impotent.

*

He saw no connection between that experience and the event, a much more important one, which took place a few weeks later. Yet the woman's image often came back to him. He dreamed about her several times in the room where he had had to put up a shade, since he slept there during the day.

He even recalled details which he did not remember having noticed, such as the brownness of her nipples and the wide pink band around them. Not only did she have hair high on her belly, but also very low down, on her thighs.

He had twenty-two francs in his pocket that afternoon. Later, in the case of other sums, he was often all at sea, for the value of money changed many times in the course of his life. He earned forty francs a month at Samuel's, which he would turn over to his mother, including the tips from the market gardeners, and Gabrielle would then give him pocket money for the week.

Twenty-two francs represented two months' savings. He had noted the shop at the lower end of the Rue de Richelieu, not far from the National Library. It was a big stationery firm with two shop windows, a whole section of which was reserved for artists' materials and which employed ten clerks in the shop alone.

He had often stopped in front of the display, looking at what he called the 'colours', for he had no idea of the various mediums, and everything fascinated him, the paints in the little white earthenware bowls lined up in iron boxes, the chalks of softer and gentler tones, the tubes in small chests, which had a palette that fitted into the cover.

It must have been five in the afternoon. He had two ways of spending his days, depending on the weather, how tired he was, his mood of the moment. There were times when he would return to the flat at about nine in the morning, go straight to bed and sleep until four or five in the afternoon. as he had done that day.

On other days, he preferred to roam about, sit on a bench, go walking in a new neighbourhood, then kiss his mother at the kerb, go home to eat, and sleep until evening.

The salesmen and saleswomen wore the same grey smocks.

There were three saleswomen, and he waited outside until they were busy with customers before entering the shop, then he went straight to the artists' counter.

'What would you like, young man?'

Because of his height everyone thought he was younger than he was, and people adopted a protective, almost gentle manner with him.

'I'd like some colours, sir.'

'Coloured pencils?'

'No. I've got some.'

He jealously preserved, without quite knowing why, the set that Pliska had once given him. He used them only on rare occasions.

'Water-colours, gouache?'

He hardly dared express his desire, fearing lest the salesman laugh at him.

'The brightest colours.'

And, after a hesitation and a furtive glance at the marvels on the shelves, he added:

'Pure colours.'

He had uttered the word 'pure' in such a tone, with such fervour, that the salesman, a middle-aged man, took an interest in him.

'If I gather correctly, you've never painted?'

'I've drawn at times with coloured pencils.'

'Has someone seen your drawings and advised you to paint?'

'No one.'

'Have you seen many paintings?'

'Never.'

He had occasionally stopped in front of picture galleries around the Rue de Seine. The paintings on display in the windows had not interested him. It had not occurred to him that one could enter, see the other paintings inside, and leave without buying anything.

'Lots of young people start with water-colours.'

He showed him an open box of them and picked up another.

'These are in tubes and those in bowls.'

'Do the colours stay just as bright?'

'Not quite. Gouache fades less.'

'Is it better?'

'It depends on what you want to do. Landscapes? Portraits?'

He dared not say 'Everything together', spots, streaks, colours next to each other, the way he saw them in the street, the kind his memory was full of.

'Of course, if you want real brilliance, the only thing is oil paint.'

He opened a chest of oils in which at least thirty tubes were set between two metal flasks.

'I don't like some of the colours.'

He pointed to them: that one ... that one ... that one ...

'Why don't you like them?' insisted the salesman, who was amused.

'They're dark and sad. They don't sparkle.'

'The simplest thing is to do what painters do. Buy an empty box and a palette, and choose your colours. Come over here and have a look.'

He took him to a glass-topped counter that Louis had not noticed, and it seemed to the boy that all the colours in the world were offering themselves to him under the glass.

'May I touch the tubes?'

'Of course.'

The salesman pulled back the pane and Louis took out a long, thin tube and read: Veronese green.

'Is that the greenest?'

'There are more than twenty kinds of green. Their brightness depends on the colours around them.'

'I understand.'

It was true. He had understood, and he spent a quarter of an hour examining the coloured circles that indicated the colour contained in each tube.

'Is it just the same inside?'

'Exactly the same. Of course, you can mix them on the palette.'

112

The names enchanted him. They were more evocative than the poems he had been taught at school: Naples yellow, burnt sienna, carmine lake, ultramarine . . .

He laid aside those that seemed to him essential, but he would have loved to buy everything in the trays.

'Do you think I have what I need?'

'In my opinion, you need some browns, some dark yellows.'

'I don't like them.'

'You also need oil and turpentine, and also, of course, a palette.'

'Are they expensive?'

'Here are some inexpensive ones. The box and palette, with two flasks, cost only twelve francs. See whether the palette is right for your hand.'

He did not know how to use it, why there was a hole in it.

'Like that, you see? The hollow of the palette against your body, the curved part on the outside. It'll be easier when your hand gets bigger.'

'How much does it all come to?'

He was radiant. He fingered the coins in his pocket. The salesman looked at each label, wrote down the figures, and added them up rapidly.

'Thirty-four francs and sixty centimes.'

Louis would not have thought that such little tubes would cost so much. A big tube of blue was marked only two francs and contained ten times as much paint as the others. Without daring to ask for an explanation, he spluttered:

'I haven't enough money. I'll be back. Be sure to keep them for me. Until what time is the shop open?'

'Seven o'clock.'

The man must have thought he wouldn't come back, and there was a touch of melancholy in his eyes as he watched Louis walk out. However, when he saw him start running as soon as he reached the pavement, he smiled confidently. From there to the Rue Mouffetard Louis slowed up a bit not more than twice, in order to catch his breath. His mother was still at her post.

'Mama!'

'What's the matter with you?'

'Nothing. Listen. It's very important. You've absolutely got to lend me fifteen francs. I swear I'll give it back to you.'

'What do you intend to do with fifteen francs?'

'You'll see. I'll tell you later. I'm in a hurry.'

She had never seen him like that. It was the first time he had ever manifested keen, insistent passion.

'Here! But don't knock yourself out like that.'

He bought others, later on, from the same salesman, who had taken a liking to him. Neither knew the other's name, but there was a kind of secret bond between them.

'Someday you'll need an easel. What do you paint on?'

'On heavy paper.'

'You'll have to try canvas.'

He showed some prepared stretchers and explained the various sizes.

'After all, you can prepare the canvas yourself, with glue and zinc white. Lots of painters do.'

He dared not believe it and yet he now lived only for that, as if the years before had been only a secret preparation. He painted near the window when he returned from work in the morning, for that was when the light was best.

If anyone had spoken to him about models, he would have been thoroughly surprised. He did not look at anything, except at times the workmen who made a din with their pickaxes demolishing the fronts of Monsieur Stieb's shoe-shop and of the tripery next to it. Scaffolds were erected. The demolishers were followed by other workers, and one afternoon there came to life the smartest-looking shop in the street, with two all-glass shop windows and a glass entrance as well, and, inside, a big room furnished with mahogany armchairs and matching stools. There was a section for ladies at the left and for gentleman at the right, and at the back one could see a dapple-grey rocking-horse for children.

Monsieur Stieb took on saleswomen, whom he picked young and pretty. Alice, who had gone back to work in the laundry, applied for a job in the shoe-shop and was taken on. It was indirectly because of Monsieur Stieb, who dressed more and more elegantly, that she found a husband, for one afternoon she had to wait on a tall, dark, slightly awkward young man. The following day, he waited for her after work. They went dancing together on Saturdays. Three months later, Alice announced to her mother that she was getting married in the spring.

'His name is Gaston, Gaston Cottereau. He's twenty-five and works in a big delicatessen in the Rue de Rennes. If only you could see what there is in the window! They make lobster in scallop shells, shrimp salad, chicken croquettes . . .'

'Where does he live?'

'For the time being, he rents a room in his boss's flat, but we're looking for a place of our own in the neighbourhood.'

'What about François?'

'Gaston doesn't want me to work after we're married, and François will live with us.'

François was a big, rosy, pug-nosed boy who resembled nobody in the family and who was already walking on his big chubby legs.

Louis hardly remembered the marriage or the wedding dinner on the first floor of a restaurant. Strangers were present, Gaston's parents, who lived at Saint-Aubin, in Nièvre. They had ruddy faces that looked as if they had been carved in wood.

He tried the next day and the following days to paint portraits of them sitting stiffly in front of the white tablecloth, and, without knowing why, he included the body of a woman lying on the cloth, a nude body resembling his sister's. The head was only a blurred outline, as if it were unimportant.

He was unsatisfied with what he painted, because it remained muddy. He refused to let himself mix colours and found it hard to place faces and objects on different planes.

There were schools. His salesman in the Rue de Richelieu had asked him whether he would enter the School of Fine Arts when he was old enough, and Louis dared not admit to him that he had only his elementary school diploma and worked at Les Halles at night. He expected to work there all his life and to be promoted little by little, for Monsieur Samuel liked him.

'Look, little one. Climb up the step-ladder and try to write figures in the columns.'

Louis did not know that the man who had been writing prices on the blackboard for years had entered the hospital the day before and probably would not come out alive. He was to undergo an operation the next day or the following day, though he did not know for what.

'I can't reach the top, sir.'

'Write on the other lines.'

Samuel called out a few figures to him at random. The chalk grated on the blackboard, the way it used to do in school. Louis followed tensely, as if his life depended on it.

'Your figures are better than poor Albert's. I can read them without my glasses. Let's see your handwriting. Here goes! Cauliflowers. Carrots. Turnips. Not so fast! Best quality peaches. Cavaillon melons. All right! You can come down. I'll tell Michel to raise the step-ladder another foot. Starting Monday, I'll give you sixty francs a month and we'll see about a raise at the end of the year.'

It was wonderful! He didn't tell his mother because he wanted to surprise her when she came to stock up. The neighbourhood tradeswomen had recognized him.

'Gabrielle! Look up there . . .'

She waved to him in surprise, but he had no time to wave back. He was catching figures on the wing, rubbing out, writing, looking down at people's heads, which appeared to him in a different light.

His work thrilled him. The look of the shed changed every moment. He could have painted for ten years without exhausting the material he had before his eyes.

Alice and her husband had found a fourth-floor flat in the Rue des Ecoles, opposite the Sorbonne.

'We even have a balcony. So François can be out in the air when I do the housework.'

She often walked with her son, holding him by the hand, to the Rue Mouffetard and chatted with her mother, who would cram her shopping bag with vegetables, but she almost never went up to the flat where she had lived so long.

There were only two of them in it now, and it was all the more comfortable in that they were hardly ever there at the same time, except on Sunday.

Louis found a second-hand bed, which he put against the wall, in Emilie's old place. He bought a night table with a cracked marble top which he got for a song.

116

When his mother's bed was pulled over to the night table, there remained a big empty space on the window side, and one day he set up an easel there, a light, cheap, deal easel for which he had been hankering a long time.

He had perhaps found a way of thinning his paint, of keeping it from being pasty, what he called smeary, though he was not sure of the result. Instead of spreading it carefully, as on a wall or door, he used a fine brush and dabbed touches of pure tones on the cardboard. For he continued to be haunted by pure colours. He never felt they were limpid enough, vibrant enough. He would have liked to see them quiver.

He was not yet ready to use canvas and found all the cardboard cartons he wanted on top of dustbins. He prepared them as the salesman had advised him. It took a lot of time, but he had no sense of time. He had never had it; events that were years apart had no chronological order in his mind.

He was sleeping warmly and voluptuously one day when he felt someone touch his shoulder and then heard his mother's voice:

'Louis! Wake up!'

He was struck by the tone of it, for it was grave, tragic.

'What's the matter, Mama?'

She stared at him. She was pale and drawn and looked as if she had suddenly been frozen by fate.

'They've declared war, Louis.'

'Where?'

'Here. In France. The Germans have attacked us. There are posters up announcing a general mobilization.'

'Do you think the Germans'll get to Paris?'

'I hope we beat them. Men are leaving, regiments are parading . . .'

He had no reaction, and he thought he heard a tone of reproach in his mother's vooice when she added:

'Vladimir will be among the first to go.'

He hadn't thought of Vladimir. His first thought had been that he was only sixteen, that he was too short to be a soldier, and that since the Germans weren't near Paris life would continue as usual.

'If the twins are in France or in the colonies, they'll be mobilized too, because they're nearly nineteen.'

She was counting on her fingers and moving her lips.

'In fact they're over nineteen, since they were born in April. They'll be pulled in right away, and if they don't show up they'll be deserters.'

'I'm sorry, Mama.'

'It's only natural. And there's Alice's husband, who's in the cavalry of the line. They're the ones who ride out ahead of the lines. He once explained it to me without realizing it would soon be happening.'

She bent over and kissed him listlessly, with her mind elsewhere.

'I wonder if Vladimir will come to say good-bye to me.'

He came in the evening, in service uniform, with his pack on his back. He seemed unimpressed by the events.

'Hello, Mama. Hello, you.'

He kissed them on both cheeks.

'I've got to get going. Have to be at the Gare de l'Est. This is no day for missing the train. See you both soon. Don't worry, we'll beat them!'

A blonde woman, heavily made up and wearing high heels, was waiting for him in the street and took his arm. Shopkeepers brought him various things, one a cheese, another half a bottle of cognac, which he crammed into his pack.

The florist handed him a carnation, and Vladimir stuck it into the end of his rifle. When he disappeared at the foot of the street, Gabrielle left the window where she had been leaning her elbows and sat down at the table.

'Hand me the wine, will you, Louis?' she murmured.

That evening she got drunk alone, dismally drunk, while groups of young people paraded in the street screaming patriotic songs and drinking songs.

## Chapter Two

The war left few traces on Louis, some memories relating mainly to his family. No one at home had ever read the papers, nor did they now, since only he and his mother were left in the flat. He tried to read them, because he heard people talk about communiqués. He tried again later, when he was older, but never managed to be interested in the news. It was just words and phrases that had no effect on him. He couldn't feel or smell or touch them. There was no vibration.

Perhaps if he had been four or five inches taller in 1914, he would have been swept up in the general frenzy and have volunteered without waiting to be called up. Then, in the trenches, the war would have entered him, would have been part of his being and, as must have been the case of so many others, would have accompanied him throughout his life.

In the Rue Mouffetard, the frenzy, apart from some singing and a few bouts of drunkenness, was practically non-existent. It was a street in which people's main concern was to get enough to eat every day, and, for those who had children, to feed them.

At Les Halles, one saw fewer and fewer young men, then middle-aged men started leaving, but the rhythm remained the same, cabbages remained cabbages, poultry was still poultry, and one continued to see sides of beef hanging from hooks and the little train from Arpajon waiting by the sheds.

He was to retain only a confused memory of historic dates, of battles whose names would be carved in stone, and he mixed up the names of the generals.

His first real memory of war, apart from the general mobilization, which he had experienced only from his window, was his sister's arrival one evening while his mother and he were having dinner together in the kitchen. Her eyes were red and dazed, and he thought her gestures theatrical. She had rushed from the doorway straight to her mother, who had had just time enough to catch her in her arms.

'Mama! Oh, Mama! It's awful . . .'

It was false. His sister wasn't like that. His mother had also, on the first day, adopted a tragic attitude that didn't become her. Both of them were perhaps sincere, but they exaggerated their gestures, like people who made speeches.

Alice sobbed on a bosom where he had never seen her lay her head, and she sobbed without speaking. Finally she pulled away and held out an official-looking paper.

'It's to inform me that Gaston's dead. He was killed in a

forest near Charleroi, in Belgium, while he was on patrol.'

To Louis, this Gaston Cottereau was a stranger, and had he lived he would have remained on the fringes of the family, just like young François, who was his sister's son but did not resemble any of them physically.

He nevertheless became conscious that evening that war really killed. For him, this was the first casualty.

'My poor child! You married at the wrong time, but there was no way of knowing, nobody could have known. Where's François?'

'I left him with a neighbour, a woman whose husband's also at the front.'

'What are you going to do?'

'I don't know yet. It seems we'll be given help, a pension. We'd hardly finished setting up the flat.'

Then she became aware of her brother's presence.

'You, Louis, you're lucky!'

She had no need to be more precise. She was alluding not to his age but his shortness. He did not remain present at the whining of the two women, who were hardly sincere, in any case not Gabrielle, who had never liked either Gaston or his family.

He left for work. In Samuel's shed nothing had changed, except that an office clerk and two stock clerks had left and been replaced.

His colours, as he said, for he never uttered the word 'paint', remained his basic concern. The war was reflected in his work in the form of flags, bugles gleaming in the sun, soldiers in red trousers, shoulder braid. Later, when the uniforms were changed, he liked the blue, which he put into several pictures.

His sister did not stay in Paris long. Gaston's parents, still remembering perhaps the Franco-Prussian War of 1870, imagined that the capital was starving and the Parisians were eating rats. They had written to Alice from their village in Nièvre asking her to come to Saint-Aubin, where they had a farm and three or four cows and where the child would be sure of being properly fed.

'I've found someone who'll rent my flat, the wife of an English officer who has some post or other in Paris.'

After a little more than a year, Louis moved to the glass cage, for another employee had been mobilized. He was earning a hundred francs a month. His mother too was taking in more money than before the war, and they felt almost rich.

As their occupations obliged them to play hide-and-seek and one couldn't light a fire in midsummer just to prepare coffee or fry two eggs, they had a gas ring installed next to the old stove, which of course would be used in winter, and after a few weeks they were so used to it that they couldn't understand how they had ever been able to do without it.

When they had dinner together, Gabrielle would sometimes fall into a melancholy reverie. It was not the violent, spectacular grief of the early days, but it was more impressive.

'Vladimir doesn't write to us. Just two little notes, simply to say that he's well and that he's been made a corporal. I'm sure he writes to that girl, who he never bothered to introduce to us and whose name we don't even know.'

Nor did they know what Vladimir had lived on between the end of his military service and the declaration of war. When he returned from his long stay in Toulon, he was a different man. He was tanned, had new mannerisms, and made gestures he had never made before, and he looked more aggressive than ever.

'Are you going back to work for Monsieur Brillanceau? I met him two months ago, and he's ready to take you on again.'

'He's likely to wait a long time.'

His smile was derisive. He had always been derisive, but not in that casual way.

'What do you expect to do?'

'I don't know. I've rented a room and I'll see what comes up.'

He made no mention of the possibility of living at home again.

'You'll stay in the neighbourhood at least?'

'I've seen enough of the neighbourhood. I'm going to live in the Rue de Clichy.'

She was timid in his presence, as if she were afraid he would get angry and go away for good.

'Will you come to see us?'

'Of course.'

'Will you leave me your address?'

'When it's definite, I'll let you know. For the time being, I'm living in a hotel.'

'Isn't it very expensive?'

'I manage.'

All the same, he had dropped in for a moment to kiss her before leaving for the front, but not without accompanying the girl who was waiting for him on the pavement.

Two brief notes in more than a year! He must have had leave, like the others, and he had certainly been in Paris.

Of course, the family was not in the habit of being effusive, and Gabrielle had led her life her own way without bothering much about the children as soon as they were old enough to stand on their hind legs.

Louis discovered little by little that the bonds between Gabrielle and her children were stronger than he had thought. Her attitude did not resemble the mother love that he heard people talk about or that one learned about in school.

It was rather as if, without her realizing it, the umbilical cord that had connected her with her children had never been completely cut.

'It's funny, Louis, that you've started to paint.'

She rarely spoke to him about his pictures. He was sure she glanced at them when she got home, but they bore so little resemblance to her idea of what a painting was that she preferred to say nothing.

'Are you planning to make it your profession?'

'It's not a profession.'

'There are some people who make a living at it. I used to know an old fellow who wore a big hat and a flowing polka-dot tie. He was a specialist.

'If I remember right, that was before you were born. I wasn't bad-looking in those days. He claimed I was beautiful, that I could earn my living as a model just by lying naked and not moving.

'I once went to pose for him in his studio near Saint-Germain-des-Prés, and he didn't even touch me. He hardly talked to me. I felt like laughing all the time, I don't know why. It seemed funny to me to be all naked for hours in front of a gentleman who didn't try to paw me. He gave me five francs and told me to come back whenever I wanted. He made a good living and had, in addition to the studio, a nice flat, well furnished, with a big balcony.'

She felt like adding: 'You ought to paint like him.'

He was already doing better work with his touches of pure colours, especially since he had begun painting on canvas. The difficulty was still to make things that seemed to have no relationship 'hang together'.

He did not try to copy reality, a chair, a street, a woman, a tram, except as an occasional exercise, and he succeeded fairly well. But that was a mere matter of images. What he would have liked to get down on canvas was reality itself, as he saw it, or rather as it composed itself spontaneously in his mind.

For example, he had put little François in the middle of the schoolyard, alone, unsteady on his chubby legs. It was a winter scene, since there was snow, but he wanted the sky to be a summer sky, and a red and yellow tram, full of faces pressed against the windows, was going by in front of the wall.

He could not have explained. It was too complicated. The salesman in the shop in the Rue de Richelieu had urged him so often that he finally went to the Rue du Faubourg-Saint-Honoré and the Rue La Boétie where there were several picture galleries.

'You'll see the best Impressionists, Cézanne, Renoir, Sisley, Pissarro. Not long ago, people made fun of them, and now you've got to be very rich to buy one of their paintings. You'll also see the Fauves, Vlaminck, Derain, and others whose names I've forgotten. One of them's an odd type, a half-tramp, who spends his life in the Montmartre bars. You can recognize his paintings a mile away.'

He had looked at the canvases exhibited in the windows and was annoyed with himself because they left him cold. They were good, of course. He felt crushed by the craftsmanship of those painters who knew where to put their spots of colour and how to give them their full value.

He was nevertheless disappointed. What he saw did not resemble what he was looking for. If he showed his paintings to the salesman, the latter would lose interest in him. Louis had finally learned his name because he had heard someone call him from the back of the shop: Monsieur Suard. He was a friend of a painter named Marquet and of another one who was younger, Othon Friesz.

'Some of them come from quite a distance to get their supplies in our shop because we have foreign brands, especially Dutch, which are hard to find in Paris.'

'Are they pure?'

'In my opinion, they fade less rapidly. The trouble with most paints is that they start getting dark, and present-day painters don't want to varnish their work. Besides, how can you varnish paint that's laid on thick?'

He was learning words, unsuspected techniques.

'Haven't you ever been tempted to work in a studio, Julian's, for example? They have good models and a teacher who gives advice.'

Monsieur Suard was as delighted by Louis's naïveté about painting as by his passion.

'It's not a matter of schools, like the Fine Arts. You go whenever you like. You bring your materials, set yourself up in front of an easel that's not being used, and you draw or paint the model. You pay by the hour.'

Louis had almost asked: 'What model?'

But remembering his mother and the painter with the big hat who specialized in street-sellers, he had understood.

'There's a studio not far from here, in the Rue du Faubourg-Montmartre.'

He had gone there one morning with his box. The light was as cold as at certain hours in Monsieur Samuel's shed, except that you never saw the light, because the place had a northern exposure. The silence was impressive, sinister. Thirty or forty people, men and women, especially girls and middle-aged men, stood or sat in front of the easels around a wooden stand on which a naked girl with skinny thighs stood with her hands clasped at the back of her neck.

Some were painting, others drawing, erasing, drawing again, while an old gentleman with pince-nez and a goatee planted himself silently behind each in turn.

124

Occasionally he would point, without saying a word, to a charcoal stroke. Or else he would grab a girl's brush and with two or three touches correct the movement of an arm or position of a leg.

'Do you want an easel?'

'No, sir. Thank you.'

He could not have worked in that atmosphere and had no need of the model. Some day perhaps, if he had the courage, he would talk to Monsieur Suard about what he had in mind, but it was impossible to explain if it wasn't down on canvas.

When he finished a picture, he would, in most cases, scrape it down with a palette knife, a smooth flexible instrument that was voluptuous to handle. After a few days of drying, he would spread a layer of zinc white and so have a new canvas, which saved him money.

'Louis, I wonder what's become of the twins.'

He too thought back to the past every now and then. At times he would conjure up the image of Emilie, of whom no one had spoken for years. His mother had precise memories about each of them, but they were not the same as his, so that when they had these conversations they did not echo each other.

'Do you remember the day when a distinguished-looking gentleman with a decoration in his lapel came in with Olivier in his arms? Olivier was unconscious. Guy and he had been playing. They'd been jumping over a bench with their feet together. Olivier missed and his head hit the pavement so hard that the gentleman, who was reading on the same bench and who might very well have been annoyed with them for disturbing him, thought he was dead.'

'Was I born then?'

'I think so. Of course! How stupid I am! You must have been at least six, since you were going to school.'

He had no recollection of the incident, any more than his mother remembered most of the events that, for him, constituted the history of the family.

'The thing that consoles me is knowing they weren't unhappy.'

He would look at her without understanding, disturbed at the fact that other memories were being mixed with his, for he no longer felt so sure of himself. They were like false notes.

'Have you forgotten that they ran away a first time and were found in a goods train, in Rouen?'

'I remember . . .'

'If the police inspector . . .'

He would listen abstractedly, irritated, unwilling to hear all the details again.

'The second time . . .'

'I know, Mama.'

She would glance at him reproachfully.

'I had to see a doctor last week because I had pains in my stomach. I didn't say anything to you about it so as not to worry you and because it was a woman's thing.'

He had heard allusions to venereal diseases and wondered whether his mother had one, which made him blush.

'It's unimportant. He was a very nice man, very understanding. He asked me questions about my life. I told him about the twins and admitted that what happened must have been my fault.

'He swore it wasn't, that neither I nor the kind of life we led had caused them to run away. Doctors know all about that kind of thing, and now I understand why the inspector was a little lenient with them.

'It's in their blood. They take after their father, who didn't get along anywhere and who ended up you know how.

'I'm sure those two were Heurteau's. I've every reason to think so. About Alice, I couldn't swear, but I'd rather she weren't.'

He was obliged to sit and listen. It made him uncomfortable. He was interested, of course, but he would have preferred that she should not speak of such things.

'There are children who run away five or six times a year. Even when they're locked up, they find a way of getting out and some get killed trying to escape by the window, like sleep-walkers. Did you know that?'

'No.'

'The thing that reassures me is that in most cases they get over it when they're older. It gives me hope of seeing them some day. Don't forget they're over twenty. They ought to be in the army. I wonder why we've never had a notice from their draft board.'

'You know, Mama, all the red tape . . .'

'All the same, it's funny. When it comes to military service, they usually know how to find people. They have enough military police for that!'

That must have been in 1916. The war had been going on for two years and people were no longer surprised.

Had Gabrielle had a premonition? A few days after that conversation, she received an official paper, as had Alice two years before, informing her that her son, Sergeant Olivier Heurteau, had been killed in front of Fort Douaumont in the course of a dangerous operation for which he had volunteered and that he had been awarded the Distinguished Service Medal posthumously.

The personal effects that had been found on him would be sent to the family later.

What intrigued both of them was that the African Battalions had a bad reputation, or at least had had before the war, for they were composed of troublemakers, delinquents, pimps from the Porte Saint-Martin district, Montmartre and elsewhere, of boys who had been in reformatories and those who had had a police record before the age for military service.

It was also odd to have news of only one of the redheads, and Gabrielle would not have been surprised to learn that they had died at the same time.

Olivier's personal effects arrived shortly thereafter. He had been the leader of the pair, the one who looked older, whereas Guy, who was as tall as his twin and had the same build, seemed milder, hesitant, and followed his brother around like a shadow.

Gabrielle and Louis learned from the service certificate that Olivier had volunteered for the African Battalions long before the war, with his 'parents' consent', from which they inferred that he had faked his mother's handwriting.

His address was given as the Rue d'Oran and his occupation

as that of agriculturist. His effects included a switchblade knife with a horn handle. The blade had been sharpened often and he must have used it in North Africa and in the trenches. An old wallet, which had lain in the mud, contained only a few bank notes, some postage stamps – why stamps, since soldiers' letters were post free? – a postcard from Algeria to an address written in an almost illegible handwriting and signed with a name that was undecipherable. Above the signature were drawn a star, a heart, and an animal that could have been a goat as well as a horse.

A blurred photograph was perhaps the key to this message, for it showed a young Bedouin woman squatting on the ground next to a donkey that was loaded with two baskets.

She looked about thirteen or fourteen and had a tattoo mark in the middle of her forehead, unless it was only a stain on the print. Her big gaping eyes were looking straight ahead with an expression of adoration. 'Don't you think she's his girl friend?'

'I don't know, Mama.'

'I don't think they're allowed to marry there while they're still in the army, especially a native woman. Besides, if he were married, she's the one they'd have sent his things to.'

The remaining items were a pipe, a pig-bladder pouch in which there was still a little tobacco, and a tinder pipe-lighter.

'Guy must have joined up the same time as he, in the same regiment. I'm going to inquire at the War Department. I'll go myself, because if I write to them they won't answer.'

She spent a whole day there, not only at headquarters, but in the offices scattered all over Paris. When she got home, she was in a state of exhaustion but was still hopeful.

'I'll find the right door sooner or later. I've never seen so many women, young and old, queueing in yards and hallways. A lieutenant, who resembles the police inspector, promised me that within a week he'd have the list of those who volunteered for the African Battalions in 1912.'

She smiled, and there was a certain pride in her expression.

'You know, Louis, it was wrong of us to think there are only criminals in the African Battalions. I asked the lieutenant. He agreed that they were made up mainly of troublemakers and boys who'd been sentenced.

'But it's different in the case of those who sign up, boys attracted by adventure and a hard life around the desert and who sleep in a tent more often than in a barrack room. He said to me, "At the front, they're our best soldiers." He knew one personally who'd become a second lieutenant and after ten years of service became a priest.'

She did get a reply, not after a week but after about a month. It was brought by an orderly, as if mail from the Ministries was too important or confidential to be entrusted to the post office. The letter confirmed the fact that Olivier Heurteau had enlisted as a volunteer on 21 October 1912, but stated that there was no record of a Guy Heurteau in the African regiments for that year or the following years.

'Do you think that means he's dead?'

'I don't know, Mama. They might have separated. Maybe Guy fell in love with a girl and married her.'

'He couldn't have done that without my consent. He wasn't of age.'

'Olivier couldn't join up either. Maybe Guy went to live in another country, in South America, for example. When he lived here, he often talked about South America.'

She shook her head sceptically. It remained a mystery to her, and Louis could tell from certain silences and a certain vague look that would suddenly come over her face that the matter preyed on her mind.

Louis was becoming more and more friendly with Monsieur Suard, and he would sometimes drop into the stationery shop in the Rue de Richelieu when he saw that the salesman was not busy, just to chat with him, without buying a tube of paint.

'It's too bad I married so young and had children right away. I have three, one of them a girl your age.

'And even so. I'm glad she's a girl. Otherwise the draft board would soon be after her!

'Remember, I'm not complaining. I myself once dreamed of being a painter. That's why I asked to be assigned to this department.

'Later, who knows, I may even become a picture dealer, I may open a small gallery. Not with big names, because that requires too much capital and there's no merit in it. With young painters that I discover. I already have a few canvases that some customers let me have cheap . . .'

Was it out of graciousness, so as not to disturb Louis, that he added:

'When you're satisfied with what you're doing, I'd be glad to see one of your paintings.'

'I'll never be satisfied. You know well enough that I'm not a real painter.'

At the beginning of 1917 – at any rate, it was the winter when it was so cold and there was a shortage of coal, the winter too when there was talk of mutiny of troops and soldiers' being shot as an example – at the beginning of 1917, Gabrielle learned from a street-seller in the Rue Saint-Antoine who had formerly worked in the Rue Mouffetard that Vladimir was in Paris.

The woman claimed she had seen him in the boulevard, not far from the Rue Montmartre, where she had gone to visit her daughter who was a saleswoman.

'I swear to you, Gabrielle, I wasn't mistaken. Don't forget that I knew him when he was a tot and that later he used to swipe peaches from my cart. He was wearing a marine's uniform, with a beret, and he had a bandage on his head. People turned around to look at him and he seemed proud of it. I yelled out to him, "Hey Vladimir! Don't you recognize your friends any more?" And he yelled back, "Hello, Aunt Emma!" That's what he used to call me when you and I were always together, with our carts side by side.'

'And to think he didn't come to see me!'

'If he was wounded, he's on sick leave. He has all the time in the world.'

'Meanwhile he's living at that awful woman's place.'

'It's just as if he were married.'

'You're right. I'm getting jealous of my children. His sister hasn't written to us once in the last two months and we've received only a photograph of her son.'

Vladimir came and even presented his mother with an oriental jewel, a charm that probably was not made of gold but that she thereafter wore proudly on her neck. He spoke of the Balkans, of Constantinople, as if he were talking about Clignancourt or the Porte des Lilas.

'Have you heard that Olivier's dead?'

'No.'

'He was a sergeant and got the Distinguished Service Medal. I have it here. Do you want to see it?'

'I've seen so many of them! What about Guy? Dead too?'

'We have no news of Guy. Nobody knows what's become of him.'

He could have said of the dead what he had just said of Distinguished Service Medals: he had seen so many!

'What about you, with your wound, didn't they give you a decoration?'

Louis shuddered when he saw his brother's face and heard the sound of his cutting voice:

'I'm not the kind of man they give medals to. Even if I were dead, like Olivier.'

'Don't you want to let me have your address in Paris, in case I have news of Guy?'

He merely answered evasively:

'I'll be back to see you before I leave.'

'When are you going?'

'When the doctors decide.'

'Is it serious?'

'A hole in the skull. They removed what they could, but there's still a piece of shrapnel somewhere.'

'Do you still have pain?'

'Occasionally.'

One afternoon by pure chance, Louis ran into an old acquaintance on the Pont Saint-Michel: the huge, colossal Monsieur Pliska, who now had a beard and whose blond hair flowed down the back of his neck. Louis would not have been sure it was he if the Czech giant had not recognized him and crushed his hand.

'Little Louis, eh? What happening?'

His French was hardly better than in the past, and he still accompanied his words with gesticulations and questioning looks.

'Your mother, Gabrielle? Gabrielle, yes?'

He remembered the pretty redhead with whom he had lived for almost two months, but he was no longer sure of her name.

'Brother Vladimir. Little sister. Big girl now?'

'She's married and has a son.'

'Me, very hard, lots trouble, because me foreigner. Two years in camp concen . . . how you say? Hard word. Concentra . . .'

'Concentration.'

'In nice country. Sun. South France, but pointy wire.'

'Barbed wire.'

'Yes. Huts bad. Soup bad. Lots little bugs. Fleas, you say? And in hair?'

'Lice?'

'Everybody lice. Now over. Me studio. Come see studio. Heavy work. Sculpture. Dealers come see sculpture. Not buy, but come see.'

Louis went with him as much out of curiosity as out of fear of offending him. They went by tram to the Boulevard Montparnasse. Pliska took him to the Rue Campagne-Première, where they entered a rather recently built house.

'Here. Lift. You know?'

There was indeed a lift, which carried them to the top floor, the sixth, where Pliska took out a key and proudly opened his door.

'My studio.'

Louis was dazzled. The room was vast and was flooded with light that streamed in through a large window that separated it from the street. Part of the sloping roof was also glazed.

'Magnificent, is no? Me work.'

He took off his jacket, waistcoat, and tie with the air of a wrestler challenging spectators from the platform of a fair booth.

Louis's gaze was attracted by a big block of clay on a rotating pedestal in the middle of the room.

'See? When finished, terrific. Terrific one says?'

For the time being, it suggested a couple locked in embrace. Louis could recognize human shapes, but without being able to tell what was a leg or an arm. He was moved. He looked at it eagerly and was filled with a sweet feeling. There was, in particular, a rather heavy mass, a rump which was already definitely modelled and which gave him a deeper impression of sensuality than the rump of a live woman.

'To sculpt very hard. Very much hard. Here . . .'

On a plain wooden slab stood a horse and rider made of bits of iron that looked as if they had been picked up in a workshop.

'Don Quisote.'

'Don Quixote?'

'Yes. Funny. No. Not funny.'

He frowned. His limpid eyes clouded over.

'Dealers say funny. Me not funny. Me and dealers . . .'

He made a show of throwing them through the glass and into the street from his top floor.

'Much work. Much make love. Not much eat because not sell. So me carry beef.'

'At Les Halles?'

'Halles, yes. Know Halles?'

When he learned that Louis worked there too, he wanted to have a drink with him and opened a bottle whose shape and label recalled an old Christmas.

'Not drink?'

'No. Too young.'

'Me, drink too much. Not good.'

He beat his chest like a gorilla and burst out laughing.

'See you Halles. You come back. You see love finished.'

What he called love was the half-ton block of clay in the middle of the studio. Although they worked so near each other at night, it was a long time before they met again, for Les Halles had sharply defined areas and varied activities, and Pliska's working hours, for example, did not coincide with Louis's.

On being promoted and getting an increase, Louis had locked himself up in a glass cage and could no longer, as in the beginning, thread his way through the market carrying messages from Monsieur Samuel to the agents in the neighbouring streets or in the big sheds.

It was unquestionably as a result of his meeting with the Czech that the idea of a studio took root in him, and from then on, when he walked in the street, he would make sure whether or not there was a big glass window or, better still, a workshop at the back of a yard.

His turn came to receive an official paper. He had to report to the district office on March 12 with a copy of his birth certificate and appear before the draft board. He did not mention it to his mother, who had been out when he found the envelope under the door. He spent an anxious week, not in fear of being declared fit for service, but at the thought that he would have to appear naked in front of men.

He was the only one in the family who was modest. His mother and sister were not at all ashamed of their nakedness, which they exhibited with a casualness that was perhaps not unmingled with satisfaction. Vladimir had begun to hide his sex organs only when he was about thirteen, and as for the redheads, they had paid no attention to them at all.

Louis had never moved his bowels in the pot, except in very early childhood, of which he had no memory.

Even though it was freezing cold on the stairs in winter, even though it was menacingly dark, just as it was in the yard, he nevertheless would go down at night when he would start feeling sick as a result of holding it in.

And when he was bathed in the tub, he always held a flannel with which he hid his genitals as long as he was not sheltered by the soapy water.

There were at least forty of them gathered in a dusty room. There were no clothes-hooks, but they were none the less ordered to undress.

'Be quick about it, boys. Another batch is due at eleven.'

He was more embarrassed when he recognized former schoolmates, three or four of them, including the lawyer's son whose name he had forgotten, the one who had left the state school to enter a private one.

'Well, well!' he exclaimed. 'The little saint!'

A wag called out, after looking Louis up and down:

'Are you sure it's not a girl?'

'We used to take him for a boy, but he's had time to change. Let's see your tool, little saint, so we can tell what you really are.'

Covering himself with his hands, he tried to turn his back to them.

'He'll have to show it when he goes by. And you know what the medical officer's going to do? He'll yank your balls and if he doesn't like you, he'll stick a finger up your behind. Don't think

134

I'm making it up. My brother was called up last year and tipped me off. Why do they call you the little saint? Do you go to confession every morning? Do you want to stay a virgin till you're married?'

The door finally opened into a larger room where men were sitting at a table covered with a green cloth. He could not distinguish them from each other. Although he did not shut his eyes, he saw only shadows, silhouettes, two horizon-blue uniforms, and a line of naked bodies.

'Step up. Stand up straight. Straighter than that. What are your hands fiddling with?'

One of the men in uniform announced:

'Five feet, three-quarters of an inch.'

There was a roar of laughter.

'Come here,' ordered the doctor.

Perhaps at the rate men were being consumed at the front, height no longer mattered? He was not afraid of being hit by a bullet, of being killed by a shell. What frightened him was the brutality, the orders that were rapped out in a snarling voice, the obligation to do what was ordered, without discussion.

He had made up his mind that if he were given a gun he would never fire it, or fire only in the air.

The medical officer dug his fingers between Louis's ribs, between his shoulder blades, then, after feeling his muscles, declared:

'Unfit. Rejected.'

He was pushed out of the room.

'What are you waiting for, my boy? Didn't you hear the doctor? The country doesn't want you.'

He let three days go by before saying to his mother, at dinner, in an expressionless tone:

'You know, Mama, I've been rejected.'

'That's no misfortune. That way, I'm sure of having one of you.'

Louis looked at her with the vague smile that intrigued them all and that did not necessarily reflect joy or gaiety.

His war was over.

# Chapter Three

His mother continued going to Les Halles every morning to stock up, but she was less often heard joking aloud in her clear, vibrant voice. He remembered the time when he would recognize its brightness amidst the hubbub in the glass-roofed warehouse, as one recognized from a distance the brightness of her hair.

His grandmother too continued pushing her cart through the dark streets in the early hours of the morning, but there were more and more days when she did not turn up and when Gabrielle, between clients, would go up to her room at the foot of the street, near Saint Médard's, to make sure she wasn't ill and didn't need anything.

Louis hardly knew that room. He had been in it two or three times, when he was little, and remembered it as being dark and crowded with furniture. There was a dining-room sideboard through whose upper doors, which were made of glass, he could see crockery. There were a table and chairs with fake-antique carvings, greenish velvet curtains with satin-stitch embroidery, and also knick-knacks, vases, statuettes, porcelain sweet dishes.

'Be careful, Louis. The last time your brother Vladimir came, he broke another saucer that I was very fond of. They're souvenirs.'

The smell of the room was different from the one at home, and he suspected the old woman of not liking to have visitors, not even her grandchildren. He had always considered her old, but she was not so very old, for the girls in the family had children early.

In the spring of 1919 Gabrielle must have been fifty-four. Her brother, the butcher, whom they pretended to ignore, though his shop was in their street, and who ignored them too, did not know that Louis was his nephew. He had been the old lady's first child. She had had him when she was about sixteen.

She had grown very thin and was becoming eccentric. Once,

136

when she had not turned up at Les Halles for a whole week, Gabrielle reassured Louis, who was worried.

'Don't be upset about Grandma. She could live on her savings. She's put aside quite a pile. She's never spent a penny. And she didn't help me in the beginning either, even when I was in a tight spot. She'd say to me, "Every man for himself! One brings up one's children until they're old enough to manage. After that, they can fend for themselves. I don't expect anything from anyone, and I have no desire when I'm old to sue you and your brother to make you give me an allowance." '

It was between eight and nine in the evening. Louis and his mother were both at home.

'What do you feel like eating, Louis? An omelette? A steak?'

'An omelette, Mama, with cheese, if there is any.'

They would sit at the table facing one another, and there would be long silences. One would have thought they were observing each other. Actually they were, or at least Louis was.

For years he had been seeing his mother with the same eyes, and she had always seemed to be the same age. Though she had hardly changed physically, for her body was still firm and her face unlined, he had the impression that a kind of greyness had invaded her.

In the past, she had never looked sad or preoccupied, and even the death of Emilie had dampened her spirits for only a few days. All in all, she had taken things as they came, enjoying what was good in life, contenting herself uncomplainingly with what was less good and ignoring the rest as if it had not existed.

Was it because her children were growing up and seeing her with new eyes that she had suddenly stopped receiving men? Yet she was still having them up when Vladimir was fifteen.

Her life had dimmed. To talk in terms of painting, like Monsieur Suard, shade was forming, dull spots on the canvas.

When Louis took her out from time to time on Saturday night, she no longer wore the lavender-blue dress which he had been so fond of. Fashion had changed with the war. Petticoats had little by little disappeared, as had heavy boned corsets, dresses that swept the ground, and shoes that were laced half-way up the leg.

Women displayed not only their ankles but half their calves and wore military-style jackets above their skirts. This caused so little astonishment that Louis had to make an effort to remember pre-war fashions.

She still undressed in his presence.

'You don't mind my going out?'

'Why, Mama?'

'You may think I'm too old.'

'You'll never be old.'

'Doesn't it bother you to see your mother running to dance halls like a bitch in heat?'

He smiled at her in a way that was meant to be reassuring.

'You, you never go out.'

'I go out during the day.'

'I've never seen you with a girl friend. Do you have one?'

'No, Mama.'

'Why not? A boy of nineteen needs women.'

He realized what was worrying her, and it reminded him of the jokes in the office of the draft board.

'Don't be afraid. I'm a man.'

She had not lost the habit of coming straight to the point.

'Do you do it?'

'Sometimes.'

'You could have it for nothing, as much as you want, especially as most men are at the front. If only you knew how women squabble over soldiers on leave!'

'It would take up too much of my time.'

That was not quite true, it expressed only part of a truth which was too complicated, which he was not sure he understood.

The memory of his impotence at the sight of a tangle of black hair had kept him for a long time from trying again. His appetite rarely had a keen enough edge to awaken his torment.

Erotic fantasies sometimes prevented him from falling asleep, as they did everyone, but he had found a method of making the physical need less acute. He made an effort at times to compose extravagant images, to see them as street scenes, as

138

spots of colour, to surround them with other details, and to create in his mind a picture of which he could have reproduced every detail.

There was a picture which he had a desire to paint but which he could not work on at the time because his mother would see it and he was ashamed of it.

Its colours would be as gay and bright as those he ordinarily used and yet, in advance, he entitled the composition 'War'.

He would start on it as soon as he had a studio, especially since the picture would be rather big. The vista would be that of the Champs-Elysées, with the greenery of the rows of trees and with bright houses whose details need not be visible, except for a profusion of flags at the windows.

The crowd would be represented by black spots dotted with blue, white, and red.

The important thing was the parade. As for the title, he hesitated between 'War' and 'The Parade', waiting for the canvas to be painted before deciding.

Ranks of soldiers, bigger than the crowd. He did not mind disproportion in his works among the figures or objects.

Naked soldiers, some of them rosy, others ghastly pale, as at the draft board. Each of them would carry a rifle and a peaked cap or helmet – he didn't know yet.

An officer, also naked, resembling the doctor, would be caracoling on a horse in front of them. They would be marching towards the Arc de Triomphe, except that it would be replaced by the dark and monumental sex organ of a woman whose legs were spread.

It would be hard to achieve. He probably would never be able to bring it off. Yet he had succeeded with a painting almost as complicated which he called 'The Little Train from Arpajon' and which, in his mind, was meant to epitomize Les Halles.

He had spoken about 'The Little Train from Arpajon' to Monsieur Suard, who said he would like to see the painting.

'As soon as I find a studio.'

'There are some available ones in Montmartre.'

'That's too far away.'

Too far away from his mother, of course, for he would go to see his mother every day, most likely would have dinner with her. He did not know how the matter could be arranged, and he foresaw that it would be painful. The actual reason for his rejection of Montmartre was that he would feel he was in a foreign country there, far away from the images he had been collecting unwittingly for nineteen years.

When he left the stationery shop one warm, humid afternoon, he had happened to pass a woman, not very tall, not young either, but plump, and with a pretty, smiling face. She had looked at him with complicity as she went by. The look was unlike that of the women who accosted men in the street. He had wondered whether he had quite understood. When he had looked back, she had too, the very same instant, and he had turned around and gone up to her.

She was wearing a blue suit with gilt buttons, and an overseas cap of the same colour, which was in fashion at the moment, was set on her curly hair.

She had not waited for him to make the first advances.

'Will you come along with me? I live only five minutes away.'

He warned her honestly that he was not rich.

'That doesn't matter. We'll arrange things.'

She looked to him about thirty. One could have taken her for a saleswoman in a store in the Grands Boulevards, or for a typist. She slightly resembled Mademoiselle Blanche, who worked with him every night in the glass cage and to whom he had never dared make a proposition, despite his desire to.

She lived in a cozy flat in a street that ran along the Palais Royal behind the Comédie Française. At the window, a canary was hopping about in a cage. The furniture and waxed floor were clean and bright.

'Do you often pick up women in the street?'

'It's the first time.'

Or almost the first. The other one had called to him and all he had had to do was follow her.

'How old are you? Sixteen? Seventeen?'

'Nineteen. People think I'm younger because of my height.'

'And because of your pretty little monkey face, eh? Do you know you've got a roguish look?'

140

She had taken off her hat and was undressing. Through an open door he could see a small dining-room beyond which must have been a kitchen.

'Are you embarrassed?'

'I don't know. A little.'

'Haven't you ever undressed in front of a woman?'

'Not entirely, no.'

'Haven't you ever made love?'

She understood his silence.

'It's nothing to be ashamed of, you know. Everyone has had to start some day. At your age, it was the same with me. I finally made up my mind. I was pretty scared and you'd be amazed if you knew what I imagined it would be like.'

She had thus far uncovered only her bosom, which was as beautiful as Gabrielle's, except that it did not have his mother's pearly sheen.

'Come and sit here.'

He sat down beside her on a couch with a yellow cover that later appeared often in his paintings.

'Do you like breasts?'

'Yes, I do.'

'Is that what excites you in a woman?'

She was speaking to him amiably, as if they were good friends who had known each other a long time.

'Don't think I'm in the habit of walking the streets. It looks like it, but it's very different. Haven't you ever been to what's called a massage establishment in the newspaper advertisements? Most of the time they're flats.

'I'm at Madame Georgette's in the Rue Notre-Dame-de-Lorette. It's quiet and discreet. There are only three or four of us, rarely five, and the customers are well behaved. They visit us regularly. You ought to drop in. One of the girls, Arlette, is just twenty-one.'

He stroked her breasts while looking at the canary in the cage, and she did not rush him. She kept talking casually. She unbuttoned his clothes little by little and he did not feel ashamed of being naked with her on the couch.

He wondered whether he wasn't going to love her. Entering

her was an experience unlike what he had imagined. It was very smooth and a feeling of well-being flowed through his whole body.

'Stay like that for a moment,' she whispered to him, stroking his hair and looking into his face with tender curiosity.

He was surprised, afterwards, that she did not act as if it were over, and they remained lying side by side, looking up at the ceiling and chatting.

'What do you do? I bet you're a student.'

'I work at Les Halles.'

'You? At Les Halles?'

'Some day I'll be a painter. I've started, but my work is bad.'

Later, she did not get dressed but put on a dressing-gown of the same blue as his mother's old dress.

He anxiously slipped his hand into his pocket, frightened at the thought that he might have to run home to get money as he had had to do the first time he bought paints.

'No. Not today. I've got another idea. Go down to the bakery. It's at the left, in the Rue des Petits-Champs. Buy some cakes, whatever you like, except chocolate cake, because chocolate doesn't agree with me. There's a grocery opposite and if you have enough money left get a bottle of port. There's no point in buying the most expensive, because I wouldn't know the difference. To me, port is port.'

Did she wonder whether he would come back or did she trust him? He read the names of the streets on the blue signs, for he was not familiar with the neighbourhood. She lived in the Rue Montpensier, and in order to get to the Rue des Petits-Champs he had to go by way of the Rue de Beaujolais.

He found the bakery and the grocery. Her odour was still on his skin, and it seemed to him that the passers-by could tell that he had made love twice.

She was leaning on the window-sill with her elbows, near the canary, when he returned with his packages, and the door opened the moment he reached the landing.

'You're very nice.'

Oddly enough, her name was Louise and his Louis.

'At Madame Georgette's, they call me Loulou.'

'May I call you Louise?'

'Would you rather? They say it sounds romantic, because of an opera.'

'My name is Louis.'

'Louis what?'

'Cuchas.'

'Is it a foreign name?'

'I don't think so. It's my mother's and grandmother's name and they were both born, just as I was, in the Rue Mouffetard.'

'Uncork the bottle. There's a corkscrew in the sideboard.'

They had gone into the dining-room. The sky above the roofs of the Palais Royal was lovely, very gentle, in spite of the heat.

She filled the glasses and handed him one, and he looked into her eyes as he drank. He did not like alcohol of any kind. It immediately made him dizzy.

'May I come back?'

'You seem to have liked it.'

'I did. I . . .'

He was at a loss for words, he felt moved, was filled with a sentiment he had had only for his mother or sister and once or twice, when they were younger, for Vladimir. He would have liked her to remain happy and gay, he hoped nothing unpleasant would happen to her.

She refilled the glasses.

'Here's to you!'

He rather liked the taste, as he did the warmth he felt in his chest and then, later, in his head. His eyes must have been shining and his ears getting red.

'You know . . .'

'A little while ago you called me Louise . . .'

'You know, Louise . . .'

It was really too difficult to thank her as he would have liked, as she deserved, to make her understand the importance of what had just happened, of the wonderful gift she had just made him and which would last all his life, he was sure it would.

There was no way of her guessing it. He would also have liked to tell her that Madame Georgette's didn't matter to him, that she was . . .

He got muddled, he spluttered, he had to control himself so that tears would not come to his eyes.

'You're a nice boy, Louis, very very decent. I'd like very much to see you again too, but don't come at the same time as today. It was just by chance that I didn't go to work this afternoon, because I had to see someone.'

'Who?' he dared ask.

'Now don't be jealous! It would surprise you if I answered that it was my uncle who comes from Tours once a month and invites me out for lunch. He's a wine-grower. My father was a wine-grower too. He was one of the first killed in 1914.'

'Like my brother-in-law.'

'He was in the cavalry of the line.'

'So was my brother-in-law.'

'I usually work until seven or eight and, since I have dinner in a restaurant in the Place Saint-Georges, I'm hardly ever here before ten or so.'

'What about in the mornings?'

'I sleep late. Then I wash and dress and make up and after that I do my shopping, because I prepare my own lunch.'

'I start work at ten in the evening.'

'Every evening?'

'Except Sunday.'

'On Sunday I go to the country with girl friends.'

'So?'

'Come and knock at my door from time to time around ten in the morning. You're not sleeping then?'

'I sleep just as well in the afternoon.'

'It doesn't matter if you find me in bed tired-looking and with my face shiny. Might as well empty the bottle, don't you think?'

He drank a third glass and half of a fourth, and when she accompanied him to the landing he was very animated.

'It's a day that ... a day that I ... Don't you think I'm ridiculous?'

'No. But it's time you had dinner. Your mother's waiting for you.'

He did not remember having told her that.

'All right, now go!'

And she looked at him pensively as he walked down the first flight.

He saw Louise again only twice. Each time he came with little cakes and a bottle of port. There were mornings when he left Les Halles feeling so sleepy that all he thought of was dropping into bed and did not even bother to lower the blind.

At other times, he was so eager to work on a painting that he could not get home fast enough.

The last time he went to see her, he did not feel that he was in form. He was acting from conviction. He rang the bell and waited. At first, there was no answer, though he heard voices inside. He rang again and there were footsteps. The door opened slightly and he caught sight of a man who had hastily slipped on Louise's blue dressing-gown.

'What is it?'

'Nothing,' he answered without insisting.

Nevertheless, a few months later he painted a picture that he entitled 'Portrait of Louise'. There was neither a face nor a body in it, only a window, a canary in a hanging cage, and, above the roofs of the Palais Royal, a sky of the softest and most dazzling blue he had ever obtained.

In October, a month before the famous Armistice Day, he feverishly awaited the evening conversation with his mother at the dinner table. He had a bad conscience, he felt like an executioner, he was ready to give in even before starting.

'I've got something to tell you, Mama.'

'You getting married too?'

When he went away, Gabrielle would be the only one left in the flat which had once been so full that everyone had to fight to defend his place.

'I'm not getting married. I don't think I ever will. I've found a studio. Wait! That doesn't mean I'm leaving you. What is it like now? We're never at home together except for dinner. Your working hours aren't the same as mine and we don't sleep at the same time. The studio will be the place where I work, you understand, the way Vladimir worked at Monsieur Brillanceau's. Remember, Mama, you didn't spend any more time with Vladimir or the twins than you do with me.'

'Where will you sleep?'

He blushed.

'First of all, I promise to come and have dinner with you every day. I'll spend my Sundays with you, either here or in my studio, where it'll be a pleasure to see you.'

'Are you taking your bed?'

'If you don't mind. I feel like working more and more. I don't go to sleep until I'm knocked out.'

'Where is it?'

'Not far from here, in the Rue de l'Abbé-de-l'Epée.'

'Is it expensive?'

'Thirty francs a month, with a lavatory.'

'Have you signed the lease?'

'I'll sign it tomorrow morning, if you allow me to.'

'And what if I don't?' she exclaimed with a burst of laughter. 'But of course, my little chick, of course I allow you to! Your wings and hackles have grown without my realizing it. And you, at the age of twenty, you blush at asking me to be free!'

'It's because of my painting, you understand?'

'Of course! Of course! It's always because of something.'

She was not crying and did not seem sad.

'When are you moving?'

'Tomorrow I'll move my things, my painting material and my canvases.'

'With my cart?'

'When you've finished work. I'll sleep here, and the day after tomorrow . . .'

He imagined how the room would look. His mother's bed in the middle of the big empty space would seem tiny. He did not yet realize how lucky he was. A month later, what with the return of the men who were still in the army, with the arrival of foreigners who were going to invade Paris and the painters who would congregate in Montparnasse, he would have found nothing equivalent to his studio without having to pay a small fortune.

It was in the yard of an old house, or rather an ancient house, not an old house like theirs. It must have been a private mansion in the past, and it had been kept in repair during its two or three centuries of existence. The walls were of stone. The spacious arch led to a cobbled yard in the middle of which stood a linden tree.

There were flats only in the front part of the building. They were occupied by middle-class people, civil servants, a dentist, a young couple, of whom the husband was a prisoner in Germany and whose three- or four-year-old son played alone in the yard.

The low part of the building, at the rear of the yard, had no doubt been a stable in the past. It had been transformed into a glass-enclosed workshop that had been occupied for fifty years by the same craftsman, a cabinet-maker, who had specialized in repairing old, precious furniture and whose clients had been the best antique dealers in the Rue du Bac, Rue de Seine, and Rue Jacob.

'He died exactly a month ago, sir. I've been in the house only ten years, but he'd already been working at the back of the yard fifty years before and maybe even earlier. People say he was married for fifteen years and that from the day he became a widower no woman was ever seen entering his place, even to do the cleaning, because he preferred to do it himself.'

The concierge spoke on in that vein as she showed him around.

'When I think that furniture was piled up to the ceiling and that now the place is empty.

'A nephew in the provinces, his only heir, didn't even bother coming to Paris for the funeral and had everything sent to the auction-rooms, including a stove the like of which I've never seen, enormous, with bronze decorations, there was always a pot of glue heating on it.

'Look! He himself built this wall. It makes a nice room. Behind it is the lavatory. He didn't call in workmen for that either.

'You're quiet, aren't you? You look as if you were. I wouldn't want one of those painters who invite friends and models at night and make a racket until dawn. You seem rather shy.'

'You know, Mama, it even has electricity!'

Even in his wildest dreams he would not have imagined such luck. The next day, radiant with joy, he took his mother's push-cart and moved out his personal belongings, which did not weigh much. The following day, he took his bed apart and tried to centre his mother's against the wall.

The concierge had given him an idea while chattering away. For several days he prowled around the rooms of the Paris auction-rooms, obviously not those in which valuable paintings, jewels, and antique furniture were sold, but the rooms containing odds and ends. He ended by unearthing a cylindrical cast-iron stove which had escaped from some provincial station and which he got for a song, and a low armchair, that had no style at all but in which he felt very comfortable.

He kept his promise to have dinner with his mother.

'You'll have to tell me how much I owe you for my meals.'

'Don't be silly, Louis. I realize why they called you the little saint. Did I make you pay for the milk that came from my body?'

'This is different. If you had to keep feeding all your children . . .'

He felt like biting his tongue off. He had just said 'all'. Only three of the five were left. Nothing was known of Guy. Vladimir merely dropped in on her every now and then for a few minutes, while the same woman waited for him in the street.

Alice had written that, after thinking it over, she did not plan to return to Paris after the war, that she had sold the furniture in her flat to her English sub-tenant, and that perhaps she would remarry in the near future. She did not send a photograph of her son François, about whom she merely said that he was in good health.

'Will you come on Sunday, Mama? There won't be much furniture. I've bought only the necessary pots and pans. The kitchen is small, a kind of cupboard, but it has a gas ring.'

She came, dressed in the clothes she wore when she went dancing on Saturday nights. She looked at everything, sniffed the smell of varnish and old wood that lingered in the studio.

'It's nice,' she admitted, more to say something pleasant than out of conviction.

'Did you see my linden tree?'

For he had incorporated it into his universe, without knowing that, like the old cabinet-maker, he would be living in its shade for fifty years and more.

'It looks big, but when I become a real painter I'll need room.'

'Why don't you hang your pictures?'

The few canvases he had kept without scraping them down so as to use them again were on the floor, facing the wall:

'Later. They're not good enough. If I saw them all the time, I'd tear them up and might never paint again.'

She went to the studio only rarely, not feeling at home there, even less than if Louis had been living with another woman. 'I'm having a visitor on Saturday night, a man who knows about painting. It's the one from whom I buy my colours, and he's given me advice. He's a friend of lots of painters and plans to set up as a picture dealer some day.'

He did not suspect that in talking that way, quietly and with a smile in spite of his inner excitement, he was moving farther away from Gabrielle than Vladimir and Alice had done.

Yet the studio was only a five-minute walk from the Rue Mouffetard. His new street had the same kind of shops as those in the one he had left. The Boulevard Saint-Michel, down which his mother pushed her cart every morning, was a few feet away, a few houses off. Just opposite were the trees, benches, and iron chairs of the Luxembourg Gardens.

'It's only nine o'clock, Mama. I have time to walk you home.'

'Why should I make you go out of your way?'

He insisted. He was wrong, for that Sunday evening, with the shops closed the windows of the flats opened and the people leaning on the window-sill and looking out, he in turn felt like an outsider. It was no longer the street whose image was fixed in his memory, an image he needed, which must not be stolen from him. He had promised his mother to go home and have dinner with her every evening and he suddenly wondered whether he would have the courage to keep his word.

All at once, things began to happen fast. It began with the visit of Monsieur Suard, who was not surprised to see paintings hanging on the walls.

'May I look?'

As chance would have it, he picked up 'The Little Train from Arpajon', and his first reaction was one of surprise, perhaps agreeable surprise, perhaps disagreeable. For several minutes he kept looking back and forth from Louis to the painting, as if he were examining the relationship between a portrait and its model.

'The fact is . . . No! . . . I was about to say something silly. . . . I'll put it in a different way. . . . I don't suppose you've tried to reproduce reality . . .'

'Why?' asked Louis simply, though he was disturbed.

'You've tried to give an impression of Les Halles, haven't you?'

'Why Les Halles?'

'The little train . . . the shed on the left and that side of beef as big as the shed . . . the cabbages in the foreground . . .'

'I didn't try to paint Les Halles.'

'Then what *did* you try to paint?'

'I don't know. I started with the little train. That's why I've called the picture "The Little Train from Arpajon". It might have been elsewhere, in a street, even in the Champs-Elyseés.'

'In a certain way, anything that's represented is real.'

'Everything is real.'

'Have you seen any of the work of Odilon Redon?'

'No.'

'He too thinks that he paints reality, and in a sense he does. Do you dream much?'

'Not when I sleep.'

'But you do dream?'

'I don't know. I walk. I sit down on a bench. I look.'

'Thinking about what?'

'About nothing.'

Was he going to reply, like Louis's first teacher, the one with the flabby mouth, that it was impossible to think about nothing?

'And this picture, this one here, what title have you given it?'

'You know, the titles I give my pictures, they're meant just for me. The way, at first, one gives one's children a name, or a nickname that changes later. This little canvas is called, in my mind, "Portrait of Louise".'

150

'Are you in love with her?'

'Not any more.'

'Did she play an important part in your life?'

'Maybe. I think so. What I can't manage to get is a certain sparkle that I'm after, the quivering space between objects. You understand?'

'I understand. Monet spent his life trying to do that.'

Louis felt a pang of disappointment. He would have liked to be the first to have had that ambition.

'But Monet tried to achieve that result with light. The object was unimportant.'

'My cabbages, my beef, my little train are *very* important.'

Monsieur Suard seemed to be musing.

'You're an odd man. I ought to say an odd young man, because you're under twenty.'

'I'll be twenty in December.'

'Does your work at Les Halles tire you?'

'It takes up my time and obliges me to sleep part of the day.'

'What's that picture, the one bigger than the others?'

'It's a painting I botched. A sketch. I intended to do it again, larger, like a fresco, when I had enough room and money.'

He turned it around reluctantly, and Monsieur Suard was even more surprised than at the sight of the first painting.

'Don't tell me the title. I want to guess. "War." Am I right?'

'I hesitated between "War" and "The Parade". I may try it again some day. The soldiers will remain naked, wearing helmets or peaked caps. I prefer the cap, because of the colour.'

'What will you substitute for the woman?'

So Monsieur Suard had guessed that it was the monstrous female sex organ that bothered him. Did he also guess why?

'I don't know yet. Maybe the Arc de Triomphe?'

'Do you need this one in order to start work on the other?'

'No. I'll work without looking at it. I know it by heart.'

'Listen, Louis. Do you mind my calling you that?'

A few months later, Monsieur Suard was to start addressing him by the familiar *tu*, but Louis never reciprocated and for many many years continued to call him Monsieur Suard.

'Of course not. I'd be delighted.'

'I'd like to buy this painting that you pretend to reject, which some day perhaps you will reject, but which I consider very important.'

'Why?'

'You're an artist and you don't have to understand. Perhaps it's better for you not to understand too much. German Expressionists worked along the same lines. They were intellectuals who knew where they were going, who were trying to express an idea. Did you know, when you were painting the soldiers, that they would be marching towards a monumental sex organ?'

'No, I didn't.'

'In your mind, towards what were they marching?'

'I don't know. At the draft board, we were naked. I added the rifle and the cap and instead of making us parade by the medical officer, I put in a lot more, in ranks.'

'That woman ... No! Don't answer. I'm not rich. I know painters who haven't exhibited yet. I buy a picture from them from time to time. Let me confess something. Just between you and me. I've stopped smoking and having apéritifs in order to buy another painting when the opportunity occurred. I offer you a hundred francs for it. Fifty this month and fifty next. If, let's say in five years, your paintings are worth more, I promise to pay you the difference.'

'That's too much. I want to give it to you.'

'I know what I'm doing. Here's fifty francs. Before coming here, I was sure I'd buy something from you, but I didn't suspect it would be such a painting.'

'Why?'

' "The Little Train from Arpajon" will have more success, not right away, but in a few years. You see, Louis, you're neither an Impressionist nor a Fauve nor a Cubist. You're not an amateur either. If, as I hope, you remain yourself, it'll be hard to classify you. I don't quite understand either, but you've got something.'

'I can't manage to get down on canvas what I'd like to. I don't think I'll ever be able to.'

'Have you a piece of paper? It's raining and I want very much to take this painting with me.'

One day, shortly thereafter, Louis was sleeping in broad daylight, as he was in the habit of doing. It would have cost too much to buy curtains for a glassed-in bay twenty-five feet long and twelve feet high.

Someone was pounding at his door, and he did not immediately enter the world of reality.

'Monsieur Cuchas! Monsieur Cuchas! Wake up!'

And the voice of the concierge literally screamed:

'The war's over!'

He thanked her without opening the door, for he was wearing only a shirt and underpants. An uproar, including singing and the blowing of instruments, could be heard coming from the Boulevard Saint-Michel. He hesitated for a moment, barefooted on the cold floor, then went back to bed and fell asleep.

In the evening, he had difficulty in getting to Les Halles, where couples were dancing in the markets. There was no dancing in the shed in the Rue Conquillière, and Monsieur Samuel, whose stomach overflowed his trousers as usual, did not say a single unnecessary word. His face was ashen. He had just learned that his son had died of Spanish influenza at a military hospital in Amiens.

Monsieur was to die later, in the midst of work, in the midst of the crowd, in the midst of the hubbub, of a stroke of apoplexy.

Former employees who had been demobilized were entitled to their old jobs. The firm had been bought by two partners who knew nothing about the business and who began by not allowing push-carts, which they considered a nuisance and unprofitable, to enter the shed.

The street-sellers of the Rue Mouffetard scattered and either chose another wholesaler or preferred to prowl about looking for bargains.

Gabrielle was among the latter, so Louis no longer saw her during the night or at dawn.

He had left the glass office and gone back to the blackboard. At times he was so tired as a result of painting most of the day that he would get mixed up in the figures that were called out to him.

One of the partners, who had made a lot of money in scrap metal, was particularly foul-mouthed and had picked Louis as scapegoat. His name was Smelke and it was hard to identify his foreign accent.

Monsieur Suard, who had paid the remainder of the hundred francs, had taken 'The Little Train from Arpajon' to show it to two or three collectors whom the painting might interest. He was beginning to build up a clientele, not of rich people who bought, in galleries, the works of established artists but of people who cared enough about painting to buy pictures with the little extra money they had, doctors, lawyers, shopkeepers, clerks.

'I'm ashamed to tell you, Louis. Among the people I know, there's only one who's interested, but he can't give more than eighty francs.'

'That's a lot, isn't it?'

'If I were you, I wouldn't accept.'

'What if it made it possible for me to leave my job at Les Halles?'

'Well in that case it's different.'

'The Little Train from Arpajon' also was gone. A time was to come when full-size reproductions of it could be bought in most bookshops, not only in France but in foreign countries as well, even in America. The exact price of the reproduction was eighty francs.

## Chapter Four

How long did he continue having dinner at his mother's home almost every day? The answer to that question, as to many others, depended on the period in which he wondered about it, for time seemed longer to him at the age of forty than at sixty. Events were placed in such or such a period, but their chronological order would sometimes vary.

His mother, who was to live on until after the Second World

War, kept making a reproach which he felt he did not deserve.

'If you'd stayed with me, if you'd kept coming to see me, I wouldn't be here with that lunatic and would have stayed in the good old Rue Mouffetard just as my mother did until she died.'

In 1945 she was living in a smart-looking cottage at Joinville, on the bank of the Marne.

'Léon's getting more and more impossible. Imagine, at his age and mine, he's becoming jealous. When he goes fishing, he fishes from in front of the house so as to keep an eye on me.'

She was over seventy and the Léon in question, her second husband, was six or seven years older. He did not look his age. He stood as straight, his shoulders were as broad and his flesh as firm as when Louis had met him for the first time.

Like the twins in the past, he had a square face and his hair was closely cropped, but it was all white.

Louis was sure that he had continued to have dinner alone with his mother for a long time and he could see himself bringing, when he had a little money, a dish that they were not in the habit of eating, a lobster, scallops in a shell, which had simply to be reheated, a cold chicken, a bottle of good wine or a small tin of fat goose liver.

Guy's letter dated from late 1919 or early 1920, and Louis and his mother had been sitting at the table. Léon had not yet entered the picture when she had taken it out of her bag.

'It's strange, Louis. You'll see. It's not his hand-writing, but he signed it.'

On the envelope were several Ecuadorian stamps.

Dear Mama,

'I suppose that now the war has been over for some time, letters are no longer censored and I can write to you without getting you into trouble. You'll be surprised to receive this letter, which I hope finds you all in good health, Excuse me for not writing to you myself. You know I was never very good at spelling since I didn't spend much time in school.

I have no news of Olivier or anyone else. I don't know if Olivier married his little Bedouin and if he still lives in Oran. When I left

155

him, he spoke of joining the Foreign Legion or the African Battalions. I hope he didn't do such a foolish thing.

Maybe you'll find the city of Guayaquil on a map of South America. It's almost opposite the Galápagos Islands. Do you remember that at home Olivier and I often used to talk about the Galápagos Islands and you didn't believe me when I said there were huge turtles hundreds of years old and so big that two persons could sit on them?

Well, they exist. Olivier and I left with the idea of living on a desert island. Unfortunately, the boat on which we stowed away put in at Algeria, where we were discovered. Then we dreamed of making enough money to leave from Dakar.

We worked as labourers and at other jobs. Olivier met a little girl who begged in the street.

I admit that, for a Bedouin, she was very beautiful. Those people generally live in the mountains and are very proud.

I wonder how that one landed in Oran and why she held out her hand in the street, with her eyes covered with flies.

Olivier didn't want to go on. We argued and I went away alone. I got to Panama, which is a funny country, where I got a job on a freighter going down the Pacific coast.

I won't go into detail because it would take time and I had lots of adventures and hardships. If I started telling my life history, poor Dorothy would never finish writing this letter that I'm dictating to her. She's very educated. She's English and was born in Quito, the capital of Ecuador, where her father was consul.

He made her go to school first in Quito, then in Panama, where there's an American school, and after that he sent her to England, where she studied the natural sciences.

She's begging me, while I'm dictating this letter, not to talk about her so much and I'm sure she's writing down everything I say. She even worked for quite a long time at the museum. When she came back here, she was on a kind of mission.

I was still trying to get to the Galápagos. I would have had to hire a boat and I hadn't sufficient money. I worked as a lift-boy in a hotel, because they built an eight-storey hotel. I managed to get along until I met Dorothy, who's eight years older than I.

We were married in a few minutes by an English clergyman, so I've become a Protestant, but it's of no importance to either Dorothy or me.

I still don't understand how she could have fallen in love with a big brute who can hardly write and whom she had to teach everything.

We now live in a bungalow, which means a wooden house, very comfortable, with all improvements, twenty miles out of town. Since the road doesn't go any farther we live right in the bush.

It's hotter than in Africa. Plants grow amazingly fast and you'll be surprised to hear that we earn our living hunting butterflies, hummingbirds, and egrets, which we send to New York and London where we sell them at very high prices.

There are also certain lizards and certain birds that we catch alive and that zoos fight to get.

Dorothy attends to the correspondence and goes with me into the bush, where you have to be very careful not only because of the jaguars but particularly the insects.

We have a comfortable life. Three half-breeds look after the bungalow and prepare our meals. I speak Spanish and English almost better than French. The thing that makes me sad is that I won't ever be able to go to see you in France, where I'd be arrested as a deserter.

I hesitated when I learned that war was declared. The consul would have paid my fare.. He was angry with me when he realized that I preferred to stay here, and for years he pretended not to recognize me.

He has forgotten about it by now, calls me Troublemaker, and only last week came to our house for whisky. Dorothy and I have no children. Let us have news about all of you. The address is at the bottom of the page. San José is the name of the nearest village.

I kiss you with all my love. Forgive me for having gone away. I couldn't help it.

Your loving son,<br>Guy

At the age of more than seventy-five, Gabrielle still kept the letter in the biscuit tin, which she had taken with her to Joinville. The Léon incident had occurred later, Louis was sure of it, in 1921 or 1922. She was still going to Les Halles. He had gone to see her at home one Sunday morning, at about ten o'clock, for she did not like either his studio or his paintings. He had found her *en déshabille,* sitting opposite a man touched with grey who seemed to be quite at home.

'Don't go away, Louis. It's not what you think. I want you to meet Léon, Léon Hanet. He's a foreman in a big plumbing firm in the Boulevard Voltaire. He's been a widower for ten years and has two married daughters. One of them's the wife of a doctor.'

The man was wearing only trousers, a white collarless shirt, and a pair of old shoes on his sockless feet.

Gabrielle laughed with embarrassment.

'Imagine, Léon has got it into his head that he wants to marry me. He makes a good living and wants me to give up my push-cart.'

She in turn was betraying the Rue Mouffetard, like the rest of the clan. The others had gone off, of course, but it had never occurred to Louis that she would not remain in their home.

'He has a nice flat in the Boulevard Richard-Lenoir. What do think of the idea? Even though I keep telling him that I'm too old . . .'

She had remarried, discreetly, without telling anyone, and their former home was invaded by a family of Poles.

Later on, newspaper articles and even biographies of him related that during the long years when his work had been un-appreciated he had never had enough to eat and that he had hunted for food in dustbins.

It was untrue. The legend grew out of the fact that he had once spoken of the couple he had seen from the window in the Rue Mouffetard. He had added that he had later been curious to know what edible food was to be found in dustbins and had opened two or three as he walked by.

As for hunger, he attached no importance to it. He had never been gluttonous. Even when he had money, he would be satisfied with milk, hard-boiled eggs, and cheese. There were times, it is true, when he had to do without. Not for years, but occasionally.

There was also a tendency to include him among what was called the Montparnasse painters, who had invaded the four-teenth *arrondissement* after the war and who could be seen and heard, talking all languages, first at the Rotonde and on the terrace of the Dôme and late at the Coupole.

These cafés were frequented not only by painters and sculp-tors in odd get-ups, men and women alike, but also by writers, poets and critics whom, before long, tourists came to gape at.

Louis had spent a few hours a day over a period of a month

in a corner of the Rotonde, sitting in front of a cup of coffee and milk without ever saying a word to anyone.

He had recognized well-known painters there, men who, especially towards the end, always arrived accompanied by a court of aesthetes and pretty girls. Some of them had conspicuous cars which would be surrounded by onlookers.

Louis had not been involved in any group. Nobody in Montparnasse knew his name. He was only a short, thin young man with tousled hair and a contented smile.

Monsieur Suard had left the stationery shop in the Rue de Richelieu too late or too soon. Too late because in 1923 or 1924 there were as many picture galleries as night clubs in Montparnasse, to say nothing of the larger and more luxurious ones that sprang up in the Rue du Faubourg-Saint-Honoré.

The value of money had changed. Formerly, when Louis lived with his mother, people counted by sous. Now they counted by hundreds and thousands of francs, and artists whom no one would mention in ten years were selling their paintings at prices higher than those paid for works by an Italian master of the Renaissance.

Monsieur Suard had also started too soon, because people had not yet begun, as was to happen later, to distinguish between what would last and what would end up at the Flea Market.

The Rue de Seine was not a bad location, but the narrow shop window with the dark green frame was stuck between a butcher's shop whose marble counters were covered with poultry and a modest fruit and vegetable shop whose baskets and crates extended, as in the Rue Mouffetard, to the middle of the pavement.

Passers-by did not notice that between the two was a picture gallery, especially since the paintings that were shown and the posters that occasionally announced an exhibition bore unknown names.

It was to that period that journalists and others alluded later when they wrote that Cuchas had lived in poverty for years.

As a matter of fact, it did go on for years, with ups and downs, until 1927 or 1928. In order to carry on, Monsieur Suard sold some of his furniture and moved from his flat at the Porte d'Orléans to a cheaper one.

When he saw Louis enter the gallery with a canvas under his arm, he was torn between enthusiasm and his despair at not having money to give him.

'Are you at the end of your tether?'

Louis would smile and shake his head.

'There's someone interested who's supposed to come back on Monday. I'm sure he'll be back. He's excited by one of your canvases, "The Baskets", but I refused to let him have it cheap. Now's the time we've got to establish your reputation, and if I sell you for less than the others no one will take you seriously.'

The bowl was full, half full, or empty, depending on the month or the week. It was a big ceramic bowl that had been used for God knows what. There was no way of telling what craftsman had fired it, in what kiln, and how he had obtained that bright metallic red which had caught Louis's eye at the Flea Market in Saint-Ouen, where he sometimes roamed about on Sundays.

He had placed it on a shelf, for the studio had gradually become cluttered with tables, stands, easels, objects that interested no one, glass paperweights in which one could see snow falling, odd-shaped bottles of all colours – in short, a collection of odds and ends, which he called his treasure.

The bowl in the studio played the role of his mother's biscuit tin. When he came home with a little money, Cuchas would put it into the bowl, whether it was in change or notes.

'See whether there's enough left in the bowl to buy some salami,' he would say, without stopping his painting.

There was often a woman with him. He had built, with his own hands, a narrow couch, for he hated to sleep with anyone.

He had never been able to say no and everyone regarded his smile, his way of tilting his head, as an acceptance.

'I bet you're a painter, aren't you?'

He wore the same suit for ten years. It was made of a kind of corduroy that had been used for labourers' trousers when he was a child. He had not chosen it in order to look like a painter but because he had always wanted such a suit. Otherwise, clothes did not matter to him and he sometimes wore the same shirt for two weeks.

'You have a look in your eyes that women must find attractive.'

He did not believe it. He didn't care. He let them have their way. They would follow him home. Three cats had taken refuge in his studio, and he accepted a woman's presence as he did theirs.

He rather liked seeing a naked body moving about in the light that streamed in through the big window. But because of the complaints of a tenant whose flat faced the yard, he had to have a curtain, and one day, when there was money in the bowl, he had one made of the cheapest material he could find, burlap.

He was neither poor nor rich. He spent his time painting, in quest of the sparkling space that he had been seeking so long and that he continued to seek all his life.

Some girl friends stayed two days, others a month or more. For a time, there were two Lesbians, one of them a Swede, who had no place to sleep. They were fond of him, especially the Swede, whom he seemed to fascinate and who compared him to a Scandinavian elf.

Why did Cuchas suddenly think of Pliska one day when Suard, who was discouraged, spoke of giving up his gallery? He had run into the Czech again a few nights before on the terrace of the Dôme amidst a group of people talking different languages. He was the biggest and strongest of the party and had such a booming voice that despite the noise in the street he could be heard at the other end of the terrace.

'You ask my first name? . . . No first name. . . . Only Pliska . . . Pliska. . . . You all hear . . .'

Though he was drunk, he nevertheless recognized Louis, to whom he called his audience's attention.

'Ask my friend. . . . Knew him child. . . . Him know Pliska great sculptor. . . . Greatest sculptor in world. . . . Him have seen "Couple". . . . No more "Couple". . . . Changed name. . . . "Procreation" . . . eh! . . . "Procreation". . . . Understand? . . .'

This 'Procreation', which was to make Pliska famous and

really launch the Suard Gallery, not in the Rue de Seine but in the Rue la Boétie, attracted the attention of an American art critic who had been commissioned by a Philadelphia millionaire to buy the best works of painting and sculpture he could find for the collector's private museum, which he intended to bequeath to his city.

That was how one of Cuchas's small canvases, entitled 'The Wedding', happened to cross the Atlantic on the same boat as the Czech's monument.

Around the age of thirty, Louis became plump, and his cheekbones filled out and slightly dulled his features. He ate almost every day at the Caves d'Anjou, a restaurant with a tin counter and cane-bottomed chairs that was frequented by truck drivers. He would always sit in the same corner, for he liked corners and felt too conspicuous or vulnerable in the middle of a room.

A glass of white wine, Monsieur Cuchas?'

The carroty cat would jump on his knees and he would stroke it mechanically. He drank little, two or three glasses of white wine a day, walked the streets, and would stop to look at a piece of wall or watch women on a scaffold. He liked benches, especially those in the little parks or small squares where there was almost never anyone and where he could sit for two hours without being aware of the passing of time.

Suard was beginning to get better prices for his paintings and the bowl was almost always full.

'Is that where you keep your money?'

'It's beautiful, isn't it? I've never managed to get the same red.'

'Anyone can dip into it.'

He shrugged. Money or no money, his life remained the same. At times when he prowled about the Rue Mouffetard, he looked as if he were walking around a magic circle.

For a long time he had been inside it and he seemed to hesitate to re-enter it. Hadn't he picked the Caves d'Anjou at the corner of the Rue Rataud because it was at the frontier of his former universe?

Vladimir was living between Marseilles and Toulon. He had a car that stopped at the studio two or three times. He was more ironic and aggressive than in the past and there was a certain disquieting heaviness in his gaze.

'Have you seen Mama?'

'I have. I don't like her man.'

'They're married.'

'I know.'

'So is Alice. She married a cattle dealer and claims she's happy.'

She too came to see him, though without her husband or children, for she had had two more since her second marriage.

'Are you in Paris alone?'

'No, all five of us came for the Motor Show.'

She had put on weight. Her gaze was lustreless.

'We're building a new house, a villa, two miles from Nevers. My husband's buying up all the grassland he can find. It's the best investment. I'm going to see Mama tomorrow.'

'Have you got her address?'

'She sent it me on a postcard.'

'She's remarried.'

'It's funny, isn't it? I'd have been embarrassed at her age.'

He would sometimes work on a painting for five or six hours at a stretch and then toss away his brush and throw himself down on his bed to cry.

Pliska encouraged him. Every time he came he was accompanied by a new girl whom he ordered, as soon as she opened her mouth:

'You not talk... Not know.... Only screw...'

He would examine the paintings one by one, carefully, with his brows knit. He was deeply moved one day when he caught sight of the box of coloured pencils he had given little Louis one Christmas Day.

'You keep?'

They were almost intact, having been used only for drawing the tree in the schoolyard and for two or three childish sketches. The dark blue one was missing. His sister had taken it one evening to copy the pattern of a skirt from a fashion magazine.

Since then he had painted another tree, the linden in the yard, 'Mr Tree'.

'Why Mister?'

What could he answer? He smiled, slightly embarrassed.

'I don't know.'

It had been the same with cabbages. He had painted lots of cabbages. Most people eat vegetables without ever having watched a cabbage or leek or young carrot actually live.

'Do you find cabbages decorative?'

'No. Not decorative.'

Journalists began coming to question him.

'Is it a memory from the time when you worked at Les Halles?'

'I don't know.'

One day when he was attending the opening of another painter's exhibition at the Suard Gallery, a voice cried out:

'Well, what do you know! The little saint!'

A man put out his hand. Louis tried in vain to attach a name to the face, which he nevertheless knew very well.

'Don't you remember? Randal. Raoul Randal, the one who fought you over a yellow marble. Is this your exhibition?'

'No.'

'I was told you'd become a painter. How's it going?'

He looked him up and down as if to judge the degree of his success from his face and clothes.

'I'm working.'

'Do you sell?'

'Sometimes.'

'That's good. What does this bird do? I don't know anything about art. I received an invitation because I've put some money into a small weekly.'

A journalist who had heard the conversation came over.

'Why did you call him the little saint?'

'Cuchas? Because at school he let everyone hit him without complaining to the teacher.

'Or maybe because he used to help his mother push her cart to Les Halles and back at three in the morning. She was a street-seller. They were very poor. If I remember right, there were two twins, older than he. They were nasty little bastards.'

Louis did not protest. He kept smiling, as he had smiled in the past when he was slapped or kicked. The story appeared in an evening paper, which the concierge brought him. She was all excited.

'Now I understand, those cats you keep, those girls who take whatever they want.'

The legend spread. Before the second war, many people were calling him the little saint and caricatures of him appeared with a halo around his head.

Until the age of forty-two he had never had any desire to travel and it was only when people began to leave Paris when the Germans were expected to arrive any hour, that he left for the south. One of his collectors, a doctor, drove him as far as Moulins but went no farther because his wife had relatives there and it was unthinkable that the Germans would get as far as that. Louis got a few lifts from lorry-drivers and also walked part of the way. In Lyons, after waiting on the platform a night and a day, he was able to get into a train that took him to Cannes, where he was unable to find a room.

The sight of the sea thrilled him. However, he was obliged to go a bit north, first to Mougins, then to Mouans-Sartoux, a real village without villas or hotels for tourists, a few miles from Grasse.

He spent the war years there. He no more read the papers than he had done during the first war. He rented a shanty which he used as a studio. Suard and his family had settled in Nice.

'Well, do you find the light bright enough and the colours pure enough?'

'I thought I did at first.'

For two years he had been trying to render the vividness of nature.

'You no longer think so?'

'The light eats everything up, it chokes everything. All that's left is a kind of mush. I'd have done better to stay in Paris.'

'We'll be there before long. Here, take this! I've brought you a bit of butter that some friends sent me.'

Before long. . . . No. . . . It lasted another three years. Suard was selling his paintings at such high prices that Louis did not know what to do with the money. People were afraid of a devaluation and were buying anything.

'Do you want me to keep it for you?'

'I don't care.'

He had his corner in the local inn, the smell of which delighted him. His stoutness had gone and never came back. In fact, when he returned to his studio in Paris, where he was surprised to find every object in its place, he began to get lean. His hair, which remained fine and loose, had turned grey. It flitted about his face and made him look thinner and more delicately modelled than when he was a child.

There were paintings of his in many museums. People were surprised to find him in that comfortless studio where he did not even want to have a telephone. He continued to wear corduroy suits, though he could no longer find the thick, warm, strong cloth of the old days.

His grandmother had died. His mother and her husband were still living in the cottage at Joinville. Nobody in the family was left in the Rue Mouffetard, and when he went back to it he recognized few faces. Monsieur Stieb was dead. So were the Dorés. The old house was still there, but a six-storey building was under construction next to it.

'You're Louis Cuchas, aren't you, the half-brother of a man named Joseph Heurteau?'

He almost said no, because of the unfamiliar 'Joseph'.

'Do you mean Vladimir?'

'So you know his nickname?'

'He was called that when I was born.'

'Why?'

'I don't know.'

That was in 1960. His hair was now white and his features had become so pure that it was as if he were disembodied and were only a limpid gaze, a gentle, disquieting smile.

Two men had come to his studio and shown him their police badges.

'How long is it since you've seen him?'

'The last time was in Cannes, during the war.'

'What was he doing?'

'I don't know.'

'Didn't you ask him what he lived on?'

'No.'

'Did he spend a lot of money?'

166

'I don't know.'

'Didn't you notice that he hung around with shady characters?'

'He was alone with his wife. I happened to run into him in a café.'

'Do you mind if we look around your studio?'

The searched everywhere, methodically. One of them admitted in discouragement:

'We didn't find anything at your mother's place either.'

'What are you looking for?'

'Drugs. Joseph Heurteau, known as Vladimir, is one of the top men in the drugs racket in France. He was run in for pimping, but now we want to give him the works.'

He heard nothing more about Vladimir for a year. He was almost at the point of making the objects on this canvas vibrate by surrounding them with air or light. Almost. Not quite. It would take years.

He learned from his mother that Vladimir had been sentenced to fifteen years hard labour.

He continued to paint all day long. In most of his paintings there were traces of his mother, his sister Alice, and even little Emilie. Nobody noticed it. The faces of the redheads also appeared several times, as did the stove, a yellow marble, the sheet with a hole in it that had separated the mattresses from Gabrielle's bed.

He would soon be seventy and walked with short steps, conscious of his fragility.

In the evening, he liked to sit in a local cinema amidst the warm crowd. When early films were shown he discovered the actors of the time when he was a young man and had hardly been aware of the existence of the cinema.

He had worked a great deal. He was still working. It would take him years more to render what he felt had always been in him.

'What exactly is your aim?'

'I don't know.'

That was the sentence that he had uttered most often in the course of his life and which he kept repeating.

Monsieur Suard was dead. His son, who had taken over the

gallery, called him Maître. Many people called him Maître.

He remembered the evening when he had thought he saw a slight cloud come over his mother's face, which had always been radiant. One of the twins was dead. Emilie was dead. Pretty Alice was fat and callous. She too was clouded over. And Vladimir had no chance of getting out of prison alive. Only one of them was left, far away, in Ecuador, and he had stopped writing. He was nearing seventy-five and his wife was over eighty. Were they still alive and were they still hunting for butterflies and birds of paradise?

At times he thought he could feel the cloud coming over him too. He would think of the mattresses, of Emilie's cot, of the Rue Mouffetard, of the push-carts arriving at Les Halles.

Had he not taken something from everything and everyone? Had he not used their substance?

He didn't know, he mustn't know, otherwise he would be unable to carry on to the end.

He continued to walk with little steps, to smile.

'May I ask you, Maître, how you see yourself?'

He did not reflect very long. His face lit up for a moment as he said, joyously, and modestly:

'As a small boy.'

*Epalinges, 13 October 1964*

# Maigret and the Headless Corpse

Translated from the French by
Eileen Ellenbogen

# Contents

# 1. The Fouled Propeller

In the faint, grey light of early dawn, the barge lay like a shadow on the water. Through the hatchway appeared the head of a man, then shoulders, then the great gangling body of Jules, the elder of the two Naud brothers. Running his hands through his tow-coloured hair, as yet uncombed, he surveyed the lock, the Quai de Jemmapes to his left, and the Quai de Valmy to his right. In the crisp morning air he rolled a cigarette, and while he was still smoking it, a light came on in the little bar on the corner of the Rue des Récollets.

The proprietor, Popaul, came out on to the pavement to take down his shutters. His hair, too, was uncombed, and his shirt open at the neck. In the half-light, the yellow façade of the bar looked more than usually garish.

Rolling his cigarette, Naud came down the gangplank and across the quay. His brother, Robert, almost as tall and lanky as himself, emerging from below deck in his turn, could see, through the lighted window, Jules leaning on the bar counter and the proprietor pouring a tot of brandy into his coffee.

It was as though Robert were waiting his turn. Exactly as his brother had done, he rolled a cigarette. As the elder brother left the bar, the younger came down the gangplank, so that they met half-way, in the road.

'I'll be starting the engine,' said Jules.

Often, in the course of a day, they would not exchange more than a dozen laconic sentences, all relating to their work. They had married twin sisters, and the two families lived on the barge, which was named *The Two Brothers*.

Robert took his elder brother's place at the bar, which smelt of coffee laced with spirits.

'Fine day,' said Popaul, who was a tubby little man.

Naud, without a word, glanced out of the window at the sky,

173

which by now was tinged with pink. The slates and tiles of the rooftops and one or two paving stones below were still, after a cold night, coated with a translucent film of rime, which was just beginning to melt here and there. Nothing seemed quite real, except the smoking chimney pots.

The diesel engine spluttered. The exhaust at the rear of the barge spurted black fumes. Naud laid his money on the counter, raised the tips of his fingers to his cap, and returned across the quay. The lockkeeper, in uniform, was at his post, preparing to open the gates. Some way off, on the Quai de Valmy, there were footsteps, but, as yet, not another soul in sight. Children's voices could be heard below deck on the barge, where the women were making coffee.

Jules reappeared on deck, and leaned over the stern, frowning. His brother could guess what the trouble was. They had taken on a load of gravel at Beauval from Wharf No. 48 on the Ourcq Canal. As usual, they were several tons overweight, and the previous night, as they were drawing away from the dock at La Villette, headed for the Saint-Martin Canal, they had churned up a good deal of mud.

As a rule, in March, there was no shortage of water. This year, however, there had been no rain for two months, and the Canal Authority was hoarding its reserves.

The sluice-gates opened. Jules took the wheel. His brother went ashore to cast off the moorings. The propeller began to turn, and, as they had both feared, thick mud, churned up by the blades, was soon bubbling to the surface. Leaning with all his weight on the boat-hook, Robert tried to head the barge towards the lock. It was as though the propeller were spinning in a vacuum. The lockkeeper, used to this sort of thing, waited patiently, clapping his hands together to keep warm.

The engine shuddered with a grinding sound. Robert looked at his brother, who switched off.

Neither of them could make out what had gone wrong. The propeller, protected by the rudder, could not have scraped the bottom. Something must have got caught in it, a loose cable, maybe, such as are frequently left lying about in canals. If that was the trouble, they were going to have a job disentangling it.

Robert went behind the boat, leaned over, and felt about in the muddy water with his hook, trying to reach the propeller. Jules, meanwhile, fetched a smaller boat-hook. His wife, Laurence, poked her head through the hatchway.

'What's up?'

'Dunno.'

Silently, the two men felt about with their boat-hooks, trying to reach the fouled propeller. After a few minutes of this, Dambois the lockkeeper, known to everyone as Charles, came down to the quay to watch. He asked no questions, but just stood by, silently puffing at his pipe, the stem of which was held together with string.

From time to time, people hurried past, office workers on their way to the Place de la République, nurses in uniform making for the Hospital of Saint-Louis.

'Got it?'

'I think so.'

'What is it? Rope?'

'I couldn't say.'

Jules Naud had certainly hooked something. He managed, after a time, to free the propeller. Bubbles rose to the surface.

Gently, hand over hand, he drew up the boat-hook and, with it, a strange-looking parcel, done up with string, and a few remnants of sodden newspaper.

It was a human arm, complete from shoulder to finger-tips, which, through long immersion, was drained white, and limp as a dead fish.

*

At Police Headquarters, 3rd Division, situated at the far end of the Quai de Jemmapes, Sergeant Depoil was just going off night duty, when he saw the lanky figure of the elder Naud standing in the doorway.

'I'm from the barge *The Two Brothers,* up near the lock at the Récollets. We were just pulling out when the propeller jammed. We've fished up a man's arm.'

Depoil had served fifteen years in the 10th *Arrondissement.* His first reaction, like that of all the other police officers to be subsequently involved in the case, was incredulity.

'A *man's* arm?' he repeated.

'Yes, a man's. Dark hair on the back of the hand, and . . .'

There was nothing remarkable in the recovery, from the Saint-Martin Canal, of a corpse which had fouled someone's propeller. It had happened before, more than once. But as a rule it was a whole corpse, sometimes that of a man, some old tramp, most likely, who had taken a drop too much and stumbled into the water, or a young thug knifed by someone from a rival gang.

Dismembered bodies were not all that uncommon either. Two or three a year were about average, but invariably, in the Sergeant's long experience, they were women. One knew what to expect right from the start. Nine out of ten would be cheap prostitutes, the kind one sees loitering in lonely places at night.

One could safely conclude, in every case, that the killer was a psychopath.

There was not much one could teach the local police about their neighbours. At the Station, they kept up-to-date records of the activities of every crook, every shady character in the district. Few crimes were committed – from shoplifting to armed robbery – that were not followed in a matter of days by the arrest of the perpetrator. Psychopathic killers, however, were rarely caught.

'Have you brought it with you?' asked Depoil.

'The arm?'

'Where is it?'

'At the quay. Can we go now? There's this load we've got to deliver, Quai de l'Arsenal. They'll be waiting for it.'

The Sergeant lit a cigarette, and went to the telephone to notify the Salvage Branch. Next, he rang his Divisional Superintendent, Mangrin, at his home.

'Sorry to get you out of bed, sir. A couple of bargees have just fished a human arm out of the canal. No! A man's. . . . That's how it struck me too. . . . What's that, sir? . . . . Yes, he's still here. . . . I'll ask him.'

Holding the receiver, he turned to Naud:

'Would you say it had been in the water long?'

Jules Naud scratched his head.

'It depends what you mean by long.'

'Is it in a very bad state?'

'Hard to tell. Two or three days, I'd say.'

The Sergeant repeated into the instrument:

'Two or three days.'

Doodling on his notepad, he listened while the Superintendent gave his instructions.

'Can we go?' repeated Naud, when he had hung up.

'Not yet. As the Superintendent quite rightly says, we don't know what else you may have picked up, and if you moved the barge, we might lose it.'

'All the same, I can't stop there for ever. There are four others already, lined up to go through the lock. And they're beginning to get impatient.'

The Sergeant had dialled another number, and was waiting for a reply.

'Hullo! Victor? I hope I haven't woken you. Oh! You're having breakfast, are you? Good. I've got a job for you.'

Victor Cadet lived in the Rue du Chemin-Vert, not far from the Police Station, and it was unusual for a month to go by without some call upon his services from that quarter. He had probably retrieved, from the Seine and the canals of Paris, a larger and more peculiar assortment of objects, corpses included, than any other man.

'I'll be with you as soon as I've got hold of my mate.'

It was seven o'clock in the morning. In the Boulevard Richard-Lenoir, Madame Maigret, already dressed, as fresh as paint and smelling faintly of soap, was busy in the kitchen getting breakfast. Her husband was still asleep. At the Quai des Orfèvres, Lucas and Janvier had been on duty since six o'clock. It was Lucas who got the news first.

'There's a queer thing!' he muttered, turning to Janvier, 'They've fished an arm out of the Saint-Martin Canal, and it's not a woman's.'

'A man's?'

'What else?'

'It could have been a child's.'

There had, in fact, been one such case, the only one, three years before.

'What about letting the boss know?'

Lucas looked at the time, hesitated, then shook his head.

'No hurry, he may as well have his coffee in peace.'

By ten minutes to eight, a sizeable crowd had gathered on the quay where *The Two Brothers* was moored. Anyone trying to get too close to the thing lying on the ground covered with sacking was ordered back by the policeman on guard. Victor Cadet's boat, which had been lying downstream, passed through the lock and came alongside the quay.

Cadet was a giant of a man. Looking at him, one wondered whether his diving suit had had to be made to measure. His mate, in contrast, was undersized and old. He chewed tobacco even on the job, and stained the water with long brown streamers of spittle.

It was he who secured the ladder, primed the pump and, when everything was ready, screwed on Victor's huge, spherical diving helmet.

On deck, near the stern of *The Two Brothers,* could be seen two women and five children, all with hair so fair as to be almost white. One of the women was pregnant, and the other had a baby in her arms.

The buildings of the Quai de Valmy were bathed in sunshine, golden, heart-warming sunshine, which made it hard to credit the sinister reputation of the place. True, there was not much new paint to be seen. The white and yellow façades were streaked and faded. Yet, on this day in March, they looked as fresh as a scene by Utrillo.

There were four barges lined up behind *The Two Brothers,* with washing strung out to dry, and restless children who would not be hushed. A smell of tar mingled with the less agreeable smell of the canal.

At a quarter past eight, Maigret finished hs second cup of coffee, wiped his mouth, and was just about to light up his morning pipe, when the telephone rang. It was Lucas.

'Did you say a *man's* arm?'

He, too, found it hard to believe.

'Have they found anything else?'

'We've got the diver, Victor, down there now. We'll have to

let the barges through fairly soon. There's a bottleneck building up at the lock already.'

'Who's on duty there?'

'Judel.'

Inspector Judel, a young policeman of the 10th *Arrondissement*, was conscientious if somewhat dull. He could safely be left in charge at this early stage.

'Will you be going yourself, sir?'

'It's not much out of my way.'

'Do you want one of us to meet you there?'

'Who have you got?'

'Janvier, Lemaire. . . . Hang on a minute, sir. Lapointe's just come in.'

Maigret hesitated. He was enjoying the sunshine. It was warm enough to have the windows open. Was this just a straightforward, routine case? If so, Judel was quite competent to handle it on his own. But at this stage, how could one be sure? If the arm had been a woman's, Maigret would have taken a bet that there was nothing to it.

But since it was a man's arm, anything was possible. And if it should turn out to be a tricky case, and he, the Chief Superintendent, should decide to take over, the day-to-day Headquarters routine would to some extent be affected by his choice of assistant, because, whoever it was, Maigret would want him to see the case through to the end.

'Send Lapointe.'

It was quite a while since he had worked in close collaboration with Lapointe. His youth, his eagerness, his artless confusion when he felt he had committed a *faux pas*, amused Maigret.

'Had I better let the Chief know?'

'Yes. I'm sure to be late for the staff meeting.'

It was March 23. The day before yesterday had been the first day of spring, and spring was in the air already – which was more than could be said in most years – so much so, in fact, that Maigret very nearly set off without his coat.

In the Boulevard Richard-Lenoir he hailed a taxi. There was no direct bus, and this was not the sort of day for shutting oneself up in the underground. As he had anticipated, he arrived at the Récollets Lock before Lapointe, to find Inspector Judel gazing down into the black waters of the canal.

'Have they found anything else?'

'Not yet, sir. Victor is still working under the barge. There may be something more there.'

Ten minutes later, Lapointe drove up in a small black police car, and it was not long before a string of glittering bubbles heralded Victor's return to the surface. His mate hurried forward to unscrew the metal diving helmet. The diver lit a cigarette, looked round, saw Maigret, and greeted him with a friendly wave of the hand.

'Found anything?'

'There's nothing more there.'

'Can we let the barge go?'

'It won't turn anything up except mud, that's for sure.'

Robert Naud, who had been listening with interest, walked across to his brother.

'Start the engine!'

Maigret turned to Judel.

'Have you got a statement from them?'

'Yes, they've both signed it. Anyway, they'll be at the Quai de l'Arsenal, unloading, for the best part of a week.'

The Quai de l'Arsenal was only a couple of miles downstream, between the Bastille and the Seine.

The overloaded barge was very low in the water, and it was a slow business getting it away. At last, however, it scraped along the bottom into the lock, and the gates closed behind it.

The crowd of spectators dispersed, leaving only a few idle bystanders who had nothing better to do, and would very likely hang around all day.

Victor was still wearing his diving suit.

'If there's anything else to find,' he explained, 'it'll be upstream. An arm's light enough to shift with the current, but the rest, legs, torso, head, would sink.'

There was not a ripple to be seen on the canal, and floating refuse lay, seemingly inert, on the surface.

'Of course, there's nothing like the current you get in a river. But each time the level is raised or lowered in the lock, there's movement, though you'd barely notice it, all along the reach.'

'In other words, the search ought to extend right up to the next lock?'

'He who pays the piper . . .' said Victor, inhaling and blowing smoke through his nostrils. 'It's up to you.'

'Will it be a long job?'

'That depends on where we find the rest of the body – assuming, of course, it's in the canal at all.'

'Why would anyone, getting rid of a body, dump part of it in the canal, and the rest somewhere else – say on some patch of waste ground?'

'Carry on.'

Cadet signalled to his mate to move the boat a little way upstream, and indicated that he was ready to be screwed into his diving helmet.

Maigret moved away, followed by Judel and Lapointe. They formed a solitary little group on the quay, observed by the spectators with the instinctive respect accorded to authority.

'You'll have to search all rubbish dumps and waste ground, of course.'

'That's what I thought,' said Judel. 'I was only waiting for you to give the word.'

'How many men can you spare?'

'Two right away. Three by this afternoon.'

'Find out if there have been any gang-fights or brawls locally in the past few days, and keep your ears open for anyone who may have heard anything – screams, say, or someone shouting for help.'

'Very good, sir.'

Maigret left the local man on guard over the human arm, which lay covered with sacking on the flagstones of the quay.

'Coming, Lapointe?'

He made for the bar on the corner, with its bright yellow paint, and pushed open the glass door, noting the name, *Chez Popaul*, inscribed on it. Several local workmen in overalls were having snacks at the counter.

The proprietor hurried forward.

'What can I get you?'

'Do you have a telephone?'

Before the words were out of his mouth, he saw it. It was on the wall next to the bar counter, not enclosed in a booth.

'Come on, Lapointe.'

He had no intention of making a phone call where it could be overheard.

'Won't you have something to drink?'

'We'll be back,' promised the Chief Superintendent, not wishing to give offence.

Along the quay there were blocks of flats and concrete office buildings, interspersed with one-storey shacks.

'There's bound to be a bistro with a proper telephone box somewhere round here.'

Walking along, they could see, across the canal, the faded flag and blue lamp of the Police Station and, behind it, the dark, massive Hospital of Saint-Louis.

They had gone about three hundred yards when they came to a dingy-looking bar. The Chief Superintendent pushed open the door. Two steps led down into a room with a tiled floor, dark red tiles of the kind commonly seen in Marseilles.

The room was empty except for a large ginger cat lying beside the stove. It got up, stretched lazily, and went out through an open door at the back.

'Anyone there?' called Maigret.

The staccato tick-tick of a cuckoo clock could be heard. The room smelt of spirits and white wine, especially spirits, and there was a faint whiff of coffee.

Someone was moving about in a back room. A woman's voice called out rather wearily, 'Coming!'

The ceiling was low and blackened with smoke, and the walls were grimy. Indeed the whole place was murky, but for faint patches of sunlight here and there. It was like a church lit only by stained-glass windows. A scribbled notice on the wall read: Snacks served at all hours, and another: Patrons are welcome to bring their own food.

There were, for the time being, no patrons to take advantage of these amenities. It was plain to Maigret and Lapointe that they were the first that day. There was a telephone box in a corner, but Maigret was waiting for the woman to appear.

When at last she did appear, she shuffled in, sticking pins in her dark, almost black hair. She was thin, sullen-faced, neither young nor old, perhaps in her early or middle forties. Her felt slippers made no sound on the tiles.

'What do you want?'

Maigret and Lapointe exchanged glances.

'Have you a good white wine?'

She shrugged.

'Two white wines. And a *jeton* for the phone.'

He went into the telephone box, shutting the door behind him, and rang the Public Prosecutor's office to make his report. The Deputy to whom he spoke was as surprised as everyone else to hear that the arm fished out of the canal was a man's.

'The diver is working upstream now. He says if there's anything more to find, that's where it will be. The next step, as far as I'm concerned, is to have Doctor Paul examine the arm as soon as possible.'

'I'll get in touch with him at once and ring you back, if that suits you.'

Maigret, having read out the number on the dial, went over to the bar. Two glasses of wine stood ready poured on the counter.

'Your very good health,' he said, raising his glass to the woman.

For all the interest she showed, he might not have spoken. She just stared vacantly, waiting for them to go, so that she might finish making herself presentable, or whatever it was she had been doing when they arrived.

She must have been attractive, once. She had, like everyone else, undoubtedly once been young. Now, everything about her, her eyes, her mouth, her whole body, was listless, faded. Was she a sick woman, anticipating a dreaded attack? Sometimes sick people who knew that, at a particular hour of the day, the pain would recur, wore that same look of apathy mixed with apprehension, like drug addicts in need of a shot.

'They're ringing me back,' murmured Maigret, sounding apologetic.

It was, of course, like any other bar or café, a public place, impersonal in a sense, yet both men had the feeling of being intruders who had blundered in where they had no right to be.

'Your wine is very good.'

It really was good. Most Paris bistros advertise a *petit vin du pays,* but this, as a rule, turns out to be a wholesale product, straight from Bercy. This wine was different. It had a distinctive regional flavour, though the Superintendent could not quite place it.

'Sancerre?' he ventured.

'No. It comes from a little village near Poitiers.'

That accounted for the slight flinty tang.

'Is that where you come from?'

She did not answer. She just stood there, motionless, silent, impassive. Maigret was impressed. The cat, which had come into the room with her, was rubbing its back against her bare legs.

'What about your husband?'

'He's gone there to get more.'

More wine, she meant. Making conversation with her was far from easy. The Superintendent had just signalled to her to refill the glasses when, much to his relief, the telephone rang.

'Yes, it's me. Did you get hold of Paul? When will he be free? An hour from now? Right, I'll be there.'

The Deputy talked. Maigret listened in silence, with an expression of deepening disapproval, as it sank in that the Examining Magistrate in charge of the case was to be Judge Coméliau. He was the most pettifogging, niggling man on the Bench, and Maigret's very own private and personal enemy.

'He says, will you please see to it that he's kept in the picture.'

'I know.'

Maigret knew all too well what he was in for: five or six phone calls a day from Coméliau, not to mention a briefing session every morning in the magistrate's office.

'Ah! well,' he sighed. 'We'll do our best.'

'Don't blame me, Superintendent. There just wasn't anyone else available.'

The sunlight had penetrated a little farther into the room, and just reached Maigret's glass.

'Let's go,' he said, feeling in his pocket for change. 'How much?'

And, outside in the street:

'Have you got the car?'

'Yes, I left it over by the lock.'

The wine had put colour in Lapointe's cheeks, and his eyes were bright. From where they were, they could see a little group of onlookers watching the diver's progress from the edge of the quay. As Maigret and the Inspector came up to them, Victor's mate pointed to a bundle in the bottom of the boat. It was larger than the first.

'A leg and foot,' he called out, and spat into the water. This time, the wrapping was in quite good condition. Maigret saw no necessity to take a closer look.

'Shall we need a hearse?' he asked Lapointe.

'There's plenty of room in the boot, of course.'

The prospect did not commend itself to either of them, but they did have an appointment at the Forensic Laboratory, a large, bright, modern building overlooking the Seine, not far from the junction of the river and the canal. It would not do to keep the pathologist waiting.

'What should I do?' Lapointe asked.

Maigret could not bring himself to say. Repressing his revulsion, Lapointe carried the two bundles, one after the other, to the car, and laid them in the boot.

'Do they smell?' asked the Superintendent, when Lapointe rejoined him at the water's edge.

Lapointe, who was holding his hands out in front of him, nodded, wrinkling his nose.

\*

Doctor Paul, in white overall and rubber gloves, smoked incessantly. He subscribed to the theory that there was no disinfectant like tobacco, and ofter, during a single autopsy, would smoke as many as two packets of *Bleues Gauloises*.

He worked briskly and cheerfully, bent over the marble slab, chatting between puffs.

'Naturally, I can't say anything definite at this stage. For one thing, there's not a great deal to learn from a leg and an arm on their own. The sooner you find the rest of the body, the better. Meanwhile, I'll do as many tests as I can.'

'What age would you say?'

'As far as I can tell at a glance, a man somewhere between fifty and sixty – nearer fifty than sixty. Take a look at this hand.'

'What about it?'

'It's a broad, strong hand, and it's done rough work in its time.'

'A labourer?'

'No. A farm worker, more likely. Still, it's a fair bet that that hand hasn't gripped a heavy implement for years. This was not a fastidious man. You can tell by the nails, especially the toenails.'

'A tramp?'

'I don't think so, but, as I say, I can't be sure till I have more to go on.'

'Has he been dead long?'

'Again, I can only hazard a guess – don't take my word for it. I may have changed my mind by tonight or tomorrow. But, for the time being, I'm fairly confident that he died not more than three days ago, at the very outside.'

'Not last night?'

'No, the night before that, possibly.'

Maigret and Lapointe were smoking too, and, as far as they could, they kept their eyes averted from the marble slab. As for Doctor Paul, he seemed to be enjoying his work, handling his instruments like a juggler.

He was changing into his outdoor clothes when Maigret was called to the telephone. It was Judel from the Quai de Valmy.

'They've found the torso!' he announced, sounding quite excited about it.

'No head?'

'Not yet. According to Victor, it won't be so easy. Because of its weight, it will probably be sunk in the mud. He's found an empty wallet and a woman's handbag, though.'

'Near the torso?'

'No, quite a long way off. There probably isn't any connection. As he says, every time he goes down, he finds enough junk to open a stall in the Flea Market. Just before he found the torso, he came up with a child's cot and a couple of slop pails.'

186

Paul, holding his hands out in front of him, was waiting before taking off his gloves.

'Any news?' he asked.

Maigret nodded. Then to Judel:

'Can you get it to me at the Forensic Lab?'

'I'm sure we can manage it.'

'Right. I'll be here, but be quick about it, because Doctor Paul . . .'

They waited outside the building, enjoying the fresh air, and watching the flow of traffic on the Pont d'Austerlitz. Across the Seine, several barges and a small sailing boat were unloading at the quayside opposite a warehouse. Paris, in the morning sun, was throbbing with youth and gaiety. It was the first real spring day. Life was full of promise.

'No tattoo-marks or scars, I suppose?'

'None on the arm or leg, at any rate. From the condition of the skin, I'd say he was not an outdoor type.'

'Hairy, though.'

'Yes. I have a fair idea of what he must have looked like. Dark, broad-shouldered, but below medium height, with well-developed muscles, and coarse dark hair on the arms, hands, legs and chest. A real son of the soil, sturdy, independent, stubborn. The countryside of France is full of men like him. It'll be interesting to see his head.'

'If we ever find it!'

A quarter of an hour later, two uniformed policemen arrived with the torso. Doctor Paul, all but rubbing his hands, got to work at the marble slab like a craftsman at his bench.

'As I thought,' he grumbled. 'This isn't a skilled job. What I mean to say is: this man wasn't dismembered by a butcher or a Jack-the-Ripper, still less by a surgeon! The joints were severed by an ordinary hack-saw. The rest of the job, I'd say, was done with a large carving knife. All restaurants have them, and most private kitchens. It must have been a longish job. It couldn't have been done all at once.'

He paused.

'Take a look at this chest. What do you see, and I don't mean hair?'

Maigret and Lapointe glanced at the torso, and looked away quickly.

'No visible scars?'

'I don't see any. I'm certain of one thing. Drowning wasn't the cause of death.'

It was almost comical. How on earth would a man found in pieces in a canal contrive to drown?

'I'll examine the organs next, and especially – in so far as it's practicable – the contents of the stomach. Will you be staying?'

Maigret shook his head. He had seen quite enough. He could hardly wait to get to a bar and have a drink, not wine this time, but a drop of the hard stuff, to get rid of the foul taste in his mouth, which seemed to him like the taste of death.

'Just a minute, Maigret. What was I saying? D'you see this white line here, and these small white spots on the abdomen?'

The Superintendent nodded, but did not look.

'That's an old operation scar. Quite a few years old. Appendectomy.'

'And the spots?'

'Now there's an odd thing. I couldn't swear to it, but I'm almost sure they're grapeshot or buckshot wounds, which confirms my feeling that the man must have lived in the country at some time or other. A smallholder or gamekeeper, maybe. Who knows? A long time ago, twenty years or more, someone must have emptied a shotgun into him. There are seven, no, eight of these scars in a curve, like a rainbow. Only once before in the whole of my life have I ever seen anything like them, and they weren't so evenly spaced. I'll have to photograph them for the record.'

'Will you give me a ring?'

'Where will you be? At the Quai des Orfèvres?'

'Yes. In my office, and I'll probably lunch in the Place Dauphine.'

'As soon as I have anything to report, I'll let you know.'

Maigret led the way out into the sunshine, and mopped his forehead. Lapointe felt impelled to spit several times into the gutter. He, too, it seemed, had a bitter taste in his mouth.

'As soon as we get back to Headquarters, I'll have the boot fumigated,' he said.

On their way to the car park, they went into a bistro for a glass of marc brandy. It was so potent that Lapointe retched, held his hand to his mouth, and, for a moment, with eyes watering, wondered anxiously whether he was going to be sick.

When he felt better, he muttered:

'Sorry about that.'

As they went out, the proprietor of the bar remarked to one of the customers:

'That's another of them come from identifying a corpse. It always takes them that way.'

Situated as he was, directly opposite the mortuary, he was used to it.


## 2. Red Sealing-wax

When Maigret came into the great central lobby of the Quai des Orfèvres he was, for a second or two, dazzled, because even this lobby, surely the greyest and dingiest place on earth, was sunlit today, or at least gilded with luminous dust.

On the benches between the office doors, there were people waiting, some handcuffed. As Maigret went past, to report to the Chief of Police on the Quai de Valmy case, a man stood up and touched his hat in greeting.

With the familiarity born of daily meetings over many years, Maigret called out:

'Well, Vicomte, what have you to say for yourself? You can't complain this time that it's just another case of someone chopping up a whore.'

The man known to everyone as the Vicomte did not seem to object to his nickname, although he must have been aware of the innuendo. He was, in a discreet way, a homosexual. For the past fifteen years he had 'covered' the Quai des Orfèvres for a Paris newspaper, a press agency, and some twenty provincial dailies.

In appearance, he was the last of the Boulevard dandies,

dressed with Edwardian elegance, wearing a monocle on a black ribbon round his neck. Indeed, it could well have been the monocle (which he hardly ever used) that had earned him his nickname.

'Have they found the head?'

'Not to my knowledge.'

'I've just spoken to Judel on the phone. He says, no. If you get any fresh news, Superintendent, spare a thought for me.'

He returned to his bench, and Maigret went into the Chief's office.

The window was open, and from there, too, one could see river craft plying up and down the Seine. The two men engaged in pleasant conversation for ten minutes or so.

The first thing Maigret saw when he went through the door of his own office was a note on his blotting pad. He knew at once what it was – a message from Judge Coméliau, of course, asking him to ring him as soon as he got in.

'Chief Superintendent Maigret here, Judge.'

'Ah! Good morning, Maigret. Are you just back from the canal?'

'From the Forensic Lab.'

'Is Doctor Paul still there?'

'He's working on the internal organs now.'

'I take it the corpse hasn't been identified yet?'

'With no head, there's not much hope of that. Not unless we have a stroke of luck . . .'

'That's the very thing I wanted to discuss with you. In a straightforward case, where the identity of the victim is known, one can tell more or less where one is going. Do you follow me? Now, in this case, we haven't the faintest idea who may be involved. Within the next hour, or the next day or two, we may be in for a nasty shock. We must be prepared for the worst, the very worst, and therefore would do well to proceed with extreme caution.'

Coméliau enunciated every syllable, and liked the sound of his own voice. Everything he said or did was of 'extreme' importance.

Most examining magistrates were content to leave matters in the hands of the police until they had completed their inquiries.

Not so Coméliau. He always insisted on directing operations from the outset, owing, no doubt, to his exaggerated dread of 'complications'. His brother-in-law was an ambitious politician, one of a handful of Deputies with a finger in every departmental pie. Coméliau was fond of saying:

'You must understand that, owing to his position, I am more vulnerable than my brother-magistrates.'

Maigret got rid of him eventually by promising to inform him immediately of any new development, however trivial, even if it meant disturbing him at his home in the evening. He looked through his mail, and then went to the Inspectors' Duty Room, to give them their orders for the day.

'Today is Tuesday, isn't it?'

'That's right, sir.'

If Doctor Paul had estimated correctly that the body had been in the Saint-Martin Canal about forty-eight hours, then the crime must have been committed on the Sunday, almost certainly during the evening or night, since it was hardly likely that anyone intent on getting rid of a number of bulky and sinister packages would be so foolhardy as to attempt it in broad daylight with the Police Station not five hundred yards away.

'Is that you, Madame Maigret?' he said playfully to his wife, when he had got her on the line. 'I shan't be home for lunch. What were we having?'

Haricot mutton. He had no regrets. Too stodgy for a day like this.

He rang Judel.

'What news?'

'Victor is having a snack in the boat. The whole body has been recovered, except the head. He wants to know if he's to go on looking.'

'Of course.'

'I've got my men on the job, but they haven't come up with anything much so far. There was a spot of trouble in a bar in the Rue des Récollets on Sunday night. Not *Chez Popaul*. Farther up towards the Faubourg Saint-Martin. A concierge has reported the disappearance of her husband, but he's been missing for over a month, and the description doesn't fit.'

191

'I'll probably be along some time this afternoon.'

On his way to lunch at the Brasserie Dauphine, he looked in at the Inspectors' Duty Room.

'Ready, Lapointe?'

He really did not need his young assistant just to share the table at which he always sat in the little restaurant in the Place Dauphine. This thought struck him as they walked along in companionable silence. He smiled to himself, remembering a question that had once been put to him on this subject. His friend, Doctor Pardon of the Rue Popincourt, with whom he and his wife dined regularly once a month, had turned to him one evening, and asked very earnestly:

'Can you explain to me, Maigret, why it is that plainclothes policemen, like plumbers, always go about in pairs?'

He had never thought about it, though, on reflection, he had to admit that it was a fact. He himself, when he was out on a case, almost always took an inspector with him.

He had scratched his head.

'I imagine it goes back to the days when Paris was a lawless city, and it wasn't safe to go into some districts alone, especially at night.'

It was not safe even today to make an arrest single-handed, or venture into the underworld on one's own. But the more Maigret had thought about it, the less this explanation had satisfied him.

'And another thing. Take a suspect who has reluctantly made some damaging admission, either in his own home or at Headquarters. If there had been only one police officer present at the time, it would be that much easier to deny everything later. And a jury will always attach more weight to evidence when there is a witness to corroborate it.'

All very true, but still not the whole truth.

'Then there's the practical angle. Say someone is being shadowed. Well, you can't watch him like a hawk and make a telephone call at the same time. And then again, more often than not, your quarry will go into a building with several exits.'

Pardon had smiled then as Maigret was smiling now.

'I'm always suspicious,' he said, 'of tortuous answers to simple questions.'

To which Maigret had retorted:

'Well, then, speaking for myself, I usually take an inspector along for company. I'm afraid I'd be bored stiff on my own.'

He did not repeat this conversation to Lapointe. One should never poke fun at the illusions of youth, and the sacred fire still burned in Lapointe. It was pleasant and peaceful in the little restaurant, with other police officers dropping in for a drink at the bar, and four or five lunching in the dining-room.

'Will the head be found in the canal, do you think?'

Maigret, rather to his own surprise, shook his head. To be honest, he had not given the matter much thought. His response had been instinctive. He could not have said why, he just had a feeling that the diver, Victor, would find nothing more in the mud of the Saint-Martin Canal.

'Where can it be?'

He had no idea. In a suitcase at a left-luggage office, maybe. At the Gare de l'Est, a few hundred yards from the canal, or the Gare du Nord, not much farther away. Or it might have been sent by road to some address or other in the provinces, in one of the fleet of heavy, long-distance lorries that the Superintendent had seen lined up in a side street off the Quai de Valmy. These particular lorries were red and green, and Maigret had often seen them about the streets, heading for the motorways. Until today, he had had no idea where their depot was. It was right there in the Rue Terrage, next to the canal. At one time during the morning, he had noticed twenty or more of them strung out along the road, all inscribed: 'Zenith Transport. Roulers and Langlois.'

When Maigret directed his attention to details of this kind, it usually meant that he was thinking of nothing in particular. The case was interesting enough, but not absorbing. What interested him more, at the moment, was the canal itself and its sur-roundings. At one time, right at the beginning of his career, he had been familiar with every street in this district, and could have identified many a night prowler who slunk past in the shadow of the buildings.

They were still sitting over their coffee when Maigret was called to the telephone. It was Judel.

'I was in two minds about ringing you, sir. I wouldn't exactly call it a lead, but one of my men, Blancpain, thinks he may be on to something. I posted him near where the diver is working, and, about an hour ago, his attention was attracted by an errand boy on a carrier bicycle. He had a feeling he'd seen him before, earlier on, more than once, at regular intervals of about half-an-hour, in fact. People have been coming to the quay all day to watch the diver. Most of them stay for a bit and then wander away, but this character, according to Blancpain, kept himself to himself, and seemed to be drawn there by something more than curiosity. Errand boys, as a rule, work to a pretty tight schedule on their rounds, and don't have all that much time to waste.'

'Has Blancpain spoken to him?'

'He was intending to, but as soon as he made a move towards him – very casually, so as not to scare him off – the lad hopped on to his bicycle, and pedalled away at top speed towards the Rue des Récollets. Blancpain did chase after him, but couldn't make much headway in a crowded street on foot – he had no transport – and finally lost him in the traffic of the Faubourg Saint-Martin.'

There was a brief silence. It was all very vague, of course. It might mean nothing. On the other hand, it could be a break-through.

'Was Blancpain able to describe him?'

'Yes. A lad of between eighteen to twenty – probably a country boy – very healthy complexion – fair – longish hair – wearing a leather jerkin and a turtle-neck sweater. Blancpain couldn't read the name of the firm on his carrier, but he was able to see that one word ended in "ail". We're checking on all the local shopkeepers who employ an errand boy.'

'What news from Victor?'

'He says that as long as he's getting paid for it, he doesn't care whether he's under water or on dry land, but he's sure it's a waste of time.'

'What about the rubbish dumps and waste ground?'

'Nothing so far.'

'I should be getting the pathologist's report shortly. I'm hoping that will tell us something about the dead man.'

At half-past two, when Maigret was back in his office, Paul

rang to report his findings, which would later be confirmed in writing.

'Do you want it at dictation speed, Maigret?'

Maigret drew a writing pad towards him.

'I've had to rely on guess-work to some extent, but I think you'll find I'm not far out. First of all, here's a description of your man as far as one can be certain in the absence of the head. Not very tall, about five foot eight. Short, thick neck and, I feel sure, round face and heavy jowl. Dark hair, possibly greying a little at the temples. Weight: eleven and a half stone. I would describe him as thick-set, stocky rather than tubby, muscular rather than fat, though he did put on a bit of weight towards the end. The condition of the liver suggests a steady drinker, but I wouldn't say he was an alcoholic. More probably the sort who likes a glass of something, white wine mostly, every hour or even every half-hour. I did, in fact, find traces of white wine in the stomach.'

'Any food?'

'Yes. It was lucky for us that his last meal – lunch or dinner, whichever it was – was indigestible. It consisted mainly of roast pork and haricot beans.'

'How long before he died?'

'Two to two-and-a-half hours, I'd say. I've sent scrapings from under his toenails and fingernails to the laboratory. Moers will be getting in touch with you direct about them.'

'What about the scars?'

'I can confirm what I told you this morning. The appendectomy was performed five or six years ago, by a good surgeon, judging from the quality of the work. The buckshot scars are at least twenty years old, and if you ask me, I'd say nearer forty.'

'Age?'

'Fifty to fifty-five.'

'Then he would have got the buckshot wound as a child?'

'In my opinion, yes. General health satisfactory, apart from the inflammation of the liver that I've already mentioned. Heart and lungs in good condition. There's a very old tuberculosis scar on the left lung, but it doesn't mean much. It's quite common for babies and young children to contract a mild form of T B which no one even notices. Well, that's about it, Maigret. If you want any more information, bring me the head, and I'll do my best to oblige.'

'We haven't found it, yet.'

'In that case, you never will.'

There, Maigret agreed with him. There are some beliefs in the Quai des Orfèvres which have been held for so long that they have come to be taken for granted. The belief, for instance, that, as a general rule, only the corpses of cheap prostitutes are found dismembered. And the belief that, although the torso is usually found, the head is not.

No one questions these beliefs, they are just accepted by everyone.

Maigret stumped off to the Inspectors' Duty Room.

'If I'm wanted, I shall be upstairs in the lab.'

He climbed slowly to the top floor of the Palais de Justice, where he found Moers poring over his test-tubes.

'Is that my corpse you're working on?' he asked.

'I'm analysing the specimens Paul sent up to us.'

'Found anything?'

The laboratory was immense, and full of pathologists absorbed in their work. Standing in one corner was the dummy used in the reconstruction of crimes, for instance, in a case of a stabbing, to determine the relative positions of victim and assailant.

'It's my impression,' murmured Moers, who always spoke in a whisper, as though he were in church, 'that your man seldom went out of doors.'

'What makes you think that?'

'I've been examining the particles of matter taken from under his toenails. That's how I can tell you that the last pair of socks he wore were navy-blue wool. I also found traces of the kind of felt used for making carpet slippers, from which I conclude that the man practically lived in his slippers.'

'If you're right, Paul should be able to confirm it, because if one lives in slippers over a long period, one ends up with deformed feet, or so my wife always tells me, and. . . .' He broke off in mid-sentence to telephone Doctor Paul at the Forensic Laboratory. Finding that he had already left, he rang his home.

'Maigret here. Just one question, Doctor. It's Moers's idea really. Did you get the impression that our man wore carpet slippers most of the time?'

'Good for Moers! I almost said as much to you earlier on, but it was just an impression, and I didn't want to set you on a false trail. It came into my mind, while I was examining the feet, that the man might have worked in a café or a bar. Barmen, like waiters and policemen – especially policemen on point duty – tend to get fallen arches, not because they do much walking, but because they stand for long hours.'

'You mentioned that the fingernails were not well kept.'

'That's true. It's not very likely that a hotel waiter would have black fingernails.'

'Nor a waiter in a large brasserie or a respectable coffee-house.'

'Has Moers found anything else?'

'Not so far. Many thanks, doctor.'

Maigret stayed in the laboratory for almost an hour, roaming about, and leaning over the benches to watch the technicians at their work.

'Would it interest you to know that there were also traces of soil mixed with potassium nitrate under the nails?'

Moers knew as well as Maigret where such a mixture was most often to be found: in a cellar, especially a damp cellar.

'Was there much of it?'

'That's what struck me. This was ingrained, occupational dirt.'

'In other words, a man who regularly worked in a cellar?'

'That would be my guess.'

'What about the hands?'

'There are traces of the same mixture under the fingernails, and other things too, including minute splinters of red sealing-wax.'

'The kind used for sealing wine-bottles?'

'Yes.'

Maigret was almost disappointed. It was beginning to look too easy.

'In other words, a bistro!' he muttered grumpily.

Just then, in fact, it seemed to him more than likely that the case would be over that same evening. He saw, in his mind's eye, the thin, dark woman who had served him with a drink that morning. She had made a deep impression on him, and she had been in his mind more than once that day, not necessarily because he had associated her with the dismembered man, but because he had recognized her as someone out of the ordinary.

There was no lack of colourful characters in a district such as the Quai de Valmy. But he had seldom come across anyone as negative as this woman. It was hard to put it into words. As a rule, when two people look at one another, an interchange of some sort, however slight, takes place. A relationship is established, if only a hostile one.

Not so with this woman. Her face, when she had seen them standing at the bar, had betrayed no trace of surprise or fear, no trace of anything, indeed, but a profound and seemingly habitual lassitude.

Or was it indifference?

Two or three times, between sips of wine, Maigret had looked her straight in the eye, but there had been no response, not so much as the flicker of an eyelash.

Yet, it was not the insensibility of a moron. Nor was she drunk or drugged, at least not at that moment. He had made up his mind there and then that he would pay her another visit, if only to discover what kind of people her customers were.

'Are you on to something, sir?'

'Maybe.'

'You don't sound exactly overjoyed.'

Maigret did not care to pursue the subject. At four o'clock, he went in search of Lapointe, who was catching up on his paper-work.

'Would you mind driving me over there?'

'To the canal?'

'Yes.'

'I hope they'll have had time to fumigate the car.'

There were brightly coloured hats in the streets already, with red this year as the dominant colour, brilliant poppy-red. The awnings, plain orange or candy-striped, were down over the street cafés. There were people at almost every table, and there seemed to be a new air of cheerful briskness about the passers-by.

At the Quai de Valmy, a small crowd was gathered near where Victor was still searching the canal bed. Among them was Judel. Maigret and Lapointe got out of the car and went over to him.

'Nothing more?'

'No.'

'No clothing?'

'We've been working on the string. If you think it would help, I'll send it up to the lab. As far as we can tell, it's just the ordinary coarse string most shopkeepers use. Quite a lot was needed for all those parcels. I've got someone making inquiries in the local hardware shops, so far without results. Then there's what's left of the newspapers that were used for wrapping. I've had them dried out, and they're mostly last week's.'

'What's the most recent date?'

'Saturday morning.'

'Do you know that bistro in the street just beyond the Rue Terrage, the one next door to the surgical instruments place?'

'*Chez Calas?*'

'I didn't notice the name; it's a murky little place below street level, with a big charcoal stove in the middle, and a zinc bar counter painted black, stretching almost from end to end.'

'That's it. Omer Calas's place.'

When it came to local landmarks, the district police had the edge on the Quai des Orfèvres.

'What sort of place is it?' asked Maigret, watching the air bubbles which marked Victor's comings and goings under water.

'Quiet. They've never given us any trouble, as far as I know.'

'Would you say Omer Calas was a townsman or a country-man?'

'A countryman, I should think. I could look up his regis-tration. It's always happening. A man comes to Paris as a personal servant or chauffeur, and ends up married to the cook and running a bistro in double harness.'

'Have they been there long?'

'Longer than I have. As far back as I can remember, it's always been much the same. It's almost opposite the Police Station, and I occasionally drop in for a drink. They do a good white wine.'

'Who looks after the bar? The proprietor?'

'Most of the time – except for an hour or two every afternoon, when he's at a brasserie in the Rue La Fayette playing billiards. He's mad keen on billiards.'

'When he's away, does the woman look after the bar?'

'Yes, they have no staff. I seem to remember they did have a little waitress at one time, but I've no idea what became of her.'

'What sort of people go there?'

'It's hard to say,' said Judel, scratching the back of his head.

'All the bistros hereabouts cater for more or less the same class of customer, and yet no two are alike. Take *Chez Popaul*, opposite the lock. It's busy from morning to night. There it's neat spirits and rowdy talk, and there's always a blue haze of tobacco smoke about the place. Any time after eight at night you're sure to find three or four women in there, waiting for their regular fellows.'

'And Omer's place?'

'Well, for one thing it's a bit off the beaten track, and for another, it's dark and rather gloomy. You must have noticed the atmosphere yourself. They get dockers from round about dropping in for a drink in the morning, and a few take their sandwiches along at lunch-time, and order a glass of white wine. There's not much doing in the afternoon, and I daresay that's why Omer goes off for his game of billiards after lunch. As I said, there are no regulars at that time, just the occasional passer-by. Trade picks up again at the end of the day.

'I've been in myself once or twice of an evening. It's always the same. A hand of cards at one of the tables, and a couple of people, no more, drinking at the bar. It's one of those joints where, if one doesn't happen to be a regular, one is made to feel out of place.'

'Is the woman Omer's wife?'

'I've never thought to ask. I can easily find out, though. We can go over to the station now, if you like, and look them up in the records.'

'I'll leave that to you. You can let me know later. Omer Calas is away from home, it seems.'

'Oh? Is that what she told you?'

'Yes.'

By now, the Naud brothers' barge had docked at the Quai de l'Arsenal, and the cargo of gravel was being unloaded by crane.

'I should be grateful if you would compile a list of all the bistros in the district, drawing my attention to any whose proprietor or barman has been absent since Sunday.'

'Do you think? . . .'

'It's Moers's idea. He may be right. I'm going along there.'

'To Calas's?'

'Yes. Coming, Lapointe?'

'Shall we be needing Victor tomorrow?'

'We can't chuck the tax-payer's money out of the window. I have a feeling that, if there had been anything more to find, he'd have found it today.'

'That's what he thinks, too.'

'Tell him he can give up as soon as he feels like it, and not to forget to let me have his report by tomorrow.'

Maigret paused on his way, to take another look at the lorries in the Rue Terrage, and read the inscription, 'Roulers and Langlois', over the great archway of the depot.

'I wonder how many there are,' he murmured, thinking aloud.

'What?' Lapointe asked.

'Lorries.'

'I've never driven into the country without finding myself crawling along behind one. It's bloody near impossible to pass them.'

The chimney pots, which had been rose-pink that morning, were now a deepening red in the setting sun, and there were pale green streaks here and there in the sky, green streaks almost the same colour as the green sea at dusk.

'Do you really believe, sir, that a woman could have done it?'

He thought again of the thin, dark woman who had poured their drinks that morning.

'It's possible . . . I don't know.'

Perhaps Lapointe felt, as he did, that it was all too easy.

Confront the men of the Quai des Orfèvres with a thoroughly tangled and apparently insoluble problem, and you will have every one of them, Maigret most of all, fretting and grumbling over it. But give them something that, at first sight, seems difficult, and later turns out to be straightforward and commonplace, and those same men, Maigret included, will not be able to contain their disappointment.

They were at the door of the bistro. On account of its low ceiling, it was darker than most, and there was already a light switched on over the counter.

The same woman, carelessly dressed as she had been in the morning, was serving two men, office workers by the look of them. She must have recognized Maigret and his colleague, but she showed no sign of it.

'What will you have?' was all she said, without so much as a smile.

'White wine.'

There were three or four bottles with drawn corks in a bucket behind the counter. Presumably it was necessary to go down to the cellar from time to time to get more. The floor behind the bar was not tiled, and there was a trap door, about three foot square, leading, no doubt, to the cellar below. Maigret and Lapointe had not taken their drinks to a table. From the conversation of the two men standing beside them at the bar, they gathered that they were not, in fact, office workers, but male nurses on night-shift at the Hospital of Saint-Louis on the other side of the canal. From something one of them said to the woman, it was evident that they were regulars.

'When do you expect Omer back?'

'You know he never tells me anything.'

She replied unselfconsciously, and with the same indifference as she had shown when Maigret had spoken to her earlier in the day. The ginger cat was still stretched out beside the stove, with every appearance of having been there all day.

'I hear they're still searching for the head!' said the man who had asked about her husband. As he spoke, he glanced at Maigret and his companion. Had he seen them on the quay earlier in the day? Or was it just that he could tell by the look of them that they were policemen?

'It hasn't been found, has it?' he went on, addressing himself direct to Maigret.

'Not yet.'

'Do you think it will be found?'

The other man subjected Maigret to a long stare, and then said:

'You're Chief Superintendent Maigret, aren't you?'

'Yes.'

'I thought so. I've often seen your picture in the papers.'

The woman still did not bat an eyelid. For all one could tell, she had not even heard.

'It's weird, carving up a man like that! Coming, Julien? How much, Madame Calas?'

With a slight nod to Maigret and Lapointe, they went out.

'Do you get many of the hospital staff in here?'

'A few.'

She did not waste words.

'Has your husband been away since Sunday?'

She looked at him blankly and asked, as though it were a matter of indifference to her:

'Why Sunday?'

'I don't know. I thought I heard . . .'

'He left on Friday afternoon.'

'Were there many people in the bar then?'

She seemed to be trying to remember. At times, she looked so withdrawn – or bored, was it? – that she might have been a sleep-walker.

'There are never many people in the afternoon.'

'Was there anyone at all? Try and think.'

'There may have been. I don't remember. I didn't notice.'

'Did he have any luggage?'

'Of course.'

'Much?'

'A suitcase.'

'What was he wearing?'

'A grey suit. I think. Yes.'

'Do you know where he is now?'

'No.'

'Didn't he say where he was going?'

'I know he must have taken the train to Poitiers. From there, he'll have gone on by bus to Saint-Aubin or some other village in the district.'

'Does he stay at the local inn?'

'As a rule.'

'Doesn't he ever stay with friends or relations? Or on one of the estates where he gets his wine?'

'I've never asked him.'

'You mean to say, that if you needed to get in touch with him urgently, to pass on some important message, for instance, or because you were ill, you wouldn't know where to find him?'

This too appeared to be a matter of indifference to her.

'Sooner or later he'd be bound to come back,' she said in her flat, monotonous voice. 'The same again?'

Both glasses were empty. She refilled them.


## 3. The Errand Boy

It was, all in all, one of Maigret's most frustrating interrogations. Not that one could call it an interrogation in the accepted sense, with life going on as usual around them. The Chief Superintendent and Lapointe stood at the bar for a long time, sipping their drinks like ordinary customers. And that was what they really were. True, one of the male nurses had recognized Maigret earlier on, and had addressed him by name, but the Superintendent, when speaking to Madame Calas, made no reference to his official standing. He would ask a question. She would reply, briefly. Then there would be a long silence, during which she completely ignored him.

At one point, she went out of the room through a door at the back, which she did not bother to shut behind her. The door presumably led into the kitchen. She was gone some time. They could hear her putting something on the stove. While she was away, a little old man came in and, obviously knowing his way about, made straight for a corner table, and took a box of dominoes from the shelf underneath. He tipped the dominoes on to the table and jumbled them up, as though intending to play on his own. The clink of the pieces brought the woman back from the kitchen. Without a word, she went to the bar and poured a pink apéritif, which she slapped down on the table in front of him.

The man waited. A few minutes later, another little old man came in and sat down opposite him. The two were so much alike that they could have been brothers.

'Am I late?'

'No. I was early.'

Madame Calas poured an apéritif of a different sort, and carried it over to the table. On the way, she pressed a switch, and a light came on at the far end of the room. All without a word spoken, as in a mime.

'Doesn't she give you the creeps?' Lapointe whispered to Maigret. That was not the effect she had on the Superintendent. He was intensely interested in her, more so than in anyone he had met for a very long time.

Had he not in his youth dreamed of an ideal vocation for himself, a vocation which did not exist in real life? He had never told anyone, had never even given it a name, but he knew now what it was he had wanted to be: a guide to the lost.

In fact, curiously enough, in the course of his work as a policeman, he had often been able to help people back on to the right road, from which they had misguidedly strayed. More curiously still, recent years had seen the birth of a new vocation, similar in many respects to the vocation of his dreams: that of the psychoanalyst, whose function it is to bring a man face to face with his true self.

To be sure, he had discovered one of her secrets, though secret was perhaps hardly the word for something that all her regular customers must be aware of. Twice more she had retreated to the back room and, the second time, he had clearly heard the squeaking of a cork in a bottle.

She drank. He was quite sure of one thing. She never got drunk, never lost her self-control. Like all true alcoholics,

205

whom doctors are powerless to help, she knew her own capacity. She drank only as much as was needed to maintain her in the state of anaesthesia which had so puzzled him at their first meeting.

'How old are you?' he asked her, when she was back at her post behind the counter.

'Forty-one.'

There was no hesitation. She said it without a trace of either coquetry or bitterness. She knew she looked older. No doubt she had stopped caring years ago about other people and what they thought of her. She looked worn out, with dark shadows under the eyes, a tremor at the corner of the mouth and, already, slack folds under the chin. She must have lost a great deal of weight, judging by her dress, which was far too big, and hung straight down from her shoulders.

'Were you born in Paris?'

'No.'

She must know, he felt sure, what lay behind his questions. Yet she did not shrink from them. She was giving nothing away, but at least he got a straight answer to a straight question.

The two old men, behind Maigret, were playing dominoes, as no doubt they did every evening at this time.

What puzzled Maigret was that she did her drinking out of sight. What was the point, seeing that she did not care what people thought of her, of slinking off into the back room to have her swig of wine or spirits, or whatever it was, straight out of the bottle? Could it be that she still retained this one vestige of self-respect? He doubted it. It is only when they are under supervision that hardened alcoholics resort to subterfuge.

Was that the answer? There was the husband, Omer Calas. He might well object to his wife's drinking, in front of the customers at least.

'Does your husband go regularly to Poitiers for his wine?'

'Every year.'

'Once a year?'

'Sometimes twice. It depends.'

'On what?'

'On our trade.'

'Does he always go on a Friday?'

'I can't remember.'

'Did he say he was going on a business trip?'

'To whom?'

'To you.'

'He never tells me anything.'

'Would he have mentioned it to any of the customers, or a friend?'

'I've no idea.'

'Were those two here last Friday?'

'Not when Omer left. They never come in before five.'

Maigret turned to Lapointe.

'Ring the Gare Montparnasse, will you, and find out the times of the afternoon trains to Poitiers. Have a word with the station master.'

Maigret spoke in an undertone. Had she been watching him, Madame Calas would have been able to lip-read the message, but she did not trouble to do so.

'Ask him to make inquiries among the station staff, especially in the booking office. Let him have the husband's description.'

The telephone box, unlike most, was not at the far end of the room, but near the entrance. Lapointe asked for a *jeton*, and moved towards the glass door. Night was closing in, and there was a bluish mist outside. Maigret, who had his back to the door, heard quickening footsteps, and turned to catch a glimpse of a young face which, in the half-light, looked blurred and very pale. Then he saw the dark outline of a man running in the direction of La Villette, followed by Lapointe, who had wrenched open the door to dash out and give chase. He had not had time to shut the door behind him. Maigret went outside, and stood on the pavement. He could now barely see the two running figures, but, even after they had disappeared from view, he could still hear their rapid footsteps on the cobbles.

Lapointe must have seen a face he recognized through the glass door. Maigret had not seen very much, but he could guess what must have happened. The fugitive fitted the description of the errand boy who, earlier in the day, had watched the diver at work in the canal, and fled when approached by a policeman.

'Do you know him?' he asked Madame Calas.

'Who?'

It was no use pressing the point. Anyway, she might well have been looking the other way when it all happened.

'Is it always as quiet as this in here?'

'It depends.'

'On what?'

'On the time of day. And some days are busier than others.'

As though to prove it, a siren sounded, releasing the workers at a nearby factory, and, a few minutes later, there was a noise in the street like a column on the march. The door opened and shut and opened and shut again, a dozen times at least. People sat down at the tables, and others, like Maigret, stood at the bar.

Most of them seemed to be regulars, as the woman did not ask what they wanted, but silently poured their usual drinks.

'I see Omer's not home.'

'No.'

She did not go on to say: 'He's out of town,' or 'He left for Poitiers on Friday.'

She merely answered the question, and left it at that. What was her background? He could not even hazard a guess. Life had tarnished her, and eroded some part of her real self. Through drink, she had withdrawn into a private world of her own, and her links with reality were tenuous.

'Have you lived here long?'

'In Paris?'

'No. In this café.'

'Twenty-four years.'

'Was your husband here before you?'

'No.'

He did some rapid mental arithmetic.

'So you were seventeen when you first met him?'

'I knew him before that.'

'How old is he now?'

'Forty-seven.'

This did not altogether tally with Doctor Paul's estimate of the man's age, but it was not far out. Not that Maigret was convinced he was on the right track. His questions were prompted more by personal curiosity than anything else. For it would surely be a miracle if, without the smallest effort on his

208

part, he were to establish the identity of the headless corpse on the very first day of the inquiry.

There was a hum of voices in the bar, and a floating veil of tobacco smoke had formed overhead. People were coming and going. The two players, absorbed in their game of dominoes, seemed unaware that they were not the only people on earth.

'Have you a photograph of your husband?'

'No.'

'Not even a snapshot?'

'No.'

'Have you any of yourself?'

'No. Only the one on my identity card.'

Not one person in a thousand, Maigret knew from experience, can claim not to possess a single personal photograph.

'Do you live upstairs?'

She nodded. He had seen from the outside that the building was a single-storey structure. The space below street level comprised the café and kitchen. The floor above, he assumed, must consist of two or three rooms, more likely two, plus a lavatory or lumber room.

'How do you get up there?'

'The staircase is in the kitchen.'

Shortly after this exchange, she went into the kitchen, and this time he heard her stirring something in a saucepan. The door burst open noisily, and Maigret saw Lapointe, flushed, bright-eyed and panting, pushing a young man ahead of him.

The little fellow, as Lapointe was always referred to at the Quai des Orfèvres, not because he was undersized, but because he was the youngest and most junior of the Inspectors, had never looked so pleased with himself in his life.

'I didn't catch him until we were right at the end of the road!' he said, grinning broadly and reaching out for his glass, which was still on the counter. 'Once or twice I thought he'd given me the slip. It's just as well I was the five hundred metre champion at school!'

The young man, too, was panting, and Maigret could feel his hot breath.

'I haven't done anything,' he protested, appealing to Maigret.

'In that case, you have nothing to fear.'

Maigret looked at Lapointe.

'Have you seen his identity card?'

'Just to be on the safe side, I kept it. It's in my pocket. He works as an errand boy for the Maison Pincemail. And he's the one who was snooping on the wharf this morning, and made a quick getaway when he saw he'd been noticed.'

'What did you do that for?' Maigret asked the young man.

He scowled, as lads do when they want to show what tough guys they are.

'Well?'

'I've nothing to say.'

'Didn't you get anything out of him on the way?' he asked Lapointe.

'We were both so puffed we could hardly speak. His name is Antoine Cristin. He's eighteen, and he lives with his mother in rooms in the Faubourg Saint-Martin.'

One or two people had turned round to look at them, but not with any great interest. In this district, a policeman bursting into a bar was quite a common sight.

'What were you up to out there?'

'Nothing.'

'He had his nose pressed against the glass,' Lapointe explained. 'The minute I saw him, I remembered what Judel had said, and I nipped out to get him.'

'If you had done nothing wrong, why try to get away?'

He hesitated, took a quick look round to satisfy himself that there were at least a couple of people within earshot, then said, with a theatrical curl of the lip: 'Because I don't like rozzers.'

'But you don't mind spying on them through glass doors?'

'There's no law against it.'

'How did you know we were in here?'

'I didn't.'

'What did you come for, then?'

He flushed, and bit his fleshy lower lip.

'Come on, let's have it.'

'I was just passing.'

'Do you know Omer?'

'I don't know anyone.'

'Not even Madame?'

She was back in her place behind the bar, watching them. But there was no trace of fear or even anxiety in her face. Had she anything to hide? If so, her nerve was beyond anything Maigret had ever encountered in a criminal or accessory to a crime.

'Do you know her?'

'By sight.'

'Don't you ever come in here for a drink?'

'Maybe.'

'Where's your bicycle?'

'At the shop. I'm off at five.'

Maigret made a sign to Lapointe, one of the few secret signs used by plain-clothes detectives. Lapointe nodded. He went into the telephone box, and rang not the Gare Montparnasse, but the police station just across the road, and eventually he got hold of Judel.

'We've got the kid here, at Calas's place. In a minute or two, the boss will let him go, but he wants someone standing by in case he makes a run for it. Any news?'

'Nothing worth mentioning. Four or five reports of scuffles in bars on Sunday night; someone who thinks he heard a body being dropped in the water; a prostitute who claims she had her handbag snatched by an Arab . . .'

'So long.'

Maigret, very bland, turned to the young man.

'What will you have, Antoine? Wine? Beer?'

'Nothing.'

'Don't you drink?'

'Not with rozzers, I don't. You'll have to let me go, you know.'

'You're very sure of yourself.'

'I know my rights.'

He was a broad-shouldered, sturdy country lad, with a wholesome complexion. Paris had not yet robbed him of his robust health. Maigret could not count the number of times he had seen kids just like him end up having coshed some poor old soul in a tobacconist's or draper's shop, to rob the till of a couple of hundred francs.

'Have you any brothers or sisters?'

'I'm an only child.'

'Where's your father?'

'He's dead.'

'Does your mother go out to work?'

'She's a cleaner.'

Maigret turned to Lapointe:

'Give him back his identity card. All in order, is it? The correct address, and so on?'

'Yes.'

The boy looked uncertain, suspecting a trap.

'Can I go?'

'Whenever you like.'

He went without a word of thanks or even a nod, but on his way out he winked furtively at the woman, a signal which did not escape Maigret.

'You'd better ring the station now.'

He ordered two more glasses of white wine. There were fewer people in the café now. Only three customers, other than Lapointe and himself, and the two old men playing dominoes.

'You don't know him, do you?'

'Who?'

'The young man who was here just now.'

Unhesitatingly, she said:

'Yes.'

It was as simple as that. Maigret was disconcerted.

'Does he come here often?'

'Quite often.'

'For a drink?'

'He drinks very little.'

'Beer?'

'And, occasionally, wine.'

'Does he usually come in after work?'

'No.'

'During the day?'

She nodded. Her unshakeable composure was beginning to exasperate the Superintendent.

'When he happens to be passing.'

'You mean when he's round this way on his bicycle? In other words, when he's out delivering?'

'Yes.'

'And what time of day would that be?'

'Between half-past three and four.'

'Does he have a regular round?'

'I think so.'

'Does he stand at the bar?'

'Sometimes he sits at a table.'

'Which one.'

'This one over here, next to the till.'

'Is he a particular friend of yours?'

'Yes.'

'Why wouldn't he admit it?'

'He was showing off, I expect.'

'Does he make a habit of it?'

'He does his best.'

'Do you know his mother?'

'No.'

'Are you from the same village?'

'No.'

'He just walked in one day, and you made a friend of him. Is that it?'

'Yes.'

'Half-past three in the afternoon. That's when your husband is out playing billiards in a brasserie, isn't it?'

'Most days, yes.'

'Is it just a coincidence, do you think, that Antoine should choose that particular time to visit you?'

'I've never thought about it.'

Maigret hesitated before asking his next question. The very idea shocked him, but he had a feeling that there were even more shocking revelations to come.

'Does he make love to you?'

'It depends what you mean.'

'Is he in love with you?'

'I dare say he likes me.'

'Do you give him presents?'

'I slip him a note from the till, occasionally.'

'Does your husband know?'

'No.'

'Doesn't he notice that sort of thing?'

'He has done, from time to time.'

'Was he angry?'

'Yes.'

'Isn't he suspicious of Antoine?'

'I don't think so.'

Entering this dark room, two steps down from the street, they had stepped into another world, a world in which all the familiar values were distorted, in which even familiar words had a different meaning. Lapointe was still in the telephone box, talking to the station master.

'Will you forgive me, Madame Calas, if I ask you a more intimate question?'

'If you want to, you will, whatever I say.'

'Is Antoine your lover?'

She did not flinch, or even look away from Maigret.

'It has happened from time to time,' she admitted.

'You mean to say you have had intercourse with him?'

'You'd have found out sooner or later, anyway. I'm sure he'll tell you himself before long.'

'Has it happened often?'

'Quite often.'

'Where?'

It was a question of some importance. Madame Calas, in the absence of her husband, had to be available to serve anyone who might happen to come in. Maigret glanced up at the ceiling. But could she be sure of hearing the door open, up there in the bedroom?

In the same straightforward manner in which she had answered all his questions, she nodded towards the open kitchen door at the back of the room.

'In there?'

'Yes.'

'Were you ever interrupted?'

'Not by Omer.'

'By whom?'

'One day, a customer wearing rubber-soled shoes came into the kitchen, because there was no one in the bar.'

'What did he do?'

'He laughed.'

'Didn't he tell Omer?'

'No.'

'Did he ever come back?'

It was intuition that prompted Maigret to ask. So far he had judged Madame Calas correctly. Even his wildest shots had hit the target.

'Did he come back often?' he pressed her.

'Two or three times.'

'While Antoine was here?'

'No.'

It would not have been difficult to tell whether or not the young man was in the café. Any time earlier than five o'clock, he would have had to leave his delivery bicycle at the door.

'Were you alone?'

'Yes.'

'And he made you go into the kitchen with him?'

For a second, there was a flicker of expression in her eyes. Mockery? Perhaps he had imagined it. All the same, he believed he could read an unspoken message there:

'Why ask, when you know the answer?'

She understood him as well as he understood her. They were a match for one another. To be more precise, life had taught them both the same lesson.

It all happened so quickly that Maigret wondered afterwards whether he had imagined the whole thing.

'Are there many others?' he asked, lowering his voice. His tone was almost confidential now.

'A few.'

Then, standing very still, not bending forward towards her, he put one last question:

'Why?'

To that question, there was no answer but a slight shrug. She was not one to strike romantic attitudes or dramatize her situation.

He had asked her why. If he did not know, it was not for her to tell him.

The fact was that he did know. He had only wanted confirmation. He had got it. There was no need for her to say anything.

He now knew to what depths she had sunk. What he still did not know was what had driven her there. Would she be equally ready to tell him the truth about her past?

That would have to wait. Lapointe had joined him at the bar. He gulped down some wine and then said:

'There is a week-day train to Poitiers that leaves at four-forty-eight. The station master says that neither of the booking-office clerks remembers anyone answering the description. He's going to make further inquiries, and ring us at Headquarters. On the other hand, he thinks we'd do better to ring Poitiers. It's a slow train, and it goes on south from Poitiers, so there would have been fewer people stopping there than had boarded the train at Montparnasse.'

'Put Lucas on to that. Tell him to ring Saint-Aubin and the nearest villages. Where there isn't a police station, let him try the local inn.'

Lapointe asked Madame Calas for some *jetons,* and she handed them over listlessly. She asked no questions. Being interrogated about her husband's movements might have been an everyday occurrence. Yet she knew what had been found in the Saint-Martin Canal, and could not have been unaware of the search that had been going on all day almost under her windows.

'Did you see Antoine last Friday?'

'He never comes on Friday.'

'Why not?'

'He has a different round that day.'

'And after five o'clock?'

'My husband is usually back by then.'

'So he wasn't here at any time during the afternoon or evening?'

'That's right.'

'You've been married to Omer Calas for twenty-four years?'

'I've been living with him for twenty-four years.'

'You're not married?'

'Yes. We were married at the Town Hall in the Tenth *Arrondissement*, but not until sixteen or seventeen years ago. I can't remember exactly.'

'No children?'

'One daughter.'

'Does she live with you?'

'No.'

'In Paris?'

'Yes.'

'How old is she?'

'She's just twenty-four. I had her when I was seventeen.'

'Is Omer the father?'

'Yes.'

'No doubt about it?'

'None whatever.'

'Is she married?'

'No.'

'Does she live alone?'

'She's got rooms in the Ile Saint-Louis.'

'Has she a job?'

'She's assistant to one of the surgeons at the Hôtel-Dieu, Professor Lavaud.'

For the first time, she had told him more than was strictly necessary. Could it be that, in spite of everything, she still retained some vestige of natural feeling, and was proud of her daughter?

'Did you see her last Friday?'

'No.'

'Does she ever come to see you?'

'Occasionally.'

'When was the last time?'

'Three or four weeks ago.'

'Was your husband here?'

'I think so.'

'Does your daughter get on well with him?'

'She has as little to do with us as possible.'

'Because she's ashamed of you?'

'Possibly.'

'How old was she when she left home?'

There was a little colour in her cheeks now, and a touch of defiance in her voice.

'Fifteen.'

'Without warning?'

She nodded.

'Was there a man?'

She shrugged.

'I don't know. It makes no difference.'

The room was empty now, except for the two old men. One was putting the dominoes back in their box, and the other was banging a coin on the table. Madame Calas got the message, and went over to refill their glasses.

'Isn't that Maigret?' one of them asked in an undertone.

'Yes.'

'What does he want?'

'He didn't say.'

Nor had she asked him. She went into the kitchen for a moment, came back to the bar, and said in a low voice:

'My meal is ready. Will you be long?'

'Where do you have your meals?'

'Over there.' She pointed to a table at the far end of the room.

'I won't keep you much longer. Did your husband have an attack of appendicitis several years back?'

'Five or six years ago. He had an operation.'

'Who did it?'

'Let me think. A Doctor Gran ... Granvalet. That's it! He lived in the Boulevard Voltaire.'

'Where is he now?'

'He died, or so we were told by another of his patients.'

Had Granvalet been alive, he could have told them whether Omer Calas had a rainbow-shaped scar on his abdomen. Tomorrow, they would have to track down the assistants and nurses who had taken part in the operation. Unless, of course, they found Omer safe and well in some village inn near Poitiers.

'Was your husband ever, years ago, involved in a shotgun accident?'

'Not since I've known him.'

'Did he ever join a shooting party?'

'He may have done, when he lived in the country.'

'Have you ever noticed a scar, rather faint, on his stomach, in the shape of a rainbow?'

She frowned, apparently trying to remember, and then shook her head.

'Are you sure?'

'I haven't seen him undressed for a very long time.'

'Did you love him?'

'I don't know.'

'How long did you remain faithful to him?'

'For years.'

She said this with peculiar emphasis.

'Were you very young when you first knew each other?'

'We come from the same village.'

'What village?'

'It's really a hamlet, about midway between Montargis and Gien. It's called Boissancourt.'

'Do you go back there often?'

'Never.'

'You've never been back?'

'No.'

'Not since you and Omer came together?'

'I left when I was seventeen.'

'Were you pregnant?'

'Six months.'

'Was it generally known?'

'Yes.'

'Did your parents know?'

In the same matter-of-fact tone, about which there was a kind of nightmare quality, she said dryly:

'Yes.'

'You never saw them again?'

'No.'

Lapointe, having finished passing on Maigret's instructions to Lucas, came out of the telephone box, mopping his brow.

'What do I owe you?' asked Maigret.

For the first time, she had a question to ask.

'Are you going?'

And, taking his tone from her, he replied,
'Yes.'

## 4. The Boy on the Roof

Maigret hesitated a long time before taking his pipe out of his pocket, which was most unlike him; and when he did, he assumed an absent-minded air, as though he had just got it out to keep his hands occupied while he was talking.

The staff meeting in the Chief's office had been short. When it was over, Maigret and the Chief stood for a few minutes talking by the open window, and then Maigret made straight for the little communicating door which led to the Department of Public Prosecutions. The benches all along the corridor in the Examining Magistrates' Wing were crowded, two police vans having driven into the courtyard a short while before. Maigret recognized most of the prisoners waiting handcuffed, between two guards, and one or two, apparently bearing him no ill-will, nodded a greeting as he went past.

By the time he had got back to his office the previous evening, there were several messages on his pad requesting him to ring Judge Coméliau. The Judge was thin and nervy, with a little brown moustache that looked dyed, and the bearing of a cavalry officer. His very first words to Maigret were:

'I want to know exactly how things stand.'

Obediently Maigret told him, beginning with Victor's search of the Saint-Martin Canal, and his failure to find the head. Even at this early stage, he was interrupted.

'The diver will be continuing the search today, I presume?'

'I didn't consider it necessary.'

'It seems to me that, having discovered the rest of the body in the canal, it's logical to assume that the head can't be far away.'

This was what made him so difficult to work with. He was not the only meddling magistrate, but he was certainly the most pig-headed. He wasn't a fool, by any means. It was said by lawyers who had known him in his student days that he had been one of the most brilliant men of his year.

One could only suppose that he had never learnt to apply his intelligence to the hard facts of life. He was very much a man of the Establishment, guided by inflexible principles and hallowed taboos, which determined his attitude in all things. Patiently, the Chief Superintendent explained:

'In the first place, Judge, Victor is as much at home in the canal as you are in your office and I am in mine. He has gone over the bottom inch by inch, at least a couple of hundred times. He's a conscientious chap. If he says the head isn't there . . .'

'My plumber is a conscientious chap, too, and he knows his job, but that doesn't prevent him from assuring me, every time I send for him, that there can't possibly be any defect in my water system.'

'It rarely happens, in the case of a dismembered corpse, that the head is found near the body.'

Coméliau was making a visible effort, with his bright little eyes fixed on Maigret, who went on:

'It's understandable. It's no easy matter to identify a torso or a limb, especially when it's been some time in the water, but a head is easily recognizable. And, because it's less cumbersome than a body, it's worth taking the trouble to dispose of it farther afield.'

'Yes, I'll grant you that.'

Maigret, as discreetly as he could, had got out his tobacco pouch and was holding it in his left hand, hoping that something might distract the magistrate's attention, so that he could fill his pipe.

He turned to the subject of Madame Calas, and described the bar in the Quai de Valmy.

'What led you to her?'

'Pure chance, I must admit. I had a phone call to make, and there was no telephone box in the first bar I went into, only a wall instrument, making private conversation impossible.'

'Go on.'

Maigret told him of Calas's alleged departure by train for Poitiers, and of the relationship between the proprietress of the bar and Antoine Cristin, the errand boy. And he did not forget to mention the crescent-shaped scar.

'Do you mean to tell me that you believed this woman when she said she didn't know whether or not her husband had such a scar?'

This infuriated the judge, because he could not understand it.

'To be perfectly frank, Maigret, I can't understand why you didn't have the woman and the boy brought in for questioning in the ordinary way. It's the usual practice, and generally produces results. I take it her story is a pack of lies?'

'Not necessarily.'

'But claiming she didn't know where her husband was or when he would return. . . . Well, really! . . .'

Coméliau was born in a house on the Left Bank, with a view over the Luxembourg. He was still living in it. How could such a man be expected to have the smallest insight into the minds of people like Omer Calas and his wife?

At last! The flicker of a match, and Maigret's pipe was alight. Now for the disapproving stare. Coméliau had a perfect horror of smoking, and this was his way of showing it when anyone had the impudence to light up in his presence. Maigret, however, was determined to outface him.

'You may be right,' he conceded. 'She could have been lying to me. On the other hand, she could have been telling the truth. All we have is a dismembered corpse without a head. All we know for certain is that the dead man was aged between forty-five and fifty-five. So far, he has not been identified. Do you imagine that Calas is the only man to have disappeared in the past few days, or gone off without saying where? Madame Calas is a secret drinker, and her lover, the errand boy, is scared of the police. Does that give me the right to have her brought to Headquarters as a suspect? What kind of fools will we look, if, in the next day or so, a head is found, and it turns out not to be the head of Omer Calas at all?'

'Are you having the house watched?'

'Judel of the Tenth *Arrondissement* has a man posted on the quay, and I went back myself after dinner last night to take a look round.'

'Did you get any results?'

'Nothing much. I stopped one or two prostitutes in the street, and asked them a few questions. It's one of those districts where the atmosphere is quite different at night from what it is by day, and I was hoping that, if there was anything suspicious going on around the café on Sunday night, one of these women would have seen or heard it.'

'Did you discover anything?'

'Not much. I did get what may be a lead from one of them, but I haven't had time to follow it up.

'According to her, the woman Calas has another lover, a middle-aged man with red hair, who either lives or works in the district. My informant, it must be admitted, is eaten up with spite, because, as she put it, "that woman takes the bread out of our mouths". If she were a pro, she said, they wouldn't mind so much. But she does it for nothing. All the men, it seems, know where to go. They only have to wait till the husband's back is turned. No one is refused, I'm told, though, of course, I haven't put it to the test.'

In the face of such depravity, Coméliau could only heave a distressful sigh.

'You must proceed as you think fit, Maigret. I don't see any problem myself. There's no need to handle people of that sort with kid gloves.'

'I shall be seeing her again shortly. And I intend to see the daughter as well. As to identification, I hope we shall be able to clear that up through the nurses who were present at the operation on Calas five years ago.'

In that connection, one curious fact had emerged. The previous evening, while Maigret was wandering about the streets, he had suddenly remembered another question he wanted to put to Madame Calas, and had gone back to the bistro. Madame Calas was sitting half-asleep on a chair, and four men were playing cards at a table. Maigret had asked her the name of the hospital where her husband had been operated on.

He had formed an impression of Calas as a fairly tough character, not at all the sort to cosset himself, fret about his health, or fear for his life. Yet, when it came to undergoing a simple operation, without complications, virtually without risk, he had not chosen to go into hospital but, at considerable expense, to a private clinic at Villejuif. And not just any private clinic, but a religious establishment, staffed by nuns.

Maigret looked at his watch. Lapointe must be there by now. He would soon be telephoning to report.

'Be firm, Maigret!' urged Coméliau, as the Superintendent was leaving.

It was not lack of firmness that was holding him back. It was not pity either. Coméliau would never understand. The world into which Maigret had suddenly been plunged was so different from the familiar world of daily life that he could only feel his way, tentatively, step by step. Was there any connection between the occupants of the little café in the Quai de Valmy and the corpse thrown into the Saint-Martin Canal? Possibly. But it was equally possible that it was mere coincidence.

He returned to his office, feeling restless and disgruntled, as he nearly always did at this stage of any inquiry.

Last night, he had been collecting and storing information without stopping to consider where it was all leading. Now, he was faced with a jumble of facts which needed sorting out and piecing together.

Madame Calas was no longer simply a colourful character, such as he occasionally encountered in his work. She was his problem, his responsibility.

Coméliau saw her as a sexually promiscuous, drink-sodden degenerate. That was not how Maigret saw her. Just what she was, he could not say yet, and until he knew for sure, until he felt the truth in his bones as it were, he would be oppressed by this indefinable uneasiness.

Lucas was in his office. He had just put the mail on his desk.

'Any new developments?'

'Have you been in the building all the time, sir?'

'With Coméliau.'

'If I'd known, I'd have had your calls transferred. Yes, there has been a new development. Judel is in a fearful stew.'

It was Madame Calas who came at once into Maigret's mind, and he wondered what could have happened to her. But it had nothing to do with her.

'It's about the young man, Antoine. I think that was the name.'

'Yes, Antoine. What's happened? Has he vanished again?'

'That's it. It seems you left instructions last night that he was to be kept under observation. The young man went straight to his lodgings, at the far end of the Faubourg Saint-Martin, almost at the junction with the Rue Louis-Blanc. The man detailed to follow him had a word with the concierge. The boy lives with his mother, who is a cleaner, on the seventh floor of the building. They have two attic rooms. There's no lift. I got all this from Judel, of course. Apparently, the building is one of those ghastly great tenements, housing fifty or sixty families, with swarms of kids spilling out on to the stairs.'

'Go on.'

'That's about all. According to the concierge, the boy's mother is an estimable woman with plenty of guts. Her husband died in a sanatorium. She has had T B herself. She claims to be cured, but the concierge doubts it. Well, when he had heard all this, Judel's man rang the Station for further instructions. Judel, not wanting to take any chances, told him to stay where he was and watch the building. He stood guard outside until about midnight. All the tenants were in by then. He went in after the last of them, and spent the night on the stairs.

'This morning, just before eight, a thin woman went past the lodge, and the concierge called out to him that this was Antoine's mother. He saw no necessity to stop or follow her. It was not until half-an-hour later that, having nothing better to do, he thought of going up to the seventh floor, to have a look round.

'It did strike him as odd then that the boy hadn't yet left for work. He listened at the keyhole, but couldn't hear a sound. He knocked, and got no answer. In the end, after examining the lock and seeing that it was anything but secure, he decided to use his skeleton keys.

'The first room he came to was the kitchen. There was a bed in it, the mother's bed. In the other room there was a bed too, unmade. But there was no one there, and the skylight was open.

'Judel is furious with himself for not having foreseen this, and given instructions accordingly. It's obvious that the kid got out through the skylight during the night, and crawled along the rooftops looking for another open skylight. He probably got out through a building in the Rue Louis-Blanc.'

'They've checked that he's not hiding in the tenement, I take it?'

'They're still questioning the tenants.'

Maigret could imagine Judge Coméliau's sarcastic smile when he was told about this.

'Nothing from Lapointe?'

'Not yet.'

'Has anyone turned up at the mortuary to identify the corpse?'

'Only the regulars.'

There were about a dozen of these, elderly women for the most part, who, every time a body was found, rushed to the mortuary to identify it.

'Didn't Doctor Paul ring?'

'I've just put his report on your desk.'

'If you speak to Lapointe, tell him to come back here and wait for me. I won't be far away.'

He walked towards the Ile Saint-Louis. He skirted Notre-Dame, crossed a little iron footbridge, and soon found himself in the narrow, crowded Rue Saint-Louis-En-l'Ile. The housewives were all out doing their shopping at this time of day, and he had difficulty in pushing past them as they crowded round the little market stalls. Maigret found the grocer's shop above which, according to Madame Calas, her daughter Lucette had a room. He went down the little alley-way at the side of the shop, and came to a cobbled courtyard shaded by a lime tree, like the forecourt of a village school or country vicarage.

'Looking for someone?' shrilled a woman's voice from a window on the ground floor.

'Mademoiselle Calas.'

'Third floor, left hand side, but she's not at home.'

'Do you know when she'll be back?'

'She very seldom comes home for lunch. She's not usually back before half-past six in the evening. If it's urgent, you can get her at the hospital.'

The Hôtel-Dieu, where Lucette Calas worked, was not far away. All the same, it was no easy matter to find Professor

Lavaud. This was the busiest time of the day. The corridors were crowded with hurrying men and women in white coats, nurses pushing trolleys, patients taking their first uncertain steps. There were doors opening on to other corridors leading heaven knows where.

'Please can you tell me where I can find Mademoiselle Calas?'

They hardly noticed him.

'Don't know. Is she a patient?'

Or they pointed down a corridor.

'Along there.'

He was told to go first in one direction and then in another, until at last he reached a corridor where stillness and silence reigned. It was like coming into port after a voyage. Except for a girl seated at a table, it was deserted.

'Mademoiselle Calas?'

'Is it personal business? How did you manage to get this far?'

He must have penetrated one of those sanctums not accessible to ordinary mortals. He gave his name, and even went so far as to produce his credentials, so little did he feel he had any standing here.

'I'll go and see if she can spare you a minute or two, but I'm afraid she may be in the operating theatre.'

He was kept waiting a good ten minutes, and he dared not light his pipe. When the girl came back she was accompanied by a nurse, rather tall, with an air of self-possession and serenity.

'Are you the gentleman who wished to see me?'

'Chief Superintendent Maigret from Police Headquarters.'

The contrast with the bar in the Quai de Valmy seemed all the greater on account of the cleanliness and brightness of the hospital, the white uniform and starched cap of the nurse.

Lucette Calas seemed more astonished than distressed. Obviously, she had not the least idea what he had come about.

'Are you sure I'm the person you want to see?'

'You are the daughter of Monsieur and Madame Calas, of the Quai de Valmy, aren't you?'

It was gone in a flash, but Maigret was sure he had seen a spark of resentment in her eyes.

'Yes, but I . . .'

'There are just one or two questions I'd like to ask you.'

'I can't spare very long. The Professor will be starting his round of the wards shortly, and . . .'

'It will only take a few minutes.'

She shrugged, looked round, and pointed to an open door.

'We'd better go in there.'

There were two chairs, an adjustable couch for examining patients, and a few surgical instruments that Maigret could not identify.

'Is it long since you last saw your parents?'

She started at the word 'parents', and Maigret thought he knew why.

'I see as little of them as possible.'

'Why is that?'

'Have you seen them?'

'I've seen your mother.'

She was silent. What more explanation was needed?

'Have you anything against them?'

'What should I have, except that they brought me into the world?'

'You weren't there last Sunday?'

'I was out of town. It was my day off. I spent it in the country with friends.'

'So you can't say where your father is?'

'You really should tell me what this is all about. You turn up here and start asking questions about two people who admittedly are, in the strictly legal sense, my parents, but from whom I have been totally estranged for years. Why? Has something happened to him?'

She lit a cigarette, saying:

'Smoking is allowed in here. At this time of day, at any rate.'

But he did not take advantage of this opportunity to light his pipe.

'Would it surprise you to hear that something had happened to one or other of them?'

She looked him straight in the eye, and said flatly:

'No.'

'What would you expect to hear?'

'That Calas's brutality to my mother had gone too far for once.'

She did not refer to him as 'my father', but as 'Calas'.

'Does he often resort to physical violence?'

'I don't know about now. It used to be an almost daily occurrence.'

'Didn't your mother object?'

'She put up with it. She may even have liked it.'

'Have you any other possibilities in mind?'

'Maybe she put poison in his soup.'

'Why? Does she hate him?'

'All I know is that she's lived with him for twenty-four years, and has never made any attempt to get away from him.'

'Is she unhappy, do you think?'

'Look, Superintendent, I do my best not to think about her at all. As a child I had only one ambition – escape. And as soon as I could stand on my own feet, I got out.'

'I know. You were just fifteen.'

'Who told you?'

'Your mother.'

'Then he hasn't killed her.'

She looked thoughtful, then, raising her eyes to his, said:

'Is it him?'

'What do you mean?'

'Has she poisoned him?'

'I shouldn't think so. We don't even know for sure whether anything has happened to him. Your mother says he left for Poitiers on Friday afternoon. He goes there regularly, it seems, to get his supplies of white wine from the vineyards round about.'

'That's right. He did even when I lived with them.'

'A body has been recovered from the Saint-Martin Canal. It may be his.'

'Has no one identified it?'

'Not so far. The difficulty is that the head has not been found.'

Was it perhaps because she worked in a hospital that she did not even blench?

'How do you think it happened?' she asked.

'I don't know. I'm feeling my way. There seem to be several men in your mother's life, if you'll forgive my mentioning it.'

'You surely don't imagine it's news to me!'

'Do you know whether your father, in childhood or adolescence, was wounded in the stomach by a shotgun?'

She looked surprised.

'I never heard him mention it.'

'You never saw the scars, of course?'

'Well, if it was a stomach wound . . .' she protested, with the beginning of a smile.

'When were you last at the Quai de Valmy?'

'Let me think. It must be a month or more.'

'Was it just a casual visit, keeping in touch with home, as it were?'

'Not exactly.'

'Was Calas there?'

'I make it my business only to go there when he's out.'

'In the afternoon, was it?'

'Yes, he's always out then, playing billiards somewhere near the Gare de l'Est.'

'Was there a man with your mother?'

'Not on that occasion.'

'Had you any special reason for going to see her?'

'No.'

'What did you talk about?'

'I can't remember. One thing and another.'

'Was Calas mentioned?'

'I doubt it.'

'You wouldn't by any chance have gone to ask your mother for money?'

'You're on the wrong track there, Superintendent. Rightly or wrongly, I have too much pride for that. There have been times when I've gone short of money, and, for that matter, food, but I've never gone to them begging for help. All the more reason not to do so now, when I'm earning a good living.'

'Can't you recall anything that was said on that last occasion at the Quai de Valmy?'

'Nothing special.'

'Among the men you saw in the bar from time to time, do you remember a fresh-complexioned youth who rides a carrier-bicycle?'

She shook her head.

'Or a middle-aged man with red hair?'

This did strike a chord.

'With small-pox scars?' she asked.

'I don't know.'

'If so, it's Monsieur Dieudonné.'

'Who is Monsieur Dieudonné?'

'I know very little about him. A friend of my mother's. He's been going to the café for years.'

'In the afternoon?'

She knew what he meant.

'Whenever I've seen him, it's been in the afternoon. But you may be wrong about him. I can't say for sure. He struck me as a quiet sort of man, the kind one thinks of as sitting by the fire after dinner in his slippers. Come to think of it, he always seems to be sitting by the stove, facing my mother. They behave like people who have known each other for a very long time. They take one another for granted, if you see what I mean. They could be mistaken for an old married couple.'

'Do you happen to know his address?'

'He's got a muffled kind of voice. I'd know it again if I heard it. I've known him get up and say: "Time to get back to work." I imagine his place of work must be somewhere near there, but I don't even know what he does. He doesn't dress like a manual worker. He might be a book-keeper, or something of the sort.'

A bell sounded in the corridor. The girl sprang to her feet.

'It's for me,' she said. 'I'll have to go, I'm afraid.'

'I may have to take up a little more of your time. If so, I'll call on you in the Rue Saint-Louis-en-l'Ile.'

'I'm never there except in the evening. Please don't make it too late. I go to bed early.'

He watched her go down the corridor. She was shaking her head slightly, puzzled by what she had just heard.

'Excuse me, mademoiselle. How do I get out of here?'

He looked so lost that the girl at the desk smiled, got up, and led him along the corridor to a staircase.

'You'll manage all right from here. Down the stairs, then left, and left again.'

'Thank you.'

He had not the temerity to ask her what she thought of Lucette Calas. He scarcely knew what he thought of her himself.

He stopped at a bar opposite the Palace of Justice for a glass of white wine. When, a few minutes later, he got back to his office, he found Lapointe waiting for him.

'Well, how did you make out with the nuns?'

'They couldn't have been nicer. I expected it to be rather an embarrassing experience, but they made me feel quite at home ...'

'What about the scars?'

Lapointe was less enthusiastic on this subject.

'In the first place, the doctor who did the operation died three years ago, as Madame Calas told us. The sister in charge of records showed me the file. There's no mention of any scar, which isn't surprising. On the other hand, I did discover one thing: Calas had a stomach ulcer.'

'Did they operate?'

'No. Apparently they always do extensive tests before an operation, and record their findings.'

'There's no reference to any distinguishing marks?'

'None at all. The sister very kindly went and spoke to the nuns who were present at the operation. None of them remembered Calas very clearly. One thought she remembered his asking for time to say his prayers before they gave him the anaesthetic.'

'Was he a Catholic?'

'No, he was scared. That's the kind of thing nuns don't forget. They wouldn't have noticed the scars.'

They were back where they started, with a headless corpse that could not be identified with any certainty.

'What do we do next?' murmured Lapointe.

With Maigret in his present disgruntled mood, he judged it wiser to keep his voice down.

Perhaps Judge Coméliau was right after all. If the man found in the Saint-Martin Canal was Omer Calas, then it might indeed be true that there was no way of getting the evidence they needed except by subjecting his wife to cross-examination. A heart-to-heart with Antoine, the lad with the bicycle, if only they could lay their hands on him, would also be helpful.

'Come on.'

'Shall I get the car?'

'Yes.'

'Where are we going?'

'To the Canal.'

On his way out, he gave instructions to the Inspectors concerned to order a search in the Tenth *Arrondissement* for a red-haired man with a pock-marked face, Christian name: Dieudonné.

The car nosed its way between buses and lorries. When they came to the Boulevard Richard-Lenoir, and were almost at Maigret's own front door, he suddenly growled:

'Take me to the Gare de l'Est.'

Lapointe looked at him in bewilderment.

'There may be nothing to it, but I'd like to check all the same. We were told that Calas had a suitcase with him, when he left on Friday afternoon. Suppose he came back on Saturday. If he's the man, then whoever killed and dismembered him must have got rid of the suitcase somehow. I'm quite sure it isn't still in the house at the Quai de Valmy, and I bet you we won't find the clothes he's supposed to have been wearing there, either.'

Lapointe nodded agreement.

'No suitcase has been recovered from the canal, nor any clothes, in spite of the fact that the dead man was stripped before being carved up.'

'And the head hasn't been found!' exclaimed Lapointe, taking it a stage further.

There was nothing original about Maigret's reasoning. It was just a matter of experience. Six murderers out of ten, if they have anything incriminating to get rid of, deposit it in the left luggage office of a railway station.

And it was no distance from the Quai de Valmy to the Gare de l'Est.

Lapointe eventually found somewhere to park the car, and he followed Maigret to the left luggage office.

'Were you on duty last Sunday afternoon?' he asked the clerk.

'Only up to six o'clock.'

'Did you take in a lot of luggage?'

'Not more than usual.'

'Have any cases deposited on Sunday not been claimed yet?'

The clerk walked along the shelves, where suitcases and parcels of all shapes and sizes were stacked.

'Two,' he said.

'Both left by the same person?'

'No. The ticket numbers aren't consecutive. The canvas holdall, anyway, was left by a woman, a fat woman. I remember her because of the smell of cheese.'

'Are there cheeses in it?'

'No, the smell has gone. Maybe, it was the woman herself.'

'What about the other one?'

'It's a brown suitcase.'

He pointed to a cheap, battered case.

'Is it labelled?'

'No.'

'Can you describe the person who handed it in?'

'I could be wrong, but I'd swear it was a country lad.'

'Why a country lad?'

'That's how he struck me.'

'Because of his complexion?'

'Could be.'

'What was he wearing?'

'A leather jerkin, if I remember rightly, and a peaked cap.'

Maigret and Lapointe exchanged glances. Antoine Cristin was in both their minds.

'What time would it have been?'

'Round about five. Yes. A little after five, because the express from Strasbourg had just come in.'

'If anyone comes to claim the case, will you please ring the Police Station at the Quai de Jemmapes immediately.'

'What if the chap takes fright and runs?'

'We'll be here, anyway, within minutes.'

There was only one way of getting the suitcase identified. Madame Calas would have to be brought to see it.

234

She looked up mechanically when the two men came in, and went to the bar to serve them.

'We won't have anything just now,' said Maigret. 'Something has been found which you may be able to identify. The Inspector will take you to see it. It's not far from here.'

'Had I better close the bar?'

'There's no need. It will only take a few minutes. I'll stay here.'

She did not put on a hat. She merely changed out of her slippers into shoes.

'Will you attend to the customers?'

'I doubt if it will be necessary.'

Maigret lingered for a moment on the pavement, watching Lapointe drive off with Madame Calas beside him. His face broke into a mischievous smile. He had never before been left all by himself in a bistro, just as if he owned it. He was so tickled by the notion that he went inside and slipped behind the bar.

# 5. *The Bottle of Ink*

The patches of sunlight were exactly where they had been the morning before. One, on the rounded end of the zinc counter, was shaped like an animal, another fell like a spotlight on a print of a woman in a red dress, holding a glass of foaming beer.

The little café, as Maigret had felt the previous day, like so many of the cafés and bars in Paris, had something of the atmosphere of a country inn, deserted most of the week, suddenly coming to life on market day.

Although he was tempted to help himself to a drink, he could not permit himself to give way to such a childish whim. Sternly, with his hands in his pockets and his pipe clenched between his teeth, he went over to the door at the back.

He had not yet seen what lay behind that door, through which Madame Calas was always disappearing. Not surprisingly, he found a kitchen, rather untidy, but less dirty than

235

he would have expected. Immediately to the left of the door was a dresser, painted brown, on which stood an open bottle of brandy. So, wine was not her tipple, but brandy, which – since there was no glass to be seen – she presumably swigged straight out of the bottle.

A window looked on to the courtyard, and there was a glass door, which was not locked. He pushed it open. Stacked in a corner were barrels, discarded straw wrappers, and broken buckets. There were rust-rings everywhere. Paris seemed far away, so much so that it would not have surprised him to find a mass of bird-droppings, and hens scratching about.

Beyond the courtyard was a cul-de-sac, bounded on both sides by a blank wall, and presumably leading off a side road.

Mechanically, he looked up at the first floor windows of the bistro. They were very dirty, and hung with faded curtains. Was there a flicker of movement up there, or had he imagined it? It was not the cat, which he had left stretched out by the stove.

He went back into the kitchen, taking his time, and then up the spiral staircase which led to the floor above. The treads creaked. There was a faint musty smell, which reminded him of little village inns at which he had stayed.

There were two doors on the landing. He opened the first, and was in what must have been the Calas's bedroom. The windows looked out on to the Quai de Valmy. The double bed, of walnut, had not been made that morning, but the sheets were reasonably clean. The furniture was what one would expect in this sort of household, old, heavy stuff, handed down from father to son, and glowing with the patina of age.

A man's clothes were hanging in the wardrobe. Between the windows stood an arm-chair covered in red plush and, beside it, an old-fashioned radio set. The only other furniture was a round table in the middle of the room, covered with a cloth of indeterminate colour, and a couple of mahogany chairs.

No sooner had he come into the room than he felt that something was not quite as it should be. What was it? He looked searchingly about him. Once again, his glance rested on the table covered with a cloth. On it was a bottle of ink, apparently unopened, a cheap pen, and one of those blotters advertising an apéritif that are often put on café tables for the convenience of customers. He opened the blotter, not expecting to find any-thing of interest, and indeed he found nothing but three blank sheets of paper. Just then, he thought he heard a board creak. He listened. The sound had not come from the lavatory, which led off the bedroom. Returning to the landing, he opened the door to the other room, which was as large as the first. It was used as a lumber room, and was piled high with chipped and broken furniture, old magazines, glasses and other bric-à-brac.

'Is there anyone there?' he called loudly, almost certain that he was not alone in the room.

For a moment, he stood absolutely still, and then, without making a sound, shot out his arm and jerked open a cup-board.

'No tricks this time!' he said.

It did not greatly surprise him to discover that it was Antoine cowering there in the cupboard, like a trapped animal.

'I thought it wouldn't be long before I found you. Come on out of there!'

'Are you arresting me?'

The young man, terrified, was staring at the handcuffs which the Superintendent had taken out of his pocket.

'I haven't made up my mind yet what I'm going to do with you, but I'm not having any more of your Indian rope tricks. Hold out your hands.'

'You've no right. I haven't done anything.'

'Hold out your hands!'

He could see that the lad was only waiting for a chance to make a dash for it. He moved towards him, and leaning for-ward with all his weight, pinned him against the wall. When the boy had tired of kicking him in the shins, Maigret managed to fasten on the handcuffs.

'Now then, come along with me!'

'What has my mother been saying?'

'I don't know what she's going to say about all this, but, as far as we're concerned, we want to know the answers to a few questions.'

'I'm saying nothing.'

'You come along with me, just the same.'

237

He motioned him forward. They went through the kitchen and into the bar. Antoine looked round, startled by the emptiness and the silence.

'Where is she?'

'The proprietress? Don't worry, she'll be back.'

'Have you arrested her?'

'Sit down over there, and don't move!'

'I'm not taking orders from you!'

He had seen so many of them at that age, all more or less in the same plight, that he had come to expect the defiant posturing and backchat.

It would please Judge Coméliau, at any rate, that Antoine had been caught, though he himself did not believe that they would learn much from him.

The street door was pushed open, and a middle-aged man came in. He looked round in surprise, seeing Maigret very much in command in the middle of the room, and no Madame Calas.

'Is Madame not here?'

'She won't be long.'

Had the man seen the handcuffs and, realizing that Maigret was a police officer, decided that discretion was the better part of valour? At any rate, he touched his cap, muttered something like 'I'll come back later', and beat a hasty retreat.

He could not have got as far as the end of the road when the black car drew up at the door. Lapointe got out first, opened the door for Madame Calas, and then took a brown suitcase from the boot.

She saw Antoine at first glance, frowned, and looked anxiously at Maigret.

'Didn't you know he was hiding upstairs?'

'Don't answer!' urged the young man. 'He has no right to arrest me – I've done nothing. I challenge him to prove anything against me.'

Briskly, Maigret turned to Lapointe.

'Is the suitcase his?'

'She didn't seem too sure at first, then she said it was, then that she couldn't swear to it without seeing what was in it.'

'Did you open it?'

'I wanted you to be present. I signed for it, but the clerk was most insistent that he must have an official requisition as soon as possible.'

'Get Coméliau to sign it. Is the clerk still there?'

'I imagine so. I couldn't persuade him to leave his post.'

'Ring him. Ask him to try and get someone to take over from him for a quarter of an hour. That shouldn't be too difficult. Tell him to hop into a taxi and come here.'

'I understand,' said Lapointe, looking at Antoine. Would the baggage clerk recognize him? If so, it would make everything a lot easier.

'Ring Moers as well. I want him here too, with a search warrant. And tell him to bring the photographers.'

'Right you are, sir.'

Madame Calas, who was standing in the middle of the room as though she were a stranger to the place, asked, as Antoine had done before her:

'Are you going to arrest me?'

'Why should I?' countered Maigret. She looked at him in bewilderment.

'Am I free to come and go?'

'In the house, yes.'

He knew what she wanted, and, sure enough, she went into the kitchen and disappeared, making straight for the brandy bottle, no doubt. To lend colour to her presence there, she rattled the crockery, and changed out of her shoes – which must have been pinching her, since she so seldom wore them – into slippers.

When she returned to her place behind the counter, she was herself again.

'Can I get you anything?'

'Yes, a glass of white wine – and one for the Inspector. Perhaps Antoine would like a beer?'

His manner was unhurried, hesitant even, as though he had not quite made up his mind what to do next. He took a leisurely sip of wine, and then went over to the door and locked it.

'Have you the key of the suitcase?'

'No.'

'Do you know where it is?'

In 'his' pocket, she supposed.

In Calas's pocket, since, according to her, he had his suitcase with him when he left the house.

'Have you a pair of pliers or a wrench of some sort?'

She took her time getting the pliers. Maigret lifted the suitcase on to a table. He waited for Lapointe to come out of the phone box before forcing the flimsy lock.

'I've ordered a white wine for you.'

'Thank you, sir.'

The metal buckled and eventually broke. Maigret lifted the lid. Madame Calas had not moved from behind the counter. She was watching them, but did not seem greatly concerned.

In the suitcase were a grey suit of quite good quality, a pair of shoes, almost new, shirts, socks, razor, comb, toothbrush, and a cake of soap still in its wrapping.

'Are these your husband's things?'

'I suppose so.'

'Aren't you sure?'

'He has a suit like that.'

'And it's not in the wardrobe?'

'I haven't looked.'

She was no help, but, at the same time, she did not hinder them. As before, her answers to questions were curt and guarded, though, unlike Antoine, she was not on the defensive.

While Antoine was scared stiff, the woman gave the impression of having nothing to fear. The comings and goings of the police seemed to be a matter of indifference to her. They could carry on, as far as she was concerned, whatever they might discover.

'Anything strike you as odd?' Maigret said to Lapointe, while they were rummaging in the suitcase.

'You mean everything shoved in higgledy-piggledy like that?'

'Well, that's how most men would pack a suitcase. But there's something else. Calas, or so we're told, was setting out on a journey. He took a spare suit, and a change of shoes and underclothes. It's reasonable to assume that he packed the case upstairs in his bedroom.'

Two men in housepainters' overalls rattled at the door, peered in through the glass, mouthed inaudible words, and went away.

'If that is so, can you think of any reason why he should have taken his dirty washing with him?'

One of the two shirts had, in fact, been worn, as well as a pair of pants and a pair of socks.

'Do you mean you think someone else may have put the stuff in the suitcase?'

'He could have done it himself. The likelihood is that he did. But not at the start of his journey. He was packing to come home.'

'I see what you mean.'

'Did you hear what I said, Madame Calas?'

She nodded.

'Do you still maintain that your husband left on Friday afternoon, taking the suitcase with him?'

'I can only repeat what I have already told you.'

'You're sure you don't mean Thursday, Friday being when he came back?'

She shook her head.

'Whatever I say, you'll believe what you want to believe.'

A taxi drew up at the door. Maigret went to open it. As the station clerk got out, he said:

'It can wait. I won't keep you a minute.'

The Superintendent ushered him into the café. The man looked about him, taking his time over it, getting his bearings, wondering what it was all about.

His glance rested on Antoine, who was still sitting on a bench in the corner. Then he turned to Maigret, opened his mouth, and gave Antoine another searching look.

All this time, which seemed longer than it was, Antoine was scowling defiance at him.

'I really do believe,' began the man, scratching his head. He was conscientious, and there was some doubt in his mind.

'Well then! From what I can see of him, I'd say he was the one.'

'You're lying,' shouted the young man furiously.

'Maybe I ought to see what he looks like standing up.'

'Stand up.'

'No.'

'Stand up!'

Maigret heard Madame Calas's voice behind him.

'Get up, Antoine.'

The clerk looked at him thoughtfully.

'I'm almost sure,' he murmured. 'Does he wear a leather jerkin?'

'Go and have a look upstairs in the back room,' said Maigret to Lapointe.

They waited in silence. The station employee glanced towards the bar. Maigret could take a hint.

'A glass of white wine?' he asked.

'I wouldn't say no.'

Lapointe returned with the jerkin that Antoine had worn the previous day.

'Put it on.'

The young man looked to the woman for guidance, resigned himself grudgingly, and held out his wrists for the handcuffs to be removed.

'Can't you see, he's just trying to suck up to the rozzers? They're all the same. Mention the word "police", and they shake in their shoes. Well, what about it? Do you still say you've seen me before?'

'I think so, yes.'

'You're lying.'

The clerk addressed himself to Maigret. He spoke calmly, though it was possible to detect an undercurrent of feeling in his voice.

'This is a serious business, I imagine. I shouldn't like to get an innocent person into trouble. This boy looks like the one who deposited the suitcase at the station on Sunday. Naturally, not knowing that anyone was going to ask me about him, I didn't take much notice of him. Perhaps if I saw him in the same place, under the same conditions, lighting and so on . . .'

'I'll have him brought to you at the station some time today or tomorrow,' said Maigret. 'Thank you. Your very good health!'

He saw him to the door, and locked it after him. There was,

in the Chief Superintendent's attitude to the case, a kind of diffidence that puzzled Lapointe. He could not have said when he had begun to notice it. Perhaps the previous day, right at the start of the inquiry, when they had come together to the Quai de Valmy, and pushed open the door of the Calas bistro.

Maigret was pursuing his investigations in the normal way, doing all that was required of him, but surely with a lack of conviction that was the last thing any of his subordinates would have expected of him? It was difficult to define. Half-heartedness? Reluctance? Disinclination? The facts of the case interested him very little. He seemed to be wrapped up in his thoughts, which he was keeping very much to himself.

It was particularly noticeable here in the café, especially when he was talking to Madame Calas, or furtively watching her.

It was as though the victim were of no account, and the dismembered corpse meant nothing to him. He had virtually ignored Antoine, and it was only with an effort that he was able to attend to the routine aspects of his work.

'Ring Coméliau. I'd rather you did it. Just give him a summary of events. You'd better ask him to sign a warrant for the arrest of the kid. He'll do it in any case.'

'What about her?' asked the Inspector, pointing to the woman.

'I'd rather not.'

'What if he insists?'

'He'll have to have his own way. He's the boss.'

He had not bothered to lower his voice, in spite of the presence of the other two, whom he knew to be listening.

'You'd better have a bite to eat,' he advised Madame Calas. 'It may not be long before you have to go.'

'For long?'

'For as long as the Judge thinks fit to hold you for questioning.'

'Will they keep me in prison?'

'At the Central Police Station to begin with, I expect.'

'What about me?' Antoine asked.

'You too. But not in the same cell!' Maigret added.

'Are you hungry?' Madame Calas asked the boy.

'No.'

She went into the kitchen just the same, but it was to have a swig of brandy. When she came back, she asked:

'Who will look after the place when I'm gone?'

'No one. Don't worry. It will be kept under supervision.'

He was still watching her with that same thoughtful expression. He could not help himself. It seemed to him that he had never encountered anyone so baffling.

He had experience of artful women, some of whom had stood up to him for a long time. In every case, however, he had felt from the first that he would have the last word. It was just a matter of time, patience and determination.

With Madame Calas, it was different. She did not fit into any category. If he were to be told that she had murdered her husband in cold blood, and had carved him up single-handed on the kitchen table, he would not have found it impossible to believe. But he would not have found it impossible to believe, either, that she simply did not know what had become of her husband.

There she was in front of him, a living creature of flesh and blood, thin and faded in her dark dress, which hung from her shoulders like a shabby window-curtain. She was real enough, with the fire of her inner life smouldering in her sombre eyes, and yet there was about her something insubstantial, elusive.

Was she aware of the impression she created? One would say so, judging from the cool, perhaps even ironic manner in which she, in her turn, appraised the Chief Superintendent.

This was the reason for Lapointe's uneasiness a little while back. The normal process of conducting a police inquiry with a view to apprehending a criminal was being overshadowed by the private duel between Maigret and this woman.

Nothing which did not directly concern her was of much interest to the Chief Superintendent. Lapointe was to have further proof of this when, a minute or two later, he came out of the telephone box.

'What did he say?' asked Maigret, referring to Coméliau.

'He'll sign the warrant and send it across to your office.'

'Does he want to see him?'

'He presumed you'd want to interrogate him first.'

'What about her?'

'He's signing two warrants. It's up to you what you do with the second one, but if you ask me . . .'

'I see.'

Coméliau was expecting Maigret to go back to his office, and have Antoine and Madame Calas brought to him there separately, so that he could grill them for hours, until they gave themselves away.

The head of the dead man had still not been found. There was no concrete proof that the man whose remains had been fished out of the Saint-Martin Canal was Calas. All the same, they did now have strong circumstantial evidence, namely the suitcase, and it was by no means unusual to obtain a full confession, after a few hours of interrogation, in cases where the cards were more heavily stacked against the police.

Judge Coméliau was not the only one to see the matter in this light. Lapointe was of the same opinion, and he could scarcely hide his astonishment when Maigret instructed him: 'Take him to Headquarters. Shut yourself up with him in my office, and get what you can out of him. Don't forget to order some food for him, and something to drink.'

'Will you be staying here?'

'I'm waiting for Moers and the photographers.'

Looking unmistakably put out, Lapointe motioned to the young man to stand up. As a parting shot, Antoine called to Maigret from the door:

'I warn you, you'll pay for this!'

At the Quai des Orfèvres, at about this time, the Vicomte, having poked his nose into most of the offices in the Palace of Justice, as he did every morning, had started on the Examining Magistrates.

'Any news, Monsieur Coméliau? Have they still not found the head?'

'Not yet. But I can tell you more or less officially that the identity of the victim is known.'

'Who is it?'

Coméliau graciously consented to give ten minutes of his time to answering questions. He was not altogether displeased that, for once, it was he and not Maigret whom the press was honouring with its attentions.

'Is the Chief Superintendent still there?'

'I presume so.'

Thus it came about that news of the inquiries in progress at the Calas bistro and the arrest of a young man, referred to only by his initials, appeared in the afternoon editions of the newspapers, two hours after the Vicomte's interview with Coméliau, and the five o'clock news on the radio included an announcement to the same effect.

Left on his own with Madame Calas, Maigret ordered a glass of wine at the bar, carried it across to a table, and sat down. As for her, she had not moved. She had remained at her post behind the bar where, as proprietress, she had every right to be.

The factory sirens sounded the mid-day break. In less then ten minutes, at least thirty people were crowded round the locked door. Some, seeing Madame Calas through the glass, indicated by gestures that they wanted to speak to her.

Suddenly, Maigret broke the silence.

'I've seen your daughter,' he said.

She looked at him, but said nothing.

'She confirmed that she last came to see you about a month ago. I couldn't help wondering what you found to talk about.'

It was not a question, and she did not choose to make any comment.

'She struck me as a sensible young woman, who has done well for herself. I don't know why, but I had the feeling that she was in love with her boss, and might be his mistress.'

Still she did not flinch. Was it of any interest to her? Did she feel any affection for her daughter, even the smallest remnant?

'It can't have been easy at the beginning. It's tough going for a girl of fifteen, trying to make her own way, alone, in a city like Paris.'

She was still looking at him, but her eyes seemed to see through and beyond him. Wearily, she asked:

'What is it you want?'

What, indeed, did he want? Was Coméliau right after all? Ought he not to be engaged at this very moment in making

Antoine talk? As for her, perhaps a few days in a police cell were just what was needed to bring about a change of heart.

'I'm wondering what made you marry Calas in the first place, and, even more, what induced you to stay with him all those years.'

She did not smile, but the corners of her mouth twitched, in contempt, perhaps, or pity.

'It was done deliberately, wasn't it?' went on Maigret, not quite sure himself what he meant.

He had to get to the bottom of it. There were times, and this was one of them, when it seemed to him that he was within a hair's breadth, not merely of solving the mystery, but of sweeping aside the invisible barrier that stood between them. It was just a question of finding the words which would evoke the simple, human response.

'Was *the other one* here on Sunday afternoon?'

This, at least, did get results. She started. After a pause, she was reluctantly compelled to ask:

'What other one?'

'Your lover. Your real lover.'

She would have liked to keep up the pretence of indifference, asking no questions, but in the end she yielded:

'Who?'

'A red-haired, middle-aged man, with small-pox scars, whose Christian name is Dieudonné.'

It was as though a shutter had come down between them. Her face became completely expressionless. What was more, a car had drawn up at the door. Moers, and three men with cameras, had arrived.

Once again, Maigret went to the door and unlocked it.

Admittedly, he had not triumphed. All the same, he did not consider that their tête-à-tête had been altogether a waste of time.

'Where do you want us to search, sir?'

'Everywhere. The kitchen first, then the two rooms and the lavatory upstairs. There's the courtyard as well, and, of course, the cellar. This trap door here presumably leads to it.'

'Do you believe the man was killed and dismembered here?'

'It's possible.'

'What about this suitcase?'

'Go over it thoroughly. The contents too, of course.'

'It will take us the whole afternoon. Will you be staying?'

'I don't think so, but I'll look in again later.'

He went into the telephone box and rang Judel at the Police Station opposite, to give him instructions about having the place watched.

When he had done, he said to Madame Calas:

'You'd better come with me.'

'Shall I take a change of clothing, and things for washing?'

'It would be advisable.'

She stopped on her way through the kitchen for a stiff drink. Soon, she could be heard moving about in the bedroom above.

'Is it safe to leave her on her own, sir?'

Maigret shrugged. If a crime had been committed here, steps must have been taken long before this to remove all traces of it, and dispose of anything incriminating.

All the same, it did surprise him that she should take so long getting ready. She could still be heard moving about, turning taps on and off, opening and shutting drawers.

She paused again in the kitchen, realizing no doubt that this was the last drink she would get for a long time.

When at last she reappeared, the men gaped at her in amazement, which in Maigret's case was mixed with a touch of admiration.

In the space of twenty minutes or less, she had completely transformed herself. She was now wearing a most becoming black coat. Under her carefully brushed hair and charming hat, her face seemed to have come to life. Her step was lighter, her carriage more upright. There was self-respect, even a hint of pride, in her bearing.

Was she aware of the sensation she was creating? Was there, perhaps, a touch of coquetry in her make-up? She did not smile, or show any sign of being amused at their astonishment. She looked inside her bag to make sure she had everything, and then, drawing on her gloves, said, almost in a whisper:

'I'm ready.'

She was wearing face-powder and lipstick. The scent of Eau de Cologne, mingled with the fumes of brandy on her breath, seemed somehow inappropriate.

'Aren't you taking a suitcase?'

She said no, almost defiantly. Would it not be an admission of guilt to take a change of clothing? At the very least, it would be an acknowledgement that there might be some justification for keeping her in custody.

'See you later!' Maigret called out to Moers and his assistants.

'Will you be taking the car?'

'No. I'll get a taxi.'

It was a strange experience, walking by her side, in step with her, there in the sunlit street.

'The Rue de Récollets would be the best place to find a taxi, I imagine?'

'I expect so.'

'I should like to ask you a question.'

'You surprise me!'

'When did you last take the trouble to dress as you are dressed now?'

She looked thoughtful, obviously trying to remember.

'Four years ago or more,' she said at last. 'Why do you ask?'

'No particular reason.'

What was the point of explaining, when she knew as well as he did? He managed to stop a taxi just as it was driving past. He opened the door for her, and got in beside her.

# 6. The String

The truth was that he had not yet made up his mind what to do with her. If anyone but Judge Coméliau had been in charge of the case, things would have been different. He would have been prepared to take a risk. With Coméliau, it was dangerous. Not only was he finicky, a stickler for the rules, scared of public opinion and parliamentary criticism, but he had always mistrusted Maigret's methods, which he considered unorthodox. It had come to a head-on collision between them more than once in the past.

Maigret was well aware that the judge had his eye on him, and would not hesitate to hold him responsible if he were to step out of line or if anything, however trivial, should go wrong.

He would have much preferred to leave Madame Calas at the Quai de Valmy until he had a clearer insight into her character, and some clue as to her connection, if any, with the case. He would have posted a man, two men, to watch the bistro. But then Judel had posted a constable outside the tenement in the Faubourg Saint-Martin, and what good had that done? The boy Antoine had got away just the same. And Antoine was just an overgrown kid, with no more sense than a thirteen-year-old. Madame Calas was a different proposition. The newspapers in the kiosks already carried the story of the little café and its possible connection with the crime. At all events, Maigret had seen the name Calas in banner headlines on the front pages. Suppose, for instance, that tomorrow morning the headlines read: '*Madame Calas disappears*'. He could just imagine his reception on arrival at the judge's office.

While pretending to look straight before him, he was watching her out of the corner of his eye. She did not seem to notice. She was sitting up very straight, and there was an air of dignity about her. As they drove through the streets, she looked out of the window with interest and curiosity.

Just now she had admitted that she had not worn her street clothes for at least four years. She had not told him what the occasion was on which she had last worn her black dress. Perhaps it was even longer since she had been in the centre of town, and seen the crowds thronging the Boulevards.

Since, on account of Coméliau, he was not free to do as he liked, he had had to adopt a different procedure.

As they were approaching the Quai des Orfèvres, he spoke for the first time.

'Are you sure you have nothing to tell me?'

She seemed a little taken aback.

'What about?'

'About your husband.'

She gave a slight shrug, and said confidently:

'I didn't kill Calas.'

She called him by his surname, as country women and shop-keepers' wives often call their husbands. But, in her case, it seemed to Maigret to strike a false note.

'Shall I drive up to the entrance?' the taxi-driver turned round to ask.

'If you will.'

The Vicomte was there, at the foot of the great staircase, in company with two other journalists and a number of photographers. They had got wind of what had happened, and it was useless to try and conceal the prisoner.

'One moment, Superintendent.'

Did she imagine that Maigret had tipped them off? She held herself erect, as they took photographs, even following her up the stairs. Presumably Antoine, too, had undergone this ordeal.

They were upstairs in his own domain, and still Maigret had not made up his mind. In the end, he made for the Inspectors' Duty Room. Lucas was not there. He called to Janvier.

'Take her into an empty room for a few minutes and stay with her, will you?'

She could not help hearing. The Superintendent felt oppressed by the mute reproach of her look. Was it reproach, though? Was it not rather disillusionment?

He walked away without another word, and went to his own office, where he found his desk occupied by Lapointe, in shirt-sleeves. Facing the window, Antoine was sitting bolt upright on a chair, very flushed, as though he were feeling the heat.

Between them was the tray sent up from the Brasserie Dauphine. There were dregs of beer in the two glasses, and a couple of half-eaten sandwiches on plates.

As Maigret's glance travelled from the tray to Antoine, he could see that the boy was vexed with himself for having succumbed. No doubt it had been his intention to 'punish' them by going on hunger-strike. They were familiar with self-dramatization in all its forms at the Quai des Orfèvres, and Maigret could not help smiling.

'How is it going?' he asked Lapointe.

Lapointe indicated, by a lift of the eyebrows, that he was getting nowhere.

'Carry on, lads.'

Maigret went across to Coméliau's office. The magistrate was on his way out to lunch.

'Well, have you arrested the pair of them?'

'The young man is in my office. Lapointe is dealing with him.'

'Has he said anything?'

'Even if he knows anything, he won't talk, unless we can prove something against him, and rub his nose in it.'

'Is he a bright lad?'

'That's exactly what he isn't. One can usually make an intelligent person see sense in the end, or at least persuade him to retract self-contradictory statements. An idiot will just go on denying everything, even in the teeth of the evidence.'

'What about the woman?'

'I've left Janvier with her.'

'Will you be dealing with her yourself?'

'Not for the moment. I haven't got enough to go on.'

'When do you expect to be ready?'

'Tonight, maybe. If not, tomorrow or the next day.'

'And in the meantime?'

Maigret's manner was so bland and amiable that Coméliau wondered what he was up to.

'I came to ask your advice.'

'You can't keep her here indefinitely.'

'That's what I think. A woman especially.'

'Wouldn't the best thing be to have her locked up?'

'That's up to you.'

'But you would prefer to let her go?'

'I'm not sure.'

Frowning, Coméliau considered the problem. He was furious. Finally, as though he were throwing down a challenge, he barked:

'Send her to me.'

Why was the Chief Superintendent smiling as he disappeared down the corridor? Was it at the thought of a tête-à-tête between Madame Calas and the exasperated judge?

He did not see her again that afternoon. He merely went into the Inspectors' Duty Room, and said to Torrence:

'Judge Coméliau wants to see Madame Calas. Let Janvier know, will you?'

The Vicomte intercepted him on the stairs. Maigret shook him off firmly, saying:

'Coméliau's the man you want to see. He'll be making a statement to the press, if not immediately then very shortly, you can take my word for it.'

He stumped off to the Brasserie Dauphine, stopping at a bar for an apéritif. It was late. Almost everyone had had lunch. He went to the telephone.

'Is that you?' he said to his wife.

'Aren't you coming home?'

'No.'

'Well, I hope you'll take time off for lunch.'

'I'm at the Brasserie Dauphine. I'm just about to have something.'

'Will you be home for dinner?'

'I may be.'

The brasserie had its own distinctive blend of smells, among which two were dominant: the smell of Pernod around the bar, and that of coq-au-vin, which came in gusts from the kitchen.

Most of the tables in the dining-room were unoccupied, though there were one or two of his colleagues lingering over coffee and Calvados. He hesitated, then went across to the bar and ordered a sandwich. The sun was still shining brilliantly, and the sky was clear, but for a few white clouds scudding across it. A sudden breeze had blown up, scattering the dust in the streets, and moulding the women's dresses against their bodies.

The proprietor, behind the bar, knew Maigret well enough to realize that this was not the time to start a conversation. Maigret was eating absent-mindedly, staring into the street with the mesmerized look of a passenger on board ship watching the monotonous and hypnotic motion of the sea.

'The same again?'

He said yes, probably not knowing what he had been eating, ate his second sandwich, and drank the coffee which was put in front of him before he had even ordered it.

A few minutes later, he was in a taxi, heading for the Quai de Valmy. He stopped it at the corner of the Rue de Récollets, opposite the lock, where three barges were lined up, waiting to go through. In spite of the filthy water whose surface was broken from time to time by unsavoury-looking bubbles, there were a few anglers, tinkering with their floats as usual.

As he walked past *Chez Popaul*, with its yellow façade, the proprietor recognized him, and Maigret could see him, through the window, pointing him out to the people at the bar. All along the road, huge long-distance lorries were parked, bearing the name 'Roulers and Langlois'.

On his way, Maigret passed two or three little shops, of the sort to be found in all densely populated, residential districts of Paris. In front of one a trestle, piled high with fruit and vegetables, took up half the pavement. A few doors farther on, there was a butcher's shop which seemed to be empty, then, almost next door to *Chez Calas*, a grocer's shop, so dark that it was impossible to see into it.

Madame Calas must have had to go out sometimes, if only to do her shopping. These presumably were the shops she went to, wearing her slippers no doubt, and wrapped in the coarse, black, woollen shawl that he had noticed lying about in the café.

Judel must have interviewed the shopkeepers. The local police, being known to them, inspired more confidence than the men from the Quai des Orfèvres.

The door of the bistro was locked. He peered through the glass, but could see no one in the bar. Through the open kitchen door, however, he could see the flickering shadow of someone moving about out of sight. He rapped his knuckles on the glass, but had to knock several times more before Moers appeared, and seeing him there, ran to unlock the door.

'I'm sorry. We were making rather a lot of noise. Have you been waiting long?'

'It doesn't matter.'

It was he who remembered to lock the door again.

'Have you had many interruptions?'

'Most people try the door and then go away, but some are more persistent. They bang on the door, and go through a whole pantomime to be let in.'

Maigret looked round the room, then went behind the bar to see if he could find a blotting pad, like the one advertising an apéritif that he had seen on the table in the bedroom. There were usually several of these blotters dotted about in cafés, and it struck him as odd that here there was not even one, though the place was well supplied with other amenities, including three games of dominoes, four or five bridge cloths, and half-a-dozen packs of cards.

'You carry on,' he said to Moers. 'I'll be back shortly.'

He threaded his way through the cameras set up in the kitchen, and went upstairs, returning with the bottle of ink and the blotting pad.

He sat down at a table in the café, and wrote in block capitals:

'CLOSED UNTIL FURTHER NOTICE.'

He paused after the first word, thinking perhaps of Coméliau closeted at this very minute with Madame Calas.

'Are there any drawing pins anywhere?'

Moers answered from the kitchen:

'On the left-hand side of the shelf under the counter.'

He found them, and went out to pin his notice above the door. Coming back, he felt something brush against his leg, something alive, and looked down to see the ginger cat gazing up at him and mewing.

That was something he had overlooked. If the place was going to be left unoccupied for any length of time, something would have to be done about the cat.

He went into the kitchen, and found some milk in an earthenware jug, and a cracked soup plate.

'Who can I get to look after the cat?'

'Wouldn't a neighbour take it? I noticed a butcher's shop on my way here.'

'I'll see about it later. Anything interesting, so far?'

They were going through the place with a fine toothcomb, sifting through the contents of every drawer, searching every corner. First Moers, examining things under a magnifying glass or, when necessary, his portable microscope, then the photographers, recording everything on film.

'We began with the courtyard, because, with all the junk

there is out there, it seemed the most likely place to choose if one had something to hide.'

'I take it the dustbins have been emptied since Sunday?'

'On Monday morning. All the same, we examined them thoroughly, especially for traces of blood.'

'Nothing?'

'Nothing,' repeated Moers, after a moment's hesitation.

Which meant that he thought he might be on to something, but was not sure.

'What is it?'

'I don't know, sir. It's just an impression that all four of us had. We were discussing it when you arrived.'

'Go on.'

'Well, there's something peculiar about the set up, at least as far as the courtyard and the kitchen are concerned. This isn't the sort of place you'd expect to find spotlessly clean. You only have to open a few drawers to see that everything is stuffed in anyhow, and most of the things are thick with dust.'

Maigret looked about him. He saw what Moers meant, and his eyes brightened with interest.

'Go on.'

'There was a three days' pile of dirty dishes on the draining board, and several saucepans. There's been no washing up done since Sunday. An indication of slovenly habits, you might think. Unless it's just that the woman lets things slide when her husband's away.'

Moers was right. She wouldn't bother to keep the place tidy, or even particularly clean.

'In other words, one would expect to find dirt everywhere, dirt accumulated over a period of a week or ten days. In fact, in some drawers and inaccessible corners, we did find dirt that had been there even longer. In general, however, there was evidence that the place had been recently and extensively scrubbed, and Sambois found a couple of bottles of bleach in the courtyard, one of them empty and, judging from the condition of the label, recently bought.'

'When would you say this spring-cleaning had been done?'

'Three or four days ago. I can't be more definite until I've made one or two tests in the lab, but I should know for certain by the time I come to write my report.'

'Any fingerprints?'

'They bear out our theory. Calas's prints are all over the drawers and cupboard, only on the inside, though.'

'Are you sure?'

'Well, at any rate, they are the same as those of the body in the canal.'

Here, at last, was proof that the dismembered corpse was that of the proprietor of the bistro in the Quai de Valmy.

'What about upstairs?'

'Nothing on the surface, only inside the wardrobe door and so on. Dubois and I have only been up there to look round. We'll make a thorough job of it later. What struck us was that there wasn't a speck of dust on any of the furniture, and that the floor had been thoroughly scrubbed. As for the bed, the sheets were changed recently, probably three or four days ago.'

'Were there dirty sheets in a laundry basket, or anywhere else?'

'I thought of that. No.'

'Was the washing done at home?'

'I couldn't see any evidence of it. No washing machine or copper.'

'So they must have used a laundry?'

'I'm almost sure of it. So unless the van called yesterday or the day before . . .'

'I'd better try and find out the name of the laundry. The neighbours will probably know.'

But before the words were out of Maigret's mouth, Moers had gone over to the dresser and opened one of the drawers.

'Here you are.'

He handed Maigret a bundle of bills, some of which bore the heading: 'Récollets Laundry'. The most recent was ten days old.

Maigret went into the telephone box, dialled the number of the laundry, and asked whether any washing had been collected from the bistro that week.

'We don't call at the Quai de Valmy until Thursday morning,' he was told.

So the last collection of laundry had been on the previous Thursday.

No wonder it had struck Moers as odd. Two people do not live in a house for almost a week without soiling some household linen. Where was it then, and in particular where were the dirty sheets? The ones on the bed had certainly not been there since Thursday.

He was looking thoughtful when he went back to join the others.

'What was it you were saying about the prints?'

'So far, in the kitchen, we have found prints belonging to three people, excluding yourself and Lapointe, whose prints I know by heart. The prints most in evidence are a woman's. I presume they're Madame Calas's.'

'That can easily be checked.'

'Then there are the prints of a man, a young man I should guess. There aren't many of them, and they are the most recent.'

Antoine, presumably, for whom Madame Calas must have got a meal in the kitchen, when he turned up in the middle of the night.

'Finally, there are two prints, half obliterated. Another man's.'

'Any more of Calas's prints inside the drawers?'

'Yes.'

'In other words, it looks as though very recently, on Sunday possibly, someone cleaned the place from top to bottom, but didn't bother with turning out drawers and cupboards?'

They were all thinking of the dismembered corpse, which had been recovered piecemeal from the canal.

The operation could not have been undertaken in the street or on open ground. It must have taken time, and each part had been carefully wrapped in newspaper, and tied with string.

What would any room look like, after being used for such a purpose?

Maigret's remorse at having delivered Madame Calas into the merciless clutches of Judge Coméliau was beginning to subside.

'Have you been down to the cellar?'

'We've been everywhere, just to get our bearings. At a glance, everything looked quite normal down there, but there again, we'll be going over it thoroughly later.'

He left them to get on with their work, and spent some time in the café roaming about, with the ginger cat following him like a shadow. The bottles on the shelf reflected the sun, and there were warm pools of light on the corner of the bar counter. He remembered the great stove in the middle of the room, and wondered whether it had gone out. He looked inside, and saw that there were still a few glowing embers. Mechanically, he stoked it up.

Next, he went behind the counter, studied the bottles, hesitated, and then poured himself a glass of Calvados. The drawer of the till was open. It was empty except for a couple of notes and some small change. The list of drinks and prices was posted near the window to his right.

He consulted it, took some loose change out of his pocket, and dropped the money for the Calvados into the till. Just then he caught sight of a figure beyond the glass door, and gave a guilty start. It was Inspector Judel peering in.

Maigret went to unlock the door.

'I thought you'd probably be here, sir. I rang Headquarters, but they didn't seem to know where you'd gone.'

Judel looked round, and seemed surprised at the absence of Madame Calas.

'Is it true, then, that you have arrested her?'

'She's with Judge Coméliau.'

Judel caught sight of the technicians at work in the kitchen, and jerked his chin in their direction.

'Have they found anything?'

'It's too early to say.'

And it would take too long to explain. Maigret could not face it.

'I'm glad I found you here, because I didn't want to take action without your authority. I think we've found the man with red hair.'

'Where?'

'If my information is correct, practically next door. Unless, that is, he's on night shift this week. He's a storeman with Zenith Transport, the firm . . .'

'Rue de Récollets. I know. Roulers and Langlois.'

'I thought you would wish to interview him yourself.'

Moers called from the kitchen:

'Can you spare a minute, sir?'

Maigret went over to the door at the back of the café. Madame Calas's black shawl was spread out on the kitchen table, and Moers, having already examined it through his magnifying glass, was focusing his microscope.

'Take a look at this.'

'What is it I'm supposed to see?'

'You see the black wool fibres, and those brownish threads like twigs, intertwined with them? Well in fact, those are strands of hemp. It will have to be confirmed by analysis, of course, but I'm quite sure in my own mind. They're almost invisible to the naked eye, and they must have rubbed off on to the shawl from a ball of string.'

'The same string that . . . ?'

Maigret was thinking of the string used to parcel up the remains of the dismembered man.

'I could almost swear to it. I don't imagine Madame Calas very often had occasion to tie up a parcel. There are several kinds of string in one of the drawers, thin white string, red string and twine, but not a scrap of string anything like this.'

'I'm much obliged to you. I take it you'll still be here when I get back?'

'What are you going to do about the cat?'

'I'll take it with me.'

Maigret picked up the cat, which did not seem to mind, and carried it outside. He considered entrusting it to the grocer, but decided that it would probably be better off with the butcher.

'Isn't that Madame Calas's cat?' asked the woman behind the counter, when he went in with it.

'Yes. I wonder if you'd mind looking after it for a few days?'

'So long as it doesn't fight with my own cats.'

'Is Madame Calas a customer of yours?'

'She comes in every morning. Is it really her husband who . . .?' When it came to putting such a grisly question into words, she baulked, and could only look towards the canal.

'It looks like it.'

'What's to become of her?'

And before Maigret could fob her off with an evasive answer, she went on:

'Not everyone would agree with me, I know, and there are plenty of grounds for fault-finding, but I think she's a poor, unhappy creature, and, whatever she's done, she was driven to it.'

A few minutes later, Maigret and Judel were in the Rue de Récollets, waiting for a break in the stream of lorries leaving the depot, to cross over safely to the forecourt of Roulers and Langlois. They went to the glass box on the right, on which the word 'Office' was inscribed in block letters. All round the forecourt were raised platforms, like those in a railway goods yard, piled high with boxes, sacks and crates, which were being loaded on to the lorries. People were charging about, heavy packages were being roughly manhandled. The noise was deafening.

Maigret had his hand on the door knob when he heard Judel's voice behind him:

'Sir!'

The Superintendent turned round to see a red-haired man standing on one of the platforms, with a narrow log-book in one hand and a pencil in the other. He was staring intently at them. He was broad-shouldered, of medium height, and wearing a grey overall. He was fair-skinned with a high colour, and his face, pitted with small-pox scars, had the texture of orange-rind. Porters loaded with freight were filing past him, each in turn calling out a name and number, followed by the name of a town or village, but he did not seem to hear them. His blue eyes were fixed upon Maigret.

'See that he doesn't give us the slip,' said Maigret to Judel.

He went into the office, where the girl at the inquiry desk asked him what she could do for him.

'I'd like to speak to someone in authority.'

There was no need for her to reply. A man with close-cropped, grey hair came forward to find out what he wanted.

'Are you the manager?'

'Joseph Langlois. Haven't I seen you somewhere before?'

No doubt he had seen Maigret's photograph in the papers. The Chief Superintendent introduced himself, and Langlois waited in uneasy silence for him to explain his business.

'Who is that red-haired chap over there?'

'What do you want him for?'

'I don't know yet. Who is he?'

'Dieudonné Pape. He's been with us for over twenty-five years. It would surprise me very much if you'd got anything against him.'

'Is he married?'

'He's been a widower for years. In fact, I believe his wife died only two or three years after their marriage.'

'Does he live alone?'

'I suppose so. His private life is no concern of mine.'

'Have you his address?'

'He lives in the Rue des Ecluses-Saint-Martin, very near here. Do you remember the number, Mademoiselle Berthe?'

'Fifty-six.'

'Is he here all day, every day?'

'He puts in his eight hours, like everyone else, but not always in the daytime. We run a twenty-four-hour service here, and there are lorries loading and unloading all through the night. This means working on a three-shift system, and the rota is changed every week.'

'What shift was he on last week?'

Langlois turned to the girl whom he had addressed as Mademoiselle Berthe.

'Look it up, will you?'

She consulted a ledger.

'The early shift.'

The boss interpreted:

'That means, he came on at six in the morning and was relieved at two in the afternoon.'

'Is the depot open on Sundays as well?'

'Only with a skeleton staff. Two or three men.'

'Was he on duty last Sunday?'

The girl once more consulted her ledger.

'No.'

'What time does he come off duty today?'

'He's on the second shift, so he'll be off at ten tonight.'

'Could you arrange to have him relieved?'

'Can't you tell me what all this is about?'

'I'm afraid that's impossible.'

'Is it serious?'

'It may be very serious.'

'What is he supposed to have done?'

'I can't answer that.'

'Whatever you may think, I can tell you here and now that you're barking up the wrong tree. If all my staff were like him, I shouldn't have anything to worry about.'

He was far from happy. Without telling Maigret where he was going or inviting him to follow, he strode out of the glass-walled office and, skirting the lorries in the forecourt, went over to Dieudonné Pape.

The man stood motionless and expressionless, listening to what his boss had to say, but his eyes never left the glass box opposite. Langlois went to the storage shed, and seemed to be calling to someone inside, and indeed, within seconds, a little old man appeared, wearing an overall like Pape, with a pencil behind his ear. They exchanged a few words, and then the new-comer took the narrow log-book from the red-haired man, who followed the boss round the edge of the forecourt.

Maigret had not moved. The two men came in, and Langlois loudly announced:

'This is a Chief Superintendent from Police Headquarters. He wants a word with you. He thinks you may be able to help him.'

'I have one or two questions to ask you, Monsieur Pape. If you'll be good enough to come with me.'

Dieudonné Pape pointed to his overall.

'Do you mind if I change?'

'I'll come with you.'

Langlois did not see the Superintendent out. Maigret followed the storeman into a sort of corridor that served as a cloakroom. Pape asked no questions. He was in his fifties, and seemed a quiet, reliable sort of man. He put on his hat and coat, and, flanked on the right by Judel and on the left by Maigret, walked to the street.

He seemed surprised that there was no car waiting for them outside, as though he had expected to be taken straight to the Quai des Orfèvres. When, on the corner opposite the yellow façade of *Chez Popaul*, they turned not right towards the town centre, but left, he seemed about to speak, but then apparently thought better of it, and said nothing.

Judel realized that Maigret was making for the Calas bistro. The door was still locked. Maigret rapped on the glass. Moers came to let them in.

'In here, Pape.'

Maigret turned the key.

'You know this place pretty well, don't you?'

The man looked bewildered. If he had been expecting a visit from the police, he had certainly not expected this.

'You may take off your coat. We've kept the fire going. Take a seat, in your usual place if you like. I suppose you have your own favourite chair?'

'I don't understand.'

'You're a regular visitor here, aren't you?'

'I'm a customer, yes.'

Seeing Moers and his man in the kitchen with their cameras, he peered, trying to make out what was going on. He must have been wondering what had happened to Madame Calas.

'A very good customer?'

'A good customer.'

'Were you here on Sunday?'

He had an honest face, with a look in his blue eyes that was both gentle and timid. Maigret was reminded of the way some animals look when a human being speaks sharply to them.

'Sit down.'

He did so, cowering, because he had been ordered to do so.

'I was asking you about Sunday.'

He hesitated before answering: 'I wasn't here.'

'Were you at home all day?'

'I went to see my sister.'

'Does she live in Paris?'

'Nogent-sur-Marne.'

'Is she on the telephone?'

'Nogent three-one-seven. She's married to a builder.'

'Did you see anyone other than your sister?'

'Her husband and children. Then, at about five, the neighbours came in for a game of cards, as usual.'

Maigret made a sign to Judel, who nodded and went to the telephone.

'What time was it when you left Nogent?'

'I caught the eight o'clock bus.'

'You didn't call in here before going home?'

'No.'

'When did you last see Madame Calas?'

'On Saturday.'

'What shift were you on last week?'

'The early shift.'

'So it was after two when you got here?'

'Yes.'

'Was Calas at home?'

Again, he hesitated.

'Not when I came in.'

'But he was, later?'

'I don't remember.'

'Did you stay long in the café?'

'Quite a time.'

'How long would that be?'

'Two hours, at least. I can't say exactly.'

'What did you do?'

'I had a glass of wine, and we talked for a bit.'

'You and the other customers?'

'No, I talked mostly to Aline.'

He flushed as he spoke her name, and hurriedly explained:

'I look upon her as a friend. I've known her for a long time.'

'How long?'

'More than ten years.'

'So you've been coming here every day for ten years?'

'Almost every day.'

'Preferably, when her husband was out?'

This time he did not reply. He hung his head, troubled.

'Are you her lover?'

'Who told you that?'

'Never mind. Are you?'

Instead of replying, he asked anxiously:

'What have you done with her?'

And Maigret told him outright:

'She's with the examining magistrate at the moment.'

'Why?'

'To answer a few questions about her husband's disappearance. Don't you read the papers?'

As Dieudonné Pape sat motionless, lost in thought, Maigret called out:

'Moers! Take his prints, will you?'

The man submitted quietly, appearing more anxious than frightened, and his fingertips, pressed down on to the paper, were steady.

'See if they match.'

'Which ones?'

'The two in the kitchen. The ones you said were partly rubbed out.'

As Moers went out, Dieudonné Pape, gently reproachful, said:

'If all you wanted to know was whether I had been in the kitchen, you only had to ask me. I often go in there.'

'Were you there last Saturday?'

'I made myself a cup of coffee.'

'What do you know about the disappearance of Omer Calas?'

He was still looking very thoughtful, as though he were hesitating on the brink of some momentous decision.

'Didn't you know he'd been murdered, and his dismembered corpse thrown into the canal?'

It was strangely moving. Neither Judel nor Maigret had been prepared for it. Slowly, the man turned towards the Superintendent, and gave him a long, searching look. At last he said, gently reproachful still:

'I have nothing to say.'

Maigret, looking as serious as the man he was questioning, pressed him:

'Did you kill Calas?'

And Dieudonné Pape, shaking his head, repeated:

'I have nothing to say.'

# 7. The Cat

Maigret was finishing his meal, when he became aware of the way his wife was looking at him, with a smile that was maternal and yet, at the same time, a little teasing. At first, pretending not to notice, he bent over his plate, and ate a few more spoonfuls of his custard. But he could not help looking up in the end:

'Have I got a smut on the end of my nose?' he asked grumpily.

'No.'

'Then why are you laughing at me?'

'I'm not laughing. I'm smiling.'

'You're making fun of me. What's so comical about me?'

'There's nothing comical about you, Jules.'

She seldom called him 'Jules'; only when she was feeling protective towards him.

'What is it, then?'

'Do you realize that, during the whole of dinner, you haven't said a single word?'

No, he had not realized it.

'Have you any idea what you've been eating?'

Assuming a fierce expression, he said:

'Sheep's kidneys.'

'And before that?'

'Soup.'

'What kind of soup?'

'I don't know. Vegetable soup, I suppose.'

'Is it because of that woman you've got yourself into such a state?'

Most of the time, and this was a case in point, Madame Maigret knew no more about her husband's work than she read in the newspapers.

'What is it? Don't you believe she killed him?'

He shrugged, as though he were carrying a burden and wished he could shake it off.

'I just don't know.'

'Or that Dieudonné Pape did it with her as his accomplice?'

He was tempted to reply that it was of no consequence. Indeed, as he saw it, this was not the point. What mattered to him was understanding what lay behind the crime. As it was, not only was this not yet clear to him, but the more he knew of the people involved, the more he felt himself to be floundering.

He had come home to dinner instead of staying in his office to work on the case, for the very reason that he needed to get away from it, to return to the jog-trot of everyday life, from which he had hoped to go back with sharpened perceptions to the protagonists in the Quai de Valmy drama. Instead, as his wife had teasingly pointed out, he had sat through dinner without opening his mouth, and continued to think of nothing but Madame Calas and Pape, with the boy, Antoine, thrown in for good measure.

It was unusual for him to feel at this stage that he was still a long way from a solution. But then, in this case, the problems were not amenable to police methods.

Murders in general can be classified under a few broad headings, three or four at most.

The apprehension of a professional murderer is only a matter of routine. When a Corsican gangster strikes down a gangster from Marseilles in a bar in the Rue de Douai, the police have recourse to standard procedures, almost as though tackling a problem in mathematics.

When a couple of misguided youths commit robbery with violence, injuring or killing an old woman in a tobacconist's shop, or a bank clerk, it may be necessary to pursue the assailants through the streets, and here too there is a standard procedure.

As to the *crime passionnel,* nothing could be more straightforward. With murder for financial gain, through inheritance, life assurance or some more devious means, the police know themselves to be on solid ground as soon as they have discovered the motive.

Judge Coméliau, for the present, was inclined to the view that financial gain was the motive in the Calas case, perhaps because he was incapable of accepting the idea that anyone outside his own social sphere, especially people from a neighbourhood like the Quai de Valmy, could have any but the crudest motives.

Given that Dieudonné Pape was the lover of Madame Calas, Dieudonné Pape and Madame Calas must have got rid of the husband, partly because he was an encumbrance, and partly to get hold of his money.

'They have been lovers for ten years or more,' Maigret had objected. 'Why should they have waited all that time?'

The magistrate had brushed this aside. Maybe Calas had recently come into possession of a substantial sum of money. Maybe the lovers had been waiting for a convenient opportunity. Maybe there had been a row between Madame Calas and her husband, and she felt she had put up with enough. Maybe . . .

'And suppose we find that, except for the bistro, which isn't worth much, Calas had nothing?'

'The bistro is something. Dieudonné may have got fed up with his job with Zenith Transport, and decided that he would prefer to end his days dozing in front of the fire in his carpet slippers in a cosy little café of his own.'

Here, Maigret had to concede, was a possibility, even though remote.

'And what about Antoine Cristin?'

The fact was that the judge was now lumbered not with one suspect but two. Cristin too was Madame Calas's lover, and if anyone was likely to be short of money, it was he rather than Pape.

'The other two were just making use of him. You'll find that he was their accomplice, mark my words.'

This, then, was the official view – or at least the view prevailing in one examining magistrate's office – of the Quai de Valmy affair. Meanwhile, until the real facts were brought to light, all three of them were being kept under lock and key.

Maigret was the more disgruntled in that he reproached himself for not having stood up to Coméliau. Owing to indolence perhaps, or cowardice, he had given in without a struggle.

At the outset of his career, he had been warned by his superiors always to be sure of his ground before putting a suspect through a rigorous cross-examination, and experience had confirmed the wisdom of this advice. A properly conducted cross-examination did not consist in drawing a bow at a venture, or hurling accusations at a suspect for hours on end, in the hope that he would break down and confess.

Even a half-wit has a kind of sixth sense, which enables him to recognize at once whether the police are making accusations at random or have solid grounds for suspicion.

Maigret always preferred to bide his time. On occasion, in cases of real difficulty, he had even been willing to take a risk rather than arrest a suspect prematurely.

And he had been proved right every time.

'Contrary to popular belief,' he was fond of saying, 'being arrested can be something of a relief to a suspected person, because, from then on, he does at least know where he stands. He no longer has to ask himself: "Am I under suspicion? Am I being followed? Am I being watched? Is this a trap?" He has been charged. He can now speak in his own defence. And, henceforth, he will be under the protection of the law. As a prisoner, he has his rights, hallowed rights, and nothing will be done to him which is not strictly in accordance with the rules.'

Aline Calas was a case in point. From the moment she had crossed the magistrate's threshold, her lips had, as it were, been sealed. Coméliau had got no more out of her than if she had been the gravel in the hold of the Naud brothers' barge.

'I have nothing to say,' was all she would utter, in her flat, expressionless voice.

And, when he persisted in bombarding her with questions, she retorted:

'You have no right to question me, except in the presence of a lawyer.'

'In that case, kindly tell me the name of your lawyer.'

'I have no lawyer.'

'Here is the membership list of the Paris Bar. You may take your choice.'

'I don't know any of them.'

'Choose a name at random.'

'I have no money.'

There was therefore no choice but for the Court to nominate counsel for her, and that was a slow and cumbersome process.

Late that afternoon, Coméliau had sent for Antoine who, having held out against hours of questioning by Lapointe, saw no reason to be more forthcoming with the magistrate.

'I did not kill Monsieur Calas. I didn't go to the Quai de Valmy on Sunday afternoon. I never handed in a suitcase at the left luggage office of the Gare de l'Est. Either the clerk is lying or he's mistaken.'

All this time, his mother, red-eyed, clutching a crumpled handkerchief, sat waiting in the lobby at Police Headquarters. Lapointe had tried to reason with her, and, after him, Lucas. It was no good. She was determined to wait, she repeated over and over again, until she had seen Chief Superintendent Maigret.

She was a simple soul, who believed, like many of her kind, that it was no good talking to underlings. She must, at all costs, see the man at the top.

The Chief Superintendent could not have seen her then, even if he had wanted to. He was just leaving the bar in the Quai de Valmy, accompanied by Judel and Dieudonné Pape.

'Don't forget to lock up, and bring the key to Headquarters,' he said to Moers.

The three men crossed by the footbridge to the Quai de Jemmapes, only a few yards from the Rue des Ecluses-Saint-Martin, behind the Hospital of Saint-Louis. It was a quiet neighbourhood, more provincial than Parisian in character. Pape was not handcuffed. Maigret judged that he was not the man to make a run for it. His bearing was calm and dignified, not unlike that of Madame Calas herself. He looked sad rather than shocked, and seemed withdrawn, or was it resigned?

He said very little. He had probably never been a talkative man. He answered, when spoken to, as briefly as possible. Sometimes he did not answer at all, but just looked at the Chief Superintendent out of his lavender-blue eyes.

He lived in an old five-storey building, which had an appearance of respectability and modest comfort.

As they passed the lodge, the concierge got up and peered at them through the glass. They did not stop, however, but went up to the second floor. Pape went to a door on the left, and opened it with his key.

There were three rooms in the flat, bedroom, dining-room

and kitchen. There was also a large store-cupboard converted into a bathroom. It surprised Maigret to see that there was a proper fitted bath. The furniture, though not new, was less old-fashioned than that of the house in the Quai de Valmy, and everything was spotlessly clean.

'Do you have a daily woman?' Maigret asked in surprise.

'No.'

'You mean you do your own housework?'

Dieudonné Pape could not help smiling with gratification. He was proud of his home.

'Doesn't the concierge ever give you a hand?'

There was a meat-safe, fairly well stocked with provisions, on the kitchen window-sill.

'Do you do your own cooking as well?'

'Always.'

Above the sideboard in the dining-room hung a large gilt-framed photograph of Madame Calas, so much like those commonly to be seen in the houses of respectable families of modest means that it lent an air of cosy domesticity to the room.

Recalling that not a single photograph had been found at the Calas's, Maigret asked:

'How did you come by it?'

'I took it myself, and had the enlargement made somewhere in the Boulevard Saint-Martin.'

His camera was in the sideboard drawer. On a small table in a corner of the bathroom, there were a number of glass dishes and bowls and several bottles of developing fluid.

'Do you do much photography?'

'Yes. Landscapes and buildings, mostly.'

It was true. Going through the drawers, Maigret found a large number of views of Paris, and a few landscapes. There were a great many of the canal and the Seine. Judging from the striking effects of light and shade in most of the photographs, it must have cost Dieudonné Pape a great deal in time and patience to get the shots he wanted.

'What suit were you wearing when you went to your sister's?'

'The dark blue.'

He had three suits, including the one he was wearing.

'We shall need those,' Maigret said to Judel, 'and the shoes.'

Then, coming upon some soiled underclothes in a wicker basket, he added them to the rest.

He had noticed a canary hopping about in a cage, but it was not until they were leaving the flat that it occurred to him that it would need looking after.

'Can you think of anyone who might be willing to take care of it?'

'The concierge would be only too pleased, I'm sure.'

Maigret fetched the cage, and took it to the lodge. The concierge came to the door before he had time to knock.

'You're surely not taking him away!' she exclaimed in a fury.

She meant her tenant, not the canary. She recognized Judel, who was a local man. Possibly she recognized Maigret, too. She had read the newspapers.

'How dare you treat him like a criminal! He's a good man. You couldn't hope to find a better.'

She was a tiny little thing, of gipsy complexion and sluttish appearance. Her voice was shrill, and she was so enraged that it would not have surprised him if she had sprung at him and tried to scratch his eyes out.

'Would you be willing to look after the canary for a short time?'

She literally snatched the cage out of his hand.

'Just you wait and see what the tenants and all the other people round here will have to say about this! And for a start, Monsieur Dieudonné, we'll all be coming to see you in prison.'

Elderly working-class women quite often hero-worship bachelors and widowers of Dieudonné Pape's type, whose well-ordered way of life they greatly admire. The concierge followed the three men on to the pavement, and stood there sobbing, and waving to Pape.

Maigret turned to Judel:

'Give the clothes and the shoes to Moers. He'll know what to do. And I want the bistro kept under supervision.'

In giving instructions that a watch should be kept on the

bistro, he had nothing particular in mind. It was just to cover himself if anything were to go wrong. Dieudonné Pape waited obediently on the edge of the pavement, and then fell into step with Maigret, as they walked alongside the canal in search of a taxi.

He was silent in the taxi, and Maigret decided not to question him further. He filled his pipe, and held it out to Pape.

'Do you smoke a pipe?'

'No.'

'Cigarette?'

'I don't smoke.'

Maigret did, after all, ask Pape a question, but it had, on the face of it, nothing to do with the death of Calas.

'Don't you drink either?'

'No.'

Here was another anomaly. Maigret could not make it out. Madame Calas was an alcoholic. She had been drinking for years, presumably even longer than she had known Pape.

As a rule, a compulsive drinker cannot endure the companionship of a teetotaller.

The Chief Superintendent had encountered couples very like Madame Calas and Dieudonné Pape before. In every case, as far as he could remember, both the man and the woman drank.

He had been brooding abstractedly over this at dinner, unaware that his wife was watching him. And that was not all, by any means. Among other things, there was Antoine's mother, whom he had found waiting in the lobby at the Quai des Orfèvres. Handing Pape over to Lucas, he had taken her into his office.

He had not forgotten to instruct Lucas to let Coméliau know that Pape had been brought in:

'If he wants to see him, take him there. Otherwise, take him to the cells.'

Pape, poker-faced, had gone with Lucas into an office, while Maigret led the woman away.

'I swear to you, Superintendent, that my son would never do a thing like that. He couldn't hurt a fly. He makes himself out to

274

be a tough guy because it's the done thing at his age. But I know him, you see. He's just a child.'

'I'm sure you're right, madame.'

'In that case, why don't you let him go? I'll keep him indoors from now on, and there won't be any more women, I promise you. That woman is almost as old as I am! She ought to know better than to take up with a lad young enough to be her son. It's shameful! I've known for some time that there was something going on. When I saw he was buying hair-cream, brushing his teeth twice a day, and even using scent, I said to myself . . .'

'Is he your only child?'

'Yes. And I've always taken extra care of him, on account of his father having died of consumption. I did everything I could for him, Superintendent. If only I could see him! If only I could talk to him! Surely, they won't try to stop me? They wouldn't keep a mother from her son, would they?'

There was nothing he could do but pass her on to Coméliau. He knew it was cowardly, but he really had no choice. Presumably she had been kept waiting all over again, up there in the corridor, on a bench. Maigret did not know whether or not the judge had finally granted her an interview.

Moers had got back to the Quai des Orfèvres just before six, and handed Maigret the key of the house in the Quai de Valmy. It was a heavy, old-fashioned key. Maigret put it in his pocket with the key to Pape's flat.

'Did Judel give you the clothes and the shoes?'

'Yes, I've got them in the lab. It's blood we're looking for, I suppose?'

'Mainly, yes, I may want you to look over his flat tomorrow morning.'

'I'll be working here late tonight, after I've had a bite to eat. It's urgent, I imagine?'

It always was urgent. The longer a case dragged on, the colder the scent, and the more time for the criminal to cover his tracks.

'Will you be in tonight?'

'I don't know. In any case, you'd better leave a note on my desk on your way out.'

He got up from the table, filling his pipe, and looked uncertainly at his armchair. Seeing him so restless, Madame Maigret ventured:

'Why not give yourself a rest for one night? Put the case out of your mind. Read a book, or, if you'd rather, take me to the pictures. You'll feel much fresher in the morning.'

With a quizzical look, he said:

'Do you want to see a film?'

'There's quite a good programme at the Moderne.'

She poured his coffee. He could not make up his mind. He felt like taking a coin out of his pocket and tossing for it.

Madame Maigret was careful not to pursue the subject, but sat with him while he slowly sipped his coffee. He paced up and down the dining-room, taking long strides, only pausing from time to time to straighten the carpet.

'No!' he said at last, with finality.

'Will you be going out?'

'Yes.'

He poured himself a small glass of sloe-gin. When he had drunk it, he went to get his overcoat.

'Will you be late home?'

'I'm not sure. Probably not.'

Perhaps because he had a feeling that he was about to take a momentous step, he did not take a taxi or ring the Quai des Orfèvres to order a police car. He walked to the underground station, and boarded a train for Château-Landon. He felt again the disturbing night-time atmosphere of the place, with ghostly figures lurking in the shadows, women loitering on the pavements, and the bluish-green lighting in the bars making them look like fish-tanks in an aquarium.

A man standing a few yards from the door of *Chez Calas* saw Maigret stop, came straight up to him, and shone a torch in his face.

'Oh! Sorry, sir. I didn't recognize you in the dark.'

It was one of Judel's constables.

'Anything to report?'

'Nothing. Or rather there is one thing. I don't know if it's of any significance. About an hour ago, a taxi drove past. It slowed down about fifty yards from here and went by at a crawl, but it didn't stop.'

'Could you see who was in it?'

'A woman. I could see her quite clearly under the gas-lamp. She was young, wearing a grey coat and no hat. Farther down, the taxi gathered speed and turned left into the Rue Louis-Blanc.'

Was it Madame Calas's daughter, Lucette, come to see whether her mother had been released? She must know, from the newspaper reports, that she had been taken to the Quai des Orfèvres, but no further details had been released.

'Do you think she saw you?'

'Very likely. Judel didn't tell me to stay out of sight. Most of the time, I've been walking up and down to keep warm.'

Another possible explanation was that Lucette Calas had intended going into the house, but changed her mind when she saw that it was being watched. If that were the case, what was she after?

He shrugged, took the key out of his pocket, and fitted it into the lock. He had some difficulty in finding the light switch, which he had not had occasion to use until now. A single light came on. The switch for the light at the far end of the room was behind the bar.

Moers and his assistants had put everything back in its proper place before leaving, so that there was no change in the little café, except that it felt colder, because the fire had been allowed to go out.

On his way to the kitchen, Maigret was startled to see something move. He had not heard a sound, and it took him seconds to realize that it was the cat, which he had left with the butcher earlier in the day.

The creature was rubbing its back against his legs now, and Maigret, bending down to stroke it, growled:

'How did you get in?'

It worried him. The back door, leading from the kitchen to the courtyard, was bolted, and the window was closed too. He went upstairs, turned on the light, and found that a window had been left open. There was a lean-to shed, with a corrugated iron roof, in the back yard of the house next door. The cat must have climbed on to it, and taken a flying leap over a gap of more than six feet.

Maigret went back down the stairs. Finding that there was a drop of milk left in the earthenware jug, he poured it out for the cat.

'What now?' he said aloud, as though he were addressing the animal.

They certainly made an odd pair, alone in the empty house.

He had never realized how deserted, even desolate, a bar could look with no one behind the counter and not a customer in sight. Yet this was how the place must have looked every night after everyone had gone, and Monsieur and Madame Calas had put up the shutters and locked the door.

There would be just the two of them, man and wife, with nothing left to do but put out the lights and go upstairs to bed. Madame Calas, after all those nips of brandy, would be in her usual state of vacant torpor.

Did she have to conceal her drinking from her husband? Or did he take an indulgent view of his wife's addiction to the bottle, seeking his own pleasures elsewhere in the afternoons?

Maigret suddenly realized that there was one character in the drama about whom almost nothing was known, the dead man himself. From the outset, he had been to all of them merely a dismembered corpse. It was an odd fact that the Chief Superintendent had often noticed before, that people did not respond in the same way to parts of a body found scattered about as to a whole corpse. They did not feel pity in the same degree, or even revulsion. It was as though the dead person were somehow dehumanized, almost an object of ridicule.

He had never seen Calas's face, even in a photograph, and the head had still not been found, and probably never would be.

The man was of peasant stock, short and squat in build. Every year he went to the vineyards near Poitiers to buy his wine. He wore good suits, and played billiards in the afternoon, somewhere near the Gare de l'Est.

Other than Madame Calas, was there a woman in his life, or more than one perhaps? Could he possibly have been unaware of what went on when he was away from home?

He had accidentally encountered Pape, and, unless he were

crassly insensitive, he must have seen how things stood between Pape and his wife.

The impression they created was not so much of a pair of lovers as of an old married couple, united in a deep and restful contentment, born of mutual understanding, tolerance, and that special tenderness which, in the middle-aged, is often a sign that much has been forgiven and forgotten.

Had he known all this, and accepted it philosophically? Had he turned a blind eye or, alternatively, had there been scenes between him and his wife?

And what about the others who, like Antoine, were in the habit of slinking in to take advantage of Aline Calas's weakness? Had he known about them too, and if so, how had he taken it?

Maigret was back behind the bar, his hand hovering over the bottles on the shelf. In the end he took down a bottle of Calvados, reminding himself that he must leave the money for it. The cat had gone over to the stove, but instead of dozing as it usually did, was restless, bewildered to find no heat coming from it.

Maigret understood the relationship between Madame Calas and Pape. He also understood the role of Antoine and the casual callers.

What he did not understand at all was the relationship between Calas and his wife. How and why had those two ever come together, subsequently married, and lived with one another for so many years? And what about their daughter, in whom neither of them seemed to have taken the slightest interest, and who appeared to have nothing whatever in common with them?

There was nothing to enlighten him, not a single photograph or letter, none of those personal possessions which reveal so much about their owners.

He drained his glass, and grumpily poured himself another drink. Then, with the glass in his hand, he went and sat at the table where he had seen Madame Calas sitting, with that settled air which suggested that it was her usual place.

He tapped out his pipe against his shoe, refilled it and lit it. He stared at the bar counter, the glasses and bottles, and the feeling came over him that he was on the brink of a revelation. Maybe it would not answer all his questions, but it would answer some of them at least.

What kind of a home was this, after all, with its kitchen where no food was served, since the Calas's ate their meals at a table in a corner of the café, and its bedroom which was only used to sleep in?

Whichever way you looked at it, this was their real home, this bar, which was to them what the dining-room or living-room is to an ordinary family.

Was it not the case that on their arrival in Paris, or very soon after, they had settled here in the Quai de Valmy, and remained ever since?

Maigret was smiling now. He was beginning to understand Madame Calas's relationship with her husband, and more than this, to see where Dieudonné Pape came into it.

It was very vague still, and he would not have been able to put it into words. All the same, there was no denying that he had quite shaken off his earlier mood of indecision. He finished his drink, went into the call box, and dialled the number of the Central Police Station.

'Chief Superintendent Maigret speaking. Who is that? Oh! it's you, Joris. How is your new arrival getting on? Yes, I do mean the Calas woman. What's that? Oh! What are you doing about it?'

It was pitiful. Twice she had called for the guard, and each time she had begged him to get her something to drink. She was willing to pay anything, anything at all. Maigret had not foreseen the terrible suffering that this deprivation would cause her.

'No, of course not . . .'

It was not possible for him to suggest to Joris that he should give her a drink in breach of the regulations. Perhaps he himself could take her a bottle in the morning, or have her brought to his office and order something for her there?

'I'd like you to look through her papers for me. She must have been carrying an identity card. I know she comes from somewhere round about Gien, but I can't remember the name of the village.'

He was kept waiting some time.

'What's that? Boissancourt-par-Saint-André. Boissancourt with an "a"? Thanks, old man. Good night! Don't be too hard on her.'

He dialled Directory Inquiries, and gave his name.

'Would you be so kind, Mademoiselle, as to find the directory for Boissancourt-par-Saint-André – between Montargis and Gien – and read out the names of the subscribers.'

'Will you hold on?'

'Yes.'

It did not take long. The supervisor was thrilled at the prospect of collaborating with the celebrated Chief Super-intendent Maigret.

'Shall I begin?'

'Yes.'

'Aillevard, Route des Chênes, occupation not stated.'

'Next.'

'Ancelin, Victor, butcher. Do you want the number?'

'No.'

'Honoré de Boissancourt, Château de Boissancourt.'

'Next.'

'Doctor Camuzet.'

'I'd better have his number.'

'Seventeen.'

'Next.'

'Calas, Robert. Cattle-dealer.'

'Number?'

'Twenty-one.'

'Calas, Julien, Grocer. Number: three.'

'Any other Calas?'

'No. There's a Louchez, occupation not stated, a Piedboeuf, blacksmith, and a Simonin, corn-chandler.'

'Will you please get me the first Calas on the list. I may want the other later.'

He heard the operator talking to the intermediate exchanges, then a voice saying:

'Saint-André Exchange.'

Boissancourt-par-Saint-André 21 was slow to answer. At last, a woman's voice said:

'Who's speaking?'

'Chief Superintendent Maigret here, from Police Headquarters, Paris. Are you Madame Calas? Is your husband at home?'

He was in bed with influenza.

'Have you a relation of the name of Omer Calas?'

'Oh, him! What's happened to him? Is he in trouble?'

'Do you know him?'

'Well, I've never actually met him. I don't come from these parts. I'm from the Haute-Loire district, and he left Boissancourt before my marriage.'

'Is he related to your husband?'

'They're first cousins. His brother is still living here. Julien. He owns the grocer's shop.'

'Can you tell me anything more about him?'

'About Omer? No, I don't know any more. What's more I don't want to.'

She must have hung up, because another voice was asking:

'Shall I get the other number, Superintendent?'

There was less delay this time. A man's voice answered. He was even more uncommunicative.

'I can hear you perfectly well. But what exactly do you want from me?'

'Are you the brother of Omer Calas?'

'I did have a brother called Omer.'

'Is he dead?'

'I haven't the least idea. It's more than twenty years, nearer twenty-five, since I last heard anything of him.'

'A man of the name of Omer Calas has been found murdered in Paris.'

'So I heard just now on the radio.'

'Then you must have heard his description – does it fit your brother?'

'It's impossible to say after all this time.'

'Did you know he was living in Paris?'

'No.'

'Did you know he was married?'

Silence.

'Do you know his wife?'

'Now, look here, there's nothing I can tell you. I was fifteen when my brother left home. I haven't seen him since. He's never written to me. I just don't want to know. I'll tell you who might be able to help you: Maître Canonge.'

'Who is he?'

'The notary.'

When, at last, he got through to Maître Canonge's number, a woman's voice, that of Madame Canonge, exclaimed:

'Well, of all the extraordinary coincidences!'

'I beg your pardon?'

'That you should ring at this moment! How did you know? Just now, when we heard the news on the radio, my husband was in two minds whether to get in touch with you by telephone or go to Paris and see you. In the end, he decided to make the journey, and he caught the eight-twenty-two train, which is due in at the Gare d'Austerlitz shortly after midnight. I'm not certain of the exact time.'

'Where does he usually stay in Paris?'

'Until recently the train went on to the Gare d'Orsay. He always stayed at the Hôtel d'Orsay, and still does.'

'What does your husband look like?'

'Good-looking, tall and well-built, with grey hair. He's wearing a brown suit and overcoat. He has his brief-case with him, and a pigskin suitcase. I still can't imagine what made you think of ringing him!'

Maigret put down the receiver with an involuntary smile. Things were going so well that he considered treating himself to another drink, but thought better of it. There would be plenty of time to have one at the station.

But first, he must ring Madame Maigret, and tell her that he would be late getting home.


## 8. The Notary

Madame Canonge had spoken no more than the truth. Her husband really was a fine-looking man. He was about sixty, and in appearance more like a gentleman farmer than a country lawyer. Maigret, waiting at the end of the platform near the barrier, picked him out at once. He stood head and shoulders above the other passengers on the 12.22 train, and walked with a rapid stride, his pigskin suitcase in one hand and his brief-case in the other. His air of easy assurance suggested that he knew his way about, and was probably a regular traveller on this particular train. Maigret noted all this when he was still quite a long way off.

Added to his height and impressive build, his clothes set him apart from the other passengers. He was almost too well-dressed. To describe his coat as brown was to do less than justice to its colour, which was a soft, subtle chestnut such as Maigret had never seen before, and the cut was masterly.

His fresh complexion was set off by silvery hair, and even in the unflattering light of the station entrance he looked well-groomed, smooth-shaven, the kind of man whom one would expect to complete his toilet with a discreet dab of Eau de Cologne.

When he was within fifty yards of the barrier, he caught sight of Maigret among the other people meeting the train, and frowned as though trying to recapture an elusive memory. He, too, must often have seen the Chief Superintendent's photograph in the newspapers. Even when he was almost level with Maigret, he was still too uncertain to smile or hold out his hand.

It was Maigret who stepped forward to meet him.

'Maître Canonge?'

'Yes. Aren't you Chief Superintendent Maigret?'

He put down his suitcase, and shook Maigret's hand.

'It can't be just a coincidence that I should find you here, surely?'

'No. I telephoned your house earlier this evening. Your wife told me that you were on this train, and would be staying at the Hôtel d'Orsay. I thought it advisable, for security reasons, to meet the train rather than ask for you at your hotel.'

The notary looked puzzled.

'Did you see my advertisement?'

'No.'

'You don't say! The sooner we get out of here the better, don't you think? I suggest we adjourn to my hotel.'

They got into a taxi.

'The reason I'm here is to see you. I intended to ring you first thing tomorrow morning.'

Maigret had been right. There was a faint fragrance of Eau de Cologne blended with the lingering aroma of a good cigar.

'Have you arrested Madame Calas?'

'Judge Coméliau has signed the warrant.'

'What an extraordinary business!'

It was a short journey along the quayside to the Hôtel d'Orsay. The night porter greeted Maître Canonge with the warmth due to a guest of long standing.

'The restaurant is shut, I suppose, Alfred?'

'Yes, sir.'

The notary explained to Maigret, who knew the facts perfectly well:

'Before the war, when the Quai d'Orsay was the terminus for all trains on the Paris–Orléans line, the station restaurant was open all night. It was very convenient. A hotel bedroom isn't the most congenial place in the world. Wouldn't it be better if we talked over a drink somewhere?'

Most of the brasseries in the Boulevard Saint-Germain were closed. They had to walk quite a distance before they found one open.

'What will you have, Superintendent?'

'A beer, thanks.'

'And a liqueur brandy for me, waiter, the best you have.'

Having left their coats and hats in the cloakroom, they sat at the bar. Maigret lit his pipe, and Canonge pierced a cigar with a silver pen-knife.

'I don't suppose you know Saint-André at all?'

'No.'

'It's miles from anywhere, and there are no tourist attractions. If I'm not mistaken, according to the afternoon news-bulletin, the man who was carved up and dropped in the Saint-Martin Canal was none other than that swine Calas.'

'Finger-prints of the dead man were found in the house in the Quai de Valmy.'

'When I first read about the body in the canal, although the newspapers hadn't much to say about it then, I had a kind of intuition, and I toyed with the idea of ringing you even then.'

'Did you know Calas?'

'I knew him in the old days. I knew her better, though – the woman who became his wife, I mean. Cheers! The trouble is, I hardly know where to begin, it's all so involved. Has Aline Calas never mentioned me?'

'No.'

'Do you really think she's mixed up in the murder of her husband?'

'I don't know. The examining magistrate is convinced of it.'

'What has she to say about it?'

'Nothing.'

'Has she confessed?'

'No. She refuses to say anything.'

'To tell you the truth, Chief Superintendent, she's the most extraordinary woman I've ever met in my life. And, make no mistake, we have our fair share of freaks in the country.'

He was clearly accustomed to a respectful audience, and he liked the sound of his own voice. He held his cigar in his elegant fingers in such a way as to show off his gold signet ring to the best advantage.

'I'd better begin at the beginning. You'll never have heard of Honoré de Boissancourt, of course?'

The Superintendent shook his head.

'He is, or rather was until last month, the "lord of the manor". He was a rich man. Besides the Château de Boissancourt, he owned some fifteen farms comprising five thousand acres in all, plus another two and a half thousand acres of woodland and two small lakes. If you are at all familiar with country life, you can visualize it.'

'I was born and brought up in the country.'

And what was more, Maigret's father had been farm-manager on just such an estate.

'Now I think you ought to know something of the ante-cedents of this fellow, Boissancourt. It all began with his grandfather. My father, who, like myself, practised law in

Saint-André, knew him well. He wasn't called Boissancourt, but Dupré, Christophe Dupré, son of a tenant-farmer whose land-lord was the former owner of the château. Christophe began by dealing in cattle, and he was sufficiently ruthless and crooked to amass a considerable fortune in a short time. You know his sort, I daresay.'

To Maigret, it was as though he were re-living his own child-hood, for his village had had its Christophe Dupré, and he too had amassed great wealth, and had a son who was now a sena-tor.

'At one stage, Dupré gambled heavily in wheat, and the gamble paid off. With what he made on the deal, he bought one farm, then a second and a third, and by the end of his life the château and all the land attached to it, which had been the property of a childless widow, had passed into his hands. Chris-tophe had one son and one daughter. The daughter he married off to a cavalry officer. The son, Alain, came into the property on his father's death, and used the name of Dupré de Boissancourt. Gradually the Dupré was dropped and, when he was elected to the County Council, he changed his name by deed poll.'

This, too evoked memories for Maigret.

'Well, so much for the antecedents. Honoré de Boissancourt, the grandson of Christophe Dupré, who was, as it were, the founder of the dynasty, died a month ago.

'He married Emile d'Espissac, daughter of a fine old family who had fallen on hard times. There was one daughter of this marriage. The mother was killed in a riding accident, when the child was only a baby. I knew Emile well. She was a charming woman, though no beauty. She sadly under-rated herself, and allowed her parents to sacrifice her, without protest. It was said that Boissancourt gave the parents a million francs, by way of purchase price one must assume. As the family lawyer, I am in a position to know that the figure was exaggerated, but the fact remains that a substantial sum of money came into the pos-session of the old Comtesse d'Espissac as soon as the marriage contract was signed.'

'What kind of a man was Honoré?'

'I'm coming to that. I was his legal adviser. For years, I have been in the habit of dining at the château once a week, and I've shot over his land ever since I was a boy. In other words, I know him well. In the first place, he had a club foot, which may explain his moody and suspicious disposition. Then again, his family history was known to everyone, and most of the county families refused to have anything to do with him. None of this was exactly calculated to bring out the best in him.

'All his life he was obsessed with the notion that people despised him, and were only out to cheat and rob him. He was for ever on the defensive.

'There is a turret-room in the château, which he used as a kind of office. He spent days on end up there, going through the accounts, not only those of his tenants, but all the household bills as well, down to the last farthing. He made all his corrections in red ink. He would poke his nose into the kitchen at meal-times, to make sure that the servants weren't eating him out of house and home.

'I suppose I owe some loyalty to my client, but it's not as if I were betraying a professional secret. Anyone in Saint-André could tell you as much.'

'Was he the father of Madame Calas?'

'Exactly.'

'What about Omer Calas?'

'He was a servant at the château for four years. His father was a drunken labourer, a real layabout.

'Which brings us to Aline de Boissancourt, as she was twenty-five years ago.'

He signalled to the waiter as he went past the table, and said to Maigret:

'Join me in a brandy this time, won't you? Two *fines champagnes*, waiter.'

Then, turning back to the Superintendent, he went on:

'Needless to say, you couldn't possibly have any inkling of her background, seeing her for the first time in the bistro in the Quai de Valmy.'

This was not altogether the case. Nothing that the notary had told Maigret was any surprise to him.

'Old Doctor Petrelle used sometimes to talk to me about Aline. He's dead now, unfortunately, and Camuzet has taken over the practice. Camuzet never knew her, so he wouldn't be any help. And I myself am not qualified to describe her case in technical terms.

'Even as a very young child, she was different from other little girls. There was something disturbing about her. She never played with other children, or even went to school, because her father insisted on keeping her at home with a governess. Not one governess, actually, but at least a dozen, one after the other, because the child somehow contrived to make their lives a misery.

'Was it that she blamed her father for the fact that her life was so different from other children's? Or was there, as Petrelle believed, much more to it than that? I don't know. It's often said that girls worship their fathers, sometimes to an unnatural degree. I can't speak from my own experience. My wife and I have no children. But is it possible, I wonder, for that kind of adoration to turn into hatred?

'Be that as it may, she seemed prepared to go to any lengths to drive Boissancourt to distraction, and at the age of twelve she was caught setting fire to the château.

'She was always setting fire to things at that time, and she had to be kept under strict supervision.

'And then there was Omer. He was five or six years older than she was, tough and strong, a "likely lad" as country-folk say, and as insolent as you please as soon as the boss's back was turned.'

'Did you know what was going on between them?' inquired Maigret, looking vaguely round the brasserie, which was now almost empty, with the waiters obviously longing for them to go.

'Not at the time. I heard about it later from Petrelle. According to him, when she first began taking an interest in Omer she was only thirteen or fourteen. It's not unusual in girls of that age, but as a rule it's just calf-love, and nothing comes of it.

'Was it any different in her case? Or was it just that Calas, who wasn't the kind to allow his better feelings to stand in his way, was more unscrupulous in taking advantage of her than most men would be in a similar situation?

'Petrelle, at any rate, was convinced that their relationship was suspect right from the start. In his opinion, Aline had only one idea in her head, to defy and wound her father.

'It may be so. I'm not competent to judge. I'm only telling you all this, because it may help you to understand the rest of the story.

'One day, when she was not yet seventeen, she went to see the doctor in secret, and asked him to examine her. He confirmed that she was pregnant.'

'How did she take it?' asked Maigret.

'As Petrelle described it, she gave him a long, hard look, clenched her teeth, and spat out the words:

' *"I'm glad!"*

'I should tell you that Calas, meanwhile, had married the butcher's daughter. She was pregnant too, of course, and their child was born a few weeks earlier.

'He carried on with his job at the château, not being fitted for any other work, and his wife went on living with her parents.

'It was a Sunday when the news burst upon the village that Aline de Boissancourt and Omer Calas had vanished.

'It was learnt from the servants that, the night before, there had been a violent quarrel between the girl and her father. They could hear them in the breakfast-room, going at it hammer and tongs for over two hours.

'Boissancourt, to my certain knowledge, never made any attempt to find his daughter. And, as far as I know, she never communicated with him.

'As for Calas's first wife, she suffered from fits of depression. She dragged on miserably for three years. Then, one day, they found her hanging from a tree in the orchard.'

The waiters by now had stacked most of the chairs on the tables, and one of them was looking fixedly at Maigret and the notary, with a large silver pocket-watch in his hand.

'I think we'd better be going,' suggested Maigret.

Canonge insisted on paying the bill, and they went out into the cool, starlit night. They walked a little way in silence. Then the notary said:

'What about a nightcap, if we can find a place that's still open?'

Each wrapped in his own thoughts, they walked almost the whole length of the Boulevard Raspail, and eventually, in Montparnasse, found a little cabaret which appeared to be open, judging from the bluish light shining into the street, and the muffled sound of music.

'Shall we go in?'

They did not follow the waiter to a table, but sat at the bar. The fat man next to them was more than a little drunk, and was being pestered by a couple of prostitutes.

'The same again?' asked Canonge, taking another cigar out of his pocket.

There were a few couples dancing. Two prostitutes came across from the far end of the room to sit beside them, but they melted away at a sign from Maigret.

'There are still Calases at Boissancourt and Saint-André,' remarked the notary.

'I know. A cattle-dealer and a grocer.'

Canonge sniggered:

'Suppose the cattle-dealer were to grow rich in his turn, and buy the château and the land for himself. What a laugh that would be! One of the Calases is Omer's brother, the other is his cousin. There is a sister as well. She married a policeman in Gien. A month ago, just as he was sitting down to his dinner, Boissancourt dropped dead of a cerebral haemorrhage. I went to see all three of them in the hope that one or other might have news of Omer.'

'Just a moment,' interposed Maigret. 'Didn't Boissancourt disinherit his daughter?'

'Everyone in the district was convinced that he had. There was a good deal of speculation as to who would inherit the property, because, in a village like ours, most people are more or less dependent on the château for their livelihood.'

'You knew, I daresay.'

'No. Boissancourt made several wills over the past few years, all different, but he never deposited any of them with me. He must have torn them up, one after another, because no will was found.'

'Do you mean to say his daughter inherits everything?'

'Automatically.'

'Did you put a notice in the papers?'

'In the usual way, yes. There was no mention of the name Calas, because I couldn't assume that they were married. Not many people read that kind of advertisement. I didn't think anything would come of it.'

His glass was empty, and he was trying to catch the barman's eye. There had evidently been a restaurant car on the train, and he must have had a couple of drinks before reaching Paris, because he was very flushed, and his eyes were unnaturally bright.

'The same again, Superintendent?'

Maigret, too, had perhaps had more to drink than he realized. He did not say no. He was feeling fine, physically and mentally. It seemed to him, in fact, that he had acquired a sixth sense, enabling him to penetrate the mysteries of human personality. Had he really needed the notary to fill in the details? Might he not, in the end, have worked the whole thing out for himself? He had not been far from the truth a few hours earlier. Why else should he have put that call through to Saint-André?

Even if he had not dotted the 'i's and crossed the 't's, the impression he had formed of Madame Calas had been very close to the truth. All that he had been told confirmed this.

'She's taken to drink,' he murmured, prompted by a sudden urge to have his say.

'I know. I've seen her.'

'When? Last week?'

This was another thing that he had worked out for himself. But Canonge would not let him get a word in edgeways. In Saint-André, no doubt, he was used to holding forth without interruption.

'All in good time, Superintendent. I'm a lawyer, remember, and in legal circles matters are dealt with in their correct order.'

He guffawed at this. A prostitute sitting at the bar leaned across the unoccupied stool between them, and said:

'Won't you buy me a drink?'

'If you like, my dear, but you mustn't interrupt. You might not think it, but we are discussing weighty matters.'

Mightily pleased with himself, he turned to Maigret.

292

'Well, now, for three weeks there was no answer to my advertisement, other than a couple of letters from cranks. And, in the end, it wasn't the advertisement that led me to Aline. It was pure chance. I had sent one of my guns to a firm in Paris for repair, and last week I got it back. It came through a firm of long-distance road-hauliers. I happened to be at home when it was delivered. In fact, I opened the door myself.'

'And the hauliers were Zenith Transport?'

'How did you know? You're quite right. I invited the driver in for a drink, as one does in the country. Calas's grocery store is just opposite my house in the Place de l'Eglise. We can see it from our front windows. The man was having his drink, when he suddenly noticed the name over the shop:

' "Would that be the same family as the people who have the bistro in the Quai de Valmy?" he said, half to himself.

' "Is there a Calas in the Quai de Valmy?"

' "It's a funny little place. I'd never set foot in it until last week, when I was taken there by one of the storemen." '

Maigret was willing to take a bet that this storeman was none other than Dieudonné Pape.

'He didn't happen to say whether the storeman had red hair?'

'No. I asked him if he knew the Christian name of this Calas. He thought about it for a bit, and then said he vaguely remembered seeing it over the door. I asked, could it be Omer, and he said yes, that was it.

'At any rate, next day, I left by train for Paris.'

'The night train?'

'No. The morning train.'

'What time did you go to the Quai de Valmy?'

'In the afternoon, shortly after three. The bistro is rather dark, and when I first saw the woman, I didn't recognize her. I asked her if she was Madame Calas, and she said she was. Then I asked her Christian name. I got the impression that she was half-drunk. She does drink, doesn't she?'

So did he drink, not as she did, but enough, all the same, to make his eyes water now.

Maigret had an uneasy feeling that they had just had their glasses refilled, but he was not too sure. The woman had moved to the stool next to the notary, and was lolling against him with her arm through his. For all the expression on her face, she might not have heard a word of what he had said.

' "Your maiden name was Aline de Boissancourt, is that right?" I said.

'She didn't deny it. She just sat there by the stove, staring at me, I remember, with a great ginger cat on her lap.

'I went on:

' "Your father is dead. Did you know?"

'She shook her head – no sign of surprise or emotion.

' "As his lawyer, I am administering his estate. Your father left no will, which means that the château, the land, and all he possessed comes to you."

' "How did you get my address?" she asked.

' "From a lorry driver who happened to have been in here for a drink."

' "Does anyone else know?"

' "I don't think so."

'She got up and went into the kitchen.'

To take a swig from the brandy bottle, of course!

'When she got back, I could see that she had come to some decision.

' "I don't want anything to do with the money," she said, as though it was of no importance. "I suppose I can refuse it if I want to?"

' "Everyone has the right to renounce an inheritance. Nevertheless . . ."

' "Nevertheless what?"

' "I would advise you to think it over. Don't make up your mind here and now."

' "I've thought it over. I refuse it. I imagine I also have the right to insist that you keep your knowledge of my whereabouts to yourself."

'All the while she was talking she kept peering nervously into the street, as though she were afraid someone would come in, her husband, perhaps. That's what I thought, at any rate.

'I protested, as I was bound to do. I told her I hadn't been able to trace anyone else with a claim to the Boissancourt estate.

294

' "Perhaps it would be best for me to come back another time and talk things over again," I suggested.

' "No. Don't come back. Omer mustn't see you here. I won't have it."

'She was terrified.

' "It would be the end of everything!" she said.

' "Don't you think you ought to consult your husband?"

' "He's the very last person!"

'I tried to argue with her, but it was no use. As I was leaving, I gave her my card. I said that, if she changed her mind in the next few weeks, she could telephone or write, and let me know.

'A customer came in then. He looked to me very much at home in the place.'

'Red-haired, with a pock-marked face?'

'Yes, I believe he was!'

'What happened?'

'Nothing. She slipped my card into her apron pocket, and saw me to the door.'

'What day was it?'

'Last Thursday.'

'Did you see her again?'

'No. But I saw her husband.'

'In Paris?'

'In my study at home, in Saint-André.'

'When?'

'On Saturday morning. He arrived in Saint-André on Friday afternoon or evening. He first called at the house on Friday evening, about eight. I was out, playing bridge at the doctor's house. The maid told him to come back next day.'

'Did you recognize him?'

'Yes, although he had put on weight. He must have spent the night at the village inn, where, of course, he learnt that Boissancourt was dead. He must also have heard that his wife was heir to the property. He lost no time in throwing his weight about. He insisted that, as her husband, he was entitled to claim the inheritance in the name of his wife. As there was no marriage contract in this case, the joint-estate system applies.'

'So that, in fact, neither could act without the consent of the other?'

'That's what I told him.'

'Did you get the impression that he had discussed the matter with his wife?'

'No. He didn't even know that she had renounced the inheritance. He seemed to think she'd got hold of it behind his back. I won't go into the details of the interview, it would take too long. What must have happened is that he found my card. His wife probably left it lying around. Very likely, she forgot I'd given it to her. And what possible business would a lawyer from Saint-André have in the Quai de Valmy unless it were to do with the de Boissancourt estate?

'It was only while he was talking to me that the truth gradually dawned on him. He was furious. I should be hearing from him, he said, and stormed out, slamming the door.'

'And you never saw him again?'

'I never heard another word from him. All this happened on Saturday morning. He went by bus to Montargis, and caught the train to Paris from there.'

'What train would that be, do you think?'

'Probably the one that gets in to the Gare d'Austerlitz just after three.'

Which meant that he must have arrived home at about four, or earlier if he took a taxi.

The notary went on:

'When I read about the dismembered body of a man recovered from the Saint-Martin Canal, right there next to the Quai de Valmy, it shook me, I can tell you. I couldn't help being struck by the coincidence. As I said just now, I was in two minds about ringing you, but I didn't want to look a fool.

'It was when I heard the name Calas mentioned in the news this afternoon, that I made up my mind to come and see you.'

'Can I have another?' asked the girl next to him, pointing to her empty glass.

'By all means, my dear. Well, what do you think, Superintendent?'

At the word 'Superintendent', the prostitute started, and let go of the notary's arm.

'It doesn't surprise me,' murmured Maigret, who was beginning to feel drowsy.

'Come now, don't tell me you've ever known anything like it! Things like that only happen in the country, and I must say that even I . . .'

Maigret was no longer listening. He was thinking of Aline Calas, whom he was now able to see in the round. He could even imagine her as a little girl.

He was not surprised or shocked. He would have found it hard to explain what he felt about her, especially to a man like Judge Coméliau. On that score, he had no illusions; he would be listened to tomorrow with amazement and disbelief.

Coméliau would protest:

'They killed him just the same, she and that lover of hers.'

Omer Calas was dead, and he certainly had not taken his own life. Someone, therefore, had struck him down, and subsequently dismembered his body.

Maigret could almost hear Coméliau's acid voice:

'What can you call that but cold-blooded? You can't imagine, surely, that it was a *crime passionnel*? No, Maigret, you've talked me round before, but this time . . .'

Canonge held up his brimming glass:

'Cheers!'

'Cheers!'

'You look very thoughtful.'

'I was thinking about Aline Calas.'

'Do you think she took up with Omer just to spite her father?'

Even to the notary, even under the influence of several glasses of brandy, he could not put his feelings into words. For a start, he would have to convince him that everything she had done, even as a kid in the Château de Boissancourt, had been a kind of protest.

Doctor Petrelle, no doubt, would have been able to express it better than he could. To begin with, the fire-raising; then, her sexual relations with Calas, and finally, her flight with him in circumstances where most other girls would have procured an abortion.

This too, perhaps, had been an act of defiance? Or revulsion?

Maigret had often tried to persuade others, men of wide experience among them, that, of all people, those most likely to come to grief, to seek self-abasement and degradation with morbid fervour, almost with relish, are the idealists.

To no avail. Coméliau would protest:

'If you said she was born wicked, you'd be nearer the truth.'

At the bistro in the Quai de Valmy, she had taken to drink. This, too, was in character. And so was the fact that she had remained there without ever attempting to escape, allowing the atmosphere of the place to engulf her.

Maigret believed he understood Omer too. It was the dream of so many country lads to earn enough money in domestic service, or as a chauffeur, to become the proprietor of a bistro in Paris. For Omer the dream had come true.

It was a life of ease, lounging behind the bar, shuffling down to the cellar, going to Poitiers once or twice a year to buy wine, spending every afternoon playing billiards or *belote* in a brasserie near the Gare de l'Est.

There had not been time to investigate his private life. Maigret intended to go into that in a day or so, if only to satisfy his own curiosity. He was convinced that, when he was not indulging his passion for billiards, Omer had had a succession of shameless affairs with local servant girls and shop assistants.

Had he counted on inheriting the Boissancourt property? It seemed unlikely. He must have believed, like everyone else, that de Boissancourt had disinherited his daughter.

It had taken the notary's visiting-card to arouse his hopes.

'I've had to do with all sorts in my time,' Canonge was saying, 'but what I simply can't understand – indeed, I confess it's quite beyond me, my dear fellow – is how, with a fortune landing in her lap out of the blue, she could bring herself to turn it down.'

To Maigret, however, it seemed perfectly natural. As she was now, what possible use could she make of the money? Go and live with Omer in the Château de Boissancourt? Set up house with him in Paris or elsewhere – the Côte d'Azur for instance – in the style of rich landowners?

She had chosen to stay where she was, in the place where she felt safe, like an animal in its lair.

Day had followed day, all alike, punctuated by swigs of brandy behind the kitchen door, and Dieudonné Pape's company in the afternoons.

He too had become a habit, more than a habit, perhaps, because he knew. She need not feel ashamed with him. They could sit side by side in companionable silence, warming themselves by the stove.

'Do you believe she killed him?'

'I don't think so.'

'It was her lover, then?'

'It looks like it.'

The musicians were putting away their instruments. Even this place had to close some time. They found themselves outside in the street, walking in the direction of Saint-Germain-des-Prés.

'How far have you to go?'

'Boulevard Richard-Lenoir.'

'I'll walk with you part of the way. What could have induced the lover to kill Omer? Was he hoping to persuade her to change her mind about the estate?'

They were both unsteady on their feet, but quite up to roaming the streets of Paris, which they had to themselves but for an occasional passing taxi.

'I don't think so.'

He would have to take a different tone tomorrow with Coméliau. At the moment, he suddenly realized, he was sounding quite maudlin.

'Why did he kill him?'

'What would you say was the first thing Omer would do when he got back from Saint-André?'

'I don't know – lose his temper, I imagine, and order his wife to accept the inheritance.'

Maigret saw again the table in the bedroom, the bottle of ink, the blotter, and the three sheets of blank paper.

'That would be in character, wouldn't it?'

'No doubt about it.'

'Supposing Omer ordered her to write a letter to that effect, and she still refused?'

'He'd have thrashed her. He was that sort – a real peasant.'

'He did resort to violence on occasion.'

'I think I can see what you're getting at.'

'He doesn't bother to change when he gets home. This is Saturday afternoon, round about four. He marches Aline up to her room, orders her to write the letter, uses threatening language, and starts knocking her about.'

'At which point the lover shows up?'

'It's the most likely explanation. Dieudonné Pape knows his way about the house. He hears the row in the bedroom, and rushes upstairs to Aline's rescue.'

'And does the husband in!' finished the notary, with a snigger.

'He kills him, either deliberately or accidentally, by hitting him on the head with something heavy.'

'After which, he chops him up!'

Canonge, who was distinctly merry, roared with mirth.

'It's killing!' he exclaimed. 'I can't help laughing at the thought of anyone carving up Omer. I mean to say, if you'd known Omer . . .'

Far from sobering him up, the fresh air, on top of all he had drunk, had gone to his head.

'Do you mind walking back with me part of the way?'

They faced about, walked a little way, and then turned back again.

'He's a strange man,' murmured Maigret, with a sigh.

'Who? Omer?'

'No, Pape.'

'Don't tell me he's called Pape, on top of everything else!'

'Not just Pape, Dieudonné Pape.'

'Killing!'

'He's the mildest man I've ever met.'

'No doubt, that's why he chopped up poor old Omer!'

It was perfectly true. It took a man like him, self-sufficient, patient, meticulous, to remove all traces of the crime. Not even Moers and his men, for all their cameras and apparatus, had been able to find any proof that a murder had been committed in the house in the Quai de Valmy.

Had Aline Calas helped him scrub the place from top to

bottom? Was it she who had got rid of the sheets and clothes, with their tell-tale stains?

Pape had slipped up in one particular: he had not foreseen that Maigret would be puzzled by the absence of dirty linen in the house, and would make inquiries of the laundry. But how could he have foreseen that?

How had those two imagined their future? Had they believed that weeks, possibly months, would elapse before any part of Calas's body was found in the canal, and that by then, it would be beyond identification? That was what would have happened if the Naud brothers' barge had not been weighed down by several extra tons of gravel, and scraped the bottom of the canal.

Where was the head? In the river? In a drain? Maigret would probably know the answer in a day or two. Sooner or later, he was convinced, he would know everything there was to know, but it was of merely academic interest to him. What mattered to him was the tragedy and the three protagonists who had enacted it, and he was certain he was right about them.

Aline and Pape, he felt sure, once all traces of the murder had been eradicated, had looked forward to a new life, not very different from the old.

For a while, things would have gone on as before, with Pape coming into the little café every afternoon for a couple of hours. Gradually, he would have spent more and more time there. In time, the neighbours and customers would have forgotten Omer Calas, and Pape would have moved in altogether.

Would Aline have continued to receive Antoine Cristin and the other men in the kitchen?

It was possible. On this subject, Maigret did not care to speculate. He felt out of his depth.

'It really is good night, this time!'

'Can I ring you tomorrow at your hotel? There are various formalities to be gone through.'

'No need to ring me. I shall be in your office at nine.'

*

Needless to say, the notary was not in Maigret's office at nine, and Maigret had forgotten that he had said he would be. The Superintendent was not feeling any too bright. This morning, in response to a touch on the shoulder from his wife, he had opened his eyes, with a feeling of guilt, to see his coffee already poured out for him on the bedside table.

She was smiling at him in an odd sort of way, with unusual maternal tenderness.

'How are you feeling?'

He could not remember when he had last woken up with such a dreadful headache, always a sign that he had had a lot to drink. It was most unusual for him to come home tipsy. The annoying thing was that he had not even been aware that he was drinking too much. It had crept up on him, with glass after glass after glass of brandy.

'Can you remember all the things you were telling me about Aline Calas in the night?'

He preferred to forget them, having an uneasy feeling that he had grown more and more maudlin.

'You talked almost like a man in love. If I were a jealous woman . . .'

He flushed, and was at some pains to reassure her.

'I was only joking. Are you going to say all those things to Coméliau?'

So he had unburdened himself about Coméliau as well, had he? Talking to Coméliau was, in fact, the next item on the agenda – in somewhat different terms, needless to say!

'Any news, Lapointe?'

'Nothing, sir.'

'I want you to get an advertisement into the afternoon edition of the newspapers. Say that the police wish to interview the young man who was given the job of depositing a suitcase at the Gare de l'Est last Sunday.'

'Wasn't that Antoine?'

'I'm sure it wasn't. Pape would realize that it had much better be done by a stranger.'

'The clerk says . . .'

'He saw a young man of about Antoine's age, wearing a leather jerkin. That could be said of any number of young men in the district.'

'Have you any proof that Pape did it?'

'He'll confess.'

'Are you going to interrogate them?'

'At this stage of the proceedings, I imagine, Coméliau will be wanting to do it himself.'

It was all plain sailing now, a mere matter of putting questions at random, or 'fishing', as they called it among themselves.

Anyway, Maigret was not at all sure that he wanted to be the one to drive Aline Calas and Dieudonné Pape to the wall. Both would hold out to the bitter end, until it was no longer possible to remain silent.

He spent nearly an hour upstairs in the judge's office. He rang Maître Canonge from there. The telephone bell must have woken the notary with a start.

'Who's there?' he asked, in such comical bewilderment that Maigret smiled.

'Chief Superintendent Maigret.'

'What time is it?'

'Half-past ten. Judge Coméliau, the Examining Magistrate in charge of the case, wishes to see you in his office as soon as possible.'

'Tell him I'll be right over. Shall I bring the Boissancourt papers?'

'If you will.'

'I hope I didn't keep you up too late?'

The notary must have got to bed even later. God knows where he landed up after I left him, thought Maigret, hearing a woman's sleepy voice asking: 'What's the time?'

Maigret returned to his office.

'Is he going to interrogate them?' Lapointe asked.

'Yes.'

'Starting with the woman?'

'I advised him to start with Pape.'

'Is he more likely to crack?'

'Yes. Especially as he was the one who struck Calas down, or so I believe.'

'Are you going out?'

'There's something I want to clear up at the Hôtel-Dieu.'

It was a small point. Lucette Calas was in the operating theatre. He had to wait until the operation was over.

'I take it you've read the papers, and know of your father's death and your mother's arrest?'

'Sooner or later, something of the kind was bound to happen.'

'When you last went to see her, was it to ask for money?'

'No.'

'What was it, then?'

'To tell her that, as soon as he gets his divorce, Professor Lavaud and I are going to be married. He might have asked to meet my parents, and I wanted them to be presentable.'

'Don't you know that Boissancourt is dead?'

'Who's he?'

She was genuinely bewildered.

'Your grandfather.'

Casually, as though the matter were of no importance, he said:

'Unless she's convicted of murder, your mother is heir to a château, eighteen farms, and goodness only knows how many millions.'

'Are you quite sure?'

'Go and see Maître Canonge, the notary, at the Hôtel d'Orsay. He's administering the estate.'

'Will he be there all day?'

'I imagine so.'

She did not ask what was to become of her mother. As he walked away, he gave a little shrug.

Maigret had no lunch that day. He was not hungry, but a couple of glasses of beer settled his stomach more or less. He shut himself up in his office the whole afternoon. In front of him on the desk lay the keys to the bistro in the Quai de Valmy and Pape's flat. He polished off a mass of boring administrative work, which he usually hated. Today, he seemed to be taking a perverse delight in it.

Each time the telephone rang he snatched it off the hook with uncharacteristic eagerness, but it was after five o'clock before he heard the voice of Coméliau on the line.

'Maigret?'

'Yes.'

There was a note of triumph in the magistrate's voice.

'I have had them formally charged and arrested.'

'All three of them?'

'No. I've released the boy Antoine.'

'Have the other two confessed?'

'Yes.'

'Everything?'

'Everything that *we* suspected. I decided that it would be a good idea to start with the man. I outlined my reconstruction of the crime. He had no choice but to confess.'

'What about the woman?'

'Pape repeated his admissions in her presence. It was impossible for her to deny the truth of his statement.'

'Did she have anything else to say?'

'No. She just asked me, as she was leaving, whether you had seen to her cat.'

'What did you say?'

'That you had better things to do.'

Maigret could never forgive Judge Coméliau for that.

# The Man with the Little Dog

Translated from the French by
Jean Stewart

# The Blue Notebook

*Wednesday, November 13*

Was last Sunday's incident as important as I am tempted to think? It is really an exaggeration to call it an incident. A chance encounter in the street. An unknown couple amidst the Parisian crowd. An exchange of glances.

And yet, for the last three days, my mood has changed and decisions which I had thought final no longer appear so. I am not being dramatic or sentimental about these. I am just a very ordinary man amongst the countless millions of others who are alive, who are being born or dying as I write these words, not to mention the hundreds of thousands of millions of beings more or less like myself who have walked on the same earth, breathed the same air, known the same seasonal rhythm.

I should have written in any case, but before last Sunday I only envisaged a letter, a longish one perhaps, addressed to nobody, since I have nobody to send it to.

Yesterday, however, after closing the shop, I went to the stationer's over the way to buy a school notebook. They showed me blue ones and pink ones, green ones and yellow ones. I chose the blue one, probably because of a patch of clear sky which on Sunday, at about three in the afternoon, appeared above the Panthéon.

My letter would have had a very different tone from what I now propose to write. It's true that I cannot tell what tone I shall adopt tomorrow or the following days, or in the weeks to come, for I foresee that it may take a long time and that I shall allow myself some respite.

On Saturday I had made up my mind. I was calm and serene, and I watched the end coming with a kind of irony, such as my letter would have disclosed. I wondered how to begin.

'I, Félix Allard, forty-eight years of age, living at no. 3, Rue des Arquebusiers, Paris IIIe . . .'

Should I have added, as though making my will, 'being of sound mind and body . . .'?

Of sound mind, I could vouch for that, although I don't know what goes on in other people's heads and therefore find it hard to decide what is normal and what isn't.

That was the tone I propose to adopt. A light tone, with touches of sarcasm here and there, a sarcasm directed against myself and nobody else.

Now that I am slowly blackening the first page of this note-book I am as calm as usual, vaguely smiling, but I couldn't swear that I am not feeling faintly disturbed.

Because of the couple I met on Sunday? It may be.

The best thing is to give a brief account of that day. I woke up as usual at six o'clock, and it was still dark. As usual, again, as soon as I stretched out my arm towards the switch, Bib, lying at my feet on the bedcover, started creeping up alongside my body, wagging his scrap of a tail, and when he reached my face, gave two or three joyful yelps.

Then we had a little chat. . . . Of course Bib doesn't really talk, any more than other dogs do. I do the talking and he answers in his own way. For instance when he's had enough of my early-morning effusions, he tugs at the sheet to uncover me and then springs down on to the floor.

I slipped on my dressing-gown, thrust my bare feet into slippers and went towards the door. All these movements, performed every day at the same time, mean nothing at all, I know, to most people; they take on the gravity of a ritual for a man living alone with his dog, particularly if that man, after weighing the pros and cons and after mature consideration, has decided to pack it up.

In the course of my life I have known other habits, other traditions. I have been woken in the mornings by the smell of coffee and my mother's footsteps in the kitchen, later by an alarm-clock, then by the movements and the animal warmth of a woman's body. A baby's whimperings have roused me from sleep, or the patter of a child's footsteps in the next room. Later

310

on. . . . If I begin like that I shall never end, and I might give a misleading impression of harbouring regrets.

I have no regrets at all, about anything, I hasten to assert. And no shame either, although I know this declaration will shock some people. It's true, for the time being. I don't try to foresee what I shall think tomorrow, even less to what conclusion I shall come, if I ever do. The conclusion, after all, is irremediably the same for all of us.

Bib ran in front of me down the staircase, an old unpolished staircase of rough, greyish wood. We had just two floors in the empty house to go down, one behind the other. The enamel plaque on the first floor belongs to a small firm making artificial flowers, which, on working days, employs about fifteen girls. On the ground floor there is a wholesale merchant of waterproofs, manufactured somewhere around Montluçon.

There is no concierge, and no other tenants. Bib and I are alone every evening from six o'clock onwards, and all day Sunday.

I unhooked the chain, drew the bolt and turned the big key which never leaves its lock. Bib slipped through as soon as the opening was wide enough to allow him to pass, and rushed across to the corner of the house opposite, where he lifted his leg.

It had been raining. Not heavily, just enough to darken the pavements and bring a breath of dampness to this tail-end of night. I stood in the doorway lighting a cigarette, for I always carry cigarettes and matches in my dressing-gown pocket. I wasn't thinking of anything. I looked at nothing in particular. Bib and I, the street-lamp at the corner, the two other lamps along the street, we were all part of the setting.

The Rue des Arquebusiers is not like other streets. For one thing, it forms a right angle. Starting from the Boulevard Beaumarchais, it stops suddenly after a hundred yards or so, just where I live, and then goes on in a different direction towards the Rue Saint-Claude, where it comes up against other buildings.

In the Rue Saint-Claude there is a church, the church of the Holy Sacrament, whose bells I can hear. Or rather I ought to be able to hear them, but I no longer notice them.

Bib ran backwards and forwards from one pavement to another, sniffed at the dustbins and the tyres of stationary lorries, while, leaving the door ajar, I went slowly back into the flat, where I opened the shutters before lighting the gas stove and putting the water on to boil.

Things had gone on just like this for nearly eight years – the first two years without Bib – and I did that morning what I had done several thousands of times. I went into the minute *cabinet de toilette* which, like the rest of the flat, had a sloping ceiling, and, looking into the mirror which reflected the electric light bulb, I ran the comb through my hair.

It has grown thin, and turned a colour to which I cannot get accustomed. It is no longer fair, but neither is it that silvery, silky grey that you see on some men of my age. It is the drab, dirty colour of old sacking, and the white skin of my scalp shows through.

I wonder if other people, as they grow old, experience the same surprise when they look at themselves in the mirror each morning. I see myself looking so ugly that I sometimes make a face at myself. Perhaps I have never been handsome; yet for a good part of my life I was able to meet my reflection without repugnance, if not with secret satisfaction. I was tall and muscular, broadly built like all the Allards.

Have I grown shorter? It looks like it. My big body has become flabby, my face is puffy and unhealthy, and my eyes remind me of a cod's eyes on a fishmonger's slab.

Don't misunderstand me. I am not complaining, I'm not lamenting my fate, and it would be quite wrong to think I have any regrets about the past.

I am simply clear-sighted, capable of looking at myself in the glass and saying out loud:

'You're ugly!'

And sometimes adding:

'You make me sick!'

Without bitterness, without nostalgia, and above all without resentment towards fate or towards man's lot. I accepted things a long time ago. The word *accepted* is not quite correct, since I couldn't have done anything else. I don't care for *resigned myself*. Let's just say that I learnt to put up with things.

I heard the water boiling in the kitchen and I poured it gradually into the filter of the coffee-pot. I had no need to go as far as the window to know that Bib, after sniffing at everything there was to sniff at, would come solemnly back to the house and push open the door with his head. After which, according to a habit formed right at the beginning, he would close it in the same way before coming up the stairs.

Bib was wet and had his rainy-morning smell. He threw a glance at the old stove in which, since it was a mild morning, I had not lit a fire.

In autumn and winter I light one every Sunday, for we spend most of the day at home. During the week I light it only when I get back from work, about half-past six in the evening. Did Bib know that it was Sunday, and was he wondering why today was different from other Sundays?

In fact, we ought both of us to have been living our last Sunday on earth. I had made up my mind to this several weeks ago. To begin with I had not fixed a date. I had merely said to myself, when I looked at myself in the glass in the morning, particularly while I was shaving:

'When I've reached a certain point . . .'

In my mind, this meant two or three months' respite. I know the point beyond which I don't want to go, but it is difficult to determine it exactly. I ran the risk, by postponing it continually, of finding myself one day without strength or will-power.

I really thought, that Sunday morning, that I had found out everything about myself.

'Today, Bib old boy, we're going for a long walk . . .'

I like to pretend that he understands whatever I say and answers in his own way, with his tail or his ears or his eyes. The word *walk* is one that he knows well, and he displayed his joy by scampering about excitedly.

I laid the table, for I still put on a tablecloth at mealtimes, wishing to keep up a certain decorum, or rather a minimum of self-respect.

The sky was already showing pale through the skylight. Almost all the buildings along the street are warehouses or workrooms and very few people live in them. And all of these must have been having a long lie-in that morning. Even in the

Boulevard Beaumarchais there were not many cars about, for it wasn't much of a day for going into the country.

It was a typical early November Sunday, I would have said a typical All Saints' Day if All Saints' had not been over. It reminded me of the cemetery at Puteaux and the smell of chrysanthemums, then, years later, of walks in the Bois de Boulogne with a child's hand in mine.

The paper wrapping of the *biscottes* crackled and Bib waited for his. The saccharine tablets made tiny bubbles in my coffee.

Everything was as mild and drab as the sky, and in thousands of kitchens people were eating breakfast like myself and wondering what to do with their Sunday.

I knew what I should do with mine. I had to begin with my routine, which meant doing the housework. Nobody else saw to that. I might have afforded a charwoman for an hour or two every morning. My budget could have stood it, particularly since chance has made me almost wealthy.

Is it my reluctance to see a stranger touch my belongings and intrude, however slightly, into my life with Bib, that prevents me? I'm not sure of that. I must admit that I find a secret satisfaction in cleaning out my burrow, as I call it, in keeping it neat and tidy, making my bed, sweeping up the dust, washing the red tiles of the kitchen and toilet with soapy water and, once a week, polishing the floor of my bedroom and my den. Besides which, the wax polish smells good.

Bib follows me with his eyes, moves out when I reach the corner where he is sitting and, from time to time, I speak to him, saying whatever comes into my head. Like so many other people I have spent part of my life with a woman. There were vacant hours in the evening and on Sunday mornings, particularly before the children were born, not unlike this one, and when I try to recall what we could have said to one another I find nothing very different from my conversation with Bib.

After a certain time Bib, too, demands attention. My wife used to ask me suddenly, as if waking from a dream: 'What are you thinking about?'

I don't believe I ever once told her the truth. Not because I felt impelled to lie, or to hide anything whatsoever from her, but because my answer would have meant nothing. The most commonplace of thoughts are connected with others, with ancient or recent memories, with fleeting impressions, and I have never felt capable of defining my state of mind at a moment's notice.

I am no more capable of doing so today, when I try to reconstitute that Sunday, recent though it was. It's now Wednesday evening. I am at home, in that 'den' whose floor I was polishing on Sunday morning when Bib decided it was time for a walk. I have been writing for a long time, under the lamp which glows warm on my forehead, and the ash-tray is full of fag-ends, the air thick with drifting smoke. Bib, lying in my armchair, is pretending to sleep, peeping through half-closed eyes when he thinks I'm not watching him.

To be accurate, to be truthful, one would have to remember every minute and convey its colour, its rhythm, its sounds and smells.

Day had dawned, soft and grey as I had expected, rather the colour of a tombstone – without any macabre implications.

I remember seeing Bib go up to his basket of toys and choose a red rubber ball his favourite, pick it up daintily between his teeth and then deposit it at my feet.

'Let's play!'

We played for a quarter of an hour while, along the pavements, people were hurrying to Mass.

\*

I have just paused for another quarter of an hour, again on account of Bib. He is surprised at being left in my armchair for so long and I wonder if he has ever seen me writing, for it's years since I wrote letters to anyone. I feel he is watching me, trying to define what has altered about my attitude.

My den is a narrow room and has a sloping ceiling with a skylight in it. Some people might call it an attic. Wherever possible I had put up deal shelves and, little by little, filled them with books. A table serves as a desk and, apart from the old leather armchair I bought at a public auction, the only piece of furniture is a straw-bottomed chair.

A quarter of an hour ago Bib jumped down on to the floor

with a hesitant air, then, after rubbing against my legs, lay down on his back and shammed dead. This is a favourite trick of his, which, like his other tricks, he already knew before we met, for I taught him nothing, not even how to shut the ground floor door. When he lies down like that, his whole body stiff, it means: 'You're forgetting me . . .'

Or else: 'I'm feeling lonely. . . . Pay attention to me . . .'

As soon as I got up he went to fetch one of his balls – he prefers them to rubber bones – and put it into my hand. After which he went into a corner and stood facing the wall.

Then I had to go into the bedroom and look for some more or less unfamiliar place to hide the ball. There aren't so many of them, and he knows them all. That's why he would rather play this game outside, on the embankment or in a square like the Place des Vosges, where there's always some small boy who volunteers to hide the object.

'Ready, Bib!'

I had not originally envisaged living with a dog. I spent several months in my flat without any company at all. One evening I brought back a goldfish in a bowl, and for a number of weeks I enjoyed its silent presence. I would even speak to it, too, as to a human being.

When I found it dead I bought another, then a third. I followed the salesman's directions scrupulously. None the less my goldfish always died after a few weeks and that was when the idea of buying a dog occurred to me.

I took an afternoon's leave and went to the strays' home at Gennevilliers. I had not decided what sort of dog I wanted and I might just as easily have come back with a cat.

When I went in, some of the animals jumped excitedly in their cages. Others ignored me. Most of the dogs were fairly big, some of them huge; there was even a Great Dane, which seemed to have a glass eye.

When my glance fell on a kind of miniature poodle, not very pure-bred, with a grey coat speckled with brown and squat little legs, I saw him stretch out on his back as he has just been doing, close his eyes, stiffen all his limbs and lie there like a corpse.

'That's a trick,' explained the keeper. 'He's trying to attract your attention . . .'

'Is he young?'

'I couldn't tell you his exact age, but to judge by his teeth he must be at least three, maybe four. I shouldn't be surprised if he'd been a circus dog . . .'

He snapped his fingers.

'Somersault for the gentleman, Clebs!'

The animal hesitated, watched me for a moment, then made up its mind to perform a perilous backward leap.

'Do you call him Clebs?'

'I call them all that because I don't know their names.'

A few minutes later the little stumpy-legged dog was running along behind me on the end of a string. But when we tried to get on to the bus I was informed that animals are not allowed to travel either on buses or on the Métro unless they are carried in a basket or bag.

I sought out a hardware shop. I found one of those holdalls of brown canvas such as footballers use to carry their gear and, borrowing a pair of scissors in the shop, I made two holes in it. Later, I was to cover these with coarse muslin.

I did not want to call him Clebs like all the others. That evening, in my bedroom, where he had already sniffed every nook and cranny, I tried out a number of names on him, watching his reactions, and when I came to Bib he seemed satisfied. Had it once been his name, or did he like the sound of it?

Next day I took him along to the bookshop and Madame Annelet, who still got about with the aid of a stick, exclaimed:

'Whatever's that?'

'It's a dog. He's called Bib.'

'Have you just picked him up on the pavement?'

'I went to choose him at the strays' home.'

'Do you mean to keep him?'

'Yes.'

'And to bring him here every day?'

'Certainly.'

She dared not protest, because she couldn't do without me. She was not fond of animals, that was obvious. She looked me up and down several times as if to take my measure and compare my frame with that of the tiny creature.

'It's funny . . .' she sighed at last.

'What's funny?'

'That you should have chosen such a very small dog, an old lady's dog. A psychoanalyst would probably find it interesting.'

She is an old woman herself and I, in spite of appearances, am a man of forty-eight. No matter. They got used to one another. Bib soon understood that any familiarity would be unwelcome and that he must keep his distance. At Madame Annelet's, in the Boulevard Beaumarchais, he never ventures on to an armchair, still less on to the bed where the old lady spends a good part of her days. Nor does he ever lick her hand, nor bring her his ball to beg her to play with him.

On other Sundays I take my time preparing my lunch, and I eat it by the window before going to spend the afternoon outside. Bib noticed with surprise that I did not light the fire, that I shaved and dressed earlier than usual and that, at eleven o'clock, I told him:

'Get your bag, Bib!'

He went to fetch the brown holdall on the bottom shelf of one of the bookshelves, while I put on my overcoat and took my hat.

If I mention chiefly material details, it is through a sort of reserve or, if you like, through a loathing for sentimentality. Actually this Sunday walk was going to be a last pilgrimage for me; let's call it a farewell walk, and say no more about it.

I was not unhappy, nor nostalgic. I saw things as they really are, as though through the indifferent eye of a camera, and I saw myself, too, without pity or indulgence.

I was living through my last Sunday, and that was all. My father, my mother, my grandfathers and grandmothers before them, had had their last Sunday, their last Monday, their last Tuesday and so on. That didn't make saints or martyrs or heroes out of them. As for choosing one's date, there was nothing very original about that either.

If I had previously decided to write a letter 'to whom it may concern', it was by way of a gesture, a joke, as though to cock a snook, and also in order to unburden myself of a few trifles weighing on my mind.

Are they still weighing on my mind? I doubt it. That's all over. I'm a quiet, respectable person. For Madame Annelet my employer, I am Félix, her assistant, on whom she can depend, a man whose past history she knows and whom she cannot get used to considering as she does the rest of mankind.

For other people, for the local tradesmen and the proprietors of the small restaurants where I sometimes treat myself to a meal, I am Monsieur Félix, who lives at no. 3, Rue des Arquebusiers.

And for those who see me go past at a regular time accompanied by Bib, I suppose I am 'the man with the little dog'.

For a certain woman, I am an ex-husband; for a certain boy and girl, I am a father whom they scarcely remember, and about whom they're not supposed to talk.

And for three other people, a woman and two other children, I am not quite sure.

The plane trees on the Boulevard Beaumarchais had lost half their leaves. There were still few cars about and we walked, Bib and I, as far as the Place de la République, where we waited for the bus. When it stopped, I merely had to open the bag and Bib jumped into it, just as the conductor was about to tell me that dogs are not allowed. It amuses us to wait like this for the last moment, and there are nearly always some passengers who burst out laughing at the conductor's discomfiture . . .

My original idea, on the previous day, had been to devote this last walk to Puteaux, where I was born and where I lived up to the age of twenty-five, in the Rue Bourgeoise, close to the church of Sainte-Clothilde, which is being pulled down. Was this rather too much like a pilgrimage? I had been back to Puteaux several times. I had also been past the flat where I lived later at Neuilly, in the Boulevard Richard-Wallace, and had felt no sort of emotion. Is it absurd or romantic to say that I was seeking myself there, in vain?

Although I am not really old, there have been several Félix Allards who appear to me increasingly distinct from one another, and some of whom I can no longer recognize or understand.

We got off the bus at the Place Blanche and I let Bib off the leash. Along the Rue Lepic I wished it had not been Sunday, so that I could have enjoyed once more the barrows lined up beside the pavements, and the smell of fruit and vegetables and of the meat on the butchers' stalls, and all the bustle of the market. Almost alone on the pavement, we walked towards the Place du Tertre, pausing whenever I felt out of breath.

Why my final goal was the Place du Tertre I am unable to explain, for the place is not connected with any of my memories, any significant episode in my life.

In spite of the lateness of the season there were tables laid outside, covered with check cloths, and a brazier here and there, and many people were already eating, provincial Frenchmen for the most part or foreigners whom artists were inviting to have their portraits painted.

'You'll take lunch?' asked a sullen waiter.

'Yes.'

'An apéritif?'

I said yes again, and ordered a Suze. For years I have drunk neither wine nor spirits, on doctor's orders. Why have I kept up this régime lately, since I had already made my decision? Out of habit? Or an indirect method of self-punishment? Punishment for what? This morning I put saccharine in my coffee, instead of sugar. And yet I have sugar at home for Bib, who doesn't have to follow a diet.

The choice of a Suze was more unexpected. I uttered the name without thinking, although I had only drunk it once in my life, in a village whose name I don't know, somewhere between Le Mans and Angers.

I was in the car with Anne-Marie, a convertible, the first I had ever bought. I couldn't say whether or not Anne-Marie was already pregnant with Philippe. The inn, just outside the village, looked like a small farm, with a huge sow in a sty and an orchard full of white poultry.

It was very hot. The low, dark dining-room looked out both on to the road and on to the orchard, where I can clearly picture the bean-poles. The proprietress was a pot-bellied woman in black.

'Can we have lunch?'

'Why shouldn't you be able to?'

'What can you give us?'

'To begin with, some pâté with radishes and cucumber. If you like I can open a tin of sardines. Then I can fry you a chicken . . .'

'That's fine.'

'What'll you drink in the meantime?'

Throughout one's life, one speaks and listens to sentences like that, and a few of them remain, for no reason, imprinted in some corner of one's brain.

On the dresser I could see bottles, most of which bore labels that were unfamiliar to me. Two men sat with their elbows propped on a table, a cattle-dealer and a farmer as I guessed, in front of glasses filled with a strange-coloured liquid.

'What are they drinking?'

'Suze.'

'Give me a Suze too. What about you, Anne-Marie?'

'I'll try it . . .'

It suddenly seems queer to me to think that I called her *tu*, that we slept in the same bed for years, that two children, who will soon be grown up, have in their veins my blood mingled with hers.

Things seem important at the time, and one fine day you realize that they have left no trace. I cannot visualize her face or figure in that inn parlour, which seemed dark in contrast with the sunlight that beat so fiercely on the countryside.

We must have talked. What did we say? All that comes back to my mind's eye is the *patronne*, in the courtyard, amongst her ruffled poultry, catching one and then another, finally choosing a chicken that seemed ready for eating and then chopping off its head on a block of wood. That was the chicken we were to eat, and a girl of about twelve began plucking it, in the midday sunshine.

Why did I order a Suze at the café in the Place du Tertre? I did not ask for chicken to follow, but calf's liver with fried potatoes, and I drank half a bottle of rosé wine. Bib, who had eaten before we left, got his share of meat notwithstanding, and as people were watching him from the neighbouring tables he could not resist showing off with a few dangerous somersaults.

I had known the Place du Tertre and the Sacré-Coeur twenty

or thirty years ago. If I'm not mistaken, my parents brought me here with my sister to 'see the panorama of Paris' while I was still at the primary school, that's to say before I was eleven years old. I fancy there had been fewer tables on the terraces, fewer painters with easels set up along the pavements, but I had not come in search of memories.

I wanted to spend my last Sunday in a different way from other Sundays, and the idea suddenly occurred to me of looking down on Paris from the heights once again. The open-air lunch had followed as a matter of course. That was all. Bib wondered why I didn't play at hiding his ball; I had no wish to make a public spectacle of myself.

'Off we go, Bib . . .'

I stopped for a longish while in front of the Sacré-Coeur, amidst the crowd of people going up and down the steps, the vendors of souvenirs and postcards, the nuns, priests or curates in charge of crocodiles of Sundayschool children.

I stared at the roofs which, under the blank sky, showed every hue of grey and rose-red. I caught myself automatically picking out monuments, like a tourist, and I thought of all the generations which. . . . No, that was morbid! It was better to look at people's faces, almost all of them devoid of expression. Men, women, children, scraps of remarks almost always the same: 'Pity there's no sun. . . . We could have seen as far as . . .'

Bib was bewildered at being taken for a walk so different from our usual Sunday walks, with long pauses on park benches and gravel walks in which to scratch. He could see nothing but legs moving, feet and yet more feet through which he had to thread his way carefully.

'This way, Bib . . .'

He thought for one moment that I wanted to go up in the funicular, and immediately looked at his bag, ready to jump into it. I chose rather to go down the steps which other people were slowly climbing, most of them pausing to take a breather every few steps.

Then I saw them. Dozens of couples must have crossed my path, but none had caught my attention. These two were climbing up very slowly and, seen from above, seemed even more misshapen than they really were. The man's head struck me first, a monstrously huge head, a hydrocephalous head such as one usually sees only in medical text-books, the skin as smooth and pink as a baby's, without a single hair, the eyes protuberant and lashless.

Below a fairly normal trunk could be seen two tiny legs, so flabby that they seemed to be dangling, and he hobbled along with the aid of two sticks, flinging one foot to the right and the other to the left as if each step he had climbed was a great achievement. Every time, he bent his head as he took off, and raised it afterwards to measure the distance he still had to cover, as though the white mass of the Sacré-Coeur up there was the ultimate goal of his whole existence.

He may have been thirty, or forty, or more. He was something outside the world of normal men. It was no doubt a miracle that he was still alive. As for his companion, a swarthy little woman with irregular features, she wore surgical boots one of which, with iron fittings, came up to her knee.

She kept one hand on the man's arm, less to support him, clearly, than out of affection, and each time he got up another step she smiled at him to thank or congratulate him for his effort.

Our meeting was actually very brief, although I slowed down my pace and stopped long enough to light a cigarette.

I was going down, and they were coming up. When I was within three or four yards of them they paused for a moment and the man with the monstrous head and flabby legs asked his companion, in an amazingly light and gentle voice: 'You're not too tired?'

He smiled at her with a smile such as I have never seen on any human face, a smile that reminded me of the ecstatic faces of certain Buddhas, and she exclaimed eagerly: 'Oh no . . . I'm all right.'

They looked at one another as though to rejoice in each other's happiness, and then they looked up at the Sacré-Coeur. Finally they turned round, hand in hand, to look at Paris, which lay stretched at their feet and which, at that instant, belonged to them.

I went past them without making a sound and when I turned

to look back, a few steps lower down, they had resumed their slow, laborious upward climb, with the cripple's fingers still holding the arm of the man with the lashless eyes.

## Friday, November 15

Yesterday I wrote nothing, and this left me vexed and disappointed. I am under no obligation to write in this blue notebook every evening. I have not made a formal vow to do so. I thought myself free, released. The fact remains that when you've done something once at a set time, it becomes a habit, almost a duty.

When I had finished the washing up and adjusted the key of the stove for the evening, Bib looked at me questioningly; as soon as I moved towards my den, he ran in there ahead of me and, without waiting for my leave, leapt on to my armchair.

I had indeed intended to write. I sat down at my table, I pushed the lamp to the right distance and opened the notebook at the page where I had left off on Wednesday. Did I make a mistake in re-reading the closing paragraphs?

'*You're not too tired?*'

'*Oh, no, I am all right!*'

Then I sat there motionless, brooding over these two remarks. I won't go so far as to say that they had lost their magic. I could still visualize those faces, those eyes. It was the worse handicapped of the two, an almost monstrous creature, who could only by a miracle have got beyond the stage of childhood, who was worrying about his companion.

What disturbed me and fostered my ill-humour was the feeling of having been taken in. True, they had spoken these two sentences. They had stared up at the white shape of the Sacré-Coeur as if they had been waiting for this moment all their lives. Then, hand in hand, they had turned round to look at the panorama of Paris.

But what happened after? What had happened before? What happened every day and at every other hour? They had not taken the funicular, on purpose, perhaps out of self-mortification, perhaps on account of a vow, or simply to test their own strength. Right up to the moment when I had lost them from sight, they had won.

A few minutes, a few hours of exaltation. Each of them, surely, transferred his personal joy to the other; each of them felt the need of a witness.

Pen in hand, I pondered sullenly, but found nothing to write. I would not, I could not accept the existence of such communion. At all costs I wanted to reduce it to a commonplace phenomenon and I searched my memory for moments of the same quality.

What will have become of the man with the baby's skin by the time he is forty-eight, my own age! He'll probably be dead. But where? And how? With what thoughts in that huge head, what expression in those lashless eyes?

Will the woman with the orthopaedic boots be there still, holding his hand? And what will be her fate, eventually? A little lame old woman in a garret like mine, only poorer, with a geranium in a window-box for company instead of a dog, which she couldn't afford to feed?

The answer was vital to me, so much so that I regretted having gone to the Place du Tertre for my lunch on Sunday. The letter would have been so much easier to write! I should have left without regrets, I swear it. And even more, without remorse. I felt sure of myself, and at peace. I know what I'm talking about, for I have had more time than most people to think, to set my thoughts in order.

As it happens, I have always mistrusted the 'moment', striving as far as possible to imagine 'what comes after'. Isn't that what matters? Since Sunday I have been less sure of it. I have been wondering. Bib is not alone in staring at me with surprise, almost with disapproval.

Yesterday, Thursday, Madame Annelet called me several times up to the mezzanine, as she often does. As soon as I have served a customer and she hears the click of the till, she rings for me. From the floor above, she hears everything. A spiral iron staircase connects the shop with her room, where she spends more and more of her time in bed.

'What was that, Félix?'

'A lady bought a second-hand book.'

We don't sell many new books. We should never have room to keep all the latest publications. The shop sign reads:

C. ANNELET
*New and second-hand books*
*Libraries bought*

The 'C' stands for Clarisse, but she dislikes the name as much as I dislike my own, Félix. My grandfather, after all, was called Désiré, and my grandmother Joséphine.

One morning, eight years ago, when I had been back in Paris on my own for four or five weeks, searching for a livelihood, I passed in front of the narrow window of the bookshop. On the pavement, in a tray like those on the quaysides, lay piles of old books. A card had been stuck on the pane with gummed paper:

'*Young assistant needed. Apply within.*'

It was the height of summer, and the sun cast the shadow of the plane-trees over the houses. A girl went past in a light dress and I looked after her, wondering at the self-confidence with which she walked. A lock of hair curling by her cheek, her handbag clasped against her round breast, patches of sweat under her armpits, she walked towards the Place de la Bastille and the world was hers to command.

I don't know where she was off to, or what became of her. I pushed open the door, setting a bell jangling, and stood for a longish time in the semi-darkness, in front of the counter. Finally I gave a gentle cough, and then, at the back of the shop, a flower-patterned curtain was pushed aside, and a woman emerged from an inner room; she was elderly, with listless movements and with a hypnotic intensity in her gaze.

The slightest details are still vivid in my memory. To begin with, that curtain with its red flowers and green leaves on a yellow ground, hardly the sort of thing you'd expect to find in a bookshop. Through the opening I could make out a narrow room, with a window overlooking the courtyard where a carpenter was busy in front of his workshop, mending the legs of a chair.

He is still mending them. Then there were shelves full of books, and more books piled up on the floor. What struck me particularly was the chaise-longue upholstered in an aggressive purple as unexpected as the flowers on the curtain.

As for the woman who stood there staring at me with her black eyes, she reminded me of a fortune-teller rather than of a bookseller.

I could not imagine her among other people in the street, although at that period she still walked about without too much difficulty. Now, eight years later, I still don't know her age. She might be a woman of sixty, prematurely aged; or, what's more likely, a woman of seventy-five or eighty who has decided to keep on living and finds the energy to do so.

'I've just read your notice about the job . . .'

She looked me over from head to foot, and did not seem to find it funny that a mature man should apply for a young assistant's job. She seldom seems surprised at anything. She watches, she tries to understand, and I realized at once that she must have experienced a great deal, known many men in every sort of situation, and that without leaving her stuffy back room she has never lost contact with life.

'The young assistant, eh?'

'I am only forty years old.'

'Some of those years must have seemed like two.'

I must have turned pale. I was sure she had guessed and, resolved not to tell her any secrets, I prepared to go back on to the Boulevard.

With the indifference of a clairvoyante, she went on:

'Your affairs are no concern of mine. What I need to know is whether you know anything about books.'

She had not said about literature, but about books, and this detail struck me.

'I studied literature for three years at the Sorbonne.'

It was her turn to be somewhat taken aback.

'Have you been a teacher?'

'No. I gave up my studies when my father died, to carry on his business.'

Most people glance at you surreptitiously or, if they look you in the face, try to assume a neutral or smiling expression. This woman, on the contrary, was scrutinizing me quite shamelessly, and I quickly guessed that she was trying to recall something.

'Have you put on a lot of weight lately?'

It was true, and I nodded.

'You used to live in Neuilly, and your name is . . .'

'Félix Allard.'

There was a pause, and her lips twitched in a faint smile.

'Life's a funny business! Come in this way . . .'

She drew back the curtain a little further to let me in to the untidy room behind the shop. On a small table there were tea things, with some half-eaten toast, and a pile of magazines.

'Clear the chair. Put the books on the floor, anywhere. I can't stand up for long at a time. That's why I put the notice in the window.'

She was wearing a dark dress, much too wide for her thin shoulders. Her chest and arms were painfully thin, too. By contrast, her body from the hips down had thickened and, when she lay stretched out on the chaise-longue, my glance fell involuntarily on her swollen legs, which she hurriedly covered with a red plaid rug.

'Have you gone back to your family?'

'No.'

'In that case I suppose you're living by yourself? Have you found anywhere to live?'

'Just round the corner in the Rue des Arquebusiers, over the waterproof merchant's.'

'How d'you feel about things?'

'I feel nothing at all.'

'You haven't seen anybody again?'

'I've not tried to see anyone at all.'

This was only partly true. It all depends on what is meant by seeing again. She lit a cigarette.

'Do you smoke?'

And, pushing the packet of Gitanes towards me:

'You're sure nobody sent you here?'

'I told you, I saw the notice as I went past.'

'Are you going to try and make a fresh start?'

'It depends on what you mean by that.'

'A job . . . friends . . . perhaps a woman?'

'In that case, I should not be here.'

It's hard to explain. We were exchanging commonplace and

superficial remarks, but we had none the less made contact at a deeper level. It was not what we said that mattered and, if she was curious about me, I was equally so about her. The difference was that I was applying for a post which she could offer or refuse me and that I had not the right to ask any questions.

Now, particularly since I had been admitted into that dubious back room, I felt an almost passionate desire to be accepted.

'If I understand rightly, you've grown used to living alone and you can put up with it?'

'That's about it.'

'It's the same with me.'

She told me no more about herself that first day.

'I suppose I needn't be afraid of your pinching money out of the till?'

I merely smiled. Words were becoming increasingly pregnant with meaning.

'I suppose, moreover, that you haven't any great expenses. If I'm asking for a young assistant, it's because I can't offer much salary . . .'

She was miserly, as I immediately guessed, but not from love of money: miserly as people are, who have been short of money, who know what it means to have empty pockets and nothing to eat, those who have experienced real poverty and are permanently haunted by the dread of relapsing into it.

'You realize that most employers would ask for references?'

'It's usual.'

'And that, on learning your past, they'd be reluctant to engage you?'

'I've discovered that by experience.'

'You seem to be a calm sort of person. I hate noise, and sudden fits of high spirits or bad temper. I don't expect to be loved and I don't care whether you like me or not. People don't interest me and my ideal would be to live in an aquarium . . .'

About everything she said, as about the expression in her eyes, there was something simple, frank and yet aggressive. Actually, I now wonder whether it was not her use of the word aquarium that morning that made me buy my first goldfish.

'One more question. How d'you manage about women?'

And as I could not find an answer right away:

'I've got a maid of about twenty, a plump, saucy little piece, who can't see a man, even a man like yourself, without making up to him. What happens at night in her room on the sixth floor doesn't concern me. One of these days she'll get herself pregnant like the rest of them, or else she'll leave me to try her luck on the Boulevard Sébastopol. What I won't stand for is cuddling and whispering behind doors. Have you got a mistress?'

'No.'

'D'you pick up girls in the street?'

I merely shrugged vaguely, embarrassed by the way she played the father-confessor.

'I think we shall be able to get on together. There's no harm in trying, let's say for a fortnight. When would you like to start?'

'Whenever you like.'

'Right away, then.'

This was eight years ago. As she had foreseen, we got quite used to one another. I'd take my oath that, lying on her chaise-longue or in her bed, she can guess what I'm doing and even what I'm thinking.

I sometimes secretly call her 'the witch'. For the last few months she has seldom left her room, for her legs and feet have swollen even more. She can no longer wear shoes or even slippers and she almost has to be carried about.

As I have mentioned, her bedroom is immediately over the bookshop; it is just as untidy as the room at the back of the shop. The whole flat is low-ceilinged, squeezed in as it were between the ground floor and the first floor. It includes a bathroom no bigger than my own, a kitchen, a dining-room and another room used as a junkroom.

She has had five or six maids in succession, mainly Breton girls, like the present one, Renée, who is only seventeen. On the grounds that Renée has not enough to do Madame Annelet lends her, or rather hires her out, for a couple of hours each afternoon to the third floor tenants, a young couple, the husband working at the Ministry of Justice and the wife as sec‹ retary to a lawyer.

Even in her bed, with an old bed jacket over her bony shoulders, Madame Annelet still exudes astonishing energy. It is five years since she drove away her last doctor in a rage, shout‹ ing after him the filthiest words I have ever heard uttered by a woman.

Since then she has followed no regimen, refused all medicine; she eats with a greedy, almost voracious appetite, and always keeps food within reach, toast, cakes, sweets, preserved fruit, anything that's edible.

She must have books too, and she buries herself in them eagerly as soon as she has finished the weekly magazines, which she reads from cover to cover.

'Isn't there anything else down there about Marie Antoinette?'

She knows all the queens of old, particularly their love stories, and it's getting quite hard to find books to satisfy her.

'I don't care a rap for war and politics, Félix. What I want ...'

I know what she wants. I search the shelves. I come back with a pile of musty-smelling old books. The outside of the shop is painted blue, like this notebook. I have the key to it.

It's my job, at eight o'clock every morning, to fetch the crank from under the counter and go out again to raise the shutter. Renée then helps me to take out the second-hand box and stand it on the pavement, steadying it with a couple of wedges.

Bib has his place under the counter, close to the crank, and he has learnt not to stir when a customer comes in with a dog. He merely sniffs the other animal's tracks when it has gone.

A bell has been fixed up to summon me to the mezzanine. Madame Annelet sees me emerge through the floor, head and shoulders and trunk, and sometimes I don't need to go right up. I tell her:

'A young man wanted a pocket edition of Montaigne ...'

She listens, not always bothering to look at me, and goes on reading and nibbling something or other.

\*

As I expected, Bib has just interrupted me. He wants to play. He has already formed the habit of breaking into my writing sessions. The first time, I showed some irritation, as I used to in the old days with my children when they demanded the same story every evening. Now I have plenty of time, for my system requires less and less sleep.

I believe I wrote that whereas Madame Annelet knows pretty well everything about me, I know very little about her. Once, however, a few months after my first visit to the bookshop on the Boulevard Beaumarchais, she told me something about her life.

'I've been married too, Félix . . .'

Her voice was hard, her eyes devoid of feeling.

'At thirty-five, just imagine, I took it into my head to marry a man called Emile Doyen, who was forty, about your age, and looked as quiet as yourself. His job was a quiet one, too: proof reader at the Crescent Press, where he spent days or nights in a glass cage bent over proofs.'

'Had you already got the bookshop?'

'Not yet. I was thinking of starting up a little business again . . .'

No reference to what she had done before that. A blank of at least thirty-five years, which she never made any attempt to fill in for my benefit.

'I set up under my maiden name, for I'm a careful person and I'd bought the stock with my own savings. One week my husband would go off in the morning and come back at night; next week he'd be on night shift and leave me after supper, to wake me up at dawn.'

Her monotonous delivery, her expressionless face, seemed deliberately to emphasize the uneventfulness of her married life. She never mentioned the words love or affection. There was not one portrait of a man in the house; nor any picture of herself or any of her relations, no snapshot taken with friends on some seaside or mountain holiday.

'It lasted ten years.'

'What happened?' I asked politely.

'One morning he sent a messenger to collect his belongings, informing me by letter that he'd decided to ask for a divorce, that he took all the blame and would stand all the costs, and giving me the name and address of his solicitor.'

I haven't Madame Annelet's insight nor, perhaps, her knowledge of life. I got the impression, however, that she had just revealed the crucial point, and I started from this to reconstitute her story. Was it true? Was it false? After several cross-checks, I'm inclined to think that, except for a few details, it was as close as possible to reality.

'Do you know for whom he left me, at the age of fifty? For a kid of seventeen, who sold newspapers in the street wearing a man's trousers and an old jacket of her father's. As soon as he was legally entitled to, he married her.'

'What became of them?'

'I imagine they're still together. She may have given him children, I don't know and I don't care, and he's probably still on the printing job, for printers are a long-lived lot.'

It was not so much her words as her tone that struck me. Under the muted, deliberately even voice one was aware of sarcasm and repressed hostility, at the same time, paradoxical though this may seem, as a kind of indifference or rather detachment, painfully acquired because it was vitally necessary.

She had certainly lied to me by asserting that she had been thirty-five and Doyen forty when she married him. The contrary was more than likely. From certain reckonings, I put her age at that period at forty-five.

She was born in Paris, she often told me so and I believe it, but I also believe that it was practically in the gutter, and certain phrases she hās let slip suggest that it was in the neighbourhood of the Porte Saint-Martin.

Had she frequented the unsavoury hotels of that district, outside which prostitutes pace like sentries on their high heels; or the Boulevard de Sébastopol, to which she had often alluded when speaking of her servant girls?

'When I was in Nice . . .' or else 'That reminds me of Narbonne . . .'

She knows almost all the towns in the Midi, and she refers to them in a very special way. She never visited them as a tourist, she has no relatives there, she has never brought back anything by way of a souvenir from any of them.

When she was twenty, thirty, forty years old, brothels were still flourishing and there was no suggestion of closing them. That is where I picture her, most convincingly, as one of the girls first and then as the Madame's second-in-command, while she was still personable and attractive.

She did not speak about women as other women do. She had a more intimate, more physical acquaintance with them. One could sense that she had seen them stark naked, under a harsh light, hurrying to the washroom while their client pulled on his clothes again.

She took somewhat the same attitude towards her successive maids, and one day when she did not know I was in the stairway I overheard her tell a little brunette, who only stopped two months:

'You had a man last night. You still smell of it.'

Each of us has his own hierarchy, the upward path that is available to him. She followed hers, by dint of sheer will-power, from the Porte Saint-Martin to the brothels of Nice, Béziers and Avignon, until at last, in her mature years, dressed in silk and decked with jewels, she presided over an establishment in neighbourhood of the Madeleine or the Rue de Richelieu.

The final stage, surely, must have been to settle down herself, and run a regular business. She must have chosen, among her clients or elsewhere, a quiet decent man who would bring her the necessary respectability. I don't exclude the possibility that Emile Doyen may have been found through the small ads column.

Now she was married, and her name deleted from the police list of public prostitutes. She owned her own bookshop and lived there, with a maid of her own.

She may well have been beautiful once, to judge by the contempt with which she refers to other women's figures. Nor is she any less critical of the male anatomy. She has seen naked bodies of every sort and age and in every position.

And then, in due course, her face becomes wrinkled and her breasts pendulous, and her legs begin to swell.

I may be mistaken, it doesn't matter since I'm not harming anyone and she will certainly not read these words. A woman of this sort must have fought fiercely against age, rejecting it to the end as she still rejects illness.

... Until that letter came from Emile Doyen, quiet, insignificant Doyen whom she had expressly chosen devoid of passion or ambition, and who was leaving her for a little newspaper-seller picked up in that gutter from which she herself had originally sprung ...

I think it was then that she shut her windows. Literally and figuratively, for she has purposely set her bed in a position from which the comings and goings on the boulevard cannot be seen.

What goes on in the world outside has no interest for her; she rejects its sounds and its smells.

If she understood me on the very first day, I may perhaps have the same reasons for understanding her. She has shut herself in. She lives only her own private life, enriching it with stories of queens, royal favourites and famous courtesans.

I have referred to small details on which I base my theory. In the first place I found, behind the books on the highest shelf, erotic books which are only sold under the counter. During the first two years it sometimes happened that a different sort of customer pushed open the glazed door, middle-aged men for the most part, of a social class unlike our usual clientele.

They would show surprise on seeing me, hesitate and ask with some embarrassment: 'Has the business changed hands?' or else: 'Isn't Madame Annelet here any longer?'

'Madame Annelet is away for the moment. I am her assistant.'

Sometimes I would say she was unwell or tired. I could guess that she was listening, overhead.

'Can I help you?'

'No thanks, I'll call back ...'

Then I would hear the bell summoning me to the bedroom.

'What was he like?'

I would describe him, convinced that she knew immediately of whom I was speaking. She never pressed me, nor did she attempt to give any explanation.

At first I thought that the curtain between the shop and the room at the back had been installed at the same time as the chaise-longue, when Madame Annelet began to find walking difficult. On examining the curtain-rod and screws I discovered that they had been there for years and that the wallpaper behind the chaise-longue was of a much brighter colour than the rest.

Not only were erotic books for sale, but the connoisseur could study them at leisure in that back room disguised as a boudoir. In Madame Annelet's company, or in that of a younger saleswoman, or a well-trained maidservant?

I don't know, and it is none of my business. Her life and mine have nothing in common except, at the moment, complete failure, and, in the long run, a quest for solitude.

Actually, we are playing a curious game together, spying on one another, each trying to guess the other's thoughts, as happened at first between Bib and myself, and as still happens occasionally.

She has no dog, no cat, no goldfish, not even a red geranium on her window-sill. Only a maid who, in her eyes, is no different from the naked, nameless girls she used to drive into the brothel parlour.

Thursday is one of my busiest days, because of the schoolboys and girls who come on their half-holiday, in groups or singly. I know them almost all by sight and some of them by name. There are some children of local wealthy bourgeois who have an account opened by their parents and to whom I send in a bill at the end of the month.

And there is someone else who sometimes goes past the window and whom I have long expected to see open the glazed door, but who never does. He lives barely three hundred yards away. Is it because he is aware of my presence behind the counter that he buys his books elsewhere?

Ten times that afternoon, as usual, the doorbell rang.

'What was that, Félix?'

'One Stendhal, Garnier edition.'

She is used to keeping a close watch on everything. In the old days she probably asked her girls, in the same way:

'What did he ask you to do?'

I closed the shop later than usual, at half-past six, going outside with my crank to lower the iron shutter. The second-hand box had been brought in, with Renée's help, and I carried the day's takings upstairs. A smell of cassoulet came from the kitchen. It was very hot in the bedroom and Madame Annelet's thin chest was almost bare under her bedjacket. After counting the notes and replacing them in the envelope, she remarked without looking at me, as if it was a matter of no consequence:

'You're thinking of leaving me, Félix?'

Only then did she lift her eyes to mine, and I thought I read real anxiety in them. Surprised by her question, I did not reply immediately, and she added, with the curt laugh that she only uses in self-mockery:

'You know I hate strange faces . . .'

She jerked her head towards the kitchen, where the maid was moving about.

'I don't care as far as the girls are concerned. They're all alike and if I kept them too long they'd become unbearable.'

That meant that, in my case, things were different.

'What makes you think I intend to leave you?'

'I don't know. I've been aware of it for some time.'

And suddenly, to my amazement:

'When did you see the doctor?'

'Last time? About six weeks ago.'

'What did that idiot tell you?'

Too late to draw back. The unexpectedness of the questions took me off my guard. I tried to remain evasive.

'Nothing fresh . . .'

'Which means?'

I was wearing my overcoat, for I had only meant to go up for a second, and I must have looked ridiculous, standing there tall and limp, with my head almost touching the low ceiling, in front of that bedridden woman with the dyed hair.

'How long does he give you?'

'A couple of years, possibly three,' I mumbled shamefacedly.

'Including everything?' She knew I would understand these words. Not two years before becoming an invalid, confined to bed or taken to hospital. No! Two years for everything, two years to the end.

I nodded, and I felt her shudder, her whole body tense with

indignation. Raising herself on one elbow, she almost screamed at me, in a voice which had regained its vulgarity:

'And you were fool enough to believe him. Admit it, eh?'

'He told me . . .'

'Men are all the same. You believed him, I know, I've been reading it in your face for days. He's put that idea into your head and I can see it gaining hold on you. Don't you know, you idiot, that one doesn't die till one wants to?'

It was no longer to me that she was speaking but to herself, and she was quivering from head to foot, so that the tension was hardly bearable.

'D'you hear what I'm telling you? It's a matter of will-power. Take me, for instance. I don't want to die and I know I shan't die until I want to, although I take none of their filthy drugs and follow none of their diets. But you, a great strapping fellow, you turn white as a sheet because a charlatan with a diploma tells you you've only two years left! And he must have said it quite seriously, the bastard, with a face like an undertaker's.

'Don't you realize that it's sheer murder? Next gentleman, please! Put out your tongue! Let's feel your pulse! When I prod you here, does it hurt? I thought so. And here? Aha! And your bowels? Oho! I bet you're breathless when you run for a bus. Undress. You smoke, needless to say. You eat all sorts of rubbish, bread and butter and sweet things. Not surprising! Lie down. Like that, yes. Don't move . . .

'Oh, Félix, when I think that you let yourself be taken in like all the rest! You broke into a sweat, you watched the eyes of the gentleman who was stuffing his rubber-gloved finger up your backside. He didn't? That surprises me. Those chaps love sticking their fingers up holes . . .

'Two years, possibly three, on condition you give up smoking and sex, and live on unsalted rusks and noodles, eh?

'Doctors can go to hell as far as I'm concerned, and I shall live to bury the lot of them.'

She relaxed as suddenly as she had grown tense. Now she stared up at the ceiling and remarked in quite a different voice:

'Were you going to do it?'

I didn't ask her what. I said nothing. She added after a silence:

'When?'

'I don't know.'

I was crestfallen; I felt like a small boy. Then, once more, she gave her brittle laugh.

'That's better already. Well, Félix, when you decide to, be kind enough to give me a week's notice so that I can find a substitute for you. And this time, I promise you, I'll make sure he's not a sick man.'

Was it because of this conversation that yesterday evening I was incapable of writing in this notebook? On Sunday, in Montmartre, two scraps of talk had disturbed me so much that the whole question had been reopened.

'*You're not too tired?*' '*Oh no . . . I'm all right . . .*'

And on Thursday the witch, in a fit of rage, had flung at me:

'*Don't you know, you idiot, that one doesn't die until one wants to?*'

Come on, Bib! Time for bed. Tomorrow is another day.

*Saturday, 16 November, 2 a.m.*

I HAVE decided to get up. Since I went to bed about midnight, I've been lying awake and, even when I grew drowsy, I still remained conscious. Even when my thoughts took the shape of dreams I could see myself lying there in bed, flabby and unhealthy, under the sloping ceiling, and I could feel Bib's weight against my left leg.

I often drift between sleep and wakefulness like that. Some nights I look at the time five or six times, reckoning how long it is until morning brings back my routine, and I can go and open the front door downstairs for Bib to run into the street.

At one point, after switching off the light, I did in fact think about my dog. I don't like calling him a dog. I've been living with him for five years. He was thought to be three or four when I brought him back from the strays' home. He must be about nine, then, more than half way through a poodle's normal span.

In fact, we're the same age, he and I. His back is growing stiffer, his body thicker, but he still keeps on playing with his little ball and doing his tricks – shamming dead and, more rarely, turning back-somersaults.

For one moment I thought I saw him, on my bed, grown as large and bulky as myself, with his big head close to my face, peering into it with morose curiosity.

This was not the only unpleasant picture that passed through my mind. I recalled Madame Annelet too, in her bedroom, raging against death. Everything she said about it, all her furious defiance, sprang from fear. Panic seized her at the thought of suddenly becoming an inert, decaying thing that people would shove underground as fast as possible to get rid of it.

Does she sleep more peacefully than I, who am not afraid of dying? Does she wait impatiently for the first signs of daylight? On Thursday evening I was crestfallen in her presence, not knowing what to say, as sometimes used to happen to me in my father's. I visualized my father, perhaps not exactly as he used to be. I recalled the courtyard of our house at Puteaux, where I spent so many hours reading in the sunshine, with my chair tipped backward and my feet on the whitewashed planks.

'You're going to break that chair, Félix!'

I tried to picture my mother.

Why? Why? Questions, more and more questions, which I thought I'd answered once and for all, whereas just as many of them are still pressing.

I slipped out of bed. I did not need to turn on the light, for the moon is almost full and it is light enough in the attic for me to make out Bib's recumbent form and his half-open eyes.

At first he thought I was going to the toilet. When he saw me move towards the window he hesitated, as I used to hesitate with my parents, torn between a selfish desire to relapse into sleep and his duty – I suppose he considers it a duty – to follow me.

I was fond of my father and mother. I have been 'fond' of a certain number of people. What does that mean, exactly?

Before sitting down at my table to write these lines I have just spent a quarter of an hour standing looking at the street, its houses, its shop-signs and its three lamps. The sky is clear and cloudless. All day it was a smooth pale blue, with a cold sun that hardly cast any shadows. Now it is silvery, with a huge moon over the rooftops, and everything is a vast empty stillness, bathed in a neutral light that reminds me of the light over a dentist's chair.

The difference between Madame Annelet and myself ... I resent the place she has taken in my thoughts; I resent, too, the fact that she thinks about me as she does. I resent the way she looks at me as if she guessed everything, without deigning to ask me if she's right or not.

My mother was like that, and as thin and dark too. My grandfather Désiré Allard, taller and broader than myself, never forgave my father for marrying a puny little woman who played the piano and the violin, and I am not sure that my father himself did not come to regret it in the end.

Madame Annelet fought hard to pull herself out of the crowd, to secure a small scrap of space where at last she had nobody to consider but herself. Is she aware that five million Parisians are breathing and eating and working all round her, so close that in spite of her closed windows she's obliged to breathe their breath?

Does she ever think that, just as she's falling asleep, whole populations are waking up on the other side of the globe, that trains and ships and aircraft, twenty-four hours out of the twenty-four, are making their way through the darkness or in the dazzling daylight?

She lives really alone. I don't. With my forehead pressed against the pane, just now, I was staring at the greyish walls in the moonlight, the closed shutters, the empty balconies, and thinking of the human beings inside their boxes.

I needed no effort to picture another house-front, in the Place des Vosges, three windows on the second floor, not so tall as the first-floor windows. I have never been into that flat. It must contain pieces of furniture bought by myself, carpets chosen by me.

As far as I can judge from the outside it is not large, two bedrooms probably, besides the living-room, the kitchen and the bathroom.

The children are too old now to share the same bedroom. Unless he sleeps on the living-room divan, which would surprise me, Philippe must have a room of his own, which implies that Anne-Marie and Nicole, who'll be fourteen this month, must sleep in the same room.

Do they sleep in the bed which was Anne-Marie's and mine? The thought leaves me quite unmoved. I can see them in the same cold light that shines over the rooftops of Paris tonight. Philippe and Nicole are my children. Like other fathers, I paced the corridors of the nursing-home while they were fighting their way into the world.

There's another apartment about which I think, nearer by, in the Boulevard Beaumarchais, not to the right of the Rue des Arquebusiers, like the bookshop, but on the left, towards the Place de la République.

They only settled there two years ago, Monique, who is three years older than Anne-Marie, that's to say forty-three, Daniel who is seventeen and his sister Martine, fifteen.

They live on the fourth floor and a balcony runs from end to end of the building, divided by a spiked railing, since there are two flats on each floor.

Three human groups, if you can call Bib and myself a human group. I'm forgetting the shop in the Boulevard Beaumarchais where, willy-nilly, I form part of Madame Annelet's group.

But the connections between them? I can't find the right word. I almost said the vibrations. On Sunday afternoon you could feel the vibrations between the two cripples climbing the Saint-Pierre steps, like those sent out by chords played on some great organ.

There they are in their various pigeon-holes, and Renée, Madame Annelet's maid, in hers on the sixth floor. Each of them is breathing and dreaming, like Bib, who has just been waving his paws and uttering little whimpers. Things aren't happening as they should. I don't mean in life, but in this notebook, whose pages I go on blackening in a depressed and irritable mood. My idea, when I started it, was to make everything clear, not only to others, if they should chance to read it, but to myself. I was almost sure I could do so.

I merely had to state my case, sincerely, cruelly if need be, in order to get at the truth. Doesn't each one of us, at some point in his life, feel the need to put things in focus? Doesn't each of us feel different from the rest, and suffer from not being understood?

Take any woman, the most intelligent, stable and virtuous in the accepted sense of the word. Look at her with a grave and anxious air. I have done so, all men have done so.

'I'm trying to understand you . . .'

'To understand what?'

'You must know; I'm not the first to have told you . . .'

Whoever you are, you'll find her listening to you.

'You're different from other people. . . . One's aware of something in you . . .'

It's just the same with a man, whether he's a genius or a fool.

'I'm sure that if you were to write the story of your life . . .'

A tiny little planet floating in a space formed of nobody knows what, among millions of other little planets, warmer or colder than itself, a minute individual, who'll soon be nothing more than stuff to be got rid of with disgust, gravely undertakes to write the story of his life.

Of what life? Of his own private life, of course! Of what goes on in what he's pleased to call his mind.

At school, he was always being told: 'Félix, you're quite wrong to think yourself cleverer than the rest. Rules are made for everybody . . .'

They taught him, too: 'You must love your parents.'

And respect them. And obey them. They aren't just a man and a woman sitting in front of you eating their soup; they are a father and a mother.

As for Grandfather, he is a sort of patriarch or apostle, such as you see in stained-glass windows.

'Show me your mark-book. You've gone down another place. . . . You're only fifth.'

Fifth out of what?

'What's happening? Why are you working less well this term? Don't forget that your whole future depends on . . .'

And it's true. You have to choose a career, find a niche somewhere or other, on one floor or another, at Puteaux or Neuilly, in a cell of the Melun Gaol or a lodging in the Rue des Arquebusiers. Or else, like Madame Annelet, work your way up from the brothels of southern and south-eastern France to the smart Parisian establishment and the bookshop in the Boulevard Beaumarchais.

One fine day, or one fine evening, you happen to be sitting at a café terrace, or on a bench, or walking along the pavement, with somebody you did not know the day before.

'What are you thinking about?'

'About you. . . . You're a strange person . . .'

'Strange in what way?'

'Do you often go for a walk with a girl and not say a word to her?'

'This is the first time.'

'Why with me?'

'I don't know . . .'

Because she is different, of course. And then she tells you about herself, and you lose no time in telling her about yourself too. You each enlarge on what makes you different: different skin, different nose and eyes and ears, above all a different mouth, and you can't wait to taste the difference; then breasts, and sex, and sighs and moans all have to be tried out, for they are different too.

'I love you.'

'I love you more.'

'I wonder how it happened?'

'It had to happen.'

The horrible icy moonlight is growing quite poetic.

'What would have become of us if fate hadn't brought us together?'

'My life wouldn't have been the same.'

'Nor mine.'

'It would have been empty, like most people's. So few know what real love is.'

'How dreadful for them.'

'Luckily they don't realize it.'

'D'you think so?'

'If they realized it, they'd shoot themselves.'

'You're amazing.'

344

'I love you!'

I can hardly imagine such a conversation taking place between my father and mother, since it's of them that I am thinking. Still less between my grandfather and my grandmother.

'When there'll be just the two of us together . . .'

To be two together in a home, or a room, or a hovel. To go on talking about oneself, each considering his own story the most important.

'If you should ever stop loving me . . .'

'Don't talk like that, it's impossible! . . . The thought of being alone again . . .'

That's the point! Not to be alone. To be a couple, so as not to be alone. Why not three, five, ten, a hundred?

'Some day, darling, we'll have a child . . .'

'Oh yes . . . a child of our own! . . . Can you imagine it? . . . Yours and mine! . . . Just our own!'

'I love you!'

'Me too!'

The crowd is no longer a hostile swarm, a mass of individuals each bitterly defending his own position. The crowd is a witness: faces turning back to watch a couple in one another's arms.

'Did you see that big fellow with the funereal expression? The way he stared at us!'

'He was envious . . .'

An old woman smiling tenderly, a small boy sniggering.

'What shall we call it?'

'If it's a boy . . .'

'And if it's a girl?'

'I want it to be a boy, and to look like you . . .'

There are three of you. There are four of you. It drives one wild, do you understand? It drives me wild that things happen like that, and that I need to write it down. There is a woman with two children in the Place des Vosges. There's another, also with two children, under a roof in the Boulevard Beaumarchais which I could see from here if this house were a little taller. And for all of these I am, after a fashion, responsible.

For the past eight years I have had no contact with them. It's unlikely that they know I am here. In any case, they never think of me; I don't exist for them, why should they exist for me?

Responsible, did I write? For whom, for what is one responsible? Each of us does what he can, myself like the rest, just as my boss – since I now have a boss – did what she could.

'And my grandfather?' a child will ask some day, amidst a world which I shall never know.

'We won't talk about your grandfather.'

'Why? Was he bad?'

What can they say? Who knows? Perhaps they'll get out of it with:

'You see, he wasn't quite like other people . . .'

Perhaps that is why I want to know, and why I want others to know. I'm doing this badly. I shall be awkward to the end of my days. Meanwhile, it's cold. I am not sleepy. I've no wish to go back to bed. I shall relight the fire, make myself a cup of coffee, sit down in front of this table again and, probably, spend the rest of the night here.

I hate that moon hanging just over my head, immediately above the skylight. I hope that it'll shortly move away and that I shan't see it any more.

No, Bib, it's not time to get up. Don't pay any attention to your master. Go to sleep, good dog!

*

One May morning, about eleven o'clock, I came out of Melun Gaol with a suitcase in my hand, and found myself in the square before Notre-Dame, having for over four years seen only the rooftops, and towers of the church. The air was fresh, the sun already warm, and the first person I met was an old gentleman with a white moustache wearing a panama hat.

I was neither bewildered nor excited. I chiefly stared at the paving-stones, the sidewalks, the houses, listened to the sound of footsteps, then, crossing the square, I went into a clean little café at the corner of a narrow street. Behind the pewter-topped counter the *patron*, in shirt-sleeves and blue apron, was arranging his bottles.

I might equally well have been in some bistro in Puteaux or in the Latin quarter. The smell was the same, the colour of the floor and of the few tables, the notice about being drunk and disorderly stuck up on the wall between advertisements for apéritifs.

'A glass of white wine.'

'Dry?'

'All right.'

I had not come for the sake of the white wine. I had come to renew contact, and the *patron* realized this. Without having seen me cross the square he knew where I had come from. He'd served others like me. I don't know how he recognized us, by our colour perhaps, or the look in our eyes.

'Well, it wasn't too bad, was it?'

I said no. It was true. Time had not seemed long for me and I wonder, in retrospect, whether it did not seem shorter than at any other period of my life.

'Paris?'

'Yes.'

'Nobody to meet you?'

'No.'

I thanked him, for nothing in particular, maybe for having spoken to me; then I paid for my drink and made my way towards the station, pausing a moment on the bridge to watch the waters of the Seine flow by.

I had not the curiosity to turn back and look at my prison for the last time, nor to try and pick out the roof of my section.

At the station I had a longish wait for a train, and I took advantage of it to eat a ham sandwich and drink another glass of white wine.

It was then, I believe, that I understood that I no longer looked at things and people in the same way. I had already foreseen this; now I was experiencing it. I saw men and women, faces and hands, trolleys, luggage, trucks standing on the lines, lilacs in bloom in a garden; I heard sounds and voices; I recognized the smell of sandwiches, of beer drawn from the barrel, of wine and alcohol. But I stayed detached from it all. It was all something outside me and did not concern me.

True, there was nobody to meet me when I came out of gaol. But were all those who had left before me so desperately keen to find somebody waiting at the gate? Possibly out of vanity, in some cases, just as certain people like to be seen off or met at the station.

Through the window I saw familiar landscapes once again: a stretch of the Seine here and there, a lock with boats, a fisherman with his rod at the foot of an embankment, gravel quarries. It's the line to the Riviera; I had often travelled on the Blue Train, and on the return journey it was at Melun that the *wagon-lits* waiters used to wake us up with coffee.

It might be supposed that I was full of plans, that I'd had plenty of time to sketch out my future. The contrary is true. I was as blank as an empty page, indifferent to everything except to ridiculous details such as the newspaper my neighbour was reading, the conversation of two soldiers on leave, or some market-gardeners I had glimpsed for one moment in a huge plot irrigated by a score of fountains.

There are plenty of hotels round the Gare de Lyon, but I have always disliked the neighbourhood of stations. You're not really inside the town, or else you're no longer in it, and yet you don't feel you're anywhere else.

I had no reason to choose one district rather than another. I know nobody at Puteaux now. Neuilly is nothing but a memory, and I sometimes wonder whether it was really I who lived there.

I walked straight ahead, as I should have done if I'd arrived at the Gare du Nord or the Gare Montparnasse. I found myself beside the river, then I walked alongside the Arsenal dock and finally reached the Bastille.

Then I began looking at the signs of the cheaper hotels, for my suit-case, which I kept shifting from one hand to the other, was beginning to feel heavy, and eventually I went into the white-painted, narrow entrance of a hotel in the Rue Castex, close to the Rue Saint-Antoine.

The *patronne*, wiping her pudgy hands, scanned me closely. I had not noticed before that human beings watch one another suspiciously before making contact. There is a pause, while furtive glances are exchanged.

'For one night?'

'I'd rather have a room by the week or the month, if it's not too expensive.'

'Are you French?'

'Yes.'

'You're alone?'

'Yes.'

Something about me worried her, something she could not understand, but she none the less showed me a room overlooking the courtyard. I went for a snack in the Rue Saint-Antoine. I drank yet another glass of white wine, then I lay down, fully dressed, and was surprised on waking to find that night had fallen.

I spent a whole week walking about, venturing a little farther each time, now taking the bus to the Place de l'Opéra, another time to the Châtelet, and so on. . . . It did not rain once all that week. The weather was set fair. Women wore light, bright-coloured spring dresses. I had forgotten the special way women walk when they have just shed their winter clothes, as if they derived a kind of sexual excitement from this state of undress which makes them unconsciously provocative.

On the Monday or Tuesday I ended up in the waiting-room of Maître Forniol, my solicitor, who lives in an imposing, comfortable building in the Boulevard Haussmann. I recognized the secretary he already had at the time of my trial. Have I changed so much that, for her part, she failed to recognize me?

'Have you an appointment?'

'No.'

She handed me a pad and pencil: name, purpose of visit, with dotted lines for the answers, just like in a Government office. I merely signed my name.

'I think that will be enough,' I said.

She read my name without surprise or curiosity, as if it suggested nothing to her.

'I'm afraid you may have to wait some time. Maître Forniol is in conference.'

In the old days I, too, had always been in conference when certain people called.

'I'll wait.'

I sat down, alone in the waiting-room, and stayed there doing nothing. That's something I have learnt: not to move, to remain perfectly blank. I heard the telephone ringing, the secretary's voice, and a man's voice muffled behind a baize door.

An articled clerk came through, carrying files under his arm, a new young man whom I did not know. He seemed surprised to find somebody in the room.

'Are you waiting for Maître Forniol?'

'Yes.'

'Has his secretary seen you?'

'Yes.'

What made him frown as he looked at me? I had no spots on my nose, nor smuts on my face. I was respectably dressed, waiting motionless on my chair.

He went in through the baize door which, a little later, somebody whom I could not see from where I was pushed open a little to glance at me. At last the secretary, Mademoiselle Emma or Irma, I forget which, came to fetch me.

'Maître Forniol will see you now.'

She took me into the office, which was empty, showed me a chair and disappeared. In the next room, the door of which was ajar, somebody was talking.

'Don't worry, my dear fellow ... I'll ask for a fortnight's adjournment, which will give us time to work on you know who. ... Yes, yes of course! ... You can depend on it. ... Our opponents can't attempt anything before ...'

He was speaking into the telephone in exactly the same voice with which he had spoken to me four years earlier.

'No. Unfortunately I've no free evening this week, but please give my wife's kind regards to yours. ... Above all, don't do anything, wait till you hear from me. ... It'll be all right ...'

The same words, too, as near as made no difference. Now he was whispering to somebody, and a few minutes later he came in, quite unlike his voice, with the grave and preoccupied air of a man overburdened with responsibilities.

He has not changed at all. He is still young and dapper. I stood up because at Melun you acquire the habit of standing up as soon as the door opens.

He glanced at me and could not restrain a look of surprise.

'So you see you've come out ...' he began.

He made a mental reckoning as he sat down behind his desk.

'In fact, you've had your sentence remitted? If I'm not mistaken, you were to have been released in . . .'

'Six months.'

He did not ask how I was; still less did he bother to simulate cordiality.

'My secretary will have told you that I'm . . .'

'Extremely busy. I shan't waste your time.'

It seemed as if my presence disturbed or embarrassed him. Yet at the Assizes he had defended me with ardour, even with passion.

'What can I do for you?'

I wondered if he was going to pull out his wallet.

'Are the children still living with my wife?'

He became even more guarded, as though I were really becoming an adversary.

'Why do you ask me that?'

'Does it surprise you?'

He took his time, fiddling with an ivory paperknife and looking at me with some annoyance.

'Look here, Allard . . . I needn't remind you of your position and I suppose you were sent the papers in due course . . .'

I remained impassive and expressionless. It was he who was put out of countenance and began pulling at the lobe of his ear.

'Your wife has not asked for a divorce, as she could have done, so as not to bear a different name from her children . . .'

'Even if we were divorced I'd have authorized her to keep mine . . .'

He glanced at me severely, shocked at my daring to make such a remark. In his opinion, I ought not to be here, I should have had the decency to disappear and, above all, to keep quiet.

'The fact remains that she merely asked for a separation order. Subsequently, on the advice of one of my colleagues she ensured her peace of mind by requesting that you forfeit your paternal rights, by virtue of the law of July 24, 1889 . . .'

He concluded, throwing out his hands:

I did not bat an eyelid; why should I, since I already knew? Forfeiture of paternal rights. Law of July 24, 1889, article 2.

Perhaps he was refreshing his memory when he was muttering in the next room a few minutes before.

'Under the circumstances . . .'

'Do you know where they live?'

He picked up the paperknife again.

'I can tell you that I know where Madame Allard and her children are living. I saw them less than two months ago and they are quite well. Now, if you'll excuse me, I'm due at the Law Courts . . .'

'You refuse to give me their address?'

'Why do you wish to know it? You have no legal or moral right to disturb their existence and, for my part, I consider myself bound to . . .'

'I've got nothing to say to Anne-Marie. I don't wish to see her nor to discuss anything whatsoever with her. Nor do I intend to confront the children and announce to them: I'm your father . . .'

I did not raise my voice. I was neither angry nor disgusted. Those words, too, have lost all meaning for me.

'It might happen that from time to time, with all requisite prudence, I should want to see the children from a distance. Since, according to you, this can't be done, I shall make inquiries elsewhere . . .'

I suppose it was my calmness, my absence of emotion that impressed him, together with the fact that he was in a hurry and feared lest I should detain him by my insistence.

'Will you give me your word that this is really your intention and that you won't go any further?'

I rose from my seat.

'You don't need my word. You're forgetting about the forfeiture of paternal rights . . .'

'If I reminded you of that . . .'

'You had every right to do so.'

'Listen . . .'

He rose, too, and showed me to the door, muttering: 'Forget about this visit. I haven't seen you. They live at 23, Place des Vosges.'

'They're not short of anything?'

'Nothing at all.'

352

'Is she working?'

'You're asking too many questions and I'm already ten minutes late. Excuse me. I've still got to make a telephone call.'

He did not shake hands with me.

'Irma, be kind enough to show out Monsieur . . .'

Irma was her name, then. As for mine, he left it unmentioned, merely substituting . . .

Ten days previously I had chosen a small hotel in the Rue Castex, at the corner of the Rue Saint-Antoine, and now I discovered that Anne-Marie was living in the Place des Vosges with the children. Four hundred yards away, five hundred maybe? It didn't matter.

Forniol need not have worried. Philippe was eight years old then, Nicole six. I saw them at a distance being taken to school by a nursemaid.

And I also saw Anne-Marie, who now owned a small green car and who, apart from having cut her hair, had scarcely altered. She was working at that time at a couturier's in the Faubourg Saint-Honoré and since then has set up her own boutique near St Philippe-du-Roule.

I never felt tempted to go closer to them, still less to make myself known. If I chance to speak of them now, as night is drawing to a close and the time has almost come to open the door for Bib, it is in order to return indirectly to the subject of myself.

I was not interested in eight-year-old Philippe, still less in his sister.

'They're your children . . .'

They are Anne-Marie's too. And there was a time, indeed, when we thought the world of them.

'He's got your nose . . .'

'Maybe my nose, but he's got your expression . . .'

Mine, yours, it always comes back to that. I once saw, in some documentary film, millions of spermatozoa struggling ferociously to be the first to pierce the ovum. One of them won; the others were wasted.

From that battle a child was born. My children, then, since they are mine, go to school, with other children who have their grandfather's or grandmother's nose or expression.

I turned my attention to finding somewhere to live, and chance made me discover this place which is just right for me, in a district of warehouses and small tradesmen that reminds me of Puteaux.

On the left, in the street, are the Magasins Réunis, who own at least twenty lorries. Elsewhere there is a candlestick-maker's. Opposite my place, a cheap restaurant with a façade painted sky-blue and the inscription *'Chez Rose'*.

One day I read the notice in the bookshop window, and little by little I organized my life. I had already put on weight at Melun, which was nobody's fault, nor that of the regulations of the prison services. I went on putting on weight, and looking puffier and uglier, particularly in the mornings, but I did not feel unwell.

I had no wish for anything, nor for any contact with people. I had reached a state of serenity. Having asked myself questions, I had eventually answered them in a way which satisfied me. It was pointless to return to them.

This did not prevent me from going, from time to time, to sit on a bench in the Place des Vosges, from which I could occasionally catch sight of the children.

Winter came, and summer, longer days, shorter days, different fruit and vegetables on the barrows in the Rue Saint-Antoine or the open-air market in the Boulevard Richard-Lenoir, overcoats or jackets, Easter holidays, summer holidays, beginning of term. Suddenly we would be selling books about shooting or the cooking of game, or people would be ordering Christmas cards. And as the years went by Madame Annelet spent less and less time up and about, and ate more and more.

I don't intend any irony. I went on preparing my morning coffee, feeding my goldfish, which was doomed to die none the less, and which would have been most surprised to learn that a dog would shortly take its place. And who's going to take *my* place, in my goldfish bowl?

Philippe started going to the Lycée Turgot in the Rue de Turbigo. He altered in appearance, in his way of walking, in his expression. He grew taller and thinner, with the prominent bones I used to have at his age.

This was the moment when he must be growing aware of his

own existence. At all events, in my own case, it was at his age that I first made the discovery.

In a very short while, by the time I had been to choose a dog at Gennevilliers, sold books, raised the shutter in the morning, got used to new maids, and carried up the day's takings to Madame Annelet, Philippe had turned sixteen and he is now preparing his baccalaureate. For his last birthday his mother bought him a motor-cycle. The first few days he never tired of buzzing like a big fly round the railings in the Place des Vosges.

He has bought himself a leather jacket. On Thursdays he forgathers with a gang of boys and girls at a café close to the Place de la République, where there are nothing but youngsters drinking fruit juice and listening to the juke-box.

I myself used to have a bicycle to get to the Lycée Pasteur at Neuilly, since there was no lyceé at Puteaux.

I . . . I . . .

I watch Philippe, and I also watch Daniel, who entered the same lycée when, with his mother and sister, he came to live in the Boulevard Beaumarchais.

Daniel, who is a year older, is in a different form. He belongs to a different set. I don't know whether they know each other. I compare; I observe; I keep hidden; I wonder . . .

Six o'clock. Bib has sensed this and jumped off the bed. The fire has gone out again. When I have been down to open the door, I shall heat some water for my coffee . . .

*Sunday, 17 November 11 a.m.*

The rain has been falling hard since midday yesterday, in great cold drops, blackening the house-fronts, pouring down the window-panes, choking the drainpipes, and wherever you look the sky is thick, so dark that this morning the lights are on everywhere.

I'm quite glad when it rains on Sunday. Not because I envy the people who, at the first gleam of sun, rush off into the country. I used to have a car, even several at one time. I know the road to Deauville and Le Touquet, the road to the Riviera, and the best places to eat on the way. I envy nobody.

If I don't dislike seeing it rain when people are at leisure, it is because one then feels that all the pigeon-holes are full, the houses brimming over with human life.

Yesterday evening Bib and I had been almost alone as we walked along the pavements, except for an occasional figure darting from the door of a block of flats to a waiting car which promptly drove off.

The cinemas must have been crowded, and the restaurants and dance-halls, and no doubt resigned processions under umbrellas were pacing up and down in front of the brightly-lit gateways of the Champs-Elysées and the Grands Boulevards.

There were some blank spaces in the house-fronts, some darkened windows, some empty dwellings. Daniel, hugging the walls, had made his way to the Métro. I suppose he was going to the cinema. His mother and sister stayed in their flat where, at eleven o'clock, the lights were still on. I don't know what they were doing.

In the Place des Vosges, nobody went out. Several cars were parked alongside the pavement and I saw one draw up, from which a young couple got out. Was there a party going on, on the second floor? It's quite likely, for shadows passed to and fro behind the curtains, as if people were dancing.

I went back to the Boulevard Beaumarchais and stood for a while sheltering in a gateway in the hope of seeing Daniel come home. Bib, who was soaked, eventually put on such a miserable expression that I abandoned my post.

This morning we went out again, without hurrying, walking at a steady pace along the empty streets. Sometimes I caught a glimpse of a face behind the net curtains; somebody was watching us and wondering what we were doing in the rain.

I suppose many people have taken advantage of the rain to sleep, those who have no children to wake them at crack of dawn. Others listen half-heartedly to the radio, which is indistinguishable from that in the flat next door or that on the floor above. One thing I'm practically certain of, Philippe is not reading a book.

I was thinking about him as I sat on a wet bench far enough from his window for his mother not to recognize me if she should happen to look out. I have never seen Philippe with a book other than his school textbooks. Daniel is different, and I'd wager that last night he went not to a local cinema nor to one of the big ones that show the latest pictures, but to some film society or avant-garde theatre.

The drops of rain hit the pavement so violently that they bounce back and water gets into one's shoes, soaking one's socks and trouser turn-ups. I have put my overcoat to dry by the fire, where Bib is drying himself too. He is feeling cross. I am not; but neither am I cheerful. I don't feel like singing; have I ever felt like singing? My mood is none the less one of quiet contentment, as with certain forms of physical pain which one eventually comes to enjoy.

It often rained when I was a child. That's an idiotic remark. I mean that when I cast back my mind I remember a lot of rain, days like today when the whole family stayed at home, particularly when I was very young, when we had not yet acquired our van nor central heating, and the cold obliged us all to take refuge in the only warm room.

Will Philippe and Daniel and the two girls retain as few memories of their early childhood as I have done? And yet I have been told I was a lively, wide-awake child, given to asking awkward questions.

I was born in January 1915, at the height of the first world war. My father, then aged thirty, being a building contractor, was called up to help construct the defences of Paris. Then Louise, my sister, was born, two years later, while the war was still on.

We were still living in the same old house with my grandfather, my grandmother and one of my aunts, Léonore, who was unmarried.

I gather my grandmother was a handsome woman, buxom in the taste of the time. She was the daughter of an innkeeper at Chatou, where my grandfather, who was then a foreman, used to go boating on Sundays.

There is a family album with brass-bound corners containing their portraits, together with those of uncles, aunts and cousins whom I do not know. At Chatou, my grandmother was known as *la belle Joséphine*.

Hers must have been the first death in the family in my lifetime. I was about four. I only remember the ringing of the choirboy's bell when, at nightfall, the priest came to administer extreme unction.

I know nothing about the funeral, but I watched the undertakers' men removing the black, silver-trimmed hangings. I can also remember seeing, that afternoon, men in their Sunday best in the seldom-opened parlour. They were drinking brandy out of tiny glasses – I can still smell it – and smoking cigars, and they soon turned me out of the room.

My grandfather was among them. Somebody said: 'You must be sensible about it. You gave her a happy life and fine children and I'm sure she's happy where she is.'

Meanwhile the women, forgathering in the kitchen which was always rather a dark place, were drinking coffee and eating cakes.

When I went to primary school and began to learn the history of the Gauls I nicknamed my grandfather Vercingetorix because of his big drooping moustache which must once have been red, but which I only remember white.

I recall other funerals, not at home but among our relations, with my mother wearing a crape veil over her face and my father usually in black, unless he was in his working clothes.

The most important incident concerned the old house and the new one. My grandfather had built, in the waste plot which adjoined and continued our courtyard, a house facing the Rue du Four, parallel to the Rue Bourgeoise.

As it was his profession, he must have built it with love, putting stained glass in the staircase windows, ceramic ornaments on the brick façade and setting pink tiles alternately with almost black ones on the roof.

I tend to get my dates confused. I might be able to remember them; my sister Louise must be able to say at what date such and such an aunt married, and the age of her children or of some cousin when he died.

I wonder if it was, and still is, through indifference on my part, or if, even as a child, I watched it all without feeling that I belonged to it.

I did not, on the other hand, feel alien to it. I was never the kind of boy who rebels against family life or against his milieu.

I accepted its rites; I accepted those of my neighbourhood, where I played in the street with my small friends, some of whose names and faces, such as Popet's, I can still remember.

I played marbles, I bowled hoops, I whipped tops; later on, I was for a short time in the school football team. I was not unsociable.

'You're teasing your sister, Félix!'

Apparently I behaved unkindly to her, I was jealous of her and deliberately rough. On such occasions I was sent into the yard, which was full of ladders, sacks, and building materials, or into the street, where the fencing was still up.

The story of the two houses was a complicated and somewhat mysterious one, for it was only mentioned in whispers in front of my sister and myself. My grandmother died at about the time when the new house had been completed. My grandfather at first stayed on with us in the old one, while my aunt Julie, married to a man called Cassegrain who already owned two lorries and became a large-scale carrier, settled in the new one.

Cassegrain was a rip, they said. He was loud-mouthed and given to drink, and would admit nobody's superiority. He was a fool, endowed with incredible vitality, and could not endure opposition. Was it true that one day he came across the yard and, finding my mother by herself, tried to take advantage of the opportunity?

For weeks, there was whispering at nights after my sister and I had gone to bed, with occasional raised voices.

'Poor Julie! To have landed with a man like that! And such lovely children she's got . . .'

She had two at the time, one of them a baby who spent all day in a perambulator which was moved about to catch the sun. All communication ceased between the two houses. Other incidents must have occurred, for the courtyard was subsequently divided in two, first with a wooden fence painted green and then with a wall.

I don't know exactly how old my grandfather was when he decided to divide up his property between his son and his daughters. My father inherited the business, under certain conditions, and undertook to look after the old man to the end of his days.

I can picture all this like some landscape distortingly reflected in the waters of a pond. At what point did Aunt Léonore, the only unmarried member of the family, go off one night leaving a letter to say she was not coming back? I myself never saw her again. I heard tell that she was living in Marseilles, then Algiers. As for Vercingetorix, he found it very boring in our home, with a skinny daughter-in-law who played the piano and cooked his food in an unfamiliar way.

The question was debated at a family gathering and eventually Grandfather went over to the other side of the wall to live with his daughter Julie in the new house.

Considering what had happened over Cassegrain, this was an act of treachery. The family was split into two camps.

I went to school by now. I was one of the three best pupils in my class, which seemed as natural to me as it did to my parents. My chief rival for the first place was one Godard, who later became an engineer in the Water Supply Department and must by now be a municipal councillor of Puteaux, if not indeed Mayor.

Was it on my teacher's advice that I was sent to the Lycée Pasteur? I used to read a great deal, as yesterday's and today's rain reminded me. When it rained, when it was cold, and we were all shut up in the same room, I used to thrust my fingers in my ears so as not to be disturbed in my reading.

I had violin lessons from my other grandfather, Justin Périnel, who had a bush of hair, flushed cheekbones and a feverish look in his eyes. He was a poorer than we were, and took his pupils in a parlour that was so heavily upholstered and so cluttered with knick-knacks and ornaments that I always felt stifled there.

He died of turberculosis. Vercingetorix declared that the same fate awaited my mother, who however lived until the end of the second world war.

'What do you want to be when you grow up?'

'A teacher.'

'A teacher of what?'

'I don't know.'

My examining magistrate, a sensitive man, trying to understand, a little too hard maybe, asked me a certain number of questions about my childhood, precisely because, I imagine, he suspected my case to be less simple than it seemed.

He did not try to hide his sympathy nor his curiosity, in spite of our respective situations. One day, after a fairly long interrogation as to the facts, he asked me:

'What was your ambition when you were young?'

'To become a teacher.'

He did not ask of what, but why. I had never thought about that. I had assumed it to be quite natural. Besides, I had originally dreamed of becoming a bus conductor. I told him this. And when he spoke to me afterwards, with a thoughtful air, I guessed which textbooks of psychology he had been reading.

'Don't you find it odd? A teacher is *in* the class, but not part of it. I mean he's not one of the rank and file, he doesn't belong to the group.'

'It had never occurred to me,' I apologized.

He added with a laugh: 'Many boys want to become bus conductors or policemen because of the uniform. In your case, I think I discern a point in common with the teaching profession. The conductor is *in* the bus but he, too, belongs in a different category from the passengers around him . . .'

I'll leave these arguments to other people. For a long time now, I have given up trying to learn about life or myself through books.

Latin was not my own choice originally. My mother would have liked me to be a doctor. She lived in terror of the scaffolding, the soaring walls, the planks stretched across the void along which my father walked like a circus acrobat when supervising men at work on a building.

There had been six or seven workmen in my grandfather's day, but soon we had twenty of them, sometimes thirty at busy periods. Father spent less and less time in his working clothes, and more and more sitting in his little office, amid a growing heap of green files, with his jacket off, his shirt-sleeves turned up and his tie loosened.

My sister was taking piano lessons and used to practise several hours a day. The sound is a familiar one to me, like the noise of our first van, which had to be started with the aid of a crank and which was often stubborn.

Shortly afterwards a lorry replaced the handcarts.

When I had to choose, I opted for Latin and Greek. Was this because the teacher had stressed the difficulties of Greek? Many are called, he had said, but few are chosen, implying that Greek was the supreme attainment; I was also attracted by the mysterious quality of the writing.

My examining magistrate might perhaps maintain that this was yet another attempt of mine to escape from life – from the life of the group, of course. Greek classes were the most sparsely attended, and among the senior boys who were preparing their *bachot* there were only six or seven doing Greek, and you saw them in the courtyard chatting to the master on an equal footing.

My grandfather Allard died while I was in the fourth or fifth form. He had been increasingly dissatisfied of late with his life with the Cassegrains, despite his affection for his daughter Julie. The house was noisy, his son-in-law an insolent vulgarian, and he came more and more frequently to take refuge with us.

He died in the courtyard, on the other side of the wall, sitting in his chair. His pipe had dropped from his hands. They spoke of heart disease. I took so little part in family life that I don't know much about it. When I was not studying I was reading. I often read a book a day, sometimes two or even three during the holidays.

I watched my sister growing into a young girl, with some astonishment, and I was surprised by the way she talked about boys. From the sexual point of view I was not precocious, and it was in the company of a school-fellow, Ledoux, more enterprising than myself, that at fifteen I made my first approaches to a woman, a pro whom we'd had our eyes on for several days.

'Both of you?' she had exclaimed.

Our naïvety amused her. Subsequently, as though by mutual agreement, Ledoux and I avoided one another.

In 1930 – I'm practically sure of the date – we spent a month at the seaside. My father drove us to Dieppe, where he had rented a floor in a villa, and he had to leave us – my mother, my sister and myself – after a few days, for summer was always his busiest time.

I hear the rain falling, I smell the odour of the dog and of my overcoat drying, and of my own skin, for the stove gives out a considerable heat. Like the one we had at Puteaux, you can never set it at just the temperature you want.

I have other memories which I might recall. What I should find interesting would be to compare them with those that Philippe and Daniel will have some day of the same period in their lives. Don't people say that it is the period that matters most and on which the rest of our lives depends?

For my own part, I cannot recognize myself in the schoolboy I once was, perhaps because I did not try to live my own life but buried myself deeper and deeper in books.

I remember one evening seeing my father – a powerfully built man with a ruddier complexion than ours – come back from one of his building sites with chalk dust in his hair and on his shoulders. It must have been winter-time, since I was not working in my bedroom but in the parlour, where a fire was now lit.

I was preparing a Greek composition and he bent over the page which I was covering with the signs he found so mysterious. He stood behind me and I could not see him. I was none the less conscious of his satisfaction and pride, of a sort of respect suddenly felt by him for his son.

My childhood was not an unhappy one, neither was it dreary or disturbed. I have as many sunny memories as cloudy ones; in the courtyard for instance, on a chair tipped back with my feet on a pile of planks and a book in my hand, and all the noises of the house, those of Puteaux and of the tugs along the Seine, running through my brain to be recorded there without my knowledge.

*

It is three o'clock, and it's still raining. My overcoat, which dries slowly, weighs twice as much as usual, and as I have no other there is no question of going out again. I think, moreover, that another walk through puddles would scarcely appeal to Bib.

Some time ago, one Saturday evening when I carried up the daily packet to the mezzanine floor, Madame Annelet asked me:

'What do you do on Sundays, Félix?'

I simply replied: 'Nothing.'

She looked at me insistently, and I concluded that she had understood. She does nothing either. She does nothing all week save read magazines and historical novels. Since she has become practically tied to her room I have the impression, every Saturday evening, that she's going to send for me.

On Sunday mornings she still has Renée. But the girl goes off immediately after lunch, for she has her free afternoon and evening as well as another evening during the week. There is nobody on the ground floor, where the shutters remain closed. Madame Annelet can't fall back on ringing for me. A cold supper is laid out by her side. On a day like today, except for the patter of rain and the noise of passing buses, absolute silence must reign.

For some little time now, my walks with Bib have been curtailed on account of my health. As recently as two years ago we used to walk along the embankment as far as Charenton, looking at the barrels behind the railings at Bercy, and the canal-boats moored one behind the other, and pausing beside the occasional angler.

We know all the benches well. And I also know all the pavement seats outside the cafés where I pause as soon as the sun breaks through a little, and sometimes order a glass of white wine, which never tastes the same as that which I drank when I came out of Melun Gaol.

I am amazed whenever I have to consider dates. I am now forty-eight. More precisely, I shall be forty-nine in January. Most men of my age are better preserved than I am, and I'm a premature old man.

This has no connection with the rather vague question I'm asking myself: how have I spent my life, how has time passed during those thirty years since my *bachot* and my entry into the Sorbonne?

On the one hand, I cannot recognize myself in the young man I then was, and, on the other, I feel as if it were yesterday. I am sometimes shocked at the idea that a life can bring so little, can pass almost without leaving any trace.

At eighteen, at twenty, when I was still given to daydreaming, I had constructed a little personal theory which was neither scientific nor philosophical, but which fascinated me.

From a physics lesson I had gathered that a certain exchange takes place between bodies that come into contact with one another, that friction, for instance, leaves its mark upon objects.

So I imagined that we leave our mark in the places through which we pass during our lives, somewhat as game leaves a trail which dogs recognize by sniffing the air. No, not a smell, a different sort of trail, or rather a succession of ghosts, drifts of ectoplasm.

I discovered long ago that nothing of the sort happens, that the only images of us that survive – and for how short a time! – are the distorted, often caricatural images floating in the memories of those who have known us.

It's not for this reason that I dog the footsteps of Philippe and Daniel; the proof being that I never show myself to them. The last time they saw me they were less than six years old and I was still a fine-looking man, well dressed and not yet overweight.

All that I'm doing is watching them grow up and convincing myself that they are turning into men. At their age, hadn't I too begun to think myself a man?

My entry into the University gave rise to no family arguments. Since I had embarked on the study of Classical languages, it was the obvious and only course to take. My father was rather sorry that his only son would not eventually carry on his business, but in his heart he was proud of me.

I took him, late one afternoon, to the Rue des Ecoles, and he stepped respectfully on the ancient paving-stones in the courtyard.

'Why, they've put up a statue to Victor Hugo!'

Nothing could have touched him more, Hugo being one of the few authors familiar to him. Seeing Pasteur at the other end of the steps reassured him still further, as if, between two such men, I was in good hands.

I showed him the amphitheatres, whose names he read on the pediments: Turgot, Richelieu, Guizot. ... He sat down for a moment on one of the seats, in a lecture-room where we were alone and where, none the less, he lowered his voice as if in church.

I might have become a schoolmaster. This career, on which I had decided at an age when I did not even understand the meaning of the term, would probably have suited me.

At the Santé prison, where I stayed during the preliminary investigation of my case, I was asked to give elementary lessons to some young delinquents. I agreed. For reasons unknown to me, lack of space no doubt, I was soon transferred to Fresnes, where I stayed only a few weeks and where I had no other occupation than arguing with my lawyer, Maître Forniol.

Once I had been sentenced to five years hard labour I was taken to Melun where, theoretically, I should have undergone six months' solitary confinement. Such are the administrative regulations. You live alone in a cell, day and night, seeing nobody except, once a day, the chief warder and, once a month, the Director or his assistant. Silence is obligatory.

For longer sentences than mine the period of solitary confinement is a whole year, and I've heard it described as a nightmare by most prisoners.

The prison doctor, who looked in from time to time, was surprised not to find me depressed, and indeed seemed worried by my indifference. As I learnt later, he went so far as to recommend that a special watch be kept on me lest I should try to commit suicide.

'I get the impression that you're not reacting,' he told me one day. 'Do you sleep normally? Don't you sometimes get a choking feeling?'

'No.'

'Are you eating all right?'

'Whatever I'm given.'

'Have you had any visitors from outside?'

'No.'

'Or any letters?'

'None either.'

He wanted to make me tell him, to see in what tone I should speak, although he knew all about me from my record, in which all such things were put down.

'No discomfort? No pain anywhere?'

No. I had been given the choice between various manual tasks, and for lack of a proper vocation I had chosen to cut out puppets.

'Do you get your daily walk?'

In the yard; it was compulsory. You saw nothing but walls and bricks. As you walked you heard, like an echo, the footsteps of other men walking in other parts of the star-shaped yard. There was nobody to be seen but the warder in the centre, gloomy, indifferent, doing his job.

'If I were you I'd ask to be seen by the neurologist. You're entitled to it. I can't force you; but it would at least enable you to spend a few days under observation in the infirmary.'

'My nerves are perfectly sound.'

I had no desire to be questioned by a specialist. I had been asked so many questions during the last six months, and had been watched as if I presented some problem. The Director took an interest in me, too; like the doctor, he was baffled by my total lack of reaction.

This was due, no doubt, to the fact that prisoners from a certain social class usually complain, demand special treatment, either fall ill or pretend to do so.

For hundreds of years monks have chosen a way of life not unlike this. And how many city-dwellers deliberately choose an even stricter routine than that of the prison?

'I don't imagine you'll be kept long in the cell, Allard. In my last report I've suggested curtailing your period of solitary confinement, and I've stressed your good conduct.'

What good conduct? Did they expect me to hit the chief warder during his visit?

'According to your record, you've done some advanced literary studies. Would you like to be attached to the library? The man who's been our librarian for six years is due to be released next week. The post is a responsible one, for it involves not merely distributing books haphazard but guiding readers, particularly young prisoners.'

I did the job for nearly four years. It was rather like being a schoolmaster, after all, and I recognized the same smell of old paper as in the Bibliothèque Sainte-Geneviève. Almost all my fellow prisoners had visitors. I expected none. I never had a single visitor, and I did not mind; far from it!

I followed a monotonous curriculum, just as I do today in my somewhat larger prison which includes the Rue des Arquebusiers, a bit of the Boulevard Beaumarchais, the Place des Vosges and the banks of the Seine.

I still follow rules which I have laid down for myself, or which have been laid down for me, and I remain confined within invisible walls.

Last Sunday I allowed myself to interrupt my programme by going for lunch to the Place du Tertre, and as far as I can judge it did not suit me.

It's strange, surely, that my recollections of the Sorbonne convey the same impression of routine. My life was apparently as free as possible. I was past the stage when my parents could worry about me. They knew nothing about the time of my classes, the work I was doing or the complicated set-up of the various examinations and diplomas.

They trusted me, they felt no anxiety about me, being chiefly concerned about my sister, who had begun to lead her own life and assume an independent air.

'If only she could find some steady lad who'd help me and take over the business some day!' my father would sigh.

I entered the Sorbonne in 1932. I was a tall, lanky adolescent of whom nobody would have foretold that he would eventually become a mass of unhealthy fat, on whom any garment would look shapeless.

I still had my room in the old house, and the shelves were crammed with books as in my present den.

At the Lycée Pasteur I had been an outstanding pupil, and my teachers were confident of my success. What happened to me during the following spring, that of 1933?

I am quite incapable of saying. I had chosen the compulsory subjects for candidates for the teaching profession, and had drawn up my programme.

At first I was passionately interested in philosophy, and all winter I kept up my Greek, as well as studying ancient and medieval history.

The tram still ran in those days, and I used to take it early in the morning, with my books tucked under my arm, and read them during the journey to Paris.

I took notes at lectures, and would usually lunch in some cheap restaurant before going to my next class.

When the weather improved and the days grew longer I formed the habit of sitting at an open-air café terrace or in the Luxembourg garden, and not returning to Puteaux before nightfall.

I went about in a daze. I became absorbed into the spring, the light, the warmth, the coming and going of the crowd. I watched the passers-by and followed them with my thoughts as though to reconstitute their life-stories.

I suppose that was the nearest I ever came to what is called happiness. The outside world permeated my skin; shadow and sunlight, the trees in the squares, the continuous movement along the Boulevard Saint-Michel, as well as the smell of beer and the click of billiard balls.

During two whole months, I read my books only inattentively, my eye soon distracted by the sight of a beggar, a red or a white dress, a child's boat sailing on the water of the pond. I could have spent an hour without boredom, watching anything living – an ant, a bee, a flower.

I had been trained in the discipline of the Lycée, and here I was let loose in a world of movement and colour in which I could enjoy myself without having to render an account to anyone.

I failed, by one mark, my French Literature exam, although the subject was an easy one: the theatre during the first half of the eighteenth century. I did not tell them at home. I had just made the acquaintance of a red-haired girl who worked as maid for a doctor in the Faubourg Saint Germain; I had to sit waiting in the evenings, on the edge of her iron bed on the seventh floor, until her employers had finished dinner and she had done the washing-up.

On her account, I spent only one week at Dieppe with my mother and sister, on the pretext that I had some indispensable work to do in Paris. Ironically enough, I quarrelled with the girl a few days later. It took me a fortnight to find somebody else, and I spent the time tramping through the deserted summer streets.

The whole of this period is bathed, in my memory, in a kind of luminous haze. Nothing mattered. Nothing was important. I would leap at random on the platform of a bus, to go wherever it took me. I would stare into shop windows, sit down in cafés. If I mentioned billiards just now, it's because I played the game for two or three months, on the first floor of the Cluny Brasserie.

My parents' chief source of worry was still my sister; they treated me as a grown man, and nobody had any doubts as to my future.

Yet by the end of the second winter I was only aiming at the *Licence ès lettres libre,* and thus had given up all thoughts of the teaching profession.

I was not unduly alarmed. I did sometimes have a moment of panic, when I thought about it.

'What are you going to do later?'

I'd heard that question so often! Well, between the ages of nineteen and twenty-and-a-half, I never put it to myself. I deliberately ignored it. I chose subjects as the fancy took me, and in this way I put myself down for a course on sociology to which I went only three times, and I nearly took up Chinese. The Sorbonne was merely an excuse, a background, a way of life.

For years we had had no servant in the house. My grandmother had never had one, nor my aunts, so far as I knew. It was less a question of money than a moral attitude; a woman must run her own house and prepare the meals.

My grandfather had built suburban villas in the traditional craftsman's way, brick by brick. My father, right from the start, had equipped himself for building in reinforced concrete, and when he got an order for a six-storey building he increased his stock and rented some land just outside Puteaux.

These changes must have coincided more or less with my parents' engagement of a maid and their purchase of a new car, no longer a van but a real car with four doors. Inevitably I demanded to take a driving test and, once I had got my licence, I borrowed the car more and more frequently.

I had companions, but no friends. I went with girls, but never long with the same one. In spite of the car, I didn't act the rich man's son. I had little pocket money and although I liked being well dressed I did not attach over-much importance to this.

As I write, trying to isolate this three-year period, I feel increasingly amazed at my own unawareness. I ought to have realized that sooner or later I should have to tell my parents that I had only managed to secure two diplomas, one in medieval history and the other in the general history of philosophy. These led nowhere, opened no professional doors. Teaching was now out of the question and I had learnt nothing else.

I had read, had read almost everything that mattters. I had discussed for hours, sitting in the smoke-filled room of the Café d'Harcourt or outside on the terrace. I had argued for hours about Russian, English and American writers, about the lives of great men, about evolution, and so forth.

And what else? I lived in the moment, taking my fill of selfish and fleeting pleasures.

The streets fascinated me, but I could also sit still in a square, my eyes half closed, enjoying the sun's warmth on my eyelids and feeling perfectly happy.

At eighteen, my sister became engaged to a commercial traveller called Noblet, and I believe my parents heaved a great sigh of relief at the idea that they would soon be rid of their responsibility.

I don't know where or how the couple met, which proves how much I had lost contact with my family. I merely remember the wedding and the small flat they went to live in, in the Rue Lamarck in Montmartre.

I don't know, either, if my father tried to persuade Noblet to go into his business. The fact remains that a few years later the latter bought a hardware business in Rouen – why Rouen, I wonder? – where he now owns the town's biggest household-goods store.

They have four children. I have only seen the two eldest, both as dark-haired as their father but with the blue eyes of the Allards, as they say in my family.

I still had to do my military service for which, as a student, I had been granted a postponement. And I also had to earn my living.

Meanwhile I was quite happy just to breathe in life as, when I was a small child, apparently I used to breathe the smell of an orange for hours and burst into tears when anyone attempted to peel it.

# The Yellow Notebook

*Monday, 18 November 9 p.m.*

Yesterday I had to cramp my writing, for I had reached the end of my notebook and had no other. Today I went to buy one at the stationer's, and chose a yellow one for a change. I am rather worried at having written so much without realizing it. It won't do for this to become a mania, and for notebooks to accumulate. And I don't like my complacency, the pleasure I seem to take in talking about myself. When I bought the yellow notebook I vowed that there won't be any others, that this shall be the last, that under no circumstances will this self-assessment I have undertaken become an excuse.

It has stopped raining. During the night the wind began to blow violently, and Bib and I, living under the roof as we do, had the full benefit of it.

This morning it was blowing full gale. The papers talk of ships in difficulties on the Channel, of havoc wrought on the Atlantic seaboard, of a factory chimney collapsing somewhere in Normandy, and trains held up by the trees and telegraph poles lying across the rails.

In our district, a number of tiles have been blown off and lie shattered on the pavement, and from time to time a few more come down. I am always excited by seeing the forces of Nature let loose; on other days, I seldom glance out of the bookshop window, but today I turned to look out at the pavement dozens of times.

It was fascinating to observe the attitudes of people in the street. Those going towards the Bastille leaned back, with their coats blown tight against their shoulders as the wind drove them on, whereas those going towards the Place de la République bent forward. Several times I witnessed the scene of some gentleman running after his hat, bending with outstretched hand to pick it up just as it went racing off again.

We had few customers; I expected this, and so did Madame Annelet, who feels nervous and ill at ease when the wind blows, and kept on sending for me. Renée looked as if she hadn't slept, which reminded me of the little redhead in the Boulevard Saint-Germain. I wonder what became of her. I ask myself that about everyone, male or female, who has ever crossed, or come into contact with, my life.

If they feel the same curiosity about myself, what sort of fate do they ascribe to me?

At exactly seven minutes past eleven – I looked at the time on the electric clock that stands above the flowered curtain – the telephone rang. I picked up the receiver and said hullo.

'Is that Annelet's, the bookshop?'

'Yes.'

A woman's voice which I did not recognize. Some of our customers give their orders by telephone, not many of them.

After a slight hesitation, as it seemed to me, the voice went on:

'Who is speaking?'

'The assistant.'

This time the hesitation was so unmistakable that I, in my turn, asked:

'Did you wish to speak to Madame Annelet?'

She has the telephone beside her bed. The two instruments are connected to the same line, so that she can listen to all conversations, which she unfailingly does, as I presently found out.

'You are Monsieur Allard?' the voice insisted.

Since I left Melun nobody has rung me, except the few customers I have mentioned, who know me as Monsieur Félix. I said yes, with some reluctance.

'Félix Allard?' the voice insisted.

'Yes.'

Another pause. We had not been cut off, however, for I could still hear the sound of breathing. At last a click told me the receiver had been replaced. Madame Annelet allowed time for me to get over my surprise, ask myself questions and construct hypotheses. I am convinced that she must have exercised great self-control not to ring for me immediately. She waited

373

five minutes before pressing the bell. I went up. Renée was tidying the room. The vacuum cleaner stood unused on the carpet.

'Do you know who that was, Félix?'

I have grown used, at long last, to being looked at like that, with those unmoving eyes that miss no trace or agitation or untruthfulness, no inner movement however vague and fleeting. One has the impression of being naked, or surprised in some humiliating posture, in the lavatory for instance. My sister had the habit of suddenly opening the bathroom door when I was on the toilet. It never worried her to be seen thus.

'No. I've no idea.'

'You didn't recognize the voice?'

'I tried to. I'm still trying, without success.'

'It wasn't your wife's?'

'Certainly not. My wife's voice is high-pitched.'

'She might have disguised it on purpose.'

'Not to that extent.'

Nor was it the voice of Monique – Daniel's mother, who lives a little way down the Boulevard Beaumarchais.

'Have you picked up anybody lately?'

'No. I've not been near a woman for three months. I've not wanted to.'

'Somebody who knows you may have seen you coming in here or going out, or caught sight of you through the window.'

'It's possible.'

'Are you frightened?'

'Of what?'

I was disturbed and uneasy none the less, and I still am. She went on, lighting a cigarette:

'It must be somebody who knew you long ago, and, since you have altered, isn't sure that it's really you. It's highly probable that you will soon meet this woman or that she will write to you.'

One of the few customers we had that day came in at that moment and I went down into the shop to serve him. I did not go upstairs again until shortly before lunch time.

'Tell me, Félix. There's something I've been wanting to ask you ever since you told me of your intention.'

'What intention?'

I was at a loss. I felt as remote as I used to feel, sitting on a chair in the Luxembourg gardens.

'Of going away for good. You must have thought about how you'll do it, surely?'

In the first place I had never taken her into my confidence. I hadn't told her about anything and it was she who had wormed it out of me. In any case, I resented her use of the future rather than the conditional tense.

'Do you own a gun?'

I smiled. She, however, remained quite serious, as though it was a matter of concern to her.

'Poison? Have you got hold of any poison?'

This was as indecent as my sister's bursting into the bathroom. I'm beginning to believe that women lack our sense of propriety. I remained evasive.

'It depends on what you call poison.'

'Sleeping tablets?'

'Perhaps.'

'You've quite decided? Aren't you afraid of changing your mind and wanting to go on living once it's too late? That must be appalling! Not to be able to move nor to call out, to lie there motionless waiting, without knowing quite how long it'll take. ... Go and eat, Félix. ... You've spoilt my lunch for me ...'

I ate mine at Rose's, the little restaurant opposite where I lived, among packers and lorry drivers. They are used to me and to Bib. He knows them, and goes up to sniff at them one after the other, wagging his stump of a tail.

Afterwards, we cut short our walk, for the wind took my breath away and my lips must have been blue.

During the afternoon there were no telephone calls. Madame Annelet did not refer to the morning call and made no fresh allusions to my death.

I myself was thinking not of my own death, but, reverting to what I wrote yesterday, of another death which changed my destiny overnight.

It was the seventh of June, one of the few dates of which I'm quite sure. A heavy, scorching midsummer sun slowed down the traffic in the streets so much that even the buses seemed to crawl. The colours were darker and denser, and the foliage of the trees along the Boulevard Saint-Michel was as still and sombre as a stage set.

At half past ten I was sitting outside a café, the D'Harcourt, in a yellow cane chair, in front of a glass of beer. A dark young woman was sitting less than a yard away from me at another small table, and had just eaten two croissants, dipping them into her *café crème*.

We glanced at one another a few times, intermittently, what I used to call question-mark glances. It was a game I enjoyed playing. It either works or it doesn't.

It worked. After a few moments she could not restrain her laughter.

'You are funny. What d'you want from me?'

'I don't know yet.'

She had a slight foreign accent. A little later I learnt from her that her name was Sonia, that her father was a Russian engineer working in Belgium, where she was born.

I had the car. Towards midday we alighted from it, Sonia and I, in front of an inn on the banks of the Seine, a few kilometres from Corbeil. We lunched outside. When our coffee was brought I went inside to whisper something to the proprietress, who handed me a key. By two o'clock, Sonia was lying naked on an iron bedstead, in a whitewashed room with closed shutters, smelling of slightly musty hay.

'Have you got a girl?'

'No.'

'You'd rather take advantage of what comes your way, like this? Have you often come to this room?'

'Only once.'

It was quite true.

'Admit that you're fond of change.'

'It depends.'

We got dressed about five o'clock, after dozing for a while. As she was thirsty we went back to the terrace and drank a bottle of white wine – Samur, I remember. I was weary, in a sort of daze. She insisted, nevertheless, on my stopping by a wood so that she could pick some broom. It all combined to produce a complex and rather sickly smell: her sweat, the broom, the white wine, the hay in the mattress . . .

I dropped her at six o'clock on the corner of the Boulevard Raspail, and in the driving mirror I could see her in the middle of the pavement, renewing her powder and lipstick, while men turned round to look at her.

I drove back to Puteaux. Leaving the car in the yard I pushed open the front door, calling out as usual: 'When do we eat?'

I fell silent immediately. I saw before me the staircase leading to the first floor, on my left the kitchen door, which should have been open, and on the right the drawing-room door. I don't know why, everything looked empty and frozen into stillness. Then, slowly and almost solemnly, the left-hand door opened and I saw my mother standing motionless before me for a moment, then she flung herself on my breast and burst into sobs.

Over her shoulder I caught sight, in the kitchen, of people whom I had not expected to see there, my sister and her husband, Aunt Julie who had not set foot in our house for several years, Victor the foreman, an old woman from the neighbourhood, and various other people, sitting or standing motionless, with expressionless faces.

'Your father, Félix! . . . Oh God! Who'd have thought this morning. . . . He was so cheerful! . . . It was the first time I had held my mother in my arms thus, not like a son, but as though I had suddenly taken my father's place.

'You know what he was like. . . He wanted to see everything for himself. . . . He was up there on the fifth floor, on a plank which. . . . Come in here!'

Carefully and noiselessly, she turned the handle of the drawing-room door. She pushed it open just as softly, and in the half-darkness I saw my father dead, already wrapped in his shroud, his hands clasped over a chaplet, an unlighted candle on either side of the bed which had been brought down from his room.

She whispered in my ear: 'Go and kiss him . . .'

I think she must have given me a slight push. I took three or four steps, I bent forward and laid my lips, furtively and without pressure, on the cold forehead.

Afterwards, I don't quite know what happened. I rushed off.

I hurried up the stairs, I flung myself at full length on my bed and tried to cry, unavailingly. My chest ached. I gnawed the bedcover.

Why should it be that day, of all days, while I had been . . .

I muttered between my teeth: 'It's my fault. . . . It's my fault. . . . It's because of me that it happened . . .'

Not only because of Sonia, the inn and that hateful broom. Because of everything. Because of my deceitfulness, those three years that I had stolen from everybody.

I thumped the bed with my fist.

'No, no, I won't . . .'

Someone touched my shoulder and I turned round in a fury.

'Whatever . . .'

It was my sister.

'Calm down, Félix. You've got to keep calm for Mother's sake. She had a frightful time. . . . She's been very brave. Don't deprive her of the little strength she has left . . .'

What right had Louise to talk to me like that? She was no longer one of the family. She had another name. She didn't live with us.

'You'd better come down. Mother's getting worried . . .'

'What are all those people doing downstairs?'

'There's old Madame Rinquet, who laid him out when they brought him back from hospital. . . . Mother was a bit beside herself . . .'

'Wasn't he . . .'

It was hard to say the word.

'Wasn't he killed immediately?'

Why was she suddenly embarrassed?

'Yes, probably. . . . We don't know. . . . Victor was in the building yard. . . . The local doctor wasn't at home, and Victor thought it best to tell the police, who sent an ambulance . . .'

I looked at her spitefully.

'And then?'

'Well, nothing. . . . When he got to the hospital it was too late and they sent him back to us here . . .'

'What time did the accident happen?'

'About half past ten . . . By twelve o'clock they'd brought him

378

back ... Mother rang me ... I hurried over with André ... He tried to reach you, he rang up the secretary's office at the Sorbonne ...'

I reddened in sudden panic, wondering what André had been told.

'They couldn't find you. ... Nobody knew where you were ...'

But I knew. When my father lay dying, I was drinking beer at a café in the Boulevard Saint-Michel and ogling my neighbour with stupid smiles.

While he was being brought home, we were speeding towards the inn on the banks of the Seine, and while the drawing-room was being turned into a mortuary chamber I was making love.

My hands still smelt of that girl and that broom. I went to wash them. I would have liked to take a bath, to purify myself. I considered myself shameful.

'What are you going to do?'

'I'm coming down ...'

'That's not what I mean. I'm talking about the future, about Mother, about the house ...'

She'd thought of everything, of course! But I remembered chiefly the way my widowed mother had quite naturally flung herself into my arms. I was as tall as my father, not quite as broad nor as tough. None the less I was now the man of the family.

'Come on. Go downstairs first ...'

And as I dried my hands I stared into the mirror at my tense face and questioning eyes.

*

It was the year of the Popular Front, I am sure of that because the funeral procession met a demonstration carrying red flags, slogans, banners waving over people's heads, and the demonstrators almost all took off their caps as they passed. I also recall seeing, on the walls, posters depicting a clenched fist.

I cannot remember what pretext my sister found for spending the night at her house with her husband. She may have been afraid that this first evening would be too painful for my

379

mother. As it happened, late that afternoon Doctor Chollet, who had looked after us from birth, dropped in to see her and gave her a sedative.

Consequently I had to dine with Louise and my brother-in-law and then sit with them for some time. I discovered then to what extent I had become a stranger. During the past year I scarcely came home except to sleep and I could count up the number of meals I had eaten with my family.

Details which ought to have been familiar to me surprised me. I hardly knew the maid, an Alsatian girl named Frida. She, too, now that my father was dead, began to treat me as the head of the house, and did not pay the same respect to Louise's husband, in her eyes a mere son-in-law.

'Have you taken any decision, Félix?'

I stubbornly refused to follow her on to that ground or discuss anything with her.

'I've got to know, though. If the business is to be sold up, I suppose Mother will come to live with us.'

Had she an ulterior motive? I'd rather not commit myself about that. I stayed with them for another half-hour out of politeness, and then pretexted a headache to go to bed.

They must have left early next morning. That has gone from my memory. But I've a clear recollection of the house with its shutters almost all closed, because of the sunlight, and the whisper of the sultry air outside.

We ate alone together for the first time, my mother and I, and as I looked at her I calculated her age. My father had been fifty-one; he was four years older than her, so that she must be forty-seven, which seemed old to me. I had been surprised, these last three days, to hear people repeat:

'To be taken so young!'

In my mind, my father had had a full life and enjoyed his fair share. I can't attempt to reconstitute our comings and goings that day. I only know that during the afternoon, when I came down from my bedroom, I found my mother in the office, a small, partially glazed room in which we seldom set foot.

I had looked for her everywhere else and I was surprised to find her absorbed in reading letters, particularly as she was wearing her glasses, which I had seldom seen. They had recently been prescribed for her for reading and writing.

'Am I disturbing you?' I asked rather awkwardly.

She smiled at me with that new smile which she kept to the end of her days, a bitter-sweet smile which irritated me more than once, particularly after a few years. I don't know why it reminded me of the colour mauve, which, when I was small, women wore for half-mourning.

'You know you never disturb me.'

'What are you looking for?'

'Victor needs a letter which must have come quite recently.'

'Would you like me to help you?'

Then, suddenly, just as she was looking at me, I took my decision.

'You know, Mother, you can count on me.'

'What d'you mean?'

'That I'm going to stay. I shall try and learn the ropes.'

'You're going to carry on your father's business?'

'Why not?'

'And you'd sacrifice your career, your studies, all the trouble you've been to?'

We were cheating, both of us. She was pretending to be surprised at my decision, although she expected it from me. I, for my part, had no alternative.

'I'm not all that keen on becoming a schoolmaster.'

'Can you see yourself climbing up scaffolding?'

'Perhaps it's not indispensable for me to do so. I should have people to help me, including Victor, who'll gradually put me in the picture.'

'You're doing it for my sake, aren't you?'

'No, no!'

That was to be the tone of our relationship for the next ten years. She kissed me effusively, but this time she did not cling to me.

'You're quite sure, Félix? You won't regret it some day?'

'Tomorrow I shall start work with Victor right away.'

His name was Victor Michou, and he was about my father's age, almost as broad as he was tall, with the neck and shoulders and biceps of a wrestler. He took considerable pride in having travelled all round France as journeyman, going from town to town, from one province to another, often on foot, to learn his trade and eventually to become master of it.

He was married to a wife who was even tinier than my mother, and their only sorrow was that they had no children.

'You'll see, Monsieur Félix! For an educated man like yourself it won't be hard. I left school at twelve myself, and it took years to get some things into this head of mine . . .'

In my father's time an accountant, Monsieur Beauchef, used to come one afternoon a week to look at the books. I got him to devote a whole day to us, then two, and he ended by working exclusively for us.

We went to the lawyer's, and I signed an agreement allowing me five years' respite before paying Louise her share of the inheritance.

This was another panel of my life, of quite a different colour from the previous one and moreover very unlike what was to come after.

My mother, to my surprise, not only took an interest in the business but was far better informed about it than I had imagined, which makes me suppose that my father must have talked to her about it when they were alone together. Perhaps he even asked her advice on occasion.

She knew the names of customers, of suppliers, of workmen, and also technical terms which I had often heard without bothering about their meaning. She knew what stage the various buildings had reached and had met several of the architects.

I have referred to a bitter-sweet smile. The word might serve to describe our whole existence. Let's say that it was pleasantly monotonous. We were fond of one another, Mother and I, but I realized that I scarcely knew her and she probably made the same discovery about myself.

'How are you going to manage about your military service, now that you're no longer a student?'

'My postponement's valid for a year. After that we'll see.'

It was Noblet, my sister's husband, who solved my problem, I'm sorry to admit, for I don't like feeling indebted to him. We have never quarrelled, but neither have we ever sought closer contact. Let's put it that I dislike seeing an outsider involved with our family concerns.

He knew a deputy or a senator, who secured a further two-year postponement for me, on the grounds of supporting a widowed mother.

Contrary to what might have been supposed, I adapted myself very well to my trade. Thanks to Victor and Monsieur Beauchef, I soon learned to draw up a building estimate, and the architects were also helpful to me.

Next, Fernand Dinaire, an active and intelligent young fellow of about thirty, with some years' experience, was signed on as works foreman when the business grew still further.

'Don't you ever think of getting married, Félix? You can't go on as you are for the rest of your life . . .'

My mother, needless to say, was not at all anxious for me to get married. We were almost like a sort of married couple. She had formed the habit of treating me as she used to treat my father, with the respect which, in certain circles, is still paid to the head of the family.

'Why don't you go out in the evenings more? It would make a change for you. At your age, you ought to be seeing friends, to know some girls . . .'

She spoke like that to sound me, for in fact I used to go out once or twice a week and had formed the habit of taking my mother to the cinema or the theatre on Saturday nights.

'Look at that girl in the third row. Don't you think she's pretty? She's got such an attractive smile!'

In 1938 we had decided together to have the house repainted outside and inside, the kitchen modernized, the office enlarged, and a second bathroom installed.

'I hardly ever see you with a book. You used to be such a reader!'

It was true. Almost overnight I had lost my taste for reading. I had emerged from my Latin-Quarter daze merely to become absorbed in another. I must be incapable of taking interest in more than one thing at a time.

I had become a serious building contractor, and my age no longer aroused suspicion. I dressed differently. I had grown broader. I walked with a firmer, more masculine step, and I spoke with assurance, sometimes, when on the job, even roughly.

I don't think I was playing a part, or that at each period of my life I have assumed the skin of some character. I did not imagine myself a building contractor; I *was* one, just as in the Boulevard Saint-Michel I had been an authentic student.

After a series of postponements, my military service none the less caught up with me. I went into barracks in August 1939, at Versailles – this, again, was thanks to my family responsibilities. When war was declared, I had not completed my training and could scarcely handle a gun.

Three weeks later, as had happened to my father in 1914, I was sent back to Puteaux and put in charge of building air-raid shelters. I was still in uniform. Some of my workmen, who had been dispersed on mobilization, had come back to me on special assignment.

When the Germans entered Paris we merely resumed our civilian dress, and my mother, terrified of seeing me taken off to Germany, patiently burned my military belongings. My helmet and gas mask must still be in the Seine, somewhere below the bridge.

Paris, which the exodus had emptied, gradually filled up again. We got used to rationing, food cards, black-out curtains over the windows, darkened streets and an oppressive atmosphere. For a time we felt as if we were outside life.

Frida accomplished miracles to provide a little butter and meat for us. An egg became a luxury. I had the same difficulty in procuring a few sacks of lime or cement.

The wisest course was to pass unnoticed, to withdraw into oneself.

I was not building anything, for lack of materials. Victor and the handful of workmen who had not been taken off to Germany could cope with the repairs and alterations which we were commissioned to do.

'If your poor father were still here . . .'

Louise's husband was very busy. We scarcely ever saw him or my sister. They were well dressed, well shod, in spite of restrictions, and seemed prosperous. I have good reason to think that

384

it was money earned on the Black Market that enabled Noblet, after the war, to set up in business at Rouen.

As for the family in the new house, on the other side of the wall, they made no secret of their activities, and when the Liberation came they vanished promptly to avoid trouble. Cassegrain's vans kept going as busily as in peace time and he even bought two new ones.

'Don't you think Julie's wrong to let him do it? I can't help thinking things will end badly one of these days. It was partly your father's and my fault for letting her marry that fellow.'

Only once was reference made to my Aunt Léonore, on the day of the North Africa landings.

'I wonder what's going to happen in Algiers, and whether Léonore is still there.'

In 1943 I had an affair, which lasted several months, with a girl I had met in a shelter during an air-raid warning. She was evidently under-nourished. Her eyes were always anxious, even when we were lying side by side in a furnished room in the Rue Washington. Her name was Irène, Irène Lautier. At all events, that was the name she told me. She used to give a start every time she heard steps on the stair.

'What are you frightened of?'

'I don't know.'

'In the street, you always seem to be afraid of being followed, and here of being arrested.'

'Hush!'

'And yet you're not Jewish?'

'What if I were?'

'You don't look Jewish.'

'Would it make any difference to you?'

'None at all.'

Before the war I had never bothered about politics. I did not join any student political group, and I was neither alarmed nor delighted by the Popular Front. Was this also laziness on my part? Wasn't it rather that mass movements do not interest me?

I felt humiliated at seeing German uniforms in Paris. I only half believed the stories of cruelty towards the Jews, distrusting one sort of propaganda as much as another.

'Listen, Félix, if you don't see me at our meeting-place on Tuesday, take this to the address I shall give you. Above all, don't go there before. Don't try to understand.'

She took off a tiny silver medallion of the Virgin which she wore round her neck.

'Give it into the right hands.'

I spent an uncomfortable Sunday because of this and on Tuesday, at the Marbeuf Métro station, I fiddled with the little medallion in my pocket. Irène never came. The address was that of a middle-class apartment in the Rue de Rennes, fourth floor, left-hand side. The building seemed half empty. Some of the tenants must have taken refuge in the unoccupied zone or in England.

I rang three times, hearing no sound on the other side of the door, and for a moment I suspected a trap. Then the door opened noiselessly and an elderly man, with hair of a dirty grey, in a collarless shirt and slippers, looked at me without saying a word.

'Monsieur Demaret?'

'Have you come from Irène?'

'Yes. She asked me to give you this.'

He did not invite me to come in. Through the crack of the door I caught a glimpse of a drawing-room with carpets rolled up, furniture covered with dust sheets and a great livid mirror over the chimney-piece.

He clenched his teeth as he held out his hand, without glancing at the object. I felt what an effort he made as he muttered: 'Thank you.'

Then he shut the door again and I heard nothing more.

If I am not mistaken, this scene took place in January 1944. A few months later came the Allied landing, the liberation of Paris, and processions down the Champs-Elysées.

There must have been a number of processions. I myself saw two of them and I am incapable of saying whether it was the Victory Parade, as they called it, or the march past of the Americans under Eisenhower, which changed the course of my life once more.

All I know is that it was the second of the two. During the first I was in the crowd at the Rond-point des Champs Elysées, squeezed against the *Figaro* building, and saw practically nothing.

On the eve of the second, Victor said to me:

'If it interests you, I can give you a tip. One of my old mates, whom I still see from time to time, is second hall porter at Claridge's Hotel. Go to see him from me, and he'll take you up on to the roof. They've a great flat roof with a balcony round it, from which you can look out over the whole of Paris, and you'll see the procession better than anyone else . . .'

I went; my mother had thought of going with me, and she only gave up the idea at the last minute, from fear of the crowds.

Victor's friend did, in fact, take me up on to the roof, by way of the back stairs and passages. Claridge's was brimful of uniforms, generals, colonels and admirals of all the Allied countries, including some Russians, whom I saw for the first time.

The only civilians there were high-ranking officials, for the hotel had been requisitioned by the Government. At every window, on every balcony, champagne and whisky were being drunk; everywhere there were laughing girls, also in uniform or else in summer dresses.

Why was the roof almost deserted? Probably the hotel guests had not thought of it, or did not know the way up. We must have been less than a dozen all told. Four Americans, with two young women whom they had certainly not known the day before, had brought up a whole case of champagne and, sitting on the roof with their backs turned to the Champs-Elysées, they were solely concerned with drinking.

I noticed one couple, at a little distance, embracing beside the balcony. I looked down at the crowd, the ranks of soldiers, the tanks, the guns, the military bands, while aeroplanes flew back and forth barely twenty yards over my head.

At one point I became aware of a presence on my right. A girl in a navy blue suit, of almost military cut, was leaning on the same balcony and looking down dreamily at the scene below.

How did I come to speak to her? I've forgotten. I must have asked her if she was French, and then if she was attached to the Army. She said no, that she was living in the hotel, that she was the secretary of a certain Desmarais, with whom she had lately returned from England. He wore the uniform of a colonel, and his post must have been an important one to entitle him to a suite at Claridge's.

'And where were you?'

'At home, in Puteaux. Shall we go for a drink?'

We tried in vain to make our way to the bar of the hotel, where somebody spilt a glass of champagne over my trousers.

'Let's go out through the back. It'll be quieter in the Rue de Ponthieu.'

I first had to protect her against indiscreet hands, and failed to prevent five or six men from embracing her avidly. They were almost all in uniform; I was not. I may have felt envious of them.

By contrast, the small bar we went into after crossing the street was a haven of peace.

'What'll you have?'

'A Scotch, without ice.'

Her name was Anne-Marie Varennes, and I was to marry her three months later.


*Wednesday, 20 November, 10 p.m.*

I did not write anything yesterday, and it was not out of laziness, nor because I had nothing to say. Ideas and memories are only too plentiful, and I am possessed with a feverish eagerness to disburden myself of them. It's as though I foresaw that I shall not get to the end, that something is going to happen which will reopen the whole question. I don't know what. I am seized with a kind of uneasiness, an indefinable anguish, and Madame Annelet's gaze is not likely to dispel it. You could swear that she knows, and that she is watching with interest the progress of . . .

Of what? Not of my illness. I speak of that to nobody. I refuse to think of it. I have always hated illness, not because it brings death closer but because it diminishes us, puts us at the mercy of other people, makes us dependent on them. Even as a schoolboy I was revolted by this idea and wished that I could die in an accident, like my father, before degeneration set in.

I spoke in all seriousness when I described my employer as a witch. Cats have the same knowledgeable air. I don't believe in clairvoyance and yet how can her attitude about my summons, yesterday morning, be ascribed to chance?

The postman calls about half past eight and invariably greets me with: 'Lovely day!' or else: 'Shocking weather!'

Yesterday, it was a lovely day. The wind had veered east and the sun broke through, still pale but almost joyous. The man laid the letters on the counter and went off.

Bills, catalogues, advertisers' leaflets. Madame Annelet gets few letters. In eight years, not one addressed to myself has come to the Boulevard Beaumarchais.

Now, yesterday morning, I actually read my own surname and christian name on an envelope of coarse paper with the Central Police Station's heading. Inside, a printed form with blanks filled in purple pencil.

*Monsieur . . .* (my name, written by hand) *is requested to appear at the Central Police Station of the 3rd Arrondissement, Rue Perrée, on* (in purple: November 21st inst.) *with reference to* (in purple again: a matter concerning him). *Please bring this form with you.*

I thrust the pink paper into my pocket and went upstairs with the bills and leaflets. There had been no rustle of paper, and only a few seconds' delay. Madame Annelet glanced at the envelopes, then looked at me.

'Is that all, Félix?'

'I nodded.

'You're sure?'

Isn't it humiliating, at forty-eight, to be caught out like a naughty schoolboy? And yet I did not blush, and my face is so flabby that any quivering was concealed in the folds of my skin.

'Why are you hiding the truth from me?'

I held out the summons and for a moment I suspected my employer of being behind the whole thing, which makes no sense.

'You have no idea what they want you about?'

'None.'

'You haven't let your dog off the leash or committed any breach of regulations? Well, in that case, we must assume it's the result of Monday's phone call, eh?'

That was most likely. In any case it was something connected with the past. The proof of that is that the paper was addressed to the bookshop and not to where I live. I am duly inscribed at the same police station, so that my address must be in their books. They never bothered to look it up, merely using the address they had been given. But who had given it them?

'Well, on Thursday you'll know the answer.'

This was not the reason, either, why I did not write in this book yesterday. I wanted to prove to myself that it had not become a sort of vice. I went for a walk with Bib, who is bewildered whenever I infringe my own rules.

Madame Annelet is not the only one who watches me live. My dog, too, acts as witness. I lingered later than usual in the Place des Vosges, which is not pleasant after night has fallen, because they shut the gates and it's impossible to sit on a bench. Anne-Marie's windows were darkened by half past six, which is unusual.

Perhaps I allowed myself a day's respite because I am coming to a difficult period? I have known many men who, apparently at least, retain the same opinion about people and things. Or if they change, it's after a long space of time, and they immediately settle down in their new way of thinking.

This is not the case with me, particularly since my trial and imprisonment. I can go further back; it must have started with Anne-Marie. I lived with her for six years. For weeks, for whole months, my opinion about her never varied. Then, all of a sudden, as a result of some minor incident, some remark, some attitude, I would see her for a while with different eyes. It even happened that the change would take place twice in a single day.

When I got up and shaved, and left her for the office or for one of my building sites, I would hum to myself happily, under the illusion that I was smiling at her from a distance and making affectionate contact with her.

At midday, when I went home, I had sometimes become an embittered, disillusioned man, who looked at her as though through an X-ray and wondered why she had come into his life.

In my first notebook I made fun of lovers' meetings.

'Why me?'

'Because you're different.'

'You're different, too.'

Then later on, a few hours or a few days later:

'I couldn't go on living without you.'

'It's a miracle that we should have met. What would have happened if . . .'

A miracle? It depends on the point of view, and my point of view has changed so often that I have become mistrustful. I don't know, then, whether my presence on the roof of Claridge's Hotel on the occasion of a military march past was a miracle or a disaster. All I know is that next day I got back to Puteaux at ten in the morning. I was thirty years old. It was not the first time I'd spent a night out. My mother spoke not a word of reproach, and her first question was: 'Have you had breakfast?'

I had drunk coffee and eaten croissants in the café-bar next to the hotel entrance. I know that my face was not my usual face. I was feverish, my skin was tense and my eyes glittering, and I was trying to conceal my inward excitement.

'Did you have a good time?'

'Very good.'

This was not quite the right term, and my mother knew it. I am convinced now that from that moment something was altered between us, and my mother foresaw the sequel, whereas I had not an inkling of it.

We had drunk a great deal, eaten something or other, and talked a great deal too, Anne-Marie and I, in the riotous revels taking place that night around the Champs-Elysées.

I have no idea what happened elsewhere in Paris, for we kept going round in a circle, indifferent to the increasingly dishevelled groups that sought to drag us into their dance.

I soon had my arm round her waist to protect her, and we walked close together. Our movements quickly harmonized, and we looked at one another from time to time so that each could see in the other's eyes the reflection of his or her own enchantment.

Her surname was Varennes. She was born in Lyons where her father, before the war, had been a journalist. As soon as the

Germans invaded Holland he had foreseen what was to come, and had taken his family to London.

In 1940 Anne-Marie, who was an only child, was seventeen. She still had to pass her second *bachot*. They found a two-roomed flat in Pimlico, close to an open-air market rather like those of Paris. The father worked at the BBC, the mother gave French lessons.

All this became entangled in my mind with the march-past of troops we had been watching. So did the blitz; she told me a lot about the blitz, the sirens, the noise of aircraft in the sky, the bombs, and the buildings that toppled down after swaying for a moment.

'What were you doing meanwhile?'

I still used the formal *vous*. *Tu* only came about four or five in the morning.

'I was learning English. My father had promised to get me into the Free French offices.'

He had not had time to. He and his wife were buried, with others, under the ruins of some church in front of which they were passing on their way to a shelter.

'I was supposed to go out with them. I don't know why I decided at the last minute to stay behind.'

I wanted to know everything. I asked one question after another. We walked till our feet ached. We would go into a bar and drink. The dance went on all round us and, even though we stood apart, we followed its rhythm and partook of its excitement.

'Monsieur Desmarais, who knew my father well, saved the situation for me by giving me a job in his office. He was head of a whole department.'

'How old is he?'

My question made her laugh.

'I don't know, I never asked him.'

'Young or old?'

'Neither old nor young. Thirty-five, maybe.'

'Was his wife with him in London?'

'No. He had embarked from Calais in the very early days and his wife hadn't been able to join him.'

'And you became his secretary?'

'Not immediately. A few months later.'

I have never seen him, and in all probability I never shall. I don't know what has become of him. I have no idea of his physical appearance – tall or short, dark or fair – and yet, for years, he was the man who loomed largest in my pre-occupations. Even today, I am not sure that I don't detest him.

He had been a titular colonel, and chief of some department or other, when we watched the march-past from Claridges Hotel, and later became an Under-Secretary of State, but I never saw his photograph in the papers, and with the first change of government he disappeared from the political scene.

Night was passing. The bars were still as full and as excited as ever. From time to time we danced like everyone else. We found ourselves back on the pavement when the roofs were beginning to be outlined against a paler sky, flushed with pink.

I dared not put the question to her. She must have thought of it herself. I was convinced that if we parted now it would all be over, that I should retain merely the memory of a rather crazy night.

'You're not tired?'

'Not at all.'

I almost suggested going to the Bois de Boulogne to watch the sun rise. We walked back and forth in front of Claridge's, each time postponing the decision, while the porter kept his eyes on us.

'He's getting on my nerves!' she suddenly burst out. 'He seems to be wondering if we're going to make up our minds . . .'

I urged her forward, gently, towards the revolving door and we found ourselves in the deserted hall.

'Which floor?' asked the lift boy.

'Sixth!' she replied.

I was afraid, physically and agonizingly afraid that something would happen to prevent us from carrying it through. We went along ever narrower passages to the back of the hotel. I looked at the shoes outside bedroom doors. She stopped me to point out a pair of tan leather boots beside a woman's shoes with inordinately high heels.

'Who is it?' I asked.

She shrugged her shoulders, implying ignorance. 'A general, for sure!'

She opened her door. I closed it behind us and without a word flung myself upon her. Did she, too, have a feeling that it was important, that what we were doing now would transform the whole of our lives?

Without meaning to, I was tense, fierce, almost cruel. I wanted to hurt her, and I clasped her as though to crush the life out of her.

Afterwards, we looked at one another as though each was asking the same question. We were pale with emotion. There was no lightness in our smiles.

'On which floor does Desmarais live?'

'On the second. . . . He moves when high officials or new delegations arrive. . . . One's never sure, on going out in the morning, of finding one's things in the same room . . .'

'Has he been up here?'

She understood.

'No.'

'And in London?'

'Yes.'

'When you were seventeen?'

'A little later.'

'In the office?'

'In his room at his hotel.'

'Was it the first time?'

'I was a virgin, yes.'

'And it went on?'

'For a few months.'

Why was my throat constricted, my chest shaken by spasms?

'Have there been others?'

'Of course.'

'And now?'

She turned her head away. We were lying side by side and I was holding her hand.

'It seems to distress you, and it's so unimportant!'

'And us, too?'

'I don't know yet. Perhaps not.'

And so, like other people, we had come to feel different. Our night together was different. We made like everyone else, but it was for different reasons!

'When was the last time?'

'Last week. Wednesday.'

'Desmarais?'

I stubbornly harked back to him.

'No. An English airman.'

'Is he still in Paris?'

'He joined his squadron next day.'

I couldn't have cared less about the English airman and the rest.

'And with Desmarais?'

'That ended a long time ago.'

'Why?'

'No special reason. It just came to an end.'

'Do you want to see *me* again?'

'I'm rather afraid to.'

How sincere was she? And I myself? How much was due to alcohol, to the atmosphere created by the procession and the hordes of revelling soldiers?

We talked without ever coming to the end of our curiosity and, when we embraced once again, we made love in a grave and slightly saddened way.

'Was it like this with . . .'

Knowing what name I was going to utter, she laid her finger on my lips and shook her head, restraining her tears.

Later I rang for the waiter, who brought us a bottle of whisky and some mineral water. It was broad daylight. The room was narrow, quite devoid of luxury, one of those rooms set aside in grand hotels for guests' chauffeurs.

'Why haven't you married?'

'I've never met a woman I wanted to marry.'

'Do you live by yourself?'

'With my mother.'

I forget what it was that made us laugh again, as we had

laughed during the previous evening. And it was in laughter that our bodies came together finally, while the hotel grew full of noises and footsteps.

'You see! I've stopped being jealous. I love you!'

I didn't ask myself if it was true or not.

'I love you too,' she answered with the same look in her eyes.

'Tonight?'

'Perhaps.'

'At our little bar in the Rue de Ponthieu?'

For we already had *our* little bar, the first we had been into.

'Eight o'clock?'

Wearing pyjamas and a blue dressing-gown with white spots, she went with me as far as the lift.

'I suppose you're going to bed?' my mother asked me.

I was not sleepy. I was still wildly excited. I none the less fell asleep at last, and when I woke, about three in the afternoon, I had a painful hangover.

*

Poor old Bib! Forgive me. After twice hiding your ball half-heartedly, without bothering to look for a difficult place, I pretended not to understand that you still wanted to play. You did not insist, but instead of going to sleep on the bed you subsided under the table at my feet. I feel that you are uneasy about all these changes in our habits. Are you wondering, as men do, what the future has in store for you?

You're *my* dog. Are you conscious of belonging to me, or do I, on the contrary, exist, in your opinion, solely in order to feed you, take you for walks and play with you? The question is not really so absurd. I ask myself much crazier ones.

Why, it has suddenly struck me: the tricks you perform so readily and which amuse me were not taught you by me. You had an earlier master, who took pains to teach you them, or found pleasure in doing so. It never occurred to me to be jealous of him.

'I want her for my own!'

By the third day, the second, perhaps the first I wanted her for my own, so desperately that I clenched my fists and scowled at passers-by in the street as if the world were conspiring to take her from me.

For my own! What does it mean, exactly? The exclusive use of her body? I should have protested indignantly if I had been told that. I wanted the whole of her, not only her present being but her past and future being.

I have even, on occasion, felt jealous of her father, because he had known her as a little girl and she had spoken of him with admiration and affection.

'Daddy was like you, strong and calm. One had the feeling that as long as he was there one had nothing to be afraid of.'

I made the same impression on everyone: strong and calm.

'I want her for my own!'

And I used to ask her suspiciously, as soon as we met again in our little bar, restored to its normal routine:

'Have you been seeing him?'

'He dictated letters to me for an hour.'

'Nothing else?'

'Of course not!'

Desmarais, as usual. I am not certain today that if he had not existed I should not have invented some other ghost.

How could I secure her more exclusively for myself, how could I feel certain of possessing her? I used to bruise her, to crush her; I made myself suffer, and I was not averse to seeing her at dawn, emptied of tears, her voice hoarse with sobbing, her face wan and swollen, with red marks on it.

What did I want from her, in addition to what she gave me? I have been trying to recall my life and to give a fairly faithful picture of it. It remains none the less basically false, because I am the only one who knows about it. And I myself am no longer sure what is true and what is less true. If I were to live another ten or twenty years the past would probably appear to me in quite a different light.

'Tell me about your life in Lyons.'

'At what age?'

At every age! But why, good Heavens, why this desperate desire to own another human being? And what about her –

must I not belong to her, too? Would she not become jealous of my mother, with whom I was still living?

She did in fact become so later, for a different reason.

'Listen, Anne-Marie. If I asked you to leave him?'

Desmarais, of course, who represented the past, the enemy, the obstacle to be overthrown.

'Do you want me to look for a different job?'

'No.'

A job implied men, one man at least, and part of her days spent out of my ken, in an atmosphere about which I knew nothing.

'I want you to be my wife.'

'I'm that already.'

'To be my wife legally; I want us to live together and never be parted.'

'Aren't you afraid, Félix?'

'Of what?'

'Of making a mistake. You've known me for one week.'

'I love you. I know that I'm incapable of living without you.'

Like everybody else, of course. And presumably this love was as exceptional as everybody else's. Nothing else mattered. My mother sighed as she watched me. Even the workmen exchanged winks behind the back of a boss who was now exultant, now morose and unsociable.

'When can you leave him?'

'Whenever I like. Here he doesn't need me any more, for he's got all the staff he wants.'

'Tomorrow, then?'

'I'll speak to him tomorrow morning.'

'I shall find you a room in Neuilly and then I shall only have the bridge to cross.'

'You know, Félix, my parents left me a little money. You won't need to keep me.'

She said it with a laugh, but the word was enough to set me off again.

'You forget you belong to me.'

'That doesn't mean that . . .'

That what? I was asking her for a couple of months to prepare my mother – as if she hadn't already prepared herself! – to fix up a pleasanter apartment in the old house, and to publish the banns. Was it important to know which of us was going to pay the rent of the room?

'I've something to tell you, Mother.'

'You're going to get married.'

'You've guessed?'

'When?'

'As soon as possible. In six weeks.'

'Are you intending to go and live elsewhere?'

'Why? Unless you dislike the idea, we shall live upstairs.'

'When are you bringing her to meet me?'

'Whenever you like. If I haven't brought her before, it's because she's very scared of you. She's shy.'

'Really?'

Hadn't my mother followed the course of our relationship from day to day, and didn't she know that at our first meeting I had stayed with Anne-Marie until half-past nine next morning? Didn't I spend almost every night out, even when for form's sake I crept back noiselessly at dawn to rumple my bed?

I resented the irony that her smile betrayed, and from that moment something went wrong between us.

The meeting took place quite satisfactorily, without display of feeling; we all remained rather on guard.

'Since you've lived in England, you must like tea. Milk or lemon?'

And I, meanwhile, was dreading some untoward incident, some blunder on the part of one or the other of them.

'What d'you think of her, Mother?'

'She's charming. She isn't quite as I had imagined her.'

'What do you mean?'

'I pictured her fair, and taller, I don't know why. She dresses well.'

'Very simply.'

We had a quiet wedding, without inviting all and sundry of the family, not even my sister Louise and her husband. I insisted on having Victor for my witness, and my works foreman was Anne-Marie's.

She had no relatives in Paris and knew no one there, apart

from her former boss and some people who had returned from London. Before the war she had been in Paris only once, at the age of fifteen, with her father and mother.

We spent a fortnight on the Riviera coast and then, back home, we tried to organize our new life. There were no scenes, no recriminations. On the surface everything went well. We ate our meals with my mother. Anne-Marie had offered to lend a hand in the office, but it had soon been made clear to her that this was a forbidden zone.

We went out a great deal, sometimes more than we wanted to, because this was the only way to be by ourselves. Not that my mother thrust herself on us, at home; on the contrary, she behaved with exaggerated tact, which made her presence all the more tangible. Rather like Bib, who is punishing me by going to sleep under the table out of sight, instead of being in his own place on the bed where I'm accustomed to seeing him.

'Do you intend to spend all your life in Puteaux, Félix?'

'I've never asked myself the question.'

'Is it essential for your business?'

'Yes and no. At the point we've now reached, I'd say no, for I've plenty of work in hand elsewhere.'

I lived in terror of hurting her feelings, distressing or offending her. Her attitude was the same towards me. She told me so.

'Are you happy, Félix?'

'I'm the happiest of men. So long as you love me!'

'Do you doubt that?'

'No.'

Yes. No. Yes. There were moments when I was not far from sharing my mother's view. My mother never expressed an opinion about Anne-Marie, but her attitude, her glances, above all her silences, were more eloquent than words.

'You'll see, my son, that soon you won't be master in your own home. She does just what she likes with you already, and this is only the beginning . . .'

Was Anne-Marie really responsible for what followed? We were dining in a restaurant one evening when a blonde young woman rushed up to my wife and embraced her effusively.

'Anne-Marie! It's you! . . .'

'Monique!'

'I've so often wondered what had become of you . . .'

'Let me introduce my husband . . .'

'Wait till I fetch mine . . .'

He had stayed at their table. His name was Cornille and it was obvious at a first glance that he felt at home everywhere.

'Imagine, Fernand, I've just run into my oldest friend, Anne-Marie Varennes, whom I've so often told you about. We used to live next door to each other on the same quayside at Lyons, when we were *so* high. . . . But forgive me! . . . I forgot you were married too. . . . What's your name now?'

'Allard. . . . My husband, Félix Allard . . .'

The four of us ate at the same table.

'Tell us! What have you done since I lost sight of you?'

I was going to endure agonies again, as I always did when she talked about London. Cornille, however, let the two women gossip and started asking me questions.

'What's your line?'

'Building.'

'That's fine! There's going to be as much building in France as in Baron Haussmann's day, and contractors will make their fortune, just as they did then.'

He was far more of a Parisian than I and I envied his easy manner.

'My concern's with advertising, but only as a springboard into big business. We're always the first to know what's brewing . . .'

They lived in a modern flat on the Quai de Passy. We acquired the habit of meeting and going to the theatre together, then having supper in some night club, where Cornille would invariably go up to greet prominent personalities and kiss ladies' hands.

The two women telephoned each other every morning and met in the afternoons to do their shopping.

'Are you very fond of Monique?'

'I'm glad to have met her again.'

'Because she reminds you of your life in Lyons?'

'No, no, Félix! You're not going to be jealous of Lyons, now? We were only little girls!'

'Weren't you in love with anyone, at fourteen or fifteen?'

'Of my drawing master, a white-haired gentleman who smelt of garlic and wore a broad-brimmed hat.'

My mother's eyes said: 'It's beginning!'

And Cornille remarked, one evening: 'I say, old man, why not *tutoyer* each other?'

'If you like.'

'D'you mind if I call your wife Anne-Marie?'

A quarter of an hour later he was dancing with her and I was dancing with Monique.

'You're jealous, aren't you?'

'Is it obvious?'

'Don't worry as far as my husband is concerned. He always seems to be flirting with every woman. It's his way; he needs to show off.'

He was a more fluent and sparkling talker than myself. I longed to be like him, to juggle as he did with life and with people.

'By the way, Félix, we must have a word one of these days. I've got a little notion that could take us a long way, you and me. You've never been to my office. Next time you're in the Champs-Elysées, come up and say hullo.'

He had to press me repeatedly, and one morning he rang up to say that he simply must see me at three o'clock. When I went there I saw, in one of the huge pale leather armchairs, a little man in black, unkempt, fat, and greasy-looking, whose sparse black hair lay in streaks across his skull, looking as though it had been painted on.

'My good friend Allard. ... My friend Mimieux. ... You don't know Mimieux, but you're going to know him. ... One of the best-informed men about what goes on in Paris, whether it's in newspapers or in banks, in Ministries or the Municipal council. ... He's a sort of *éminence grise*, a go-between, d'you understand?'

No. I did not understand yet. Mimieux had globular yellowish eyes and exuded the sickly smell of a diseased liver.

'You're well aware that in order to relieve congestion in Paris ...'

I still thought this was all idle talk.

'You must know the district of Montesson, round about Carrières-sur-Seine?'

'I've been that way.'

A quarter of an hour later, maps were spread out on the desk, and I can still recall the noises going on in the Champs-Elysées while Cornille was speaking, for it was early summer and the windows were wide open.

'D'you see this piece of land? We've an option on it and before six months are up we shall start building a block of luxury flats there, with a swimming pool, which is to be called the Résidence de la Tour. Fifty-four flats have already been sold before the first stone has been laid. The architect, one of the best in Paris, is at work. Mimieux has undertaken to obtain the requisite permits from the Ministry and the municipalities concerned, for we're on the border between two communes.

'What we're asking you today is whether you'll come in with us. You realize that it's a big undertaking, and that there's big money to be got. You'll have to find equipment and labour, unless you bring it in from abroad. After these blocks there'll be others . . .'

'You're taking me by surprise . . .'

'I wanted to give you first chance. When shall I have your answer?'

'In a week's time?'

'Say Monday. That gives you four days. On Sunday we'll go and visit the ground with our womenfolk. Of course you'll need new offices, in town preferably. Mimieux will fix you up.'

I realized, when I got home, that Anne-Marie had been informed before I had.

'Did Fernand tell you about La Tour?'

'Yes.'

'What have you decided?'

'Nothing yet.'

'Monique assures me that it's a serious proposition, and there's a big private bank involved. What's in your mind?'

'Nothing.'

'You're feeling reluctant?'

'I don't know.'

'Would you mind leaving Puteaux?'

So that, too, had been discussed. I should not only have new offices, but a new flat as well. Without my mother, obviously!

'By the way, did you know, Monique is pregnant.'

'Her husband didn't mention it.'

'She told me yesterday. Wouldn't you like us to have a baby too?'

You have to choose between one interpretation and another. My mother would doubtless have muttered: 'The minx!'

That sometimes happened to me, but I always promptly blamed myself for it.

A wife of my own! A child of my own!

'Félix!'

'Yes?'

'I love you.'

'I love you too.'

'Shall we start it now?'

She was laughing, but we were none the less emotionally excited as we flung ourselves on to the bed.

'Hush. . . . Quietly. . . . Your mother's just underneath us . . .'

By two o'clock in the morning we had almost emptied a bottle of Scotch and were discussing which district we should live in.

Tomorrow, Thursday, at four p.m., I shall know what they want with me at the Police Station.


*Thursday, November 21*

What surprised them most was to see me appear with a dog. Not only the uniformed policemen on the other side of the grey-painted counter, but the people waiting on the seats with their backs against the wall, a dozen or so men and women.

They all began by looking down at Bib's podgy little form, at my feet and legs; then their gaze travelled upward, taking in my stomach and finally resting insistently on my face, then dropped again to settle on the dog.

What was it that astonished and shocked them so?

I held out my pink paper to one of the policemen and it was passed from hand to hand, in each case provoking a frown and a glance in my direction, until finally somebody took it into another room.

'Sit down.'

Provided Bib doesn't take it into his head to sham dead or turn somersaults! There was no sort of contact between the waiting people and myself. They were silent, true, but sitting there side by side they formed a group having certain things in common. Not with me. I was an outsider.

'You're not like other people . . .'

I used to be, though, at the time when I enjoyed being told that I was not.

Now, I am not; and they all felt it, while we were waiting on the same side of the barrier, tormented by the same uneasiness, the same vague dread that one feels in places such as this.

The ordeal lasted only five minutes. Although my neighbours had arrived before me, my name was the one spoken by a clerk in plain clothes as he held open a baize-covered door.

I got up, followed by Bib on his leash, and they all went on looking at us with the same curiosity, the clerk as well and finally the Superintendent sitting behind his desk.

I am sure he was about to make some remark about the dog, but changed his mind and showed me a chair.

'Félix Allard? The same who was once convicted of manslaughter and sentenced to five years' hard labour?'

It was starting all over again, just as at the time of my trial. I was up against people whose business it is to deal with criminals. That's the word, and I am inevitably bound to use it myself.

They had tried to talk to me in an informal way, as though to one of themselves, particularly the examining magistrate, who could not help showing a certain sympathy for me. Sympathy mingled with curiosity, not with repulsion. I was not made conscious of any repulsion at that time; aloofness, rather, and embarrassment.

A man who has killed is no longer one's fellow-man. It is almost as if he had ceased to be quite human.

'How could he have done it? What does he feel? What is he thinking?'

I have perhaps become over-susceptible, and I may be

deceiving myself. Why do passers-by who know nothing about me or my story, why do insignificant people waiting on a police-station bench look at me as if my presence upset them?

Others of my age are visibly sick men, and I am not the only person who takes a small dog about. There are no marks on my face.

'I understand you work as assistant at Madame Annelet's bookshop, Boulevard Beaumarchais?'

'I've done so for the past eight years; I started a few weeks after my release from Melun.'

It disturbs me to be looked at like that.

'Do you live by yourself?'

'With my dog.'

'Do you have a permanent residence?'

'Close to the bookshop, in the Rue des Arquebusiers. I came to register myself at this very station as soon as I moved into my flat.'

He lifted the receiver of a house telephone, without taking his eyes off me.

'Please check up whether a certain Félix Allard ... Allard, yes, no H ... is registered as living in the Rue des Arquebusiers ... Thank you ... I've a few questions to ask you, Monsieur Allard. ... You were a married man with two children, I believe?'

'I still am. There has been no divorce.'

'On your release, you did not go back to your wife. Was this your own decision?'

'No.'

'Have you seen your wife again?'

'Only from a distance.'

'Have you tried to see her?'

'Not exactly. I caught sight of her one day in the Place des Vosges and I learned that she lived there with my son and daughter.'

'When did you make this discovery?'

'Shortly after I came to live in the Rue des Arquebusiers.'

'So you didn't choose this neighbourhood in order to be near the Place des Vosges?'

'No.'

'Didn't you want to see your children again?'

'Perhaps. . . . From a distance . . .'

Each of my answers surprised him and led him a little farther away from the simple truth.

'Have you never attempted to speak to them?'

'Never.'

'Nor to your wife?'

'No.'

'For fear of getting a bad reception?'

'No.'

There was a knock on the door and the official who had showed me in laid a slip of paper on the desk and went out again. This must be the confirmation of my entry in the police register.

'I see . . . I see. . . . So it wasn't deliberately, either, that you came to live close to somebody else. . . You guess to whom I am referring?'

I never flinched, but I suddenly felt very unwell.

'Chance, I am now obliged to believe, brought this other person to live in your neighbourhood. . . This person also has two children, a boy and a girl. . . Will you tell me, Monsieur Allard, why you follow them in the street, and why you sometimes keep watch in front of the building they live in?

'On Monday, when Madame Cornille learned where you work, she decided to come and see me. . . . She's a calm, level-headed person, you know that, don't you? . . . When her daughter first told her about a stranger she kept meeting, who seemed to know her, the mother put it down to a schoolgirl's imagination . . .

'But you followed the brother too, as far as the Lycée Turgot, and you frequently waited in a little café to see him come out. . . . Do you deny it?'

'No.'

'Tell me, in that case, the reason for this kind of spying.'

'It's not a question of spying. I watch them living.'

'Why?'

'I want to know what becomes of them . . .'

'Them in particular?'

'Yes.'

'The children of the man you killed?'

For decency's sake, I lowered my head. This, so I have learned, is what people expect of me.

'And also, I suppose, what becomes of the woman you have widowed?'

'Excuse me.'

'For what?'

'I hoped she would not notice me in the crowd. I have changed a lot in thirteen years.'

'Madame Cornille caught sight of you under the windows of the lawyer's office where she works, in the Rue du Bac.'

'I never tried to . . .'

I could not find any words. I was overwhelmed. If Anne-Marie had come to complain of my behaviour I should not have been affected thus.

'I'm listening, Monsieur Allard.'

'I've got nothing to say . . . I apologize once more. . . . From now on I'll take care to keep out of their way . . .'

I hardly recognized my own voice, which came from very deep down.

'I strongly advise you to. You realize, I suppose, that it is most disagreeable for a woman and her children to endure the presence of the man who . . .'

'Please . . .'

I felt my eyelids swelling. I did not want to cry. He was unaware that he had taken away the little that was left me. He must have assumed that I was troubled by remorse.

'I can see that it's not easy, in your position, to get another job and move to another district. I insist all the more strongly that you must stop annoying this family, to whom you've already done quite enough harm. . . Is that quite clear?'

'I promise . . .'

'I hope you'll keep your word for, otherwise, I should be obliged to take strong measures against you . . .'

He rose, less sure of himself than he would have liked. I got up too, mumbling: 'Thank you . . .'

For the first time, if Bib had not followed me, dragging his leash behind him, I should have forgotten him.

I went through the office where the people were waiting, and their eyes followed me to the door. The Superintendent, it suddenly occurs to me, had not said goodbye; he, too, had watched me go away without a word.

I had promised Madame Annelet to return to the shop; my place there was being taken by Renée, who, every time a customer came in, had to go up to the mezzanine to find out the price of a book.

I stopped to drink a glass of spirits on the way and, when my glance fell on Bib, I seemed to be seeing him for the first time.

I took off my coat in the back room. The dog went to take refuge in his place under the counter. I went upstairs slowly and she did not cross-question me at once. I no longer felt on familiar ground. My last links had just been severed.

'Was it your wife?'

I shook my head.

'The other woman?'

I turned to look at her in stupefaction. I had never told her about Monique's presence in the neighbourhood, nor about Daniel and Martine.

'How do you know?'

'I am capable of using the telephone directory, like anyone else. . . . When you began to change . . .'

What has changed about me?

'I asked myself some questions. Then Renée saw you hanging about in front of a certain block of flats. What does she complain of?'

'I don't know.'

'You've never tried to speak to her or to the children?'

'Never.'

I was so sure, on the contrary, that Daniel would make contact with me one day! I could have sworn he had recognized me, that he was as curious about me as I was about him.

'Does she still feel bitter against you?'

'They didn't tell me so.'

'Why did she go to the police?'

'So that I should stop following them.'

I have undergone too many interrogations not to confess right away a truth which will inevitably be extracted from me in the end.

I have stopped struggling now. I give way, perhaps out of laziness. This conversation frightened me, because I guessed what Madame Annelet was aiming at.

She did not beat about the bush.

'Are you in love with her, Félix?'

Why spoil everything deliberately? I bore no grudge against the Superintendent, who had merely done his duty. But she, with her bony shoulders, her heavily painted fortune-teller's face and her glittering black eyes ... Wasn't she seized with a moment's panic? I was staring at her, with my teeth clenched, and I am almost sure I felt tempted to clutch her throat in my great hands.

'Were you already, before ...' she insisted.

I was being left with nothing, not even the right to daydream. I did not answer. I went downstairs. I almost went off without my coat, just as a short while before I had nearly forgotten Bib at the police station. However, I waited behind the counter until the clock showed twenty-five past six, and then meekly went up the spiral stair to take her the envelope.

'Listen, Félix ...'

'I'm listening.'

'Look at me. Can you hear me?'

'Yes.'

'Promise me to be here tomorrow morning.'

What was she afraid of? She needn't worry. I had no such intention.

'Why?'

'Because I need you.'

How different words can sound, over a few years' distance! I used to say to Anne-Marie:

'You'll never leave me?'

'Why do you ask such a foolish question?'

'Because I need you!'

'I need you too, Félix!'

It was not true for either of us, but we did not know that. I have eaten nothing this evening. I only had to grill the meat over the stove and warm up the cooked vegetables I had bought this morning. I had not the heart to do so, and neither did I want to go and sit in some restaurant, convinced that everyone was watching me. Besides, I am not hungry. I prepared Bib's mess; he is increasingly puzzled by my behaviour.

I may as well admit it at once, for it will probably be evident to anyone who may read these pages one day, I bought, on my way home, a bottle of spirits – Burgundy *marc*. You can't buy whisky in the small local groceries that stay open in the evening.

I have drunk one glass. I have poured myself another, which is standing in front of me. Once, and once only, in my student days, I got drunk on *marc* with some friends, and I have never felt so wretched as next morning. Except, possibly, the day after my meeting with Anne-Marie on the roof of Claridge's.

What is there to stop me from drinking? Not a concern for my health. And was not the love between Anne-Marie and myself born of alcohol? Didn't we keep that up, both of us? Didn't those jealous fits of mine, which drove me to wound and sully her, break out when I was drunk?

I feel tempted to burn my two notebooks and begin all over again, but this time getting really to the bottom of things, probing truth to the bone. Not only the truth about myself but the truth about others too.

Nobody would understand. It would involve becoming *me*, getting into my skin, and who would want to do that? I don't feel at ease myself in this wan, flaccid skin which no longer fits me. Does Madame Annelet realize what she has just done to me?

I have emptied the second glass and since, for the past thirteen years, I have drunk almost nothing but water, I already feel the effect of it. My head is reeling a little and I see the words I am writing as though through dirty spectacles.

I have not yet spoken about the Félix Allard of the years between 1946 and 1951. He's a fellow I can scarcely recognize and whom I am ashamed of recalling. Is that his fault, and if not, whose is it?

Can you imagine what was the first thing that idiot did? It was to ask Cornille for the address of his tailor, so as to order himself some suits! Because in the set into which he was about to move, people dressed differently. Always that concern with being different! Whether at Fouquet's or Maxim's or other fashionable restaurants or nightclubs, the cut of one's clothes served as a password.

And the make of one's car, too. And the way one walked in and went to one's table, smiling to one's acquaintance with a slight wave of the hand, and the way one studied the menu card and spoke to the head waiter . . .

I had not played at being a clever schoolboy, or a student; I had been both of these. I have said so before, but it doesn't matter. Nor had I played at being the tough, blunt building contractor of Puteaux, or the lover and husband obsessed with jealousy.

Presumably the rest, too, was something I had in me. I took myself seriously. I handled a lot of business. I lived in a modern block at Neuilly, just across the river from Puteaux, in a flat like those of the film producers, stars and industrialists who were my neighbours.

I used to meet them again at the theatre and at late night suppers, then at Megève over Christmas and New Year, at Cannes or Antibes for Easter, at Deauville later and finally, when the shooting season opened, in the Sologne.

For I had taken up shooting! Anne-Marie and I went to buy ourselves guns at Gastinne-Renette's and we were given shooting lessons in the basement. I also learnt to play bridge and poker; I even took riding lessons in the Bois de Boulogne.

I had my offices in the Rue Marbeuf, with the same armchairs as Cornille, and when Philippe was born his nurse wore an English nanny's uniform.

This sort of life went on for five years. Time passed quickly. But I must really play with Bib for a moment. I haven't the right to disappoint him, and I may still need him.

*

'Ask Mimieux . . .'

'Mimieux will fix that . . .'

'Mimieux's looking after things . . .'

He reminded one of a toad. His handshake was moist and melting. He lived somewhere at the top of the Boulevard Voltaire, but I don't believe he ever entertained anyone there.

There was a Madame Mimieux, however, whom nobody ever

saw either, and I suppose she must have been as ugly as he was. They had no children.

Mimieux did not own a car and travelled only by underground, which enabled him to keep his appointments punctually. He would draw his watch from his waistcoat pocket, its lid would spring open, then he would shut it again with a snap. I always saw him wearing the same black suit and if he ever had a new pair of shoes, one wouldn't have guessed it.

'The first thing to do is to form a joint-stock company . . .'

'But . . .'

'Don't raise objections till I've explained to you . . .'

He had begun at the age of sixteen in some obscure legal office in the Rue Coquillière, near Les Halles. He had read only one book in his life, the Code Civil, which he knew by heart, and he was said to be the best-informed man in Paris on company law and the way to make use of it.

He convinced me, and I went to talk to my mother.

'Listen, *Maman* . . .'

'When are you moving?'

'That's not what I want to talk to you about. You must understand that I'm anxious to extend the business. Wasn't that what my father did when Grandfather retired? We're entering on a period . . .'

'Where do you intend to move to?'

'It's essential that the office should be in Paris. I shall keep the old warehouses, and perhaps set up others. As for yourself, if you'd like me to leave a foreman and a few workers . . .'

'It's kind of you to have thought of it, but I'm feeling tired and the rest will be good for me.'

'As regards our arrangements . . .'

'As long as you leave me the house and give me enough to live on for the rest of my days . . .'

'I've inquired in the right quarters: to secure the funds I need, particularly credit from the bank, it's essential to form a joint-stock company. Of course, you'll be allotted shares . . .'

'No, Félix. Thank you very much, but I'd rather not be mixed up in all that.'

This was the first warning note. I did not heed it. The second was sounded by Monsieur Beauchef, my accountant.

'Don't take it amiss, Monsieur Félix. I shouldn't feel at ease in your new concern.'

'What do you intend to do?'

'I shall go back to my former clients, small tradesmen and craftsmen who need my help once a week.'

Monique's pregnancy was nearing its end, and Anne-Marie was not pregnant yet. We still went out in a foursome. Cornille would dance with my wife, while Monique and I sat out, which I did not mind, for I have never been a keen dancer.

'Anne-Marie has astonishing vitality!'

I refrained from retorting: 'Just like Fernand!'

The same kind of animation inspired them both. Contact with somebody from outside acted on each of them like a spark. To go into a restaurant, to meet some acquaintance on the pavement was enough to set them going. In the space of one second they became dazzling and indefatigable.

'Did Mimieux tell you about the shares?'

'He spoke to me about them yesterday.'

'What d'you think?'

'You know I know nothing about it.'

When Mimieux explained the working of a deal, it all seemed clear and above-board. I could find no objection to raise. It was only later, before I fell asleep, that doubts and scruples occurred to me.

'Don't forget he has set more than forty companies afoot and never had the slightest trouble.'

Since I was the contractor, my name did not appear on the prospectus of the La Tour Building Society, as we had called it. A retired general was chairman of the board of directors. Nevertheless, I held one-third of the shares.

On the other hand, however, a number of shares in my own business had been blocked by the bank. I had been obliged to visit Rouen to see my sister, who had not yet received her full share of the inheritance.

I found nothing unusual about these transactions, any more than about living in the Boulevard Richard-Wallace, opposite Bagatelle.

Mimieux, the inevitable Mimieux, had produced a couple of bulldozers for me, as well as a crane and an excavator, which the American army had brought over for building wartime aerodromes.

'We've done it this time, Félix. You can open a bottle of champagne . . .'

'Done what?'

'Can't you guess?'

I looked more closely at Anne-Marie.

'Really? You're pregnant?'

I loved her. I couldn't have helped loving her. We got wildly excited and rang up the Cornilles, then went to spend the rest of the evening with them.

Every day I drove in my big American car to La Tour, where building was going on apace. Sketches had been exhibited in a shop-window in the Champs-Elysées, rented at Cornille's suggestion, and four months later every flat was sold, while I was still casting the floors of the second storey and digging the swimming-pool.

I gave Anne-Marie a small car. Philippe was born. Then I presented my wife with a diamond and my son with the most expensive English perambulator. From our windows, we were able, before long, to watch him with his nurse on the other side of the wooden fence of the Bois de Boulogne. Leaning out, I could also see my huge car, with Anne-Marie's tiny elegant one behind it.

'Are you happy?'

'Aren't you?'

Of course I said yes. I had no time not to be happy. All day, appointments and visits to the building site succeeded one another without a pause. Six people were already working in my office. I frequently lunched in town with the architects, or the suppliers, or with Cornille.

'Is that you, Anne-Marie? Sorry, darling, but I can't get home for lunch . . .'

'Poor lamb, you're working too hard! Is it still O.K. for this evening?'

Of course! Every evening there was something on, a dinner date, the opening of a new nightclub, a gala performance somewhere.

I must have loved her, since I was jealous!

During her pregnancy she sometimes asked me:

'How are you managing, poor Félix?'

For the doctor had advised against sexual relations after the third month.

'I never think about it.'

'You're sure? You don't sometimes want to go and see some other woman?'

I did; I went. Among others, I went to bed with the secretary of one of the architects, because she had big breasts, and I was surprised to see her burst out laughing at the climax. Near the Madeleine, I knew some quiet bars where one could be sure of finding pretty girls.

'D'you think you can last out till the end?'

'I'm sure of it.'

Why did I always feel compelled to lie?

'She belongs to me!' A recurrent theme. And I, theoretically, belonged to her, and Philippe belonged to us. So, later on, did Nicole, born a few months after the Cornilles' second child. It was like a race between the two families. We made a joke of it.

'Next time *we're* going to set the example!'

The first mink coat was a Christmas present. Monique had had hers a year earlier. I had become a customer of shops in the Faubourg Saint-Honoré, the Place Vendôme and elsewhere, in which at one time I would never have ventured to set foot. I ordered shirts and pyjamas by the dozen. I signed cheques. If I was in any difficulties, Cornille would say: 'Go and see Mimieux.'

And it was fixed up. Everything was fixed up. To advertise the second group of buildings, in a park near Versailles, we bought a whole page in the leading newspapers. We needed ready money to finish La Tour, where we had considerably overspent our estimates.

That was Mimieux's business. In the evenings, at weekends and on holidays, we lived in another world. The upper ten thousand? Perhaps less, perhaps more. Successful industrialists, doctors, lawyers, business men.

We had been successful. Cornille rented a shoot in the forest of Orléans, at Ingrannes, and had a modern shooting lodge built there, with huge kennels and stables. We went there for week-ends, arriving on Saturday afternoons at first, and then on Friday evenings.

All this seems to me cloudy and unreal, perhaps because I've just drunk a fourth glass of *marc*. I am going round in a circle. Since I began these notebooks, really, I've been wasting my time, through not daring to attack the real problem.

Until I was thirty the word love had no meaning for me. Then it came to mean that fever possessed me when I met Anne-Marie, and the torture I inflicted on myself through jealousy – that I inflicted on her too, by what right, I now wonder?

Was her past any concern of mine? Was I entitled to call her to account? Had I been in London during the blitz, when she suddenly found herself alone there? What had I been doing then? What was I still doing, and not only when pregnancy put her out of commission?

That did not prevent me, during my jealous attacks, from treating her like a despicable creature, and deliberately striving to strip her of any self-respect.

'Forgive me, Félix. It hurts me so to know that you're suffering on my account . . .'

And while she was dancing with Cornille, or when, late at night, they embarked on one of their interminable con-versations, Monique and I exchanged glances. We must have looked like a pair of accomplices; we were rather like mothers affectionately watching their children at play.

'They're indefatigable, the two of them!'

Evenings never seemed long enough. I felt sleepy for I had to rise early; so did Monique. We suffered patiently, united in a kind of freemasonry. I loved Anne-Marie and Monique loved her Fernand. She would say quite calmly, with a touch of resig-nation:

'It's not his fault. He needs to feel life all round him. He's bubbling over with energy!'

She was the daughter of a schoolmaster, a history teacher who, now retired and living in Lyons, was writing a fat book about the Merovingians. Wasn't that the career I had chosen myself? It seemed to me another link between herself and me.

417

'I shall wonder all my life why he married me, when I'm such a bourgeoise!'

I almost expected to hear her add: 'He ought to have married someone like Anne-Marie!'

I often thought of that, not as a possible reality but as a purely theoretical conception. And it did not shock me, although I worked myself into a frenzy at the mere name of Desmarais.

Nobody suspected or mentioned this, fortunately. Nobody guessed it, apart from that frightful witch Madame Annelet.

Not even Monique, as I am now practically convinced. We were good friends who understood one another's slightest word or glance.

'When I think that Fernand could have the prettiest girls in Paris!'

He missed no opportunity of doing so, but it was not my business to betray him. He used to tell me of his adventures and often needed me for an alibi.

'D'you mind if I ring Monique and tell her I'm lunching with you?' As he did so he would give me a wink.

'Did you notice that little brunette yesterday at the *Nouvelle Eve*? I managed to get hold of her phone number, and we're lunching together presently. Above all, don't mention it to Annie-Marie; you can never be sure with women.'

I did not mention it to Anne-Marie. We rented a villa at Deauville.

This state of things lasted for five years and I wonder what I should be like today if it had gone on longer. My mother fell ill. I used to go and see her from time to time in the old house, where my Aunt Julie, with whom she was now reconciled, often kept her company. For reasons of tact my wife only came with me on our New Year visits.

'Are you still quite happy, Félix?'

'Of course, *maman*. You're the one that should be inquired after. How's that kidney trouble?'

'Still a bit tiresome. Do you know who's been looking after me since our old Chollet died? His son, who was a doctor at one of the hospitals and who has taken over the practice.'

I saw him, a tall, solemn, rather gauche young fellow.

'Is it serious, Doctor?'

'Unfortunately, yes. I've had your mother examined by one of my former professors, who doesn't advise an operation. It would mean useless torture for her, and she'd only gain a month or two.'

She dragged on for a year, with Frida by her side, and Aunt Julie who, on account of the wall in the courtyard, had to come round by the Rue Voltaire. At the funeral, I was surprised to see Monsieur Beauchef, whose new address I had not got and whom I had not notified of her death.

I'm going round in a circle. I've nearly emptied that bottle. I thought alcohol would excite me, give me a certain energy, at all events take away my reluctance and my inhibitions.

I have never felt so weak and flabby. If it weren't for Madame Annelet's remarks running through my head, I would immediately swallow the two tubes of sleeping tablets which I have set aside, and the whole thing would be over.

She managed to frighten me, the bitch! The thought that I might change my mind when it was too late. . . . Here, above all, in a house where Bib and I are alone at night. . . . It's raining. I hear the drops falling on the skylight over my head.

The Inspector was not too harsh with me. He must have felt sorry for me. It was Monique who had gone to ask him to intervene. Anne-Marie, on the other hand, made no complaint. It's hard to imagine that she never caught sight of me in the Place des Vosges.

Why should she bother about me? She has remade her life in her own way. A woman like Anne-Marie is never in difficulties for very long. She has her family in the Place des Vosges. In her shop in the Faubourg Saint-Honoré she has a partner, a man some four or five years younger than herself.

I have seen them. I know about it. She is still young, but she'll soon have reached the danger-point and then her drama will begin, as Madame Annelet's once did. She'll fight even more fiercely than the old bookseller.

This is the woman I wanted to belong to me, to me alone. Her children are mine. I have sometimes doubted that, and sought to hold someone else responsible for them, as an excuse for looking at them with such curiosity. Philippe is like myself at his age, and that causes me embarrassment rather than pleasure. It's impossible to say as yet whom Nicole will be like. For the time being she reminds me of my sister Louise.

As for Daniel, he is the image of his mother, with her smile and her calm manner. It was partly because of this that I kept hoping to see him come into the bookshop and ask me for some book or other so as to have an opportunity of studying me at close quarters. Long before the Inspector spoke to me about it I was almost sure he had recognized me. And yet he was only five when the thing happened.

I had bounced him on my knee, as Cornille had bounced my own children on his.

I reek of *marc*. I feel I'm sweating through every pore. My mouth is thick, my hand heavy, my head full of muddled thoughts. I am drunk. A sick, drunken old man writing under a skylight through which from time to time there falls a large cold drop of water. To hell with my dog, to hell with everybody, with Madame Annelet, Anne-Marie, the children and Monique. Just so! To hell with Monique!

I imagine her at the police station, perfectly calm, sure of her rights. Of course! She works in a lawyer's office! Does she sleep with him too, as Anne-Marie does with her partner Antonio? For my wife's partner is called Antonio!

'Please excuse my bothering you, Inspector. There's a man in the neighbourhood . . .'

The bitch! Surely she realizes? Has she understood nothing? Did I really bother her so much? Did she imagine that my presence in the street was enough to pollute the air and contaminate Daniel and Martine?

'At night he walks up and down the pavement on the other side of the street, with his dog, staring up at our windows, and when it rains he takes shelter in a gateway . . .'

It was all I had left.

Damn, damn and blast! I must go and be sick, and that idiot Bib will gaze at me reproachfully once again.

I have just spent two and a half days in bed, three days without writing. At one point I decided not to add another word to these notebooks, and to destroy them. I had not been quite sincere when I pretended not to know for whom they were intended. In my heart, I was thinking of Monique. Absurd as it may seem, it was a kind of declaration of love, of a love which really *was* unlike other sorts. I should have been quite glad if Daniel, too, had read these pages some day.

Now I have recovered my calm, my peace of mind, or more exactly my indifference. I believe I am once more capable of looking at myself not from within, which might incline me to indulgence, but from without, as others see me.

I shall try to remain cold and lucid to the end.

It was on Thursday that the Inspector unwittingly dealt me the hardest blow I have yet had to endure, and Madame Annelet, as I might have expected, took advantage of it to finish me off.

I drank. I've no desire to re-read what I wrote on Thursday night. I went to bed and at six o'clock Bib woke me. Still dazed, which seldom happens to me, I got up to open the door for him and it was then that everything began to spin round me and I collapsed on the floor like some great insect.

It was not directly due to the *marc*. I have had other fits of dizziness during the last few months, less violent, which forced me to stop still in the street but allowed me to keep on my feet. It's agonizing the first few times. You get used to it. It's nothing to do with my illness. It's just an extra infirmity.

I did not lose consciousness, and what I chiefly felt was humiliation, even though nobody was there except my dog, who looked at me without understanding and uttered little yelps.

To begin with he must have thought it was a new game. I got painfully on to all fours. I tried to stand up, then, giving up the attempt, I managed, by dint of cautious movements, to climb into my bed.

It was raining. It's still raining. For four days a fine invisible rain has been falling and I have mechanically watched the water trickling down the panes. Lying in bed, I played at guessing if one of the streams would run to the left or to the right and I was almost invariably wrong.

Bib was running round in a circle, impatiently, and whimpering. I could do nothing for him. He could do nothing for me. We both had to wait. We heard the girls invading the workshop on the first floor and the lorries unloading goods on the ground floor.

Madame Annelet must have thought, when I failed to appear at eight o'clock, that I had at last committed suicide. I am no longer afraid of the word, nor ashamed of it either. At half-past eight, as I had foreseen, she sent Renée along to me, and Bib was able to dash out into the street.

'So you're ill now! Have you sent for the doctor, at least?'

What for? And how could I, since I have no telephone?

'I must go and give news of you to Madame. Is there anything I can do for you?'

I had a hangover, but as long as I lay down and kept still it was not painful nor even unpleasant. She made me some coffee, which I thought tasted nasty. She went off. At about ten, she came back with a pot of vegetable broth.

'Madame has rung up your doctor, who'll come to see you as soon as he can.'

Bib did not get back on to the bed. He settled down in the farthest corner of the room, as though he were sulking.

'Shall I light the fire?'

'Just as you like.'

Renée went backwards and forwards between the Boulevard Beaumarchais and the Rue des Arquebusiers all day. She is twenty-two; she'll live long after me. She too must think that I've had my share. Perhaps she wonders why I'm not already dead, and resents my inflicting extra work on her.

I should not, of my own accord, have sent for Doctor Heim, who lives in the Boulevard Richard-Lenoir. Since Madame Annelet had notified him, I might expect to see him arrive at any moment.

It was not until three in the afternoon that I heard his car draw up outside, then a door was slammed and his footstep sounded on the stair.

'I couldn't come any earlier, for I've had a very busy day.'

I might have died meanwhile. But of course there are others in the same case, younger men, women or children who, as the saying is, have their lives before them.

I understood him. I understood his attitude towards me, which is strictly professional, with no attempt to establish any human contact. He examined me, looked at his watch as he held my wrist, took my blood pressure, felt my abdomen and merely frowned.

'What happened?'

'I got up as usual and immediately felt dizzy and fell down.'

'Have you been following my prescriptions?'

'No.'

As a man. I don't interest him; as a patient, hardly at all, for he knows there is nothing to be done.

Why should he feel sympathetic towards me? Who could be fond of me, even in the slightest degree? The sight of me tends rather to make people uneasy, as if they guessed that within the mass of quivering flesh that I have become, decay has already set in and is slowly doing its work.

Faced with such a spectacle, they sometimes seem to be asking themselves:

'Isn't he going to shout or groan, to bite things or burst into tears?'

I don't shout or bite, nor do I burst into tears. I shed no tears in the police station.

Doctor Heim noticed the half-empty bottle of *marc*.

'Was it you who . . . ?'

Who else could have been drinking in my attic?

'Last night?'

I don't care if he feels disgust or contempt for me. I am back to where I was so short a while go, a fortnight if I'm not mistaken, before I met my two foolishly radiant monsters climbing the steps of the Sacré-Coeur.

I had vowed not to yield to sentimentality. I fear that I may have given way to it once or twice. The time I have just spent in bed has put things back in their right places. Since I have begun to tell my story, I will finish it, without self-pity.

On Saturday I tried three times to get up, carefully, holding on to the bed, and I realized that it was useless.

Renée came back several times, after hanging on to the book-shop door the notice that says: 'Closed until ... o'clock.' As with certain calendars and with car-parking meters, you turn a cardboard disc and a figure appears in the slit.

On Sunday I was able to get about in my room and I told Renée not to bother coming round in the afternoon, but to take her day off as usual. Madame Annelet and I each stayed in our hole, while thousands of people queued up outside cinemas.

Where had I got to? It doesn't matter. I'm not attempting to stick the pieces together again. Things were bound to crack up. We were living in the midst of so much money that we did not know what to do with it, yet we were always short of it.

'Ask Mimieux ...'

It couldn't last indefinitely, and I sometimes longed for the end to come as soon as possible.

'Don't you think, Fernand, that ...'

'Oh, you've always been a pessimist. Since Mimieux ...'

Mimieux waved no danger signal, merely asked for my signature from time to time, and I had acquired the habit of signing anything. In any case it was all too complicated for me.

'What is it? What are they doing in your office?'

I had seen unfamiliar faces, severe and unfriendly, in the accounts department at the Building Society, where I had gone to see Cornille.

'Specialists from the Finance Squad.'

'Does that mean danger?'

'Mimieux swears it's only a routine inspection and they'll find nothing out of the ordinary.'

They studied our books for a whole week, unvaryingly impassive and polite, then they turned up at my office in the Rue Marbeuf.

'Aren't we in order?'

'In business, one's never in order. So long as Mimieux says there's nothing to be alarmed about ...'

We got an ever-increasing number of telephone calls from clients who had bought flats and were worried to see that work had not yet begun. A paragraph in a weekly started off a slight panic. Mimieux, still travelling by underground, grew more cautious about handing out money to either Cornille or myself or our chief accountants.

As for Anne-Marie, she went on living as if nothing had happened. We went out more than ever.

'It would be bad policy not to show ourselves. People would assume that . . .'

Only Monique occasionally gave me a questioning look. I was not yet in love with her, or, if I was, I was not conscious of it. It was only at Melun that I had time to reflect and to clarify my thoughts and feelings.

It was in April. For once, we had not gone to spend the Easter holidays on the Riviera, for the Public Prosecutor's Department had politely requested us not to leave Paris and to hold ourselves at their disposal.

Spring was early that year, sunny and warmer than on previous years, and I can still see myself bringing home the first strawberries, set out in cotton wool like jewels in a case. I could not find Anne-Marie. I went into our room to change. Having no more cigarettes in my pocket I opened her bag, which she had left on a small table, to take one from the gold case I had given her.

I almost failed to notice the key which my fingers touched at the bottom of the bag. Its shape surprised me. It was neither a car key nor the key to our flat. I got a shock. It hurt, although I was not really surprised. I immediately thought of Cornille, and then I knew. I put the key back and then, after a moment's pause to compose my face, I went into the nursery where Anne-Marie was playing with the children.

'Strawberries! The first!'

On two afternoons, at the time when she usually went out, supposedly to meet Monique or to do shopping, I waited in a taxi close to the house. On the second day, she got into her little car and drove to a building in the Rue de Longchamp, where no one of our acquaintance lived.

It was three o'clock. I waited until five, and it was Cornille who came out first.

A situation which has given rise to dramas, but above all to comic plays and funny cartoons in the newspapers. She emerged a quarter of an hour later.

'What an afternoon! It's getting more and more difficult to find ready money . . .'

He never wondered why I looked coldly at him. That evening Anne-Marie lay down quite naturally in our bed.

'You admit,' the examining magistrate insisted, 'that a week elapsed between this discovery and your crime?'

I was forced to admit it, for I'd happened upon a conscientious taxi-driver who, after seeing my photograph in the papers, had rushed to the police station to make a statement.

This is very important. Well, it was important at the time. My lawyer, Maître Forniol, who received me the other day as if I had the plague, gave me, when I was in the Santé prison, a little lecture on the Penal Laws. I still know two articles of the Code by heart:

*Art. 592. Homicide committed involuntarily is termed manslaughter.*

*Art. 296 Manslaughter committed with premeditation or malice aforethought is termed wilful murder.*

'For a whole week, then, you had leisure to reflect, you gave mature consideration to your decision.'

And while a prison car took me daily to the Palais de Justice, the Trade Tribunal declared the bankruptcy of the Building Society and of my own concern, thus restraining all our possessions.

'Why did you wait so long?'

'I don't know.'

'Did the urge to kill occur to you on the first day?'

The true answer is no, and I admit it for the first time. I lied to the judge, and then to the jury, which did not prevent a sort of uneasiness hanging over the whole trial.

'You are jealous by temperament?'

'Yes, *Monsieur le Président.*'

'Your behaviour was occasionally violent?'

'Yes.'

'Towards your wife?'

'Only with her.'

'Why?'

'Because I loved her.'

Forniol lectured me.

'That's the crucial point. Premeditation means the death sentence. Otherwise, it's forced labour for a term.'

I had at some time in the past found among my father's belongings an old repeating revolver. Anne-Marie gave evidence in the witness box without once looking at me. She was not put on oath. Nor was Monique, who for her part glanced furtively at me as if something was worrying her.

'On the contrary, this week of waiting, this long week of conflict and anguish seems to me to offer proof of my client's sincerity. . . . Under the shock of his discovery he remained stupefied. . . . Little by little, as hours and days elapsed and as he watched his wife, saw how she lied while laughing and playing with the children . . .'

It was on a Friday that I made my way to the Rue de Longchamp with the big revolver in my pocket. The bachelor flat was on the ground floor, looking out on the courtyard, where a chauffeur was washing down a tenant's Rolls-Royce with a hose.

I pushed the bell, a little bone button like any other, and waited with my right hand in my pocket. I waited for some time. I could hear steps inside, the characteristic sound of bare feet on the carpet.

Cornille, who was wearing nothing but a pair of trousers, half opened the door, and then his jaw dropped. He had time to say, in amazement:

'You!'

I had pointed the gun at him and, before I fired, he opened his mouth once more. I could read on his lips the word he was trying to call out:

'No!'

I fired three bullets, point-blank. I would have emptied the barrel, if the weapon had not jammed. I caught sight of Anne-Marie running naked through the room.

The concierge watched me go past with more curiosity than alarm. She was the first person to look at me in that way. I went to the police station in the Rue de la Pompe.

'I have just killed my wife's lover.'

Maître Forniol whispered to me, during the indictment:

'The President doesn't like you . . .'

Already!

'But you'll see the jury will react favourably. They always do, in Paris, in cases of *flagrante delicto*.'

The jury did. They did not find malice aforethought. Recognizing, moreover, that there were extenuating circumstances, they reduced my sentence to five years.

I was almost sincere. My voice quivered as I spoke of Anne-Marie.

Today, Monday, when I went back to my job at the bookshop and Madame Annelet looked at me with her clairvoyante's eyes, I was on the point of saying to her:

'You needn't hunt any further!'

For she is still chasing after a truth that eludes her.

'Anne-Marie had nothing to do with it. It's even possible that I never loved Anne-Marie. I believed I did. I made myself believe it. Because . . .'

Good Lord, because, like everyone else, I needed someone, someone who belonged to me. Only she did not belong to me, any more than Philippe and Nicole. Nobody belongs to anyone else. Monique has given me further proof of that, although from her I asked nothing. Nobody has pity on anyone else, either.

In prison, one has plenty of opportunity to think. At Melun, particularly in the library, where I had my own little habits, my routine, just as I have here, and where I could at last begin to take a look at myself.

I lied to all of them, not so much to avoid a severer sentence as from fear of admitting the truth to myself. During the preliminary investigation and the trial, I had succeeded in concealing it from myself, in almost completely wiping from my memory the incident which had occurred on that Wednesday in the Champs-Elysées.

The previous Friday I had seen Fernand Cornille, and then Anne-Marie, coming out of the building in the Rue de Longchamp. On Saturday evening the four of us had gone out together. On Sunday we went to the races. On Monday and Tuesday I spent most of the time on the building sites.

On Wednesday afternoon I went to the Champs-Elysées office intending to see Mimieux, for I needed money to pacify a supplier who had turned threatening. I went through the waiting-room and the typists' room. Mimieux's door was ajar and just as I was about to push it I overheard Cornille remark:

'Allard? I'm not worrying about him. He's a weak conceited fool, who'll go on doing whatever we decide upon . . .'

I retreated on tiptoe.

'I'll call back later,' I told the office boy.

That was the heart of the matter. I understood, there, behind the door, that I had just heard the truth. I had got it, as they say, straight between the eyes.

Only, he had no right to speak it. He had no right to rob me of my dignity, of my self-esteem. Nobody has the right to do so, for without self-esteem a man ceases to be a man.

I know I behaved in the same way with Anne-Marie in the early days, when in my fits of jealousy I wantonly reviled her. But she never believed me.

I believed Cornille. I knew the truth. He forced me to know it.

The rest doesn't matter. I don't care whether he skulked for months or for years in a bachelor flat in the Rue de Longchamp to enjoy Anne-Marie's body.

What he stole from me was not my wife, but myself.

I shall not revert to this. I shall close this notebook once and for all. And I shall not even kill myself. The two tubes of barbiturate shall go down the lavatory.

I can't help it if people have to watch me decomposing more or less slowly and if some day, in hospital, I give trouble to the nurses and house doctors.

We are all robbers. We all steal lives, or parts of lives, to feed our own lives with.

The half-empty bottle no longer tempts me.

Up you get, Bib my lad! It's ten o'clock. I am not sleepy. We are both going out for a walk in the rain and we shall turn right on the Boulevard Beaumarchais, since we no longer have the right to walk under certain windows.

That's all you want. You're wagging your tail already, you idiot!

*News item*
*Paris, January 13*

*Yesterday, at half-past six in the evening, at the corner of the Boulevard Beaumarchais and the Rue du Pas-de-la-Mule, a man identified as Félix Allard, aged 49, bookshop assistant, met his death in a street accident. He had been walking along the pavement, leading a small dog on a leash, and stepped off on to the roadway, when he was knocked over by a bus which he had his back to. His head was completely crushed. According to evidence so far received, Allard was subject to fits of dizziness, and it is presumed that one of these attacks made him change his direction so suddenly that the driver of the bus was unable to brake.*

*The dog, which by a miracle escaped uninjured, has been taken to the strays' home.*

Noland, September 25, 1963.

# More about Penguins and Pelicans

# Maigret Stonewalled

*Simenon*

A simple enough case . . . on the face of it. A
commercial traveller killed in a hotel bedroom on
the Loire. But Maigret sensed falseness everywhere,
in the way the witnesses spoke and laughed and
acted, and, above all, in the manner of M. Gallet's
death, under a false name, from a shot that nobody
heard, with his own knife plunged into his heart.
And behind the falseness, as Maigret discovered,
the pathos of a man for whom nothing had ever
gone right – not even death.